HEATHER GRAHAM

Blood Red

MIRA®

MIRA

ISBN-13: 978-0-7783-2486-7
ISBN-10:   0-7783-2486-9

BLOOD RED

www.MIRABooks.com

Printed in U.S.A.

First printing: July 2007

To New Orleans.

To Sean and everyone at the Monteleone.

For Alice Duffy, with lots of love, respect and tremendous admiration.

Especially for Kate Duffy—"Duffee" will always mean pure excellence—with deepest gratitude, always.

For Christine Feehan (and clan), Cherry Adair, Molly and Kate, Brian and Kristi Ahlers, Deborah and Harvey, Lance and Rich, Debbie Richmond, Pat and Patricia, Bonnie, Kathleen, Aleka, Toni, Sally and all those who were so willing to hop on and give New Orleans and me their very best.

And for Connie and T, who get me through everything.

Prologue

There had never been a more beautiful bride, never a more picture-perfect wedding. The weather had bowed down in honor of the occasion, and there was a slight cooling breeze. The night was neither too warm nor too cold, and the time had been carefully chosen; the sun was just setting in the western sky. The bride had longed for a castle, and they had found an ancient cathedral perched atop a hill within an old fortress town.

The groom was gallantly trying to be everything the bride's fairy-tale prince should be. He had spent his adult life trying to live life by his own code, which demanded decency to his fellow human beings. He didn't bend easily to anyone's whim, but he had learned the importance of compromise, and of being compassionate. He knew himself capable of error and had learned to admit it. He could honestly say he was ready to battle for the downtrodden or the underdog, and he had lived through enough battles to see many of the errors made around him. More than anything, as he prepared to wed his stunning bride, he could say that he loved her dearly, more than life itself.

Thus…this wedding.

Whatever she longed for, a castle deep in a land foreign to him, an elegant horse-drawn carriage, or anything that could possibly complete the fantasy wedding of her heart, she could have. It helped that events had recently turned in his favor; where for many years he had worked to support what he prayed was a talent, he had suddenly discovered himself a rich man, almost overnight. And though the bride hailed from this part of the world, they had met in the United States. She had heard him playing his guitar; he had looked up and met her eyes. Life hadn't been the same from that moment on. But since many of their closest friends were still struggling financially, he and his bride had—very tactfully, they hoped—managed to treat their friends who couldn't afford the trip, providing an enjoyable respite from the rigors of life, as well as the pleasure of the wedding itself.

A lavish runner extended the length of the cathedral aisle. The groom, elegant in a black tux, stood next to his identically attired groomsmen. As the music played and the priest cleared his throat, they all looked to the rear for the entry of the bride and her party.

The flower girl was adorable, tossing petals with a somber appreciation for the great duty entrusted to her. The bridesmaids, lovely in glimmering silver offset with black trim, entered next, escorted by the groomsmen.

And then the bride…

So beautiful…

Her hair, long and lustrous, as red-gold as the sunset, fell to her shoulders, haloing her face in beauty. She wore a modern gown, but one designed in a Renaissance style, and his heart caught in his throat at the sight of her. Beneath the sheer flow of her veil, he could see her eyes shimmering, touched by a mist of tears. He smiled in return, and his heart thundered.

She moved gracefully down the aisle.

And then…

The spill of blood appeared on her dress, beginning as a tiny dot at her heart. Then it widened…widened to cover her breast, the entire bodice….

She stopped walking.

She stared at him.

There was horror on her face. Her eyes pleaded.

He started to run to her, but he couldn't reach her. A sound was rising in his ears. A storm, a siege, a rush…

The blood came then, like a tidal wave. A rush of it, as if a crimson river had exploded, broken a dam, surged down a hill…

He blinked.

He saw her face, her eyes…pleading for help.

Then the blood washed everywhere, along the aisle, up the ancient lichened walls of the cathedral. It rose higher and higher.

He was drowning in it.

Choking on it.

Far away from the distant mountains, a man awoke from a nightmare. He let out a hoarse cry and jackknifed to a sitting position. The scene in his mind had played out so realistically that he was momentarily convinced he was covered in blood. He was coughing, as if he had been fighting for breath in his sleep.

He cast off the sweat-soaked sheet that had covered him, rose, and strode to the doors to the balcony, quickly casting them open. Reality rushed in with a breath of magnolia-scented air.

Would it never stop? Would the nightmare never cease to haunt him?

It was the end of spring, the beginning of summer. Heat rose by day, and yet, by night, there was a breeze that touched his skin like a gentle hand.

He looked up at the sky. Eerie clouds veiled the moon, giving it an unearthly tinge of color.

He gritted his teeth, his features hard and determined.
It looked just as it had then....
At the blood wedding.

1

Mark Davidson watched the couple at the bar, who seemed to be like any couple at any bar.

The man leaned toward the woman. She was pretty, in a tube top that displayed sculpted abs and a short skirt that afforded a long look at longer legs. She batted her lashes now and then, lowering her head, offering a shy, even rueful, smile to the man at her side. He was tall, and dark. Despite his apparent ease with her flirtation, there seemed to be a tenseness in him, a leashed energy that, to Mark, at least, suggested something wasn't quite right.

The couple laughed together, teased each other. Body language. She'd been looking for something that evening; he'd definitely been set on action.

"Another drink, sir?" Momentarily, he was distracted by the waitress, an attractive but older woman with large eyes and a nice figure. Her voice was polite but also weary, he thought. Maybe it hadn't been easy for her over the past few years.

"Um…" He wasn't sure why she was asking. He'd barely touched the beer he'd ordered earlier. Then again, they needed to make money here, so maybe it was just a hint.

"Sorry, I guess you don't," she said with a little sigh. He had a feeling she was a native. Her accent was richly Southern.

Not that New Orleans was a city where only natives could be found. It was the kind of place people simply fell in love with, as if it had a personality all its own. Of course, some people loathed the city's free-and-easy spirit, and, he had to admit, the vomit in the streets after a particularly wild night during Mardi Gras wasn't exactly a selling point. None of that mattered to him. He loved the place, the narrow streets, the old buildings and the mixture of cultures. He loved everything about the place.

Oh, yeah. He loved everything about the place, except for…

The waitress was blocking his view, he realized. He had chosen a back table, in the shadows. He was away from the jazz band playing to the far left of the bar, near the entrance. The group was great; Mark would have happily come here just to listen to them. That was one of the things he loved most about New Orleans; some of the best music in the world could be heard here, often just by walking along the streets. Young talent, *fine* talent, often began their careers playing in Jackson Square or right on any street corner, performing in the hope that the passersby would toss their dollars in a guitar case or a hat.

There was so much to love about New Orleans.

Like the many times he had come here with Katie…

No.

He took a long swallow of the beer in front of him, lukewarm now, and gritted his teeth. He wasn't here to walk down memory lane.

"Sure, yeah, another beer. Cold, please," he said, trying to look around the waitress. But when she moved, he saw that the couple at the bar had gone.

He leaped to his feet and dug into his pocket for a bill. He handed it to her.

"Never mind," he said, heading for the door.

"Sir, your change," she protested, staring at the fifty he'd handed her.

"Keep it," he murmured, his eyes already riveted on the door to the street.

Out there the world was bright, alive with neon, laughter and the dueling beats of jazz and rock, as the music from the bars and clubs lining the sidewalks spilled into the humid air. Flashing lights advertised all manner of drinks and entertainment; old buildings seemed to peer at the rush of people with a haunting, even if decayed, elegance, despite their cloaks of commercialism.

Men and women, groups, duos, even singles, meandered down the street, some slowly, slightly inebriated, bumping into one another as they walked. Others moved with purpose.

He didn't see the couple from the bar, and he swore bitterly to himself.

Where the hell would the man have taken the girl? It wasn't as if he had to commit murder in a darkened cemetery; he could have rented a room anywhere. Hell, he might even have a place of his own here. Where? Alone, he might have moved as quickly as the wind. But he had the woman with him, slowing him down.

"Sir?"

He turned. The waitress had followed him.

"I said to keep the change," he said gently.

She smiled. "The bartender said the couple you were watching went left. The guy talked her into a late-night cemetery visit." She shrugged, a soft and thankful glow in her eyes. "Lots of assholes trying to pick up women convince them to slip into the cemeteries at night. Risky business. Drug dealers hang out there—and worse. You take care."

"Thanks," he told her. "Thank you."

Now that he had a direction, he started running down the street. So much for thinking the guy might just opt for a hotel room or the courtyard of some nice bed-and-breakfast.

As he ran, he patted a hand against the pocket of his chinos. He could feel the vial. He was armed, as well—conventionally armed—but he knew that wouldn't mean a damned thing, given what he was up against.

He reached the cemetery. Entry at night was illegal, but he scaled the fence easily, landing with a soft thud on the other side.

As he did, he heard the laughter. They were deeper into the grounds, behind the chipping stone and plaster of an above-ground tomb, with its sad angels and praying cherubs.

"Ooh, this is decadent. Creepy, and kind of exciting," a female voice said.

"Yes. I know."

"You want to…here? Right here?" she whispered. Her voice sounded a little uncertain. Now that she had come to the cemetery, perhaps she was feeling a little bit bothered by such disrespect for the dead. Or maybe it was fear of getting caught—by the police.

"You tell me," the man answered. "Do you want to feel my lips touch your flesh?"

The girl made a sound Mark couldn't identify, and he clenched his jaw tightly, seeking to control the pain and fury that swept through him. He didn't blame the girl. She might as well have been hypnotized.

"I want…yes…." she murmured.

Mark crept closer. There they were.

The man had stripped off his shirt. The girl was stretched

out on top of one of the tombs, her bare torso glistening beneath the moonlight. The man was bent over her, his hand stroking the length of her legs, his lips teasing the bare flesh of her midriff.

"Wait, please!" There was fear in the girl's voice now.

"Too late."

"No. No!"

"You're very pretty…. We could have had so much more fun first. Excitement like you've never imagined. Too bad that tonight…well, I'm really hungry. It's been a while for me, I'm afraid."

She was gasping out another protest. She had just realized she was about to die, Mark knew, and she was trying hard to scream. But terror, as sweet as sugar in the blood, was beginning to fill her, and she couldn't choke out the agony trapped in her throat.

Now!

Mark inhaled, tensing. She would be dead any second now if he didn't act. He reached into his pocket. He sprang.

He was in terrific shape, having served with the Marines before putting in several years as a bouncer while getting his own music sold. Even so, as fast as he was, the man sensed his approach. He heard the snarl of rage before he saw the man at the tomb swirl around, ready to meet him, a horrible, twisted mask of fury on his face. He saw the mouth open, the glint of the fanglike teeth in the darkness. Oddly enough, they had a fascinating opalescent glow.

He swore softly to himself. This wasn't the same man he had been trailing with such dogged determination. It was another, no doubt equally as bad.

His heart sank. And yet…

This creature was about to kill. He had to remember

justice—had to put it above revenge. He couldn't let his guard down; he couldn't falter for an instant.

Before he could reach the creature, however, the man gave a harsh laugh of amusement. "Going to shoot me?" he demanded.

"Hell, no," Mark assured him. His vial was full, and it was open. He aimed directly into the face and eyes of his opponent.

It let out a bloodcurdling cry of rage and astonishment as the holy water bathed its features. There was a flutter of shadow and darkness, a weak flapping of wings. It took off and crashed hard into a tomb.

Mark followed it. He drew the small but sharply honed stake he always carried from his pocket, then skewered the mix of shadow and substance and bat wings by the tomb.

There was a burst of misty color in the night. Dust exploding in the air, crimson with the blood of many lifetimes.

The flapping stopped. For a moment there was something of the darkened essence of a man by the grave…then there was nothing. Dirt and ash. Dust to dust.

He stood there, just staring, suddenly shaking as he broke out in a cold sweat.

Suddenly the girl started to scream. The sound jerked Mark back to reality, the here, the now. He turned. She was staring at him with wild, tearstained eyes, obviously in a state of total shock.

"Shut up," he said sharply but not unkindly.

"He was a…a vampire!" she said. She blinked in disbelief at her own words.

"Yes."

"You killed him!" she gasped. "But…he was real." She shook her head. "That's…impossible."

"I'm afraid not."

She swayed, still reeling, shaking as if she were suffering from a severe chill.

"He—he really was a vampire?"

Mark could hear sirens approaching. Someone must have heard her scream. "Yes, he was." But not the one I was looking for, he added silently.

"I don't…I can't…believe this," she said.

"We need to get out of here. The police are coming."

"Shouldn't we stay and report…um… this?"

He arched a brow at her. "You're going to report what happened here?" he asked.

She stared at him, still shaking. "Yes, but…no, it isn't real, can't be real, but…"

"It *is* real." He was trying very hard to be patient, but time was running out. He sighed. "They won't believe you, though. We have to get out of here."

Her jaw worked hard as she tried to form words. At last, still shivering, she said, "Get me over the wall, please?"

"Of course. Head that way."

He could move like the wind himself—college football—but she was still so stunned that he felt as if he were dragging dead weight. He had to urge her to help herself as he pushed her up the wall, then jumped to safety behind her and brought her back down on the sidewalk.

Back on solid pavement, she stared at him, shaking her head. "He was really a vampire?"

"Yes."

"No," she argued, then, "Yes," she said.

She was going to need some major therapy, he thought.

"You…you saved my life. I—I—oh, God, I owe you…you…"

"You and I both have to get out of here. They'll think we're junkies or thieves or something," he said flatly.

"Yes, but…I need to…to thank you somehow." Her eyes were wide, frightened; she wasn't being sexual, just grateful and unsure what to do about it.

She straightened her spine, still unable to believe what had happened, but trying for proper dignity.

"My *life*. You saved my life. I owe you something."

The patrol cars were nearly at the gates.

"You want to do something for me?" he demanded "Be careful. Don't go off into cemeteries with assholes you meet in a bar, okay?" He grabbed her hand. "Let's go."

He ran, pulling her along after him, and stayed with her down Canal Street and all the way to Harrah's.

"I don't even know your name," she told him.

"And you shouldn't," he said gently. "Go in there. Call a friend. Go home."

He turned and left her, suddenly exhausted, and more disappointed than he cared to admit.

He'd thought he'd been chasing…someone.

But he hadn't been. It was that simple.

He swore softly.

Damn, but there were a hell of a lot of foul beasts preying upon the world.

It occurred to him as he walked wearily back to his hotel that man himself could be considered one of them—even before the taint of pure evil touched upon him.

He stopped and looked at the roiling sky. He'd killed a murdering bloodsucker tonight. And it was all just beginning.

"I'm coming to get you. You're going to be mine, in a world of blood and death and darkness," Deanna Marin whispered darkly.

"Oh, for the love of God, cut it out," Lauren Crow pleaded.

"Seriously. Perhaps we'll open a door to another world, and demons will spring out and bring darkness and evil into this world," Heidi Weiss said, laughing, unable to maintain a low, threatening tone with the same success Deanna had managed.

Both Deanna and Heidi were staring across the outdoor table at Lauren with ridiculous grins on their faces. Of course, they were both holding drinks obtained from one of the bars here in Jackson Square, though she couldn't remember which one. Deanna's glass was in the shape of some kind of nuclear-material container and Heidi's looked like a naked man, buns, pecs and all. Perhaps due to a combination of alcohol and the atmosphere of New Orleans itself, they were suddenly eager to visit one of the numerous fortune-tellers who worked the area around Jackson Square with their tarot cards and crystal balls at the ready.

Lauren was delighted to be there—New Orleans was one of her favorite places in the world. Few locations offered such an artistic setting, with not just the visual stimuli but with the history of the area and liveliness of people filling the very air, as New Orleans did.

Tonight, however…

Maybe it was due to the one cosmo she'd imbibed, but instead of feeling light and giddy, she felt as if a strange sense of dread and darkness had settled over her.

"Lauren, what on earth is the matter with you?" Heidi demanded. "It's just for fun."

Lauren just didn't like the idea. She didn't know why—she wasn't particularly superstitious—but she had never wanted to have her cards read, let someone see her future in her palm, or receive any other kind of astral or otherworldly advice. Time, in her opinion, brought enough hardship without having to worry ahead of time about the bad things that could happen.

But she hated to be a wet blanket when they were here in New Orleans for a much anticipated prebridal shower for Heidi. Since they worked together at the graphic design company they had created after college, it had taken a lot of planning to get all their projects completed so they were free to take off together.

It was Heidi's party, and Lauren had promised herself that she was going to make sure everything went exactly the way Heidi wanted it to. But this desire to play with the occult was something new, and it was making her very uncomfortable.

"You said you would do anything at all this weekend to make me happy. Remember, you're my bridesmaid, so you're supposed to be my slave," Heidi teased.

"Why are you so bugged about it?" Deanna asked.

Lauren didn't know why, and she knew it was silly, but she really didn't want to look into the future.

"You can pick whomever we go to. How's that?" Heidi asked.

"Guys, I just think—"

"You need to do this just so you won't be frightened of a few dramatic effects and some spooky patter," Deanna said.

"I'm not afraid," Lauren protested quickly, but even as she spoke, she realized that in fact that was exactly it. She *was* afraid.

"Really, think about it," Deanna said. "Most of the psychics here are just college kids, trying to make a few bucks. Think of all the times we came here to draw, and how badly we needed the money people paid us for our sketches."

"I think you're forgetting the important point here. I told you. You're supposed to be my slave, remember?" Heidi said.

"Yeah, yeah, yeah," Lauren muttered. "All right. In that case, I think we should see some kind of voodoo queen. This is New Orleans, after all."

"And do you know an authentic voodoo queen?" Heidi asked, grinning.

Lauren had to smile; she couldn't help finding a certain amusement in the question. Heidi Weiss had powder-blue eyes, platinum hair and a smile a mile wild, the kind that coerced you into a good humor whether you wanted to feel cheerful or not. That grin was a little lopsided now, but just a little. They hadn't been drinking to the point of saturation, only enough not to feel any pain.

"We can walk around, look them all over," she suggested.

Lookswise, Deanna was the opposite of Heidi, with almond-dark eyes, sleek, almost blue-black hair, and now she decided to take charge. "I've got it. We'll walk around the entire Square to start. And then, if we don't see someone Lauren likes, we'll walk the entire French Quarter."

Lauren wondered if Deanna really had that much energy, or if she thought Lauren would decide more quickly if the alternative involved endless walking, since she was already—and obviously—exhausted They had arrived that morning on the red-eye from Los Angeles, and they hadn't stopped since. Lauren always felt very much at home in New Orleans, since she came from Baton Rouge, but Deanna had grown up in New York, and Heidi was from Boston. They had come often after becoming friends in college, but neither Heidi nor Deanna knew the little quirks and twists and turns of the place the way she did. They'd hit the casino early; then she'd been assigned to lead them to every little shop in the French Quarter, every place that wasn't part of a chain. Now she was tired and just wanted to get this over with.

"There," she said, pointing completely at random.

The woman she had chosen was sitting at a small portable table, facing the cathedral. She appeared to be older than they were, but beyond that, her age was indeterminate. Her hair was tied back with a scarf, and she wore a white peasant shirt and skirt. Her face was stunning, with strong features and skin a beautiful shade of gold that spoke of a multiethnic heritage. She was speaking earnestly to a man in the chair across from her, pointing to the tarot cards she was laying out before her as she spoke. She might have been at a Renaissance fair, rather than the French Quarter of New Orleans. Behind her was a small red tent that would have looked at home on a medieval battlefield. There was a table just inside it, covered with a cloth that depicted the moon and the stars. On the table was a crystal ball.

"She already has a customer," Deanna noted.

"I'm sure he won't take that long," Lauren said with a shrug. She wasn't sure why she had pointed to the woman, but now that she had, she was determined. Suddenly she realized that she *did* know why—she would have liked to draw the woman. Her face was so arresting.

"We could go to Madame Zorba right there," Heidi teased, inclining her head toward a younger woman just a few feet away.

Lauren grinned. Madame Zorba was definitely a college student.

"I like the woman over there," Lauren insisted.

"There's a good-looking gypsy guy up the street," Heidi said.

"You're engaged," Deanna teased her.

"Yeah, but you and Lauren could use a guy," Heidi said.

"Wow. Thanks," Deanna said.

"Just what I need, a gypsy," Lauren said. She didn't let her smile falter. *Heidi, damn it, you know I'm not looking to meet a guy.*

"You don't have to fall in love, pack him up and take him home with you," Heidi told her. Then she added softly, "But you could date. We're talking well over a year here."

"Thanks for the advice, Mom," Lauren murmured. She

paused, shivering suddenly, looking up. The night sky seemed to have clouded over; it had suddenly become cooler. There was a moon trying to come out, she thought, but it was shadowed by the clouds. She frowned. It was strange. There was a red glow where the moon should have been. "We may get rain tomorrow," she said.

"It's supposed to be clear all weekend," Deanna said.

Lauren shrugged. "Look at the sky."

"Um, well…could be smog," Deanna said.

"Hey, we're not in L.A.," Heidi said with a laugh.

"What—is it just called pollution when you're not in L.A.?" Deanna asked.

"It's just an angry red sky," Lauren murmured.

Heidi groaned. "Oh, Lord, we haven't even gotten to the fortune-teller yet, and she's talking about poetic doom."

"It's just strange," Lauren said.

"Is there anything weird in the wind?" Heidi teased.

"As a matter of fact, it's gotten a bit cooler," Lauren said.

"Thank God," Deanna breathed.

"You know, we could just go have another drink," Lauren suggested.

Heidi giggled. "The guy is gone. Let's go."

Lauren let out a sigh of impatience. "Just remember, you two wanted to do this. I'll do whatever you want, but I want it on record that I'm against such silliness."

"This trip is all about silliness," Heidi reminded her. "I'm going to get married. No more wild weekends with the girls. No more adventurous vacations. I mean, Barry is great, and he'd never care if I wanted a few days away with you guys, but…well, you know. And I guarantee you he's going to have one of those wild bachelor parties with strippers, and his idiot brother is going to make sure he has a lap dance—"

"I'll be happy to get you a lap dance," Lauren said.

Heidi laughed. "I don't want a lap dance. Now humor me, slave," she told Lauren.

"I'm all humor," Lauren muttered. "Let's go."

As they approached the woman, Lauren decided that she must look as on edge as she felt. Either that or she had talked herself into some kind of ridiculous paranoia, because it seemed as if the woman frowned when she saw them, as if she looked worried. Still, Lauren couldn't help noticing the strength of her features, and she wondered if she dared ask to do a sketch of her at some point.

There was no nameplate, nothing like Madame X or Madame Zenia or any other cliché, on her table. She rose, stretching out an elegant arm and offering a slender hand with elegantly polished nails. "Hello," she said simply.

"Hi," Heidi said cheerfully.

The woman stared at Heidi gravely. "You seek the future?"

"Absolutely," Heidi said, introducing herself. "I'm Heidi Weiss, and I'm about to be married. I'd love some advice."

The woman nodded, but her expression said that she read in Heidi's polite words the simple fact that she didn't really believe in what she was doing. It was all for fun.

"I'm Deanna Marin," Deanna said, stepping forward. "And this is Lauren Crow."

The woman arched a brow slightly, studying Lauren. "Crow?"

"I've been told that my great-grandfather was Cherokee," Lauren said, taking the woman's hand. There was strength in her grip. It offered a strange assurance.

"I, too, have Cherokee blood. We have the same green eyes."

"So we do," Lauren agreed, though she wasn't sure green eyes came from the Cherokee part of her background.

"You're tall…five ten?"

"Around there. Another grandfather was from the Orkney Islands. A big, tall guy, so I was told. Some Norse, some Scots."

"Ah, and thus you are redheaded."

"I like to think auburn."

The woman smiled. Lauren had to admit, she liked her, but more than ever, she didn't want a reading, didn't want to know what the future supposedly held. She wanted to ask the woman to have a drink with them instead.

"I like to think I am not turning gray. I'm Susan," the woman said.

Heidi started to giggle. "I'm so sorry," she apologized quickly. "It's just so…normal."

Susan offered a slight smile in return. "Life is normal, the cycle of life is normal, the air we breathe is normal. So many things are normal, including much that we don't understand yet."

"You have a beautiful face," Lauren heard herself blurt out.

Susan inclined her head slightly, acknowledging the compliment. When she lifted her eyes again, she smiled. "You're artists?"

"I'm a graphic designer, actually," Deanna said. "Heidi and Lauren can draw anything in the world, though. They're fabulous."

"And you'd like to sketch me?" Susan asked, looking at Lauren.

"I'd love to."

"That's not why we're here, though," Heidi said.

"Ah, yes, the future," Susan said. She lifted her hands. "What will it be? Would you like a reading of your palm? Or shall we see what's in the cards? And then, of course, there is always the crystal ball."

"We should each do something different," Deanna suggested.

"Tarot cards," Heidi said.

"I'll take a palm reading," Deanna determined.

Lauren shrugged. "Crystal ball."

Susan nodded, indicating several small fold-up chairs inside the tent. "Lauren, you are welcome to sketch. I'll begin with the bride."

Lauren always carried a small sketch pad in her handbag, but she wondered how Susan knew that, and she was slightly disturbed. Or slightly *more* disturbed, if she were being honest. Then she told herself that Susan already knew they were artists. Guessing that she carried a sketch pad was just a logical assumption. No doubt most people who did this kind of thing for a living learned how to assess people, how to read a great deal in a few words and intuit where to go from there.

Deanna had unfolded the little wooden chairs. She sat on one side of Heidi, while Lauren backed her chair away a bit and took out her sketchbook. As she sat, watching Susan instruct Heidi on how to choose her cards, she could hear the sounds around them. Music in the distance, coming from the bars. People talking, then stopping to ooh and aah at the artwork available on the street. Across from them, near the cathedral, a lone flutist had set down his cap, and now he performed a plaintive and beautiful tune.

She looked up at the sky. Clouds still rode heavy over the moon, like a red curtain in the air.

She studied Susan. The woman was soft-spoken. Elegant. Not at all what she had expected. Her pencil moved over the paper. She drew the lines first, then filled in the shades and shadows. Finally she added background, the greenery around the Square, the sidewalk, the tent, the statue of Andrew Jackson rising far behind Susan's back.

"Ugh! What does that mean?" Heidi asked, drawing Lauren's attention to the table, where Heidi had turned up a card with a skeleton.

"It's…death, isn't it?" Heidi asked.

Susan shook her head. "It often signifies change, an ending so that there can be a new beginning. You are about to end your single life. You will start into a new life."

"Whew," Heidi murmured. Though she spoke lightly, Lauren thought she was seriously relieved, and she felt a new wave of discomfort.

"What's that?" Deanna asked, pointing to another card.

"Love." Susan looked at Heidi. "You can rest assured in this—your fiancé loves you very much. You are all he has ever wanted, all he could ever need in life."

"Oh," Heidi breathed happily. "Ditto."

"Yes, I can see," Susan murmured.

"Will the wedding go off without a hitch?" Heidi asked.

"No wedding goes off without a hitch," Susan said dryly as she scooped up the cards, patting them back into a neat pile. "But you are deeply loved, and you love deeply in return."

"Thank you." Heidi rose and looked at Lauren with an expression on her face that plainly said, *See? Nothing to be afraid of.*

Lauren smiled back weakly, wondering if Heidi had really been listening. Susan hadn't said anything specific about Heidi's wedding at all—she had just generalized about weddings. And she had said the skeleton card *often* indicated a change.

Then again, Lauren told herself, maybe *she* was the one hearing words that weren't being said.

"On to the palm," Deanna said. She and Heidi changed seats. As Deanna started to sit down, she glanced at Lauren's drawing and frowned.

"What is it?" Lauren asked.

"Uh, nothing, I guess. It's a great drawing. It's just that…well, you made the skeleton card the focus of it."

"I did not!" Lauren protested, and looked down at the sketch. It was one of her best, she thought. She'd captured not just a two-dimensional image but given it great depth. She'd found the strange and arresting beauty that was Susan's. She'd caught the atmosphere of the Square. You could look at the drawing and almost hear music.

And yet…

Deanna was right. Somehow she had detailed the tarot card down to the finest line so that it unerringly drew the viewer's eye and became the focus of the picture.

"Don't draw me," Deanna whispered to her.

"Okay," Lauren assured her quietly in return.

Susan was watching them both. Deanna noticed and gave her a rueful smile. "Lauren was engaged once."

"And her young man died," Susan said.

Wow, damned good guess, Lauren thought irritably. Though it was a fifty-fifty shot. Either they'd broken up or he had died. She knew that she was just one of many young women of her day. She'd fallen in love with a soldier. He'd gone to war. They'd e-mailed for six months, and then she'd stopped receiving replies.

Until the army lieutenant had come to her house.

She'd gone through it all. The devastation, the anger. And the healing. She didn't feel that she had any terrible psychological hang-ups. She just wasn't actively looking to find love again. But if the right person came along…

Would she be ready?

She really didn't know.

"I'm so sorry," Susan said to Lauren gravely. She was

clearly sincere, making Lauren feel vaguely guilty, though she wasn't quite sure why.

"Thank you," she said, ignoring her uncomfortable feelings. "But, hey, that's the past, and we're looking to the future, right? What does Deanna's hand say to you, Susan?"

Susan studied Deanna's palm and looked up gravely.

"What?" Deanna asked impatiently.

"So far, it has told me that you do not like housework at all," Susan said.

Even Deanna laughed. "Okay, I suck. Seriously, I'm really bad, so I gave it up."

"Don't worry, she has a wonderful woman who comes in twice a week," Heidi assured Susan.

Susan traced a finger down a line in Deanna's hand.

"The life line, right?" Heidi asked.

Susan shrugged.

"It doesn't look very long," Deanna said worriedly.

Susan shook her head, looking at Deanna. "Often, things are what we make them. The line…it's like the card. It might not mean anything bad at all. It signifies change. A change in life. Heidi is getting married."

"I'm not even dating steadily," Deanna said.

"You're a beautiful woman," Susan said, sidestepping. "What else do you see?"

Susan pointed. "Here…artistic success. You are clever and determined." Susan looked up and stared hard at Deanna. "When you set your mind to something, you can make it happen. When we fail, far too often, it is because we're afraid. Remember, you have the talent and the will. Don't be put off by circumstances that seem dire. You are very strong. And there will be changes."

"Will I ever get married?" Deanna asked.

Susan shrugged. "Your palm is not telling me. I can say that you are passionate and giving, and that you are quite capable of creating fire, passion—and love—around you."

"I like that," Deanna said.

Lauren looked at her, trying to avoid Susan's eyes. *Lots of people could have said that to you,* her stern gaze said.

"Your turn," Deanna said.

"Ah, the crystal ball for our talented young artist," Susan murmured. She didn't move, though, and her eyes were downcast.

"I think Susan is tired," Lauren said.

"Oh, no, you are *not* getting out of this!" Heidi insisted.

"May I see more fully?" Susan asked.

Lauren handed her the drawing she had done.

"You are very kind," she murmured. "You have caught me on paper with great beauty."

"I want to work more on it. I'll send you a copy when I'm done," Lauren told her.

Susan nodded and handed back the drawing. Lauren flipped her sketchbook closed and returned it to her purse.

"It seems like you've had a busy night. You look tired. You really don't have to do another reading," Lauren said.

"She's trying to get out of this," Heidi explained.

Susan stood. She wasn't smiling. "I think that we must look into the crystal ball."

Heidi and Deanna started to rise.

"There is only room in the tent for one—I'm sorry. The crystal ball is quite different from the palm and the cards."

Susan waited gravely, and at last Lauren followed her into the tent, the sounds from the street and the night receding. As she sat in the chair opposite Susan, the world outside all but disappeared.

"Your fiancé, he was a soldier?" Susan asked, staring into the crystal ball.

Startled, Lauren looked at her.

"Yes."

"I'm very sorry, truly. But…there are those who believe there are certain fates we cannot avoid, and others who believe we have a hand in our own futures. Perhaps many people lived because your young man died," she said softly.

"Thank you. I'd like to think that," Lauren murmured.

"You don't date much."

"I've dated."

Susan smiled enigmatically.

"What?" Lauren asked.

"You don't date much because you feel that you meet nothing but dimwits and users since you lost your man."

"It's hard to meet the right person."

They had been chatting casually, almost as if they were engaged in a normal conversation at any one of the smaller cafés or bars in the city.

But Lauren realized that something had been subtly changing since she had come into the little tent.

The crystal ball had begun to glow, to fill with a red mist.

She stared at it, unable to tear her eyes away. She only dimly noted Susan's face, registering as if from a great distance that the other woman looked tense, even distressed.

"You must leave here…. You and your friends…must go."

"Yes," Lauren said.

But she couldn't move. It felt as if she were frozen where she sat, as if her very muscles were paralyzed.

There was something dark at the core of the crystal ball, dark and red, finding form as the milliseconds ticked by.

It was a bird. A winged thing.

Then it was not.

It took the shape of a man. Tall, the face dark, the figure imposing.

A sound seemed to rise in her ears, and she realized that it was laughter. Deep, rich, taunting—and cruel.

She heard words.

So soft at first that she couldn't understand what was being said. Then she knew.

"I'm coming for you. I'm coming to get you."

"No," Lauren murmured, struggling for sanity, for reality. Someone had heard them talking earlier. Someone had heard the words that Deanna had spoken teasingly.

"Lauren…"

The dark figure called her by name. "I'm coming to get you, Lauren…."

"No!"

"I'm coming to get you, and you'll be mine in a world of blood and death and darkness."

Susan suddenly jumped up, as if she, too, had suddenly broken the invisible bonds holding her there.

She made a strange sound and her arm flew out.

The crystal ball leaped off the table and shattered on the ground.

But even as it shattered into a thousand pieces, it seemed to Lauren that she heard a husky whisper of evil laughter.

2

She wasn't sure how she'd gotten there, but Lauren found herself outside the tent. It seemed so normal now, nothing more than a little red canvas tent again.

She was back outside just as if they had finished their session completely normally, as if she had casually strolled out after hearing some nice, normal prediction for her future. She was back outside, in the midst of the neon light and movement of the night. The very *normal* night. She could hear footsteps and laughter, bits of conversation, the sound of mules' hooves as they clattered on the pavement, drawing carriages filled with tourists.

Both Heidi and Deanna were staring at her in surprise, and that wasn't normal at all.

Lauren turned to look back inside the tent. The images she had seen now seemed ridiculous, but the shattered crystal ball was there as proof that *something* out of the ordinary had happened.

"Lauren!" Heidi said, shocked. "Susan, we're so sorry. We'll pay for your crystal ball, of course. What on earth happened?" She stepped forward, slipping an arm through Lauren's, lowering her voice to a whisper. "I knew you weren't exactly into this, but did you have to break her crystal ball?"

"It was an accident!" Lauren protested.

It *had* been an accident—and she hadn't even been the one to break it. But beyond that, she couldn't have seen what she thought she had. She had been tricked. It must have been some kind of a parlor trick, though that seemed impossible now, with all the light and noise around her.

Even now, the details of what she had seen, what she had heard, were slipping from her mind. She tried to hold on, but they were all escaping her. And she was beginning to feel like a fool.

Was she worse off—mentally or emotionally—than she had thought?

No!

Susan was still staring at her. And she didn't seem to be concerned about her crystal ball but about Lauren herself.

"Where are you girls staying?" Susan asked.

"The Old Cote," Deanna said.

Susan frowned in puzzlement. "I don't know it."

"It's a lovely place, made up of several cottages. It was kind of a family compound before the storm, but they've opened it up as an inn now as a way to recoup some of their losses. The grandmother—the family matriarch, I guess—is enjoying it, so I guess the place will stay around for a while. I found it online," Deanna said, her enthusiasm for their little discovery evident.

"But where is it?" Susan asked.

Deanna seemed a little surprised by the fortune-teller's persistent tone. "Off Conti and a good bit back from Bourbon, luckily. The noise is great when you're part of the party, but when you're trying to sleep, it can be a bit much."

"You have to move. Move into the biggest, most crowded hotel, and room together, stay together, until you can get out of New Orleans," Susan warned.

"But we're not leaving," Heidi said. "Not for several days. This is my bachelorette party."

Susan shook her head, a look of dismay on her face. She stared at Lauren, and Lauren knew that her own expression must have shown the woman that she was already feeling silly and skeptical, as if she had been the target of a trick—or a joke.

"You have to leave."

"Oh, please," Deanna said impatiently.

"I'll pay you for the damages," Heidi said, starting to sound irritated.

"You came for readings. You've had them, and now you have to leave," Susan said.

Heidi pulled out her wallet and tried to give Susan money, but the woman only backed away. Heidi set the money on the table, shaking her head. Then she linked arms with Lauren, pulling her away. "You do not get to pick the fortune-teller anymore," she said, dragging her along.

As they put some distance between themselves and the Square, Deanna burst into laughter. "Didn't you feel as if we had just walked into an old horror flick?"

"I'm sure she was going to tell us to beware the bite of a werewolf any second," Heidi agreed, and then she, too, burst into laughter.

"And you! You fell for all her tricks," Heidi told Lauren.

"I did not," Lauren protested, but silently she was thinking, *Yes, I did. It was creepy as hell in there.*

She felt like an idiot now, though, as they passed Royal Street, nearly at Bourbon. Bands were playing loudly from several corners, the sound of jazz mixing with rock.

"We need a drink," Heidi said. "Name your poison."

"Meow," Deanna said.

"What?"

"The Cat's Meow. Karaoke," Deanna said.

"You must be joking. We suck," Heidi said.

"And that's why we're perfect for karaoke," Deanna said happily.

"I need a lot more to drink for this," Lauren said. The two of them had her laughing, but karaoke was no more her style than mystical readings. "Wait!" she said, stopping in her tracks and forcing the others to stop, too.

"What?" Deanna asked.

"I'm only Heidi's slave. Heidi, you don't really want to sing karaoke, do you?"

"You bet I do!" Heidi said.

Groaning, Lauren found herself dragged into the bar.

It wasn't that bad. The host was a handsome, well-built black man with an exceptional voice. His choice of music was great; the place was hopping. The entire room actually seemed to enjoy the rendition of "Summer Nights" that Heidi and Deanna laughed their way through.

But when the two of them left the stage, Lauren was glad to see that they were feeling the effects of the noise and the crush of humanity, and were ready to go before she had to make a fool of herself in public. They left the club and headed for a darker place with soft jazz that was just down the street.

"Order me another one of those fizzy things I was drinking," Lauren said to Deanna when they had found a table. "I'm off to find the restroom."

She left her friends and made her way through the tables. When she reached the hallway that led to the facilities, she was startled when she ran straight into a man. She hadn't even realized she'd been walking with her head down, deep in thought. Still, she wasn't sure where he'd come from as she plowed straight into him.

Apologizing, looking up at last, she backed away.

He was tall, two or three inches over six feet, and definitely well built—she had almost bounced off the muscles of his chest. His hair was dark, a moderate length, and even in the shadowy hallway, it was apparent that his eyes were a deep and striking blue. She thought he was somewhere around thirty, with ruggedly striking chiseled features: high cheekbones, a long, straight nose, determined jawline and a high forehead. His mouth was generous, the kind that could harden into a thin line or curve into a quick smile.

He wasn't model-pretty. He had the look of a man who lived, and lived by his own rules, heedless of others' opinions.

"I'm sorry," she said, realizing that she was staring at him.

But then again, he was also staring at her.

"Katie," he murmured.

"Lauren," she corrected automatically.

He took a step back, deep eyes almost burning into her. "No, I'm sorry," he said. "You reminded me of someone. My mistake. Sorry," he said again. But he didn't move, and he was still staring at her.

As if he really did know her.

But he couldn't possibly. She would have remembered if she had ever crossed paths with him before.

"I…uh, need to get by," she said softly.

"Of course," he said.

But he was still staring, and she felt a blush rising to her cheeks.

She didn't know him, she was certain.

But she would like to.

She could introduce herself, of course. They were in a bar. People did things like that in bars. Some of them even went to bars specifically for the purpose of meeting people.

Some people did things like that, but she didn't. She hadn't dated in…well, only once since Ken had died. She hadn't been able to work up any interest in the print-shop owner Deanna had decided she had to meet. She just hadn't been attracted to him. Maybe her feelings had still been too raw, the sense of loss too new. She had been completely in love with her fiancé. He had made her smile, made her laugh. And she had been attracted to him from the start. There had been nothing wrong with the print-shop owner. He just hadn't been Ken. She just hadn't been attracted to him.

But this stranger staring at her, this man she didn't know from Adam? She *was* attracted to *him.*

She flushed at her own thoughts. Some people picked up strangers in bars. *She* didn't, not at this stage of her life. She was here for Heidi.

She smiled. "Honestly, I didn't mean to ram you. And I do need to get by."

"Right. Sorry." He stepped aside.

She walked past him, heading for the door marked "Madames." She couldn't help but turn back.

He was still watching her.

Great. She was heading into a ladies' room in a dimly lit corridor and a good-looking but possibly very weird guy was watching her.

She entered, closed the door and leaned against it. There was no lock on the door, only on the three individual stalls.

I should go back, make Heidi or Deanna come with me, she thought. *I'm going to be attacked in a restroom on Bourbon Street.*

She was being ridiculous, she told herself. It was just the uneasiness left over from her experience in the fortune-teller's tent. The woman was probably still laughing at the three of them. She probably ought to report Susan to the tourist board. Imagine! Trying to scare them, telling them to leave town. That was hardly good for business.

She opened the door a crack and peered out.

The man was gone. She was relieved.

And also disappointed.

She let out a sigh, irritated with herself for still feeling nervous.

She was so nervous, in fact, that she took her time, unwilling to go back out into the club right away. She splashed her face with water after she washed her hands, reminding herself that she was being ridiculous. When she finally left the restroom behind, there was no one in the hallway.

The bar had grown more crowded while she was gone. As she wended her way through the crowd, she could see that Heidi was alone at their table. Frowning, she noticed Deanna was at the bar, chatting with a tall, dark man. For a moment her heart thudded. Was it the same man?

No, not unless he had changed his shirt. The man she had met had been wearing a tailored shirt; this man was dressed more casually.

She started toward the bar and her friend. Deanna had definitely imbibed more than she had tonight, and she wasn't sure she wanted to let her friend get too close to a stranger in that condition.

On the other hand, Deanna wasn't the one getting married. She was free to flirt if she chose.

Apparently she was simply worried in general tonight, Lauren thought. She headed for the bar, but as she did, the man turned and headed out to the street.

"Hey there," Deanna said as Lauren reached her. "Her Majesty wanted more cherries for her drink," she said with a grin.

Lauren forced a smile in return. Deanna didn't seem all that drunk, she thought. In fact, she seemed more pleasantly tipsy than anything else. "Cool," Lauren responded, then asked, "Who was that?"

"Who?" Deanna frowned and flipped back a length of her long dark hair.

"The guy who was just there."

"Oh. Just a guy."

"Cute?"

"Yeah, kind of."

"And?"

"I told him I was with friends tonight," Deanna said. And she laughed. "I'm a big girl, so don't worry about me."

"I wasn't worried," Lauren lied.

"Yes, you were. And you still are. You're still tense." Deanna looked at her and sighed. "We shouldn't have made you go to that fortune-teller."

"Don't be silly."

"She was weird."

"She was striking, don't you think?" Lauren said.

"A great face to sketch, yes, but weird. Come on. Let's get back to the table. Heidi is going to want her fruit."

The band was playing exceptional jazz; it sounded as if they had been together forever. As she sat, Lauren let the music engulf her, and she smiled. She came from this state, after all. She'd been in New Orleans hundreds of times. She knew the city well. Why she was letting the antics of a Jackson Square fortune-teller disturb her, she didn't know.

"So are you ever going to tell us where the honeymoon is going to be?" Deanna asked Heidi.

Heidi shrugged. "I'll tell you guys, but not Barry's friends. A few of them are crazy enough to show up."

"Okay, where?" Lauren asked.

Heidi leaned forward, and her love for her soon-to-be husband was apparent in her gamine smile and powder-blue eyes. "Fiji," she said.

"Fiji. Wow," Lauren said.

"You really think Barry's friends might show up in Fiji?" Deanna asked.

"You never know," Heidi said. "I can guarantee you right now that we'll all probably end up in the pool at the reception, and that they'll tie cans to the car and do anything else ridiculous that guys can do. Most of those guys actually graduated from college, and some of them are even lawyers, like Barry, but honestly, they're still like a bunch of kids."

"You're not marrying them, you're marrying Barry," Deanna reminded her.

"Because he's wonderful," Heidi said, finishing the statement by biting the cherry at the end of her swizzle stick.

"He is a good guy," Lauren agreed.

"And he has some very attractive friends—silly, but attractive," Deanna added.

"I can set you up any time," Heidi promised.

"I like setting myself up. We'll see what happens at the wedding," Deanna said.

Lauren let out a yawn, then quickly apologized. "Sorry."

"It's late, isn't it?" Heidi said.

"Not for New Orleans. And this is your party," Lauren assured her.

"I know, but I think I'd like to take my party back to our nice cushy cottage," she said.

"Cool. I'm your slave," Lauren said.

They both looked at Deanna, wondering if she intended to protest.

She laughed. "Okay, I admit, I'm beat, too. But we're pathetic. I guarantee you they'll go all night at Barry's bachelor party."

"Right, but his bachelor party is only one night. We have a whole weekend. We have days left to party," Heidi said. "And shop."

"For Fiji," Lauren said.

"Yep, for Fiji," Heidi agreed. She lifted her glass, and Deanna and Lauren followed suit, clinking their glasses in a toast. "Here's to the world's best friends."

"Here's to you, too," Lauren said.

"Let's not get maudlin," Deanna said.

"If she wants to be maudlin, we'll be maudlin," Lauren reminded Deanna.

Deanna groaned. "Okay, but let's walk in a maudlin manner and get back to the B and B."

"Sounds good," Lauren agreed.

As they headed for their cottage, they talked about the shops Heidi wanted to hit in the morning.

Along Bourbon Street, everything felt fine to Lauren. It was quieter than it had been earlier, but the bars were still open, and people were moving about. Groups still spilled out of the doorways of the clubs. Hawkers were handing out flyers for the strip joints. A group that appeared to be made up of retirees was moving along at a good clip. Most of the members seemed to be couples who had spent many years together, and who still enjoyed walking hand in hand. She had to smile. It didn't seem quite the right place, but then again, who was she to say? They were definitely young at heart.

It was when they turned off Bourbon that Lauren first felt the strange stirring of unease.

The street wasn't so well lit anymore.

And it wasn't filled with people.

The sound of Heidi and Deanna's voices seemed to fade. She wasn't hearing them. Instead, she was watching.

Watching the shadows.

They seemed to be moving too much. Houses and buildings, flush against one another, a few feet away, should have been still. Instead, their shadows stretched, became too long, seemed to loom.

Then there was the breeze.

She hadn't felt it on Bourbon Street, but it was eerily noticeable now.

She quickened her pace.

"Hey!" Heidi's protest broke through her sense of isolation.

"What?" Lauren asked.

"Do we really have to *run* back?"

"I think we should hurry, yes," Lauren said.

"You told me this was a safe area," Heidi protested.

"It is. But…it's late," Lauren said.

"Look. Up ahead," Deanna said.

"What?" Lauren said, her heart quickening.

"Mounted police officer," Deanna said dryly.

"Oh." Lauren slowed her pace a bit as they passed the officer, who touched his helmet and wished them good-night, then rode on toward Bourbon Street. As soon as he was gone, she started hurrying again. She couldn't help herself.

"Lauren, slow down," Deanna begged. "My legs aren't working too well."

"That's because they want to be stretched out in bed," Lauren said.

"You two are tall—I'm not," Heidi reminded her.

Gritting her teeth, Lauren forced herself to slow down. She was frightened, and she didn't know why. And she was angry. She'd never been frightened here before in her life.

It was all because of that damn fortune-teller.

She made herself keep to a slower pace, but she couldn't stop herself from watching the shadows. And no matter how hard she tried to tell herself she was being ridiculous, she was certain the shadows were doing things shadows weren't supposed to do. She couldn't help but feel they were *watching* her.

The bed-and-breakfast, with its lovely courtyard and cottages, was straight ahead. She had to forcibly stop herself from breaking into a run.

But then they were there and she let out a sigh, praying that it wasn't audible. The cast-iron gates, dating back to the 1840s, were opened to the main manor and the old cottages surrounding it.

Theirs was the middle cottage, directly facing the pool. Lauren all but dragged her friends toward it.

"Honestly, Lauren," Heidi began to protest.

"See, we're here. Your stubby little legs can get a rest."

"Stubby little legs!" Heidi objected. "Some slave you are."

"But we're here. Aren't you glad?" Lauren demanded.

Deanna yawned, pulling out her key and opening the door. "Yeah, yeah, great, we're here." She turned around and said speculatively, "Look how good that pool looks."

"You want to go swimming—now?" Lauren demanded.

"Well, I'm sweating—since I ran back," Deanna said.

"We'd make a racket," Lauren said quickly.

"No one said that we couldn't swim at night," Heidi said.

"We've all had a fair bit to drink. No one is going to save us if we begin to drown," Lauren informed them, longing desperately to go inside and lock the door.

"She's right, you know. We *have* had too much to drink," Heidi said.

"Right," Lauren announced. She pushed the door fully open and turned on the light. They'd left the television on. She was glad. She was even happier to realize that it was showing a seventies sitcom, not some creepy horror show.

"How are we sleeping?" Heidi asked. There were two double beds in the bedroom behind the kitchen/living room area where they were standing. In the outer room, the bed was a pullout sofa.

"I'll take the bed out here, and you two can have the real beds," Lauren said. She would have taken a hard wooden floor at that moment, she was so relieved just to be back in their cottage.

"You sure? You can bunk in with one of us," Deanna offered.

"You snore when you drink," Lauren said, grinning for real at last. "I'll be fine out here."

"I do not snore!" Deanna protested.

"You do," Heidi told her, grinning. "But only when you drink," she added quickly.

"Humph," Deanna muttered, and started for the bedroom.

"I guess that means she's taking first dibs on the bathroom," Heidi said, shrugging. "I'm getting into pajamas and crashing." She gave Lauren a hug good-night. "Thanks—this is the best trip, ever."

"Absolutely," Lauren agreed, wishing she could believe it was true.

She watched Heidi walk into the bedroom, too, then turned to open the sofa bed. It wasn't so bad. The closet offered plenty of extra bedding and pillows, and she could brush her teeth and wash her face in the half bath next to the kitchen.

Clad in boxers and a T-shirt, she started to turn off the TV and the lights.

Then she hesitated.

She left the TV on, wanting the sounds of a sitcom to lure

her to sleep. She left the bathroom light on, then turned off the others. When she was done, she found herself walking to the window that looked out onto the courtyard and pool.

She had intended to reassure herself.

Instead, she felt a jolt of ice rip along her spinal cord.

There was someone out there.

A man.

Watching their cottage.

He was leaning against a utility pole out by the street, but, despite the high fence, she could see him, and she knew he was staring at the cottage.

What was worse was the fact that she knew who he was.

Tall, dark hair, piercing blue eyes.

It was the man she had crashed into at the bar.

A scream froze in her throat. But then, as if he knew he was being watched in return, he stepped away from the pole and walked away. She saw the breadth of his back for a few seconds, and then he was gone.

She realized a few seconds later that she had a death grip on the curtains, and that she was still staring out at the night, which now appeared completely calm and normal.

She bit her lower lip, wondering if she should call the police. And tell them what? That she had no evidence, but she was certain a man she had met in a bar had followed them home and stared at their cottage? Like that would be a pressing concern to men who had to deal with real problems—drugs, thugs and nasty drunks. But no matter what the police would think, she was sure that they had been…

Stalked.

She glanced toward the bedroom. The door was ajar and the room was quiet. Heidi and Deanna were probably sound asleep already.

All right, she would just call the police and ask if an officer could do a few drive-bys during the night.

They would undoubtedly think she was a jumpy freak. But better that than…

Determined, she walked over and closed the door to the bedroom. Then she did call the police, using the non-emergency number. A very polite officer took her information, assured her that she wasn't an idiot and promised that a car would check the property throughout the night.

When she hung up, she felt almost smug. She got a can of Coke from the refrigerator and curled her legs beneath her on the sofa bed to watch TV.

But as she sat there, the cold from her soda seemed to seep into her bones. She couldn't help but replay her fading memories of the strange scene in the fortune-teller's tent. Now, alone in the dark, the details seemed to be coming back.

She had the strangest feeling that the evil being in the crystal ball had been real.

And that a dozen police officers couldn't stand against the soul-stealing danger that he presented.

She had seen him. Great. Now she would think he was stalking her.

He was still in shock himself. It was impossible for anyone to look so much like Katie, and yet… It was as if his fiancée had been cloned. Even her smile, the way she flushed slightly, the slight hike of her brow…all were simply Katie.

As he walked away from the B and B, he was all too aware the woman in question was probably still watching him from the window.

Then, to his surprise, he noticed that there was a light on over the door to the main house, and several lights still blazing inside.

He made a point of walking away, then doubling back. The curtain at the cottage had dropped. He was free and clear. He walked up the porch steps of the main house and tried the door. It was open.

"Hello?"

A long hall led back to a desk. He admired the main house as he walked in; it reminded him of the Cornstalk, another bed-and-breakfast, and one of the loveliest in New Orleans. A curved stairway led to the upper rooms, while the hall branched off toward several more. He knew that each one would be a little bit different. That was the beauty of such a place. Nothing was cookie-cutter; every room would have something all its own.

"Hello!" a cheerful voice called from the end of the hall.

He walked on to the desk. A woman of about sixty, with shimmering silvery white hair, was sitting there. Papers were strewn before her, and a computer was on a table to her left.

"I saw the lights on," Mark said.

"I suppose I should lock up and go to bed, but I've discovered that I love being an innkeeper," she said. She had a great smile, dark eyes and an aura of energy about her, even as she sat still. "I'm Lilly Martin. How do you do?"

"I'm Mark Davidson, and I'm great, thanks. I think your inn is wonderful. I was hoping you might have a cottage left."

She cocked her head slightly. "You're looking for a room at 3:00 a.m.?"

He laughed. "I have a room, but I just saw your place, and I think it's enchanting."

Lilly Martin flushed with pleasure. "Thank you so much. And I do have a cottage vacant. I'm not sure I'd feel right, though. I can't just give you the room for free, but I can't really charge you for a full night, either."

"We could split the difference," he suggested.

"Lovely. Sold," Lilly said.

She turned toward the computer. "Let's see. Mark Davidson. Address and phone, length of stay, and will this be on a credit card?"

He produced his driver's license and credit card. As she looked at the information, he made a point of looking over her shoulder. The registrations for the night were up on the screen.

He scanned the screen quickly. The girls were obvious. Cottage five.

Lauren Crow, Heidi Weiss, Deanna Marin.

He leaned back, smiling.

As she typed information into the computer, Lilly asked, "Just being nosy, Mark, but what do you do for a living?"

"I'm a writer."

"Oh! Have I read anything you've written?"

He hesitated. "Probably not. I mostly do sports articles for syndication," he lied.

She glanced at him from the corner of her eye. "Hmm. And here I thought you might be an underwear model."

"What?"

She laughed. "Sorry. You look like those guys in the ads."

"Uh, thanks. I think."

"Or a ninja," she added.

"A ninja?"

She laughed. "Silly of me. Okay. Maybe a cop. Or FBI."

"Just a writer," he said. "But thanks." *Ninja?*

Within ten minutes, Lilly had him registered and he had a key to his cottage. He hesitated, though. "You really should lock up this late at night," he told her.

"I know. My kids would be angry."

"As well they should be."

"But I filled another cottage tonight, didn't I?" she asked cheerfully.

He turned to her, catching her hands. "Yes, but it's not safe, Lilly. Please, lock up much, much earlier, okay?"

She let out a soft sigh. "Yes, of course, you're right." She winked. "But don't tell on me, okay? Anyway, it's bedtime for both of us now. In the morning, coffee and croissants are served in the dining room, to your left there, or on the patio, by the pool."

"Great. Thanks. I'll go pick up my things from my dreaded chain hotel," he told her, grinning. "Then I'll be back."

After she accompanied him to the main door and watched him go, he heard her slide the bolt, and he was relieved. It worried him a bit to stay here; he hoped he wasn't putting Lilly in danger.

But if he thought that woman looked like Katie, so would Stephan. And he knew that Stephan was here. He had followed the creature's trail from Abruzzi to Cannes to Essex, then here to New Orleans. Mark was convinced that it was only a matter of time before Stephan saw the woman—if he hadn't seen her already.

Because Stephan was definitely here. He could feel it.

Mark simply hadn't expected that he would come across so many other vampires along the way. Tonight he could have sworn he had found Stephan at last, but he'd been wrong. Was he going to think that every tall, dark man he caught a glimpse of was Stephan?

It had still been a good night's work. He couldn't regret killing the vampire in the cemetery. He'd saved someone's life, at least.

And yet...

The lust for vengeance was like a fire inside him. Complicated now.

Because it was as if Katie had come back to life.

* * *

She was sleeping...dreaming, Lauren thought.

She had to be.

She was there, at the bar.

And he was there, too.

He said something, teasing her, as if they had been friends forever. No, lovers forever. She could smell something that teased her senses. Something that affected not just her flesh but her mind, awakening her sensuality from within, touching her most erotic zones.

Then he was touching her. Stroking her.

She awoke suddenly, the faint sound of a click in her ears. She realized that the television was still on; now it was an infomercial for diet pills.

The dream weighed heavily on her, but she knew that a noise, something that wasn't the TV, had awakened her.

The door. She had heard the door opening.

She leaped up, looking around. The bolt was undone, and she threw the door open, thinking only afterward that it was a stupid thing to do.

But she was glad she had done it.

Deanna was outside, standing at the end of the pool, talking aloud as if she were carrying on a conversation with someone invisible, or maybe someone who had just left.

Lauren burst out after her friend, calling her name. "Deanna!"

Deanna didn't move.

Lauren raced around in front of her, grabbing her shoulders and staring into her eyes. They were glazed. Deanna didn't even see her.

"Hey!" She gave her friend a shake. Nothing. "Deanna!" A harder shake.

Deanna started, her eyes widening in alarm. "Lauren?"

"Hey, you, what are you doing?"

"Sleeping," Deanna said, her features twisted into a mask of confusion.

"Sleep*walking*," Lauren corrected, confused herself. Deanna had never done this before, at least as far as she knew.

"Weird," Deanna said. She looked around at the foliage, the shimmering water in the pool, the shadows of the night. "I'm lucky I didn't fall in the pool and drown."

"You don't remember coming out here at all? Really?"

Deanna shook her head and groaned. "No more of those drinks with all the shots in them, bachelorette party or not."

"Good thought," Lauren agreed. She felt a chill, remembering how she had seen the man standing by the pole earlier. What if he had still been hanging around? "Let's go in.

"I'll put a chair in front of the door," Lauren said as soon as they were inside, the door safely locked behind them.

Deanna gave her a quick hug. "Thanks," she said huskily.

Deanna went back into the bedroom, and Lauren lay down again, troubled. She was so tired. Her lids became heavy. She drifted.

And dreamed.

Mark returned to the bed-and-breakfast with his car and belongings. He glanced at his watch. It was four in the morning.

Once he had parked and grabbed his overnight bag, he stood in the courtyard. Unease trickled through him.

He could smell it. Sense it.

Someone had been here.

He dropped his bag and hurried to the cottage where the girls were staying. He tried the door. Locked. He prayed to God it had remained so since he had left.

But he didn't like it. Didn't like it at all.

What if Stephan had discovered the woman, the one who looked like Katie?

He was tempted to pound on the door, to make sure the girls were all right. But all signs were that they were locked in, sound asleep, safe. If they began to think of him as a danger, an insane man, he wouldn't be able to help them.

It occurred to him that he was in a perfect position to use the women in his own quest. He was here; they were here.

The perfect bait.

No, he told himself, gritting his teeth painfully. Never bait. *Never.*

He stared at the door for a moment longer, then looked around the courtyard. Whoever had been here was gone. Long gone, probably. Regretfully, he walked softly away from the door, seeking his own cottage.

Luckily, it was right next door.

Lauren awoke to a hint of sunlight making its way through the draperies and the sound of chirping birds.

She frowned as she woke, despite the miraculous wonder of daylight. At least she hadn't had any wretched dreams about fortune-tellers or scary creatures in crystal balls. She hadn't even dreamed about Deanna walking out into the courtyard, sound asleep. Now, *that* was scary—and real.

Instead she had continued with the dream she had started before going out after Deanna, and that was very scary, as well.

And far too real.

She'd dreamed about *him.*

She flushed at the thought. It had been so bizarre. She'd been back in the bar, back at the point where she'd crashed into him. And it had been…

Incredibly erotic.

And insanely real. She had seen the walls, with their old posters of jazz greats. She had even smelled the slightly stale scent of alcohol that lingered around any bar, the hint of old smoke. She had seen the shadows and the dim light. And the man. They had looked at each other, and the next thing she had known, she'd been in his arms, no introduction, no small talk. Thankfully she couldn't remember how they had shed their clothing. But she had certainly been naked, just as he had been, in the shadowy hallway, flush against him, feeling his flesh and heat, his very life, as he pressed her against the wall. She could almost remember the feel of his lips against hers, and on her flesh. The hardness of his erection as he made love to her against the wall in a bar.

Even though it had only been a dream, it was humiliating. In a thousand years, she would never do such a thing, especially with a stranger. With a man who might be actively dangerous.

She groaned softly. She really, desperately, needed a life.

She sat up and stretched, straightened and smiled.

Daylight. Once she rose, drank some coffee and showered, surely the reality of the dream would fade. She decided that she couldn't even share it with Heidi or Deanna. It was simply too embarrassing. Too…personal.

She shook her head, rose and headed straight for the coffee machine.

Heidi and Deanna were still completely out—she could see the dark head in one bed and the blond one in the other. She opted for a shower while the other two slept on.

As the water streamed over her, she groaned softly. She wasn't afraid, exactly, but she felt uneasy in her own skin, unable to forget the pure sensuality of the dream. She could imagine his hands, the way they had felt on her bare flesh.

She finished her shower as fast as she could.

She definitely needed a life, she thought again. It was just so difficult. She was past the age of looking for fun and enjoyment while she set her career in motion. She wanted something real, commitment, respect…and, of course, passion. Something like what she'd had with Ken. Deanna was always telling her that she didn't need to make a commitment before the first date, and that she would never know if she really liked a man enough to love him if she didn't take a few chances. But it was hard to go back dating after she'd been engaged, in love and ready for the future. She loathed the idea of dating again. It was just too…uncomfortable. And potentially painful.

As Lauren poured coffee, Deanna emerged from the bedroom. She looked rumpled and still tired.

"Bless you, my child," she proclaimed. "Coffee."

"And more in the courtyard when we're ready for breakfast," Lauren said. She hesitated, then asked, "Are you okay?"

"Just tired," Deanna said.

"Well, you were rather active in the middle of the night," Lauren reminded her.

Deanna took a cup of coffee and sipped it. "I have never, ever, done anything like that before in my life."

"Alcohol," Lauren suggested.

"Sadly, I *have* been a bit wasted before," Deanna admitted.

"You don't remember anything at all?"

Deanna shook her head, but her eyes were lowered. Lauren thought there was more, but she couldn't force Deanna to tell her what it was. She could only hope that Deanna would explain more when she was ready.

Lauren walked to the door and moved the chair she had set against it. "Well, let's see what sunlight streaming on the pool does for the day, huh?" She opened the door.

A newspaper was lying on the mat.

She stooped down to pick it up and couldn't help but read the huge headline immediately.

Headless Female Corpse Found in Mississippi.

3

Mark sat in the courtyard, sunglasses in place, drinking his coffee and reading the newspaper. He felt a sense of bitter fatality because of the headline blazing at him, and nothing in the story that followed surprised him.

The headless woman was being called Jane Doe. The coroner estimated that she'd been dead a week to ten days, and she might have been disposed of at almost any point up to a hundred miles upriver. White, approximately five feet seven inches, one hundred and thirty pounds, her remains had been badly assailed by the river and the creatures that lived in it. The coroner had nothing else to say for the moment, other than that additional tests were being performed on the victim.

The head had yet to be discovered.

Mark put down the paper and sipped his coffee, staring at the door to the cottage the three women had taken. Someone had taken in the newspaper, but they had yet to emerge for the day.

He was seated at a table behind a pleasant elderly couple from Ohio. There was a pair of honeymooners to his left, Bonnie and Ralph, and a few of the other guests had come by, all cheerful, friendly and wishing him a good morning. Some of them hadn't read the paper. Some had, and had been appalled at what they read. But they all seemed able to distance themselves from the story. A lone young woman, attacked and killed. Yes, it was easy for a pretty girl to be in danger, to become a victim. From the conversations he overheard, most of them also wanted to believe that she had been a drug addict, as well, or a prostitute. Anything to ensure that whatever violence had touched her would never touch them.

That was the same sentiment he heard when the door to cottage number five opened at last and the three young women appeared. An even greater sense of unease surged through him at the sight of Lauren Crow, the woman with the auburn hair and extraordinary green eyes who reminded him so vividly of Katie. The dark-haired girl was stunning, as well, exotic and sleek. He decided that she had to be Deanna. The little blonde who looked like a petite princess had to be the one named Heidi.

Last night he had thought of them as bait, but the article in the paper forced him to think in far more brutal terms. They were targets.

Beautiful, all of them, and young. The perfect age. Pure temptation for the killer who had coldly thrown that poor girl's corpse into the Mississippi.

"Poor thing," Heidi was saying as the women approached an empty table.

"Horrible," Lauren concurred.

"Yes, but please, let's not obsess about it," Deanna said. "I forget the statistics, but just in the United States there are dozens of serial killers at work at any given time. But we'd go crazy if we worried about them all on a daily basis. Right?"

"Of course. It's just…it's just a really big headline," Lauren said.

"Well, sure. The corpse was headless," Deanna said.

"That's true. The more gruesome the crime, the bigger the headline," Lauren said.

Deanna linked arms with her, adjusting her sunglasses. "But we're smart, and we're not going to do anything stupid, like going off alone. You were the one who lectured us on safety way back in college—and we listened."

"My dad was a cop," Lauren reminded her. "I learned my lessons young."

"Right. And you taught us. None of us wander around alone at night, and we all keep an eye on who's around us at all times. We're all street smart."

"I know."

"Enough of this depressing stuff. It's time to go shopping," Heidi said. "Honestly, Lauren—my dear slave—this is my happy time. I know you always worry about the dangers of the world, but let's go shopping."

"Right, shopping," Deanna agreed.

Watching from a distance, homing in on the girls and trying to filter out other conversation, Mark took a long look at Deanna. She looked exhausted, as if she were suffering from a serious lack of sleep.

They hadn't seen him yet. He had his newspaper up in front of his face, his dark glasses in place. They were wandering slowly through the courtyard, as if unsure whether to leave or not.

"Coffee?" Deanna suggested.

"We'll get some on the way," Heidi said. "Let's go—"

"Shopping," Lauren said dryly.

"I can tell you're still worried," Heidi said with a sigh.

"It was that woman last night. The fortune-teller," Deanna said.

"We should never have made Lauren do what she didn't want to," Heidi admitted.

"It's over, and I'm all right. Let's go," Lauren said.

She walked right past him and didn't even notice him, Mark realized with relief. The other two women followed in her wake and didn't spare him a glance, either.

At the exit from the courtyard, though, Lauren paused and looked back, as if puzzled. As if she thought she should be seeing something but didn't know what.

Her eyes fell on him, and she frowned. He stared back at her through the dark lenses of his glasses.

She hesitated, and he couldn't tell whether she recognized him from the night before or not. The newspaper was shielding most of his face, and her expression was uncertain.

Deanna, concentrating on arranging the strap of her purse, plowed into her.

"Hey! I thought we were leaving," she said.

Lauren didn't respond. Instead, she walked back into the courtyard, and Mark watched her as she came toward him. "Hello," she said, looking straight at him. His heart lurched. She looked so much like Katie.

"Hi."

"We met last night," she said.

"The bar," he agreed.

"You're staying here?"

"It's a great little place. I see that you and your friends have discovered it, too." He rose, extending a hand. "You told me your name, but I didn't tell you mine. Mark Davidson."

She accepted his hand. Touching her, even so casually, sent a jolt through him.

"My last name's Crow. Lauren Crow," she said softly. She turned to her friends, who had followed and were standing behind her. "These are my friends. Deanna Marin and Heidi Weiss."

"Hi," they chimed in unison, stepping up to shake hands.

"You two know each other?" Deanna said.

"Not really. We met in the bar last night."

"Cool," Deanna said.

"We're here from L.A. Where do you call home?" Heidi asked.

"At the moment?" he replied. "I'm in the middle of relocating."

"Are you thinking about moving to New Orleans?" Deanna asked.

"It's a great place," he said.

"I guess," Deanna managed around a yawn, then excused herself quickly. "Not a lot of sleep to be had here, though."

He noticed that Lauren was just staring at him. Suspiciously.

"What do you do for a living?" Deanna asked.

Lauren elbowed her friend and gave her a reproving look, but he only laughed out loud. "It's okay. I'm a writer and a musician."

"What do you play?" Lauren asked sharply.

"Piano, guitar."

"Do you write music?" Deanna asked.

"Sometimes. But mostly I confine my writing to articles and some fiction."

"Cool," Heidi said.

"Horror novels?" Lauren asked pointedly. Those green eyes of hers didn't leave him for a second. He disturbed her, he thought. Why?

"I've tried a few different things in my day."

"Are you rich and famous?" Heidi teased.

"No, I'm sorry. Just plodding along," he told her.

"I'm not sure I believe that," Deanna said. "You probably have a pseudonym but you're not going to share it, right?"

"Nothing that deep or mysterious, I'm afraid."

"Well, nice to meet you," Lauren said. She set a hand on

Heidi's shoulder, her eyes still on him warily. "We need to get moving."

"What's the hurry?" Heidi asked.

"You said you wanted to go shopping," Lauren reminded her. "Nice to see you again, Mr. Davidson, but we need to get going."

"It was super to meet you," Deanna said. Her voice was low and throaty. Sensual.

"Absolutely," Heidi agreed. She seemed to croon the single word.

"We'll be seeing you again, I assume. After all, we are staying in the same place," Deanna said.

"Yes, we are," Lauren murmured. She didn't sound happy about the fact, he noticed.

"You're here for a few days?" Heidi asked.

"I am. Cottage six."

"That's right next door to us," Lauren said, unable to hide her surprise.

"Is it?" he inquired.

"I guess we really *will* see you," Lauren said, her suspicion and irritation evident in her tone. "But right now, we really do have to get going," she said firmly.

She turned, walking determinedly toward the street.

"See you," Deanna said, and winked.

"Later," Heidi told him.

"Sure. Enjoy New Orleans," he said, and he sat and pretended to give his full attention to his newspaper once again.

"My God, you met him last night and you didn't say anything, much less introduce him?" Heidi marveled, staring at Lauren as they headed toward Royal Street.

"I didn't exactly meet him," Lauren said. "I bumped into him."

"I only bump into eighty-year-old men with canes," Deanna said mournfully.

"He's…magnetic," Heidi said.

Lauren shot her a quick glance.

"Don't look at me like that. I love Barry, and I honestly believe we're going to beat the odds and be married forever. But if I'd bumped into that guy, I wouldn't have forgotten it. But you? You didn't say a word to us."

Lauren let out a sigh. "What on earth was I supposed to say? We didn't have drinks, we didn't go to dinner. I bumped into him in a hallway."

"I'd have mentioned it," Deanna said. She let out a sigh.

"He's staying at our B and B," Heidi commented.

"Yes."

Deanna stopped walking and laughed. "Heidi, did you hear that? Lauren, you said that one word and filled it with more suspicion than I can believe. What's the big deal? You bumped into him in New Orleans—and he's staying in New Orleans. Imagine that."

"He's staying in New Orleans at *our* B and B," Lauren said.

"I call that cool," Heidi said.

"You're engaged," Lauren reminded her.

"But not dead," Heidi said with a smile.

"What's the matter with you, Lauren?" Deanna asked. "You're not usually like this. The guy is gorgeous and he seemed nice. What's your problem?"

Lauren arched a brow and shook her head. "I don't know. I guess I was just nervous last night. And he was standing outside after we first got back last night, I'm certain. I saw him out on the street."

"He's staying where we are. He had to be on the street to get here," Heidi pointed out, a smile curving her lips.

"Cute," Lauren told her. "Then I found Deanna out by the pool—sleepwalking!"

"You were sleepwalking?" Heidi asked Deanna.

"I guess. Luckily, Lauren found me before I drowned. Then again, the water might have woken me up. Who knows?"

"We probably shouldn't have taken the red-eye," Heidi said.

"Today is going to be great," Lauren assured her. "Turn here. That clothing shop you wanted to go to is down a few blocks on the right. I want to go to that gallery across the way. I'll meet you guys in the place with the great hats in half an hour."

When they reached Heidi's goal, she shooed them inside and walked on.

New Orleans Police Lieutenant Sean Canady sat at his desk in the precinct, staring at the newspaper.

Headless corpse.

It was happening again. He groaned aloud.

"Hey, Lieutenant."

He looked up to see Bobby Munro standing in front of him.

"Hey, Bobby." He didn't ask his officer if he had seen the headline; he couldn't have helped but see it.

"The Mississippi's a big river. That body could have come from anywhere," Bobby said. "And there have been plenty of perps who behead their victims. Get rid of the head, stall the identification."

Bobby was a damned good officer, Sean thought. Young and good-looking, he was nevertheless a fine cop. He'd seen a hell of a lot already, but he hadn't become jaded. Bobby saw himself as one of the good guys, and he still believed he could create a better world.

Sean leaned back at his desk, looking up at Bobby. He'd been around a lot longer himself, and while he wasn't exactly jaded, he *was* weary. He came from this area. He knew he had the respect of his superiors, from the mayor up to the governor—hell, even up to the feds. He was given a lot of leeway in his investigations. His word was considered good. So were his instincts.

And he didn't like this.

"An organized killer, trying to hide an ID, would almost certainly have cut off the hands, as well," he said. "We've still got fingerprints, and I have a hunch we'll have an ID on our vic soon enough."

"Drug deal gone bad?" Bobby suggested hopefully.

Sean shrugged. "Keep an eye out," he said.

"Right. And you remember, Lieutenant. The Mississippi? A big, big river."

"Yeah," Sean said, smiling grimly. "But the corpse is in *our* morgue."

Lauren finished her shopping and arranged for the small piece of art she'd chosen to be delivered to the B and B, then stepped out onto Royal Street. The sun was bright. She shaded her eyes with one hand while she fumbled in her bag for her sunglasses with the other.

One of the mule-drawn carriages drove by. She blinked, then squinted against the glare. She could have sworn Deanna was in it—on the front seat, right next to the driver, who was tall and dark, and wearing a top hat.

The carriage kept going at a brisk pace.

"Deanna?" she called, following after it. But there were cars on the street, as well, and she had to move quickly back to the sidewalk and maneuver around all the people there. The carriage was far beyond her before she finally gave up trying to follow it.

Besides, it couldn't have been Deanna, she told herself. Deanna wouldn't have taken a carriage ride by herself, not when she was supposed to be shopping with Heidi.

But when Lauren made it across the street to one of her favorite clothing shops, she found Heidi in the back alone, trying on hats.

"Hey," Heidi said. "How's this?"

The straw hat she was trying on was wide-brimmed and sported a bright flower, and Heidi wore it well.

"Perfect," Lauren said. "Where's Deanna?"

"She said something about the shop next door," Heidi said. "She said she'd be right back."

"I could have sworn I just saw her in a carriage."

"Why would she take a carriage ride without us?" Heidi asked.

"She wouldn't."

"Then you probably just saw someone who looked like her," Heidi said. "You know, this place is a little pricey, but this really is a nice hat. Should I buy it?"

"Yes," Lauren said, still distracted. "I'm going to check next door."

Heidi turned and stared at her. "You sound worried."

"No, not really."

"Lauren, it's broad daylight. There are a zillion people on the streets."

"I know."

"Okay." She sighed. "Let's look for Deanna."

"Buy your hat. I'll check next door."

"Okay, I'll meet you there."

When she stepped back onto the street, Lauren was practically assaulted by music. She came to a dead halt.

There was something happening in the street. A jazz

funeral. The mule-drawn hearse, escorted by mounted police, passed just as she emerged. Behind the hearse came the mourners and, with them, the musicians. It was a spectacle not everyone got to see, something unique, sad yet wonderful, to be found in the city. Someone was about to be laid to rest in grand fashion.

The procession had to be on its way from the church to the cemetery, something of a long route from here, Lauren thought. The musicians were playing a dirge now, but she'd been to several jazz funerals in her life, and she knew that once they left the cemetery there would be a celebration of the deceased's life. Often the band would play "When the Saints Go Marching In," the old standby. It was an old custom, African beliefs blended with Western religion.

On the street, everyone had stopped, watching the procession go slowly by.

She did the same.

The mourners were black, white and all shades in between.

One of the trumpet players was a huge, handsome African-American man. As he played, his eyes lit on Lauren, and she offered him a nod of respect. Strangely, he kept watching her solemnly until he had passed her.

As soon as the funeral had moved on, people began to mill around on the sidewalks again, and cars followed slowly, until they could turn onto a different street.

Lauren found herself listening to the sad dirge until the funeral march was but a hint in the air, and the laughter on the street and sounds of a corner rock band overshadowed what had been. Then she gave herself a shake and hurried into the next store.

She saw T-shirts, voodoo potion boxes, alligator heads, votive candles and holders, but no sign of Deanna.

Nor did Heidi appear.

She walked back into the store where Heidi had been looking at the hat. Neither of her friends was there.

Irritated, she took out her cell phone. She tried Deanna's number first and got her voice mail. The same thing happened when she tried Heidi's number. Cursing silently, she left her a message, too.

She didn't want to go far; they had to be nearby somewhere. But after going in and out of a dozen shops, cafés and restaurants, her level of irritation peaked, and she gave in to the heat and her own weariness and opted for a table near the street at the last café she checked, and ordered a giant iced tea.

While she sat, she drew out her sketch pad, but before she could start working on a street scene, she found herself staring at the sketch she had made of the fortune-teller the night before.

"You ruined the whole party, you know," she said softly to the sketch. The woman was still striking, everything about her unusual, from the remembered color of her skin to the bone structure of her face.

"Talking to yourself?" someone said.

She looked up, startled, wariness slipping through her.

Their handsome neighbor from cottage six was standing by her, a pleasant smile on his face.

She didn't answer; she was torn between suspicion and an inexplicable desire to engage in conversation. Okay, maybe not so inexplicable. He *was* exceedingly attractive. Tall, everything in proportion, muscular without being musclebound, with rugged features that were classically appealing and entirely masculine. She even liked his scent, and felt oddly drawn to move nearer to him.

I would actually like to get to know him, she admitted to herself.

And then another voice chimed in. The truth was that he scared her. And maybe he scared her just because she felt such a strong sense of attraction to him.

Would she have been so afraid if it hadn't been for what had happened in the Square, the crystal ball and the illusion of genuine danger?

"Wow," he murmured, and she realized that he was looking at her sketch. "That's magnificent."

"I don't know about magnificent," she murmured, embarrassed.

He never actually asked if he could join her, and she never suggested that he do so, but he drew out the chair across from her anyway and sat down.

She was glad, she realized. She liked having him there, liked talking with him. Liked feeling his eyes on her appreciatively.

And yet she was still…wary.

Scared.

Something wasn't right.

"You're quite an artist," he said.

"It's a living," she replied.

He flashed her a smile. A very attractive smile. "Not everyone is good enough to make a living at it."

"I've been lucky."

"Are your friends artists, too?"

"Yes. Artists, graphic designers."

"You do logos, flyers, that type of thing?" he inquired politely.

"Yes, and ad layouts and so on," she agreed.

She didn't want him to leave, she realized.

What the hell was it about him that appealed to her so strongly? She wanted to touch him, make sure he was real, stroke the contours of his face, feel his heart beat under her palm.

He tapped the table near the sketch. "I've seen her. It's an incredible likeness. There's a touch of magic to her, and you've captured it."

"Thanks." She hesitated. "So you…know her?"

He shook his head. "I saw her when I was walking around. She's so unusual, so arresting, that you feel compelled to look at her. You've caught all that in this sketch."

"Thanks," she murmured.

"So you all had your fortunes told?"

"Yes."

"And?" His tone was teasing, his smile captivating.

And yet, despite his teasing tone, did she sense a note of seriousness behind it? Did he suspect that she had seen a strange vision?

Of course not.

"We're all going to live long, happy lives," she lied.

"Wonderful. So where are your friends now? Did they get lost in New Orleans?" he asked, a slight frown creasing his brow, though he still spoke lightly.

"They're not lost," she said, then added, "I've simply misplaced them."

"Worrying nonetheless," he said.

"It's broad daylight, and there are tons of people around," she countered.

A waitress came by. "I'd love a tea, too," he said, then looked at Lauren. "May I buy you lunch?"

"I should really wait."

"Until your misplaced friends are located?"

She turned her attention to the street momentarily, then looked back at him. She was startled when he set a hand over hers. Pinpricks of sensation seemed to leap like fire across her flesh, pass into her bloodstream and balloon at the center of her being like a flow of lava. She was tempted to pull her hand away, then realized that would be far too indicative of her feelings.

She stared at him instead, slowly arching a brow.

Suddenly his expression grew serious, and his tone matched it when he spoke. "Please, you may think I'm insane for saying this, but I promise you, I'm not. I'm afraid that you and your friends are in danger here."

Yes, there *had* been more to his earlier question.

"Oh, please," she said, closing her eyes for a moment against her disappointment that he'd turned out to be a loon. "Not this again."

All she wanted now was for him to go away. She'd been far too tempted to give in to the appealing fact that he seemed to find her interesting, attractive. To be pursuing her. Because she wanted to be pursued.

What she didn't want was this feeling that something was lying beneath every word he said, that he didn't actually want to be with her and was just plain crazy.

"Again?" he asked sharply.

Irritation filled her, along with an uncanny sense of fear. "The fortune-teller gave me the same line of bull. We're here for a bachelorette party, Mr. Davidson. Pure and simple. Heidi is about to get married, and the three of us have been planning this trip for ages. I can't imagine why you—a stranger— would want to ruin it for us."

He was quiet, leaning back. She could read little from his expression, because his sunglasses suddenly seemed as dark as night. She knew she should just ask him to leave her alone.

Somehow, she couldn't.

He was still touching her hand, but that wasn't what was stopping her. It was simply his presence that she couldn't resist.

"I swear to you," he said very softly, "I want nothing more than your complete safety."

"I'm not in any danger."

"Yes, you are. You saw this morning's headline."

She shook her head, a chill snaking through her. "Does that mean every single woman anywhere near the Mississippi River is in danger?"

"Yes."

"Oh, please!"

"There's a killer working the area," he said, with such assurance that she felt an ever greater sense of being encompassed of ice, despite the heat of the day.

"Are you a cop?" she asked sharply.

"No."

"FBI?"

"No."

"So exactly what *are* you?"

"I told you. A writer and a musician."

"Oh, well, that answers that, then. I'm sure you know all about serial killers, not to mention exactly how and why my friends and I are in danger."

She was stunned when he replied calmly and in a tone of such level and deep authority that it was the scariest part of it all. "I do."

She just stared at him.

The waitress brought his tea, and he thanked her, bringing Lauren back to the moment.

"I'm going to leave now," she said. "And you are going to leave my friends and me alone," she told him firmly.

He ignored her words when he spoke. "I know who the killer is. I've **known** about him for a very long time now. He was responsible for the death of my fiancée."

Lauren couldn't believe it of herself, but she didn't move. She remembered what he had said when she crashed into him the night before. The name he had spoken.

"Katie?" she said, then hesitated before going on. "The woman you think I resemble."

"Yes."

"I'm not your Katie," she told him.

A rueful smile curled his lips. "I know that," he said.

"But you think this man…killed her?"

He hesitated, then nodded.

"She died here, in New Orleans?" Lauren asked.

"No," he admitted.

"I see."

"No, you don't. Katie did see him here, on a trip. And now I'm afraid he's after you—just as he was after her."

She sighed, looking down.

He was just as attractive and possessed of all the raw sex appeal as she had thought from the beginning—and he was completely crazy. Maybe even a murderer himself.

He could be stalking her, for all she knew.

She was finally about to get up when he asked, "Did you all stay in your cottage last night, locked in, once you got home?"

"I saw you out on the street, watching us," she accused him, instead of answering.

"Did you stay in?" he repeated.

"Yes, which is none of your business," she lied.

He still seemed concerned. "I only asked because it's important," he told her quietly.

She felt oddly uncertain and was angry with herself, but for some reason she couldn't seem to walk away with things hanging between them.

And Deanna *had* been outside, sleepwalking, something

she'd never done before in her life, and Lauren had been out there with her. Not only that, she'd felt as if someone else had been out there, too, and that somehow this man knew about it.

And at the edge of her consciousness was the memory of how she had dreamed about him, and the ridiculous longing somewhere inside that, against all the evidence, he would turn out not to be crazy.

She forced a casual smile onto her face. "Okay, I'll bite. Why is it so important?"

Instead of answering, he reached into his shirt pocket. "I'd like to give you something."

"Please, I can't accept anything from you."

He smiled then, a charming smile that also managed to convey amusement. "No strings attached," he assured her.

She was almost bowled over by the unconscious sensuality of his appeal. God, how she wished he were normal. She had never met anyone like him, hadn't even dreamed that she *could* meet anyone like him, since she had lost Ken. The sound of his voice was alluring, his body language subtly provocative. If she'd met him anywhere else under any other circumstances...

"This was Katie's," he said.

She looked down at the item he'd produced from his pocket. It was a silver cross, beautifully designed and obviously antique.

"I *definitely* can't take that," she told him, staring across the table at him.

"Please."

"It's valuable."

"I would never sell it in a thousand years," he said.

She shook her head. "I can't take it."

He grinned at her suddenly. "If you were to take it and wear it, I'd feel better about your being out on the streets of New Orleans. I might even quit being such a pest."

"I think you really *are* crazy," she told him frankly.

"I'm not. Honestly."

She picked up her tea and took a long sip, suddenly aware that she had both elbows on the table now and was leaning closer to him. "Okay, look at all this from my point of view. First I run into you in a bar. Then I see you standing out on my street."

"My street, too."

"Coincidence, huh?"

He shrugged.

"Okay. Then I'm sitting here drinking tea, and suddenly there you are, too, with a crazy tale about trailing a killer. Don't you think you should go to the police if you know who the killer is?"

"Probably. I'm just not sure yet how to explain what I know."

"Because it's crazy," she suggested softly.

"I swear to you, I only want you to be safe," he said.

She groaned, looking down at her hands. "I've heard a piece of your story, and I'm not at all sure I want to hear the rest. Please…you're very attractive. But I…I really have to ask you to stay away from me."

There. She had managed it; she had said the words and told him to leave her alone.

He pulled away, straightening, his expression both resigned and regretful.

Suddenly she heard Heidi's voice. "There you are! Lauren, why haven't you been answering your phone? Oh, hi, Mark. Okay, now I know why you haven't been answering. Can we join you? Or should we get lost?"

And Heidi wasn't alone.

Deanna was with her.

Heidi's voice was teasing, the day sunny, everything normal. And yet...

4

Mark Davidson was charming, and of course both Heidi and Deanna were outrageous flirts when they wanted to be.

First, though, Lauren demanded to know where her friend had been. Deanna seemed surprised that Lauren had been so worried just because she'd wandered off and told her, "Shopping. And I'm perfectly capable of going in and out of stores alone. You're the one who left us high and dry, you know."

Ignoring that, Lauren asked, "Did you take a carriage ride?"

"A carriage ride? Why would I have taken a carriage ride?"

So whatever had so disturbed her was really nothing, Lauren thought. Maybe she needed to start worrying about herself.

Over a couple of po'boys, Mark entertained them with tales of his travels, his writing—and his playing.

"So are you good?" Heidi asked good-naturedly.

"I leave that to the listener to decide."

"I'd love to hear you play sometime," Lauren said.

He just shrugged. "So, tell me more about your business," he said.

He had quite a knack for turning the conversation away from himself, she thought—and decided not to allow it. "Mark lost a fiancée, too," she said. "Her name was Katie, and she looked like me. Or I look like her."

The table went dead silent.

"I'm so sorry," Heidi said.

"Me, too," Deanna told him. She reached across the table and squeezed his hand.

Lauren noted the way he studied her in return. Not lasciviously, more as if he were searching for something, expecting her to give herself away somehow.

"He's worried about us," Lauren added.

"Why?" Heidi asked.

"Because of that body they found in the Mississippi," Lauren said.

To her surprise, Heidi bestowed a tremendous smile on the man. "That is so sweet of you!"

"Imagine. We go on vacation and find a handsome protector," Deanna said. She turned to Lauren. "And he's in the cottage right next to ours."

They were both crazy, Lauren decided. The sun was too much for them. And the way they were flirting... She wasn't sure whether to scream or vomit.

"He thinks he knows who the killer is, that it's the same man who killed his fiancée."

"Oh, my God!" Deanna said, leaning forward and touching him gently, real concern in her eyes.

"I didn't actually say that he killed her, but he was responsible for her death," Mark said, frowning at Lauren.

"You should go to the police if you have any information at all," Heidi told him.

"You're right, I should," he said. To Lauren's surprise, he stood. "I think I'll take a stroll down to the station right now. Thanks so much for letting me join you for lunch," he said. "And I'm in cottage six, if you need me."

"Are you two insane?" Lauren asked in a vehement whisper as he walked away. When he looked back with a glance of amusement, she knew that, even at a distance, he had heard her, and she blushed.

"What is the matter with you?" Heidi demanded. "He's unbelievable."

"That would be the point," Lauren muttered.

"You're being ridiculous," Heidi announced. "He obviously has the hots for you, but if you're going to be an idiot and turn down a good man, let Deanna have a crack at him."

"Lauren, if you're not interested in him, you're going off the deep end," Deanna told her.

"Hey, I wasn't the one sleepwalking," she snapped. "And he's lying—I'll bet you he's lying. He isn't going to the police station."

"We can follow him and find out," Deanna suggested.

"Yeah, right after we pay the check. He joined us for lunch and walked out," Lauren reminded them, then waved a hand to signal the waitress.

"May we have the check, please?" Lauren asked when the woman came over.

"The gentleman gave me his credit card before he joined you," she said. "You don't have a check."

"Oh. Thanks," Lauren said, staring at her blankly.

"I'll leave the tip," Heidi offered.

"He was really generous," the waitress said. "You don't need to. Honestly."

"Thanks," Heidi told her. "We'll…we'll just add to it," she said lamely.

Lauren rose along with Deanna as their friend dug in her purse, then laid a bill on the table. "Hey, look at this," Heidi said.

It was the beautiful antique cross. He'd left it on the table, Lauren realized.

"Where did this come from?" Heidi asked curiously.

"Mr. Gorgeous left it," Lauren said. She shook her head but took the cross from Heidi. "Come on, I'm going to prove to you both that he's full of crap."

She led them quickly through the French Quarter, for once ignoring the architecture that never failed to enthrall her and the street musicians who somehow always sounded so good. When they reached the police station, Lauren opened the door to go in, then froze.

Mark Davidson was there, talking to the desk sergeant.

She backed out of the doorway, stunned.

"Ouch," Heidi protested, as Lauren stepped on her foot.

"I take it Mr. Davidson *is* inside?" Deanna said dryly.

"Yes," Lauren said, puzzled.

"See?" Deanna said.

"Something's still…not right," Lauren said.

"You always think something's not right," Deanna told her. "Lauren, you can't live your life with nothing ever being right," she added gently.

"You don't understand," Lauren tried to explain.

"Yes, we do." Both of them spoke in unison, looking at her in concern. They were convinced that she couldn't get beyond the past, and that she desperately needed to.

"No," she insisted. "I'm fine—these days. I would love to meet the right guy…or even a decent-enough wrong guy. Movies, dinner…music," she said. "Honestly, I know you don't have to plan a lifetime with someone to enjoy his company."

"You know what she needs?" Heidi said gravely to Deanna.

"I do," Deanna said.

"And that would be…?" Lauren asked.

"Sex. Wild, hot, passionate sex," Deanna said.

"Oh, please!"

"Spontaneous. Wicked," Heidi said, agreeing with Deanna.

"Can we move on?" Lauren said.

"Look—she's blushing. She *is* attracted to him," Deanna said triumphantly.

"How could she not be?" Heidi said.

"Look," Lauren insisted, "something just isn't right here."

"The fortune-teller," Deanna told Heidi gravely.

Heidi linked an arm through Lauren's. "I don't know what we're going to do with you. Wait! Brainstorm! I *do* know what we're going to do. I'm having a vision. It's me, and I'm standing at a craps table."

"You lose at craps all the time," Lauren said.

"And I have a hell of a good time doing it. Come on, slave, let's trot on back over to Harrah's. I see us sunning in the late afternoon sun later. A dip in the pool will be followed by dinner. K-Paul's tonight. Then we'll hit Bourbon Street for music and jazz. Cool?"

"Cool," Lauren said, though she didn't sound convinced. Then looked at Deanna and frowned. "You're sure you didn't take a carriage ride today? I could have sworn I saw you with a tall, dark-haired guy, like the one I saw you talking to in the bar last night."

"The cute guy?" Deanna said.

"Yeah. Were you in a carriage with him?"

"No," Deanna said.

It could be difficult to tell if Deanna was blushing, because her skin was such a beautiful shade of copper, but Lauren thought she had reddened.

As if she were lying.

"Hey, pay attention here, slaves," Heidi demanded.

They both looked at her. "Harrah's," she ordered.

Lauren let out a breath, still staring at Deanna. "Right. Harrah's," she said.

And she started to walk.

Mark had known the women would follow him, egged on by Lauren.

Luckily, they had quickly departed.

And he had gotten more of a response at the police station than he had been expecting. Of course, it had been some time since he'd been in New Orleans. Things here had changed.

At the desk, he'd informed the sergeant that he didn't have any solid information, but he knew of a European national now in the country who had been linked to various crimes overseas—crimes that left victims resembling the woman found in the Mississippi.

He had expected to give information to a bored paper-chasing officer in a cubicle somewhere.

To his surprise, he was ushered into the office of Lieutenant Sean Canady, an impressive man with steel-blue eyes and a rock-hard chin.

"I understand you have information regarding the body in the river?" Canady said, taking his seat after a handshake and indicating a chair across from his desk.

"Not exactly," Mark corrected. "But I do have reason to believe that the crime may be associated with a man named Stephan Delansky, whom I believe is in this area now."

"I see." Canady's hands were folded on his desk. "Sadly, Mr. Davidson, murder isn't unusual. Nor is decapitation, though I admit it's somewhat less common."

"No."

"So…?"

Mark took a deep breath. "There are a number of ancient

beliefs that suggest decapitation will prevent someone from becoming a vampire. And there's a modern belief that some vampires are careful to dispose of victims they aren't entirely…sure of. Population control, if you will. Survival of the…"

"Hottest? Most clever?" Canady said.

The man must think he was an idiot, Mark realized. "Yes."

Canady's eyes didn't flicker. He was either trying to humor him until the padded wagon bound for the asylum arrived, or…

Or nothing surprised him at all.

Or *maybe…*

He'd had previous experience with vampires.

"Your suggesting there's a vampire loose in New Orleans?" Canady said.

Mark shook his head. "No," he said. Then he took a deep breath. "No, I'm suggesting there are several."

"Look! He's up again!" Deanna said triumphantly, looking at Lauren with sheer pleasure in her eyes. "The Creature from the Black Lagoon. Bonus, bonus, bonus!"

Deanna loved the slot machines with bonus features. Especially this one.

They had both wandered away from the craps table after losing far too quickly, leaving Heidi, who had been making all the right bets, to play on her own.

Deanna and Lauren had scaled down to the penny machines, and though the stakes were low, they were winning.

"Isn't that just great?" Deanna asked, pointing at the Creature. "Can you believe that movie actually frightened people?"

Lauren reflected on the question. "It was a long time ago. Before they could do the kind of special effects we have now."

"I don't think that creature would have frightened me, no matter what," Deanna said, grinning.

"Cocktails?" an attractively and scantily attired waitress asked, interrupting their conversation.

Deanna looked at her watch. "Sure."

"Remember sleepwalking?" Lauren asked softly.

Deanna waved a hand in the air. "It's almost five o'clock."

"It's three o'clock."

"Close enough. Rum and Coke, please. And you, quit acting like my mom. This is supposed to be a wild weekend."

"A light beer, please," Lauren said.

"Wow. Going all out," Deanna teased.

Lauren looked hard at her friend. Deanna was supermodel gorgeous, with her height and exotic features and coloring. It would be hard to mistake her for anyone else.

"You really didn't go for a carriage ride today?" Lauren asked her.

Deanna stared at her. "No."

"Where were you?"

"Where were *you?*"

"Looking for you."

"I left Heidi trying on her twenty-fifth hat and wandered into a few stores."

Lauren was sure she could see color suffusing her friend's cheeks again.

"What aren't you telling me?" Lauren asked.

Deanna shrugged. "I ran into that guy from the bar last night."

"Oh?" Lauren felt a strange surge of unease. "That's who I thought you were with in the carriage."

"How strange," Deanna murmured, then looked at Lauren again.

"What?" Lauren persisted.

"There *was* a carriage—well, there are lots of carriages in New Orleans—and I was tempted to take a ride, but then I saw Jonas."

"Jonas?"

"The guy from the bar."

"And then?" Lauren persisted.

"We chatted, he said he hoped we'd run into each other again tonight, he left, I found Heidi and then we found you. And the hunk-next-door."

"The scary hunk-next-door," Lauren said.

Deanna let out a laugh. "You know what's scary about him?"

"What?"

"You."

"Me?"

"Yes, you. Your reaction. You're afraid to get close to anyone. You're afraid to so much as have lunch with someone. And you need to get over it. Here's what I think. You're actually attracted to this guy, sexually attracted, so you're trying to push him away. You don't want to be hurt, to lose someone again."

"Thank you, Dr. Deanna."

"Give the guy a chance, why don't you?"

"I was perfectly nice to him at lunch."

"He's looking for more than lunch. And I think you are, too."

Lauren felt her own cheeks redden. She was paler than her friend. Deanna didn't have to blink to realize she'd struck a chord.

"You feel it, don't you?"

"I feel what?"

"The desire to…well, I was going to say *jump his bones,* but it's you, so I'll just say the desire."

Lauren groaned and rose, stretching.

"Where do you think you're going? We just ordered drinks

from a hardworking waitress. At least wait for her to come back so we can get our drinks and give her a tip, huh?"

"Oh, all right," Lauren said. To kill time, she hit the button on the slot machine, then watched as five Creatures from the Black Lagoon appeared neatly in a row across the screen.

Bells started ringing.

"Fifty-*thousand* pennies!" Deanna said delightedly. "You just won five *hundred* dollars."

"Now that's cool," Lauren had to agree.

The bells were still ringing, and people around them were coming to check out her winnings. There were much larger jackpots to be had, she was certain, but fifty thousand cents was definitely fun, and most people seemed cheerful, apparently happy to see someone get the better of the house.

There was one cranky old fellow, though, who walked by them muttering, "That was my jackpot. That thing cleaned out my pockets."

At least the rest of the place seemed happy. The attendant was happy signing their sheet, and once they got their drinks and duly tipped the waitress, the cashier was happy to give them their money. It really wasn't that much. The man in front of them was cashing in five thousand in poker chips.

"It isn't the amount, it's the excitement of the win," Deanna told her.

"I'll bet you the excitement of a five-thousand-dollar win must feel pretty good, too," Lauren said, but she was laughing. It really had been fun.

And they'd all but forgotten Heidi.

"Craps tables," they said at the same time.

Their timing was great. They got there just as Heidi, who had apparently been on a roll, crapped out. The table cheered her when she got up, looking flushed and happy.

"Hey, you can't go now, lady luck!" a nicely dressed middle-aged woman called to her.

"Don't worry. The dice will come around again," a handsome young guy in a Harley Davidson jacket assured her.

"We should leave now, while we're all ahead," Deanna said.

"Why didn't you make me leave earlier, when I'd won even more?" Heidi demanded as they waited while she cashed in her chips. "How did you two do with your pennies?" she asked, her tone patronizing.

"Lauren won five hundred dollars," Deanna said.

Heidi frowned. "Five hundred dollars?"

"Yep," Deanna said proudly.

"I think I have three hundred and thirty-five," Heidi said, then grinned. "That means you pay for dinner."

"Bathing suits, sun and the pool first, right?" Lauren asked.

"You bet," Heidi agreed.

A little while later, they stepped out into bright afternoon sunlight and headed back to their B and B.

But despite the blazing sunlight, Lauren couldn't shake the feeling that they were surrounded by darkness and shadows.

"Vampires. Plural," Sean Canady said, looking steadily at Mark.

Mark was surprised that he hadn't called in the men in the white coats, though he *had* excused himself for several minutes, then returned.

Maybe the men in the white coats were already on the way.

All right, time to try another tack. "Look, I love New Orleans. It's like no other place, but there are plenty of cultists and crazies here."

"True enough," the cop agreed sagely.

I don't mean me, Mark added silently, then kept going.

"Stephan is a…cult leader. He's also psychotic, a man who never feels any regret for the pain he causes, and he can mesmerize others and turn them into killers."

"Well, thank you for your information. I appreciate your coming in."

"You haven't filled out any forms."

"I will."

"Usually cops take notes while someone is talking."

"You're familiar with police procedure?" Canady asked.

Mark hesitated just slightly, then said, "Hey, I watch television. *Law and Order.*"

"Right," Canady agreed politely. "And *CSI*. We always get our guy in just one episode, too," he said dryly.

"I assure you, you need to find this man, and stop him." He stood. There was so much more he wanted to say, but if he did, he really would risk being committed.

He frowned, noticing the chain around the lieutenant's neck. "Cross?" he asked.

"Yeah, why?"

"No reason. Just curious," Mark said.

He decided to depart quickly, before things became complicated. He'd tried, but he was still on his own against Stephan.

"Thanks for your time. Before I go, I should tell you that I'm certain he has some kind of…lair around here. Probably somewhere in the French Quarter, maybe the Garden District, or even uptown. I'll be looking for him. If you go looking for him, too, do it carefully."

The cop blinked but still betrayed no emotion.

"Good luck, Lieutenant," Mark said, shaking his head. Well, what the hell had he expected? For the lieutenant to form a posse armed with stakes and holy water?

"Back at you," the cop said as Mark turned and left.

Mark knew without looking that the steely-eyed lieutenant followed and watched him all the way out to the street.

The sun was still hot when they made it out to the pool, even though it was four o'clock. They had the place to themselves, the rest of the guests apparently having gone off to other pursuits.

Jumping into the water felt delicious, and crawling out wasn't bad, either.

Many of the lounge chairs around the pool were shaded by umbrella tops and they pulled three together. They chatted about the wedding, the city and their plans for their winnings, but not about the headless corpse that had been dragged from the Mississippi or the tall, dark strangers they had encountered in the course of the weekend.

Heidi stood at last, yawning and stretching. "I'm going to shower, okay? If I stay out here much longer I'll burn to a crisp."

"Poor, pale darling," Deanna teased her.

"Hey, you can burn, too, my copper beauty," Heidi warned.

"I know," Deanna assured her. "But you're by far the most delicate of us."

"I'm pale and I come in a small package, but I'm fierce," Heidi told her.

"Of course you are," Deanna assured her, waving a hand dismissively. "Go on. Take your shower."

After Heidi went inside, a gentle breeze suddenly arose, not chilly but balmy and, since they were still damp from the water, quite nice. Lauren felt as if she had returned to the world of the normal. She felt relaxed.

Deanna turned to her suddenly.

"Did you feel it?" she demanded tensely.

"What?"

"I could *feel* it."

"Feel what?"

"Eyes. Being watched."

Lauren stared blankly at her friend, then asked slowly and carefully, "Um…do you think Mark Davidson is watching us from his cottage?"

"No. He's not there."

"How do you know?"

"I knocked on his door while you were still changing to see if he wanted to hang with us at the pool."

Lauren digested that information. "Maybe he just didn't answer his door," she suggested.

Deanna shook her head firmly.

"How can you be so sure?"

"Because I saw the maid go into his cottage, and she left his door open. He wasn't there."

"Okay, so Mark isn't watching us. But you think someone is?"

"I don't think. I know."

Despite herself, Lauren felt her pleasant aura of peace and calm evaporate. She looked around. The breeze was rustling the foliage around the house and pool, but it wasn't as if they were in a deep, dark forest.

She stood, then walked around the courtyard, around a hibiscus and a croton; she went so far as to head to the parking lot at the rear and check the trees there.

"No one," she told Deanna, returning to her chair.

Deanna didn't seem appeased.

"Maybe someone was watching from the main house," Lauren suggested. "Maybe our hostess, checking to be sure we aren't throwing a wild pool party."

"I'm not making you understand," Deanna said.

Yes, you are. You're totally giving me the creeps, Lauren thought.

"Well, Heidi should be out of the shower by now. We can both go in. You can have first dibs. I think I'm going to brew up some coffee before you guys decide to hit the bars again."

"Okay," Deanna said, and began to gather her belongings.

Lauren did the same, then stopped. "Deanna," she said.

"Yeah?"

"Do you…do you think it was the man you ran into last night at the bar?"

"The cute guy?" Deanna asked.

"I didn't really see him. I don't know how cute he was," Lauren said.

Deanna frowned in thought, then shook her head. "No. There was nothing…creepy about him. Now, the other guy…"

"What other guy?"

Deanna hesitated. "I don't know," she said, puzzled.

"You're losing me. What are you talking about?" Lauren asked.

Deanna shook her head. "There are two guys."

"Two guys?" Lauren said, frowning. "Do you mean Mark Davidson, maybe? Mark and the man you met at the bar?"

"No, Mark is *your* guy," Deanna said.

"Then who *do* you mean?"

"I…don't really know. Maybe I had too much to drink or something, but I can't exactly remember. But I'm sure I've seen…or met…*two* men. The one at the bar last night. His name is Jonas. I like him. He's very sweet. And I ran into him today, right when…"

"Right when what?"

"What you said," Deanna told her. She sounded impatient.

"What I said about what?"

"The carriage ride."

"You *did* take a carriage ride?"

"No. But I was *tempted* to." She looked at Lauren. "This is crazy. You know what? I'm with you from now on when it comes to fortune-tellers. But…"

"But *what?*" Lauren persisted.

"There's someone else," Deanna said, troubled.

"The second man you've seen? Have you talked to him? Maybe you've just walked past him a few times or something. Deanna, I wish you made sense. I don't know what you're talking about."

"Neither do I. It's more like a feeling," Deanna murmured. "I'm sorry. I know I sound…confused. It must be the sleepwalking."

"It's okay. I'm just trying to understand."

Deanna stopped suddenly, looking around. "It's gone."

Lauren hesitated. "It?"

"Whatever was watching us."

"*Who*ever was watching us, you mean."

Deanna shivered. "No. *Whatever* was watching us." She stared at Lauren with wide eyes. "It wasn't human. I'm sure of it."

5

Looking for Stephan's hideout was like looking for the proverbial needle in a haystack, Mark thought. He might have chosen a basement in a deserted housing complex almost anywhere. Or an old warehouse. Or an abandoned industrial park.

Somehow, he had to get a better sense of where his nemesis was making his home base.

His next self-imposed task didn't seem to be any easier.

Mark wasn't at all sure how he was going to gain access to the morgue, and it wouldn't help him in the least if the attendants brought out Polaroids of the deceased or digital images, as was so often the case these days.

He was pretty good at mesmerizing people, and on someone trusting, like innkeeper Lilly Martin, he could almost guarantee success. But at the morgue, there were clerks, assistants, attendants, gurney pushers…all kinds of people to get past.

Luckily, he started out with a young woman in her mid-twenties, a picture of her husband and baby on her desk.

The entire business world knew that confident, direct eye contact brought about the best results. And she was easy to engage. Without telling too many lies, he convinced her that he had an official reason to be there and got her to agree to let him in to see the body that had been pulled from the Mississippi.

As it happened, the remains were in one of the autopsy rooms. Bad luck. But he was able to get into the back, and put on scrubs and a mask. With a clipboard in hand, he moved down the hallway, knowing exactly where he was going.

To his surprise, there was a roadblock. A human roadblock.

Most of the time that would have meant little, but this roadblock was different. It was the cop. Sean Canady.

Canady looked up, saw him and, despite the mask and the scrubs, recognized him instantly.

Hell. Now there was a chance he would be arrested. Not good.

But Canady only strode down the hallway to greet him.

No sense playing games. "Hello, Lieutenant."

"Musician and writer, huh?"

"I swear. You should hear me play."

Canady studied him for a long moment, looking into his eyes.

To Mark's amazement, the cop shrugged. "You feel you need to see the body? Let's go."

One of the assistants brought Canady some gloves. He thanked the assistant, then asked, "Who's on?"

"Doc Mordock."

"Great."

The autopsy room was like every other one of its kind. Sterile. Tile and paint in soft powder-blue. Same smell of death, antiseptics and preservatives. Water running to keep the stainless-steel tables as clean and germ-free as possible, and to enable the doctors and technicians to work on human bodies, with all their messy fluids and tissues.

Only one of the gurneys in the room held a form beneath a sheet. A man in scrubs and a mask was standing behind it.

"Sean, hey," he said.

"Doc Mordock, hi," Sean replied.

Mordock looked at Mark, a question in his eyes. "Mark Davidson," Sean said in introduction. "He's seen victims found in a similar situation. He may be able to tell us if we're looking at a killer who has struck elsewhere," he went on to explain briefly.

"Hey, he's with you. That's good enough for me," Mordock said as he pulled back the sheet.

There was always something sad and eerie about a naked corpse on a stainless-steel gurney. When the head was missing, the effect was intensified.

Mark knew there were things that Mordock could determine from the damage inflicted by the water, and the fish and crustaceans that made the Mississippi their home. He should be able to determine a time and date of death, what she had eaten for her last meal, and much, much more.

None of that mattered to Mark, though he did listen to the conversation between Mordock and Sean Canady.

"You got an ID yet?" Mordock asked.

Canady nodded. "Eloise Dryer. A few petty thefts, soliciting. She's known in a few of the local clubs, but her address is listed as a Houston hole-in-the-wall."

"So she was a prostitute?" Mark said.

"Most of the time," Canady told him.

Mark was inspecting the corpse's neck.

"Decapitated with an ax," Mordock told him. "Postmortem. But it was one clean swipe. I'm willing to bet many a man executed on the block would have given a lot to be killed with such a clean stroke."

"But she was deceased first?" Mark said.

Mordock indicated the cut. "Bloodless," he said.

There, Mark noted. A puncture mark. Not such a perfect way to hide the evidence after all. "Bloodless," he repeated, and looked at Canady.

The cop was silent. His face gave away nothing.

"She might have been killed as part of some ritual," Doc Mordock said. "God knows, there are enough kooks out there." He stared at Mark. "And I don't mean just in New Orleans. Hell, I was called out to work a case in the backwoods of the Midwest, the heart of America, and what those fellows were up to made hardened cops puke. But, yeah, I've seen the mark. Right on the jugular. She was drained like a slaughtered hog."

"That won't be in the press releases," Canady said, and looked warningly at Mark.

Mark shrugged. "I don't write press releases."

"But you do write."

"I won't be writing about this."

Apparently that satisfied Canady. "Thanks, Mordock. Put anything else you can think of in your report and give it to me as soon as you can. You still don't know where she went into the river?"

"Tech forensics are working on it, ebb and flow, all that," Mordock told him. "But she hasn't been dead that long. With the current and the river life, well, a body goes to hell pretty quickly when it's in the water. But here's something interesting—whoever tossed her didn't really care whether or not she was found. She wasn't weighted down. She was just dumped in the water."

Canady thanked the M.E. again and turned to exit the autopsy room. Mark followed him.

In the hallway, Canady stripped off his gloves, staring at Mark. "Did you get what you were after?"

"Yes. Did you?" Mark, too, stripped off his autopsy-room paraphernalia.

Canady studied him.

"Not just one vampire but lots of them, eh?"

Mark cleared his throat. "She was used for some kind of a blood rite."

When Sean didn't respond, Mark went on. "Every cult has some kind of leader, a grand priest, whatever," Mark said, studying Canady. "I get the impression you've dealt with cults before. That you know what I'm talking about."

"Come in tomorrow. You can have a sketch artist draw up a likeness of this man Stephan for me."

"Thanks," Mark said, then hesitated. Canady seemed to be a decent guy, treating him with such apparent respect. But he was afraid for the man, as well. "The thing is…okay, these guys really think they *are* vampires. They go down if they're hit with holy water, and they back away from crosses, and…unless they're planning to make a victim rise from the dead, they cut off the head to keep the population from getting out of control. I'm just worried that your people…"

Canady grinned. "My cops won't know they need to stake the guy, is that it?"

He didn't know if Canady was mocking him or not.

"Yeah, something like that," he said.

"I'll take care of it. Come by the station tomorrow, Mr. Davidson."

"Thank you. Um, Lieutenant?"

"Yeah?"

"They may not all be men."

"Pardon?"

"Vampires. They come in both sexes."

"Gotcha," Canady said. "Tomorrow."

Mark hesitated. "Like I said before, he's hiding out somewhere. He can move about by day, but it's a better time for him to rest."

"I've warned local law enforcement to be on the lookout," Sean told him. "And not just in this parish."

"Oh? Great. Just so long as they understand that they could really be in danger—"

"I know my business," Canady told him.

"Right. Well, thanks."

As soon as Mark left the morgue, he hurried back to the bed-and-breakfast. As he pulled into the lot, he saw that Deanna and Lauren, wearing bathing suits and carrying bags that he assumed held lotions and magazines, were just going into their cottage.

Lock it, he thought as the door closed behind them. *Lock it! And don't let anyone in....*

He decided they were safe enough for the time being and headed back to his car.

Just when the world seemed all nice and normal...

When Deanna and Lauren went into their cottage they found Heidi out of the shower, dressed and on her cell phone. She flashed them a smile and mouthed the word "Barry."

They both nodded; then Deanna headed into the shower, and Lauren plopped down on the sofa, turned on the television and found the news.

There was a police officer, a big handsome guy, talking to a sea of reporters, who were all struggling to get their mikes closer to the cop.

"The most important thing for anyone, but especially women, to remember is to use good judgment and common sense," the cop was saying.

"But the victim was a known prostitute," one of the reporters called out.

"The victim was a woman," the policeman said firmly. "And we don't know yet where she was killed. It might have been anywhere along the Mississippi. Folks, this is a great city. We've had our share of trouble, but we always rise back up. Right now, let's assume we're having a problem, so let's handle it intelligently. Go out, have fun. Go to dinner—gamble, if that's your passion, enjoy everything this city has to offer. Stay in groups. Don't go down dark streets on your own. Don't assume that you're safe just because the last victim was a woman or a prostitute, but don't spend your lives hiding, either. There's nothing new about predators. And there's nothing new to guard against them. Being smart is always the best defense."

The reporters all started shouting questions, speaking over top of each other. The detective lifted a hand. "There's nothing else I can say at the moment, except maybe to add this warning—don't open your door to strangers."

"Even tall, good-looking ones, Lieutenant?" one of the female reporters asked with a grin.

"Strangers of any kind, Amy," the cop said, staring hard at her, his expression grim. He'd been talking about murder and clearly hadn't appreciated her levity.

And that was that. They kept shouting, but he had turned and was walking away.

The television went off with a soft ping. Lauren looked up. Heidi had flicked it off with the remote control. "We need to listen to that man," she said firmly.

"Of course. Smart man," Lauren said.

Heidi sat down next to her. "You're getting that look that means you're taking all this too much to heart. We *are* going out."

"Yeah, and we're doing what the officer said."

"What's that?" Heidi asked, frowning.

"We're sticking together."

Heidi waved a hand in the air. "Of course. That will be easy."

Deanna popped out of the bathroom, followed by a cloud of steam. She was in a robe, her makeup bag in her hand. "It's all yours, Lauren."

"Great. Thanks." Lauren rose and walked in to take her shower. She was grateful to discover that despite Heidi and Deanna having gone before her, she still had hot water.

Be smart, the cop had said.

Smart would be getting on a plane and getting the hell away from here.

Heidi and Deanna would never do it.

But Deanna was acting even stranger than she was herself, she thought. Just what was going on? Deanna wasn't given to flights of fancy or weirdness. There were just too many tall, dark-haired men hanging around lately. Mark Davidson, almost devastatingly attractive but scary as hell. Jonas, Deanna's guy.

And then…

It wasn't human, Deanna had said.

Back up, she told herself. There were often moments when you felt you were being watched. Creepy little moments. There were times when she had been home in L.A. and felt her heart accelerate when she looked out at the darkness and the bushes rustling near her door. Fear was a natural human emotion, or, if not flat-out fear, at least unease.

They would go out tonight. They would check out the bars, and they would most definitely stay together.

But the newscast kept replaying in her mind.

Don't open your door to strangers.

* * *

He hadn't been out on the road in eons. He hadn't driven this way since he'd returned to New Orleans, and he wasn't even sure right now why the temptation to do so had become so strong.

He knew he was in the right place, though.

But the house was long gone, and nothing had been built in its stead. There was only a tangle of growth covering the property.

He wondered idly who owned it now. Easy enough to find out, he imagined.

He stared at the property for a while, then walked along the sweeping drive. Some of the oaks and magnolias remained, as did the foundation. If he closed his eyes, he could almost imagine what it had been. Hear laughter.

It had been a great house, long ago.

He turned and headed back to his car. The past couldn't be changed, but the future loomed ahead, and he damn well meant to change it.

"A hurricane, please," Deanna told their server. He was tall, ebony, and had a smile that could light up the world. He was also outrageously flirtatious, and they were being flirtatious in return.

"Hurricane," he murmured.

Deanna hesitated, afraid she had done something that was now incorrect. "People still order hurricanes, right?" she asked weakly.

The waiter offered them his killer grin again. "Yes. Hey, it's just a drink, you know? We had one bar that never closed during the whole storm. When they ran out of beer, the owners went over and picked some up at the A&P, and left an IOU. Anyway, it wasn't really the hurricane that did us in, it was the flood waters. You go right ahead and order whatever you want."

"Thanks," Deanna said. "What a face," she murmured, watching the waiter leave to get their drinks.

"Not bad buns, either," Heidi said, laughing.

They could actually hear one another speak, Lauren noticed. Maybe a lot of people had stayed inside after all. But not them. They'd overeaten at K-Paul's, then chosen a place offering smooth jazz. In fact, Lauren thought she recognized one of the musicians, a huge African-American man. He was playing a saxophone, while she could have sworn that earlier in the day he had been playing a trombone.

"Hey, you're engaged," Deanna reminded her.

"I know that. I'm still on the lookout for the two of you."

"Heidi, please," Lauren groaned.

"That's right. She's already earmarked for tall, dark and handsome in cottage six," Heidi teased.

Lauren refused to rise to the bait and instead listened to the smooth tones of the music, her gaze directed toward the band again. The big man she had seen earlier nodded, as if he recognized her, as well.

She lifted her beer to him.

He grinned, then started playing his sax again.

The bar was busy, but fairly large, and the acoustics were good. "Irene's—great place for dinner," she heard, as someone next to her recommended it to someone else. *It is,* she thought.

For a moment, it felt good just to be there.

"Deanna, he's gorgeous," Heidi said, startling Lauren from her thoughts. She looked back to her two companions. Heidi was tilting her head dramatically, indicating the waiter. "You have to make a play for him."

"Deanna is waiting for Jonas," Lauren heard herself say, then wondered why.

Deanna flushed, obvious even in the dim light, and Lauren caught her breath.

Her friend *was* waiting for Jonas.

Heidi sighed dramatically. "What a waste of hot masculinity."

"You go ahead and flirt with him, then," Deanna said.

"Heidi, you have to let *us* choose who we want to flirt with," Lauren insisted.

"I just want everyone to be as happy as I am. I want it for the whole world. Can you imagine? No mistrust, no war, because everyone would always be really happy, even the people running all the countries."

Lauren stared across the table, and Deanna tilted her beer bottle and grinned. "I think she's had a few."

"Think about it," Heidi said stubbornly. "Laugh if you want to. But let's face it, we have some world leaders out there who would definitely benefit from a better sex life."

Lauren smiled, relaxed and ready to go with the flow after three beers.

"Hear, hear," Deanna said dryly as the waiter swooped in with her hurricane. She managed a thank-you, but she wasn't even really looking at him. Her gaze was riveted on the bar.

Lauren quickly turned, trying to see what had captured Deanna's attention, and she saw him at last. Deanna's stranger.

She tensed immediately.

He was attractive. Tall, six-one or so, and lean. Just under or about thirty, with thick, dark, slightly wavy hair, one strand falling and forming a C on his forehead. He pushed it back, accepted a drink and thanked the bartender. Then he turned and saw Deanna.

He smiled. Nice smile.

Deanna stood. Hurricane in hand, she started toward the bar.

"What?" Heidi demanded.

Lauren, too, was on her feet. "It's him," she explained.

"Him, who?"

"Deanna's...crush," Lauren supplied.

"Jonas," Deanna breathed.

She followed Deanna with her eyes, but before her friend could reach Jonas, someone came between them. Like a brick wall, he was very definitely trying to prevent Jonas from rendezvousing with Deanna.

Had Mark been there all along, watching them?

Apparently so.

As she watched, Jonas reacted to whatever Mark was saying. A flicker of something like fear flashed in his eyes, and he shook his head. It looked like he was saying, "You don't understand," but she couldn't be sure.

Mark set a hand on the other man's chest, and a touch of anger, then defiance, showed on Jonas's face. She decided the time had come to intervene and hurried over to her friend.

"What the hell is Mark doing?" Deanna demanded when Lauren reached her.

"Picking a fight, it looks like," Lauren said. She looked back toward the table. Heidi had taken her own advice and was oblivious to the tension on their side of the room; she was talking to their waiter, laughing, showing him her engagement ring.

To be fair to Heidi, very few of the patrons seemed to notice that anything was going on. The music had stopped, and the lead singer was talking about the history of jazz in New Orleans, and most people's focus was on him. She looked at the big man she'd seen twice today.

He had noticed what was going on and was closely watching the two men.

And speaking softly to someone on his cell phone.

She returned her gaze to the action right in front of her.

Mark had a hand on Jonas's arm now, and his expression was tense as he used his other hand to indicate a hallway that led to the back.

"They're going to go outside and fight!" Deanna said, incredulous.

Could Deanna be right? Lauren wondered. She had noticed a narrow alley out back.

Jonas started in that direction. Mark followed.

Deanna stared.

Lauren pushed past her, irritated that Mark's protective attitude was getting out of hand.

She made her way to the hallway, past the restrooms and a delivery of beer, and out the back to a small courtyard with scattered tables, which was only half filled with people. The wrought-iron gate from the courtyard to the alley was ajar.

Lauren raced forward, pushing through it and catching up to the two men.

"You don't know anything," Jonas insisted to Mark, who had pushed the younger man up against a wall. "You don't know *anything.*"

"I intend to."

"I'm not your enemy."

"You're one of them."

"Mark!" She ran up and put a hand on his shoulder. He stiffened, teeth grating, face taut with fury and tension as he turned to her.

"Get out of here, Lauren. Now."

"I am not going to let you beat this man to a pulp," she said.

"Excuse me," Jonas interjected. "I'm not exactly a weakling," he said with a touch of indignation.

Mark turned back to him, and Jonas started to take a swing at him, but Mark was too fast. He blocked the blow coming his way, then counter-jabbed. Jonas took his fist in the jaw and sagged.

"Stop it!" Lauren shouted.

"He asked for it," Jonas insisted. Something in his eyes—in his entire demeanor—seemed to change.

He let out a hissing sound and flew toward Mark.

Lauren heard movement behind her. She swung around, expecting Deanna to go rushing past her into the fray.

But it wasn't Deanna.

It was the sax player.

"I've called the cops," he snapped. "So take your beef out of here—now!"

He had a beer in his hand and threw it at the men. It looked to Lauren as if a haze appeared between her and the men, like a mist, or a fog, rising in the shadows. She heard a hiss of fury but couldn't tell where—or who—it came from.

She could hear sirens wailing. Bourbon was closed off to normal traffic at night, but the next thing she knew, cop cars were pulling up on the cross street, and two mounted officers rode into the alley, as well.

"Fight over there," the sax player said, pointing.

"Where?" one of the mounted officers asked.

"Right there!" Lauren said impatiently, facing him fully, then turning back toward the spot where the two men had been.

But no one was there. Somehow, in the dimly lit alley, with nowhere for them to go, Mark and Jonas had managed to disappear.

She heard a car door open and close. A plainclothes police officer, tall, graying at the temples, but with steel-blue eyes and an attitude as powerful as his size, was striding into the alley.

"Hey, Lieutenant," the big musician said.

"Big Jim, what's going on?"

"A fight—the kind that looked like it could have turned bloody," Big Jim supplied.

"Between...?" the lieutenant asked.

"They were right there. This— Big Jim told them to stop and threw beer at them, and then they both...took off, I guess," Lauren said.

The steel-blue eyes settled on her. "And you are?"

"My name is Lauren Crow," she said.

He looked around.

"And you were egging on one of the participants?" he inquired.

"Of course not! I came out to tell Mark to leave the other guy alone."

"And Mark is...your boyfriend?" the lieutenant asked.

"No! He's just someone we...we met. He's staying at our bed-and-breakfast," Lauren explained quickly. Oh, God, what kind of a mess had the far-too-good-looking lunatic gotten her into?

The mounted patrolmen took off down the alley.

The lieutenant's partner got out of the car and stood silently in the background. As two more uniformed officers arrived from the second car, the lieutenant raised a hand. "I've got it, guys. Doesn't look like we've got a situation anymore, anyway."

"Sure. 'Night, Lieutenant Canady," one of them called.

"Hey, Lieutenant, you're working late," the second man said, respect in his voice.

"Yeah, well...anyway, I've got this. Thanks," Canady told him.

"Yessir." The pair spoke in unison and headed back to their car.

"Mark," Canady said. "Mark...?"

"His name is Mark Davidson."

"I see."

He had a notebook out, but he wasn't writing. "And who was the other man?"

"I don't know him. He and a friend of mine have had a few conversations," Lauren said. Oh, great. Now she was dragging Deanna into it. "She doesn't really know him, either." She looked toward the wrought-iron fence, the courtyard and the bar. Deanna was nowhere to be seen. "She's still inside, I guess. I thought he—Jonas—was going to start a fight, and…I guess I thought I could stop it."

"Is that what happened, Big Jim?" Canady asked the sax player.

"Just the way I saw it," Big Jim said.

She wanted to kiss him. She let out a sigh of relief and swore silently that she was going to have nothing more to do with Mark Davidson.

She heard the sound of hooves. The mounted officers were returning.

"If there were two guys about to tear each other's throats out, there's not a sign of them anywhere around here. Big Jim must have doused the fight right out of them," one of them said.

"Thanks, Macinaw," the lieutenant said.

"We'll be back out on Bourbon," the mounted officer told him.

The lieutenant nodded and watched them ride toward the street.

Then he startled Lauren when he took a step toward her and indicated her throat. "That's an interesting cross you're wearing. Antique."

"Uh, yes."

He stared at her, as if expecting her to say more. She swal-

lowed, not about to tell him that she had put it on after Mark
Davidson had left it on the table that afternoon. She hadn't
wanted to lose it until she had a chance to give it back.

"You should always wear it," he said quietly, then
stepped back.

"What's your bed-and-breakfast?" he asked.

She told him, and he arched a brow at her. "Did you call
in the other night to ask the patrol officers to keep an eye on
the place?"

She flushed. "Yes."

"You were afraid?"

"I…I had seen someone lurking around on the sidewalk."

He nodded, watching her intently. "So where are you from?"

"Actually, I'm originally from Baton Rouge. But I live
in L.A. now."

"I see."

What did he see?

"I'm here with friends. We're on vacation. If I can tell
you anything else, I'd be happy to. If not…I should get
back to them."

"Sure." He glanced around at his partner. "I'm officially
off, Bobby. Think I'll call it a night. Keep your eyes and ears
open for anything. I'm going to go in and watch Big Jim's next
set, have a beer."

"Sure thing, Lieutenant," his partner said. He turned and
headed back for the patrol car. "Call me if you need a ride."

"I can get him home," Big Jim said.

"Cool."

The officer walked on. "Miss Crow?" Lieutenant Canady
said, indicating that she was free to return to the bar.

"Thanks," she murmured.

She walked through the courtyard. No one seemed to have

noticed everything that had gone on only a few feet away. Then again, what had really happened?

Two men had fought briefly, then disappeared—as if into the mist.

Deanna was back at the table in earnest conversation with Heidi. Lauren headed for her chair.

Neither Big Jim nor Lieutenant Canady followed her. Big Jim went back to his place in the band, and Canady took a seat directly in front of the stage. The band members all acknowledged him with nods, smiles and, in one case, a raised glass.

The lieutenant loosened his collar and ordered a drink.

Though he seemed to be watching the band, Lauren was convinced the only reason he had come in was to see if she really was with friends. Or maybe just to keep an eye on her. She didn't understand why, but she was as unnerved by him as she had been by everything else.

Deanna leaned across the table and asked, her voice low, "What happened? That guy in the band must be sharp as a tack—I think he called the cops before the guys even made it outside. And when I was going to follow you, he stopped me and gave me this."

She produced a business card and handed it to Lauren.

"What is it?" Heidi asked.

"It's for another bed-and-breakfast," Lauren murmured. "Montresse House."

"Think he lives there?" Heidi asked with a giggle. "That would be a different way to pick up women, huh?"

"He wasn't trying to pick me up," Deanna said.

"No?" Heidi queried.

"I can tell, and you know it," Deanna told her.

"Maybe he's friends with the owner or something, and just hands out cards," Lauren suggested.

"Yeah. There's something about him that's...I don't know. Trustworthy," Deanna said.

Lauren fingered the card. "I'll put it in my wallet."

"Sure. You never know when we might come back."

Deanna's voice sounded strange. As if she was really thinking that she would *never* want to come back.

"So what happened out there?" Heidi asked again.

"Nothing," Lauren said. "The two of them yelled at one another, and then the guy from the band, Big Jim, came out and threw a beer at them. They disappeared before the cops showed up."

"Disappeared?" Deanna said in dismay.

"You can't be that hung up on this guy yet," Heidi said. "And you should both take a lesson from this—don't get involved with strange men."

They both stared at her.

She let out a sigh. "Let's go back to the cottage. The mood tonight is definitely blown. Great party we're having."

Lauren sat back, caught sight of their waiter and motioned that they needed the check.

He brought it to them, and they quickly handed him cash, then got up and headed for the door. Though his back was to them, Lauren was convinced that the cop was aware of their exit.

"Well, that was a downer," Heidi said a few minutes later as they walked through the night.

Deanna laid an arm across her shoulders. "Heidi, I'm sorry."

"No, *I'm* sorry. I just don't get it. Did the two of them know each other?" she asked.

"I don't think so," Lauren said.

"Then...?"

"Who knows?" Lauren replied.

They turned off Bourbon Street, walking briskly.

Lauren knew, somehow, that they were being followed.

She turned around. There was no one there, but it didn't matter. She knew what she knew. But she didn't have a sense of darkness or of shadows. Instead she knew that, feeling completely at home in the night, the cop was following them.

"Let's go on a riverboat cruise tomorrow," Deanna suggested.

"Cool idea," Heidi agreed. "And before we leave, I want to drive out to the zoo, too. I really love it."

"Great idea," Lauren said, turning around again. She couldn't see him, but she was sure that he was standing in the shadow of one of the nearby buildings.

They reached the courtyard of the B and B without incident. The gates creaked when Lauren opened them. They walked around the pool. The gorgeous and friendly lesbian couple from cottage three was sitting at one of the tables, sipping from plastic cups and watching the stars. Both women, Janice and Helen, were tall and blond, and modeled for a large clothing chain.

"Beautiful night, huh?" Janice called.

"It's so pretty here, just breathing in the magnolia, watching the sky," Helen offered. "Don't you think?" She seemed anxious for them to agree with her.

"Beautiful," Lauren agreed.

"Janice thinks it's kind of creepy, too," Helen added.

"Darkness and shadows," Janice said, then laughed. "I've got too much imagination. Helen doesn't mind the most gruesome horror movie, but I can only watch them at home, where I can leave the room when I can't take it anymore."

"Well, I'm going in. I'm beat," Deanna said, and walked on toward their cottage to a chorus of good-nights.

"I'll follow her," Heidi said.

"I guess we'll go in, too," Janice said. "Although we do have more champagne, if you'd like some."

"Tomorrow night?" Lauren suggested.

"Great," Janice said. "Meet you out here? I really do love this place at night. It's just that sometimes…"

"Sometimes what?" Lauren asked.

Janice shrugged and looked apologetically at Helen. "I get the feeling we're being watched."

Were they all crazy, Lauren wondered, or was their uneasiness just natural? The cottages were secluded, it was true, but the main house overlooked them. And the wall that separated the B and B from the old Victorian next door, where the bottom floor sold T-shirts, coffee and voodoo potions, and the upper floor was rented out as apartments, was tall and solid and would be hard for an intruder to scale.

"Deanna thinks she's being watched sometimes, too," Lauren said.

"What a shock," Helen said, laughing. "She's gorgeous. Imagine that. Some peeper watching a gorgeous woman."

"Let's all keep our doors locked, huh?" Lauren said.

"You bet," Helen agreed.

Lauren couldn't help but be glad that the other women had been outside to greet them—even if Janice's words had given her a start. And Helen's explanation *was* a sensible one.

They wished one another good-night and headed off toward their own cottages.

Lauren looked back toward the street when she reached her door and saw that they had indeed been followed back from the bar by a man.

But she could see him plainly. It was definitely the cop.

She turned away and went inside.

"I'm going to bed," Heidi said. She quickly hugged them both. "Forgive me for being bitchy. Tomorrow night, no fights, we just have fun."

"Absolutely," Deanna swore.

"You got it," Lauren promised.

Deanna gave Lauren a hug, too, as Heidi went into the bedroom. "You're a great friend. And I'm being a really weird one. Sorry. Love you."

"I love you, too," Lauren assured her. "And it's not you being weird. It's just that weird things have been happening, you know?"

"Yeah, I do. But do you want to know the really weird thing?"

"What?"

"In spite of tonight, I really want to see Jonas again. Don't worry, though. I'm not going back out in the night or anything. I'm wiped, too. I'm going to bed."

"Good night."

When Deanna had disappeared into the bedroom, Lauren went to the window, pulled back the curtain and looked outside again.

The cop was gone.

As she stared out, she heard a soft tapping on the door. She jumped, just managing to hold back a scream. It was probably the cop, and that was why she couldn't see him on the street.

Without thinking, she opened the door.

It wasn't the cop.

She drew breath to scream, but she never got the chance.

A hand covered her mouth, and she was dragged out into the night.

6

Sean Canady had taken the call while he was standing on the sidewalk on Conti Street, having just made sure that Lauren and her friends had gotten safely into their cottage.

"Canady here," he said.

"It's Bobby, Lieutenant. We've got trouble."

"Go on."

"We have another floater."

Sean's heart sank, and he swore silently. "Where?"

Bobby gave him the coordinates. He was thankful to hear that they weren't in the heart of the city.

"Send a car for me now," he said, and gave his exact location.

"Yessir."

"Bobby?"

"Yeah?"

Sean paused. "Headless?"

"Yeah, Lieutenant. Headless."

"Don't scream. Please, don't scream. I swear to God, I have no desire to hurt you. I'm trying to *help* you."

Thoughts plowed through her mind with the speed of lightning as she was dragged from her own doorway.

She should scream. Definitely, she should scream.

She would pretend to agree, but the minute he lifted his hand, she was going to scream bloody murder.

His eyes seemed so sincere. And he was definitely a powerful man, all muscle; if he had wanted to drag her somewhere else, he could have done it easily.

Scream.

How many women throughout history had died because they had listened to the words *don't scream?*

She wasn't an idiot.

She was the daughter of a cop, for God's sake.

"Please, if you'll just listen to me, I swear I won't touch you again. You just have to listen to me. You have to understand the danger you're in."

Actually, I want you to touch me, even if you look at me and think of Katie, even if I'm not quite sure whether you're sane or not....

Bad thought.

But when he eased his hand away from her mouth, she just stood there, staring daggers at him, shaking. Despite her promise to herself, she didn't scream.

"The cops know all about you," she warned.

"Some cops may know what I'm talking about."

"They know you're staying here."

"Please."

He didn't touch her, though she could tell he wanted to.

"Come next door. For ten minutes. And you can leave any time you want."

Not only was she not going to scream, she realized, she was going to go into his cottage with him.

Not a grave danger, she tried to reassure herself. The cottages were small and close together. If she screamed, someone would hear her.

Wouldn't they?

"If you still think I'm totally insane after listening to what I have to say, I swear…I'll leave you alone."

"I could have you arrested," she lied.

"Your lives are worth the risk."

He sounded so sincere.

She knew that the voice in her head telling her to just say no was right. Sure, she was attracted to the man, attracted in a way she had never believed she could feel again. In his presence, she felt as if her every sense was heightened, but that was a stupid reason to trust him. And yet…

"This better be quick," she said brusquely. "Wait here. I'm going to lock the door."

And to her amazement, she calmly went for her key, then made sure that the door was locked behind her when she exited the cottage, this time of her own volition. He led the twenty feet or so to his own cottage and opened his door, ushering her in.

She took a deep breath as she walked through the doorway. *Had she just signed her own death warrant?*

The cottage was like her own, with a bedroom, kitchenette, bath and living room. In their cottage, the sofa bed in the living room was made up. Here, it remained a sofa. She took a seat on the chair that faced the sofa. She was not going to let him sit next to her.

"Would you like something to drink?"

"No. You said you want to talk to me, so talk."

He sat on the couch opposite her, a coffee table between them. He leaned forward and took a breath. His eyes caught and held hers.

"You know the danger is real. A headless body was found floating in the Mississippi."

"It's hard to miss the newspaper reports," she replied.

"And I told you, I know who the killer is."

I should be suspecting that it's you, she thought. But somehow she couldn't believe that. If she had, surely she couldn't—wouldn't—have calmly walked over here.

No, he might not be entirely sane, but he *was* entirely sincere.

"How can you be so certain?" she asked him.

"Because I know Stephan."

She stared at him, as if digesting what he had said, then asked carefully, "And you're certain that what you're telling me is…real?"

"Stephan Delansky is very real," he told her quietly. "I've come here because I came across one of his…associates who told me he was coming here. With an army."

"An army?" she queried. "Who is Stephan Delansky?"

"An old enemy. But not just my enemy. A very dangerous man. Many years ago I took a trip to Kiev, in the Ukraine. I met a woman there. Katya."

"The one I remind you of."

"Yes," he said very softly, then took a deep breath. "I'm from this area originally. After I met Katya, she came back here with me. I was head over heels, and so was Katya. Katie, I called her. We were going to go back there to get married, though. To Kiev. She had always dreamed of being married in a castle, and there are some great castles over there. But while we were still here, she thought she kept seeing an old friend of hers—Stephan. I saw her speaking to him once and asked her about him, even suggested she introduce us, but he had no interest in meeting me. Meanwhile, we kept planning our wedding. But before it could take place, Katie was dead. Because of Stephan."

His voice was mesmerizing, compelling. It touched her in

some deep core over which she had no control. She wanted to listen to him, wanted to believe him.

But she couldn't help thinking that maybe the pain of his loss had made him delusional. She knew what it was like to deny the truth, to go through the fury, the agony and then the dull acceptance of loss.

Maybe he hadn't come quite so far.

"Did he shoot her? Stab her? What?" Lauren asked softly.

His head lowered for a minute. She was tempted to reach out. To touch the lush darkness of his hair.

He looked up at her again, straight in the eye.

"Stephan is a vampire."

She froze, staring at him.

Wishing that she hadn't heard him correctly.

Knowing that she had.

"I see," she said. But the only thing she saw was that he was delusional. It was so sad. The first man who had made her think she might want to at least have a relationship again, maybe even love again.

A relationship…? Okay, sex.

She told herself that she needed to get a grip. She had never been the type to indulge in casual sex.

Except there was nothing casual about this man.

Even now, after hearing him talk with complete seriousness about the existence of vampires, she still longed to reach out and touch the night-rich darkness of his hair.

He shook his head, the curve of his smile self-mocking.

"I know you don't believe me. But believe this. I know your cop, the one who showed up at the bar, the one who followed you here. His name's Lieutenant Sean Canady. I went with him today to the morgue."

"The morgue?" she repeated, staring blankly at him.

"I needed to see the body."

"The headless woman?" That thought scared the hell out of her.

"Yes."

"Let me get this straight. Lieutenant Canady, a police officer, took you in with him to see the corpse of a crime victim?"

"He did. You can ask him."

There was a note of absolute truth in his tone. She knew that Canady really had taken him in to see the corpse.

Great. The cops were crazy, too.

He lifted a hand. "Please, hear me out. The cops aren't insane any more than I am. But this is New Orleans. Voodoo central. They're aware of all kinds of cultists and weird practices going on here."

"Sure," she murmured.

She needed to get out of here. He had sworn he wouldn't stop her. All she had to do was stand up and leave.

But she didn't.

"And when you saw the body?"

"Even though she had been beheaded, you could still see the marks."

"The marks? From a vampire?"

"Yes."

She inhaled, wary, feeling as if she needed to run as fast as she could, but fascinated by the conversation despite herself.

Wishing desperately that…

That they weren't having this conversation at all.

"All right," she said. "Let's go back to what went on tonight at the bar. Deanna considers that man, Jonas, a friend. Why were you trying to beat him to a pulp?"

"Because he's a vampire."

"I thought Stephan was the vampire?"

"Stephan is one vampire, a very old one. Very powerful. He can influence people around him, command respect." He let out a sound of derision. "Just like a cult leader," he said quietly. "I think Stephan has come here with an army of vampires. And I'm convinced he knows you're here."

"And he's after me because I look like Katie?"

"I don't know if he'd been in love with her, after her, for years, or if having her simply became a matter of pride, an obsession, for him. But, yes, if I saw you and thought—even for a split second—that you were Katie, I can promise you that Stephan would have reacted exactly the same way."

She moistened her lips and spoke softly, reasonably. "All right, so...so if Stephan wants me, why is Jonas after Deanna?"

"I had hoped to find that out tonight. Deanna is beautiful. Any man would notice her in a crowd. Maybe that's all it is. Perhaps Jonas, having seen her, just wants her for himself. Or maybe Stephan has decided to pick off your friends one by one to get to you, so he's ordered Jonas to go after Deanna. And of course Stephan knows *I'm* in the area now, as well."

"How does he know that?"

Mark looked grim. "Trust me. He knows. And he's been here—on the grounds. I know that, too."

"You've seen him?"

"I've...smelled him."

Smelled?

A chill shot through Lauren. She should be laughing.

No, she should leave. Should have left ten minutes ago.

But once again, she simply watched him, amazed. There was something in his words, a calm sincerity, that was disturbing. He spoke with such an element of truth...or true belief, at least.

She sat still for a moment, then leaned forward and said,

"Mark. I know what it's like to lose someone. I was engaged myself. My fiancé was in the military, and he was killed overseas. I knew he was in danger over there, but somehow you don't believe anything terrible will happen to someone you love. He was a pilot, and his plane went down. I tried for months to believe it was a lie, a mistake, that it was someone else…but then his body came home and I had to face the truth. There are stages of grief, you know. Denial, fury, guilt…I'm sure it hurt terribly to lose Katie. I know there were days when I thought I'd lost my mind. Seriously, I'm a pacifist, but I wanted to nuke half the world."

He shook his head, dark lashes shielding his eyes. Then he offered her his rueful grin, the one that made her long to get closer to him.

"I have no desire to hurt anyone other than Stephan—and his kind."

"As in vampires."

He hesitated. "As in his kind," he repeated.

She lifted her hands. "What do you want *me* to do?" she asked.

"Let me protect you."

"You want to follow us around?"

"Yes."

She rose, thinking that she very seriously *needed* to get away from him, to listen to the voice of sanity again. At the same time, she couldn't resist being with him, near him, seeing his eyes, hearing his voice. All she wanted was for this to be a normal conversation. Like a date. She wanted to laugh with him. She wanted to be pulled into his arms…to explore the dream.

"I have to think about this," she told him.

He stood, as well. "You want to go to the police in the morning and report me as a lunatic, and you want to put your life in the hands of the authorities. But they can't help you. I'm not sure the police can even help themselves."

"Look, I'm really tired. I had a few drinks, and right now I don't know what I think." She started for the door but turned back. "And I'm not Katie."

He shook his head. "I know that. You're very different, entirely yourself." There was a husky tone in his voice, and she couldn't help the very sexual images that he aroused in her mind, even though she knew that she had to be bordering on insanity to even be considering a relationship with him.

She realized that she had needed to know he realized she was different, her own woman, and she wasn't sure why. And she was angry with herself because it was so important. She didn't intend to be a substitute for any other woman, so if…

If she did wind up in bed with him…

But she wasn't going to. For one thing, he clearly wasn't right in the head.

"So why the interest in me?" she demanded harshly. Too harshly.

"Because you're remarkable," he told her.

Suddenly it was all too much for her. "I need to get back. Heidi or Deanna might wake up, and they'll panic if I'm not there."

"Of course."

As he said the words, the night was suddenly broken by a bloodcurdling scream.

The sound of helicopters over water practically deafened Sean.

Without that, and the sounds of the workforce gathering, it might have been any other slow southern night on the river. Though he couldn't hear them, he knew that insects were chirping nearby, and there was actually a breeze off the water, carrying with it the scent of magnolias. If he closed his eyes…

He would still hear the helicopters and the shouting all around him.

A couple of kids out in a canoe had reported the grisly find; they were now huddled on the embankment, wrapped in blankets, pale and scared. Sean knew they'd had nothing to do with the murder, and he called for a couple of officers to take them home.

"Oh, man, this guy is one sick fuck," someone muttered near him.

He didn't say anything. He knew the guy wasn't sick at all. Wasn't demented. He was demonic. And smart. Sean knew he had to keep the situation under control, keep local cops thinking there was a run-of-the-mill deranged killer on the loose.

"I don't want her touched until Mordock gets here," he said, nodding to Bobby, who would see that his word was carried out as law.

He walked down closer to the water, knowing it would give him no clue. No, this guy was more than some sick fuck. He was enjoying every minute of what he was doing. Population control. Leaving just enough hints to throw the cops on the wrong track. Dumping the bodies in the Mighty Mississippi, knowing the water would wash away so many clues.

"Lieutenant? Mordock is here," Bobby called.

Sean strode back to the body. He looked down. He'd never become dispassionate. This was his city, and he loved it, fought for it. He cared for its people.

But the dead girl didn't even seem real. No head. Her skin sickly white, her flesh swollen from immersion.

Mordock looked up at him. "I'll know more after the autopsy," he said.

"What do you know now?"

"Dead two to four days, maybe. I don't think much longer."

"Decapitated before or after death?" Sean asked, but he already knew the answer.

"After."

One of the cops standing nearby crossed himself. "Thank God for that," he muttered. Then he turned around and walked away. Sean could hear him retching.

"Drained of blood?" Sean asked wearily.

"You bet," Mordock said. He looked at Sean. "Do we have another vampire cult or something on our hands?"

"Yeah. Something," Sean said. "Excuse me. I've got to call my wife."

Mark might have been big and tough and fast, but Lauren still beat him outside.

Where she saw…

Something.

A shape.

Living darkness?

At the end of the pool, looking like a large black hole in the universe, someone—or some*thing*—was in conversation with Deanna.

Deanna, looking gorgeous, was in nothing but a white cotton nightgown, her hand to her heart, staring at…

What?

Lauren couldn't see clearly, but she was sure there was something there. Something besides darkness.

Darkness that moved.

Mark flew past Lauren. She was amazed anyone so big

could move so fast and immediately thought he must have played football, then wondered how she could waste time thinking about something so inane when she was so afraid. As Mark ran, she noticed that he had pulled something from his pocket. Suddenly liquid went flying into the living darkness that lurked just behind Deanna.

Lauren came to a halt, her heart pounding. Mark had moved beyond Deanna, setting himself between her and whatever had been there. She refused to accept her feeling that she had seen a dark cloud of *evil* in the air. Someone had been there. She was simply being tricked by the shadows.

But when the liquid had flown, she was sure she had heard something.

A *hissing.*

Now the shadow was gone, and so was Mark. He didn't go out the gate, though. Like a quarterback heading down the field with the ball, he ran—and leaped over the wall separating the cottages from the next property.

She stared after him blankly for a moment.

Then she jolted back to reality. Deanna was just standing there, shaking.

"Deanna!" she cried, and rushed forward, putting her arms around her friend.

Deanna didn't move, didn't acknowledge her.

"Deanna?" she said again, tentatively.

Deanna jumped, as if suddenly awakening from a deep sleep, and stared at Lauren.

"I…" She fell silent, looking around in confusion. "I don't remember coming out here," she said, and shivered. "Was I sleepwalking again? I had a dream. I thought that I was going out to see Jonas…but then it wasn't Jonas." She sounded lost and afraid. Then, suddenly, her demeanor changed. "Were you talking to Mark Davidson? What on earth is the matter with that man? Why was he trying to hurt Jonas?" Her tone had gone from confused to impatient and irritated.

"Deanna, this is serious. And it has nothing to do with Mark *or* Jonas," she said firmly. "You were sleepwalking again. And you screamed."

"I did not!" Deanna said, shocked.

"Is everything all right?"

Lauren swung around. It was Helen; she and Janice had emerged from their cottage, clutching robes around themselves.

"Oh," Deanna groaned. "Did I wake you? Did I really scream?"

"You did," Janice said. "Someone did, anyway."

"I didn't mean to. I'm so sorry. I even watched my drinking tonight," Deanna said apologetically.

Heidi came wandering out then, half-asleep, confused. "Hey, what's going on out here?"

"It's all right," Deanna said, seeming like her usual self again, dismissing her disturbing behavior as if it were pure silliness. "You can dress me up, but you just can't take me anywhere," she said lightly. "I've had dreams my whole life, sometimes good, sometimes bad, but I never woke up the whole neighborhood before. I am so sorry."

"No problem. Good we're all nearby, huh?" Janice said cheerfully, then murmured, "That's strange. Where's tall, dark and to-die-for from cottage six? You'd think he'd be out here. He's such a..."

"Lean, mean, fighting machine?" Helen teased.

"I think he's a cop or something," Janice said.

"He's a writer and musician," Lauren corrected.

"So he says. I think he's a cop. FBI, maybe."

I think he's crazy, Lauren longed to say.

Then again, this whole night was crazy. Though the court-yard felt entirely normal now, she had to admit—no strange eyes watching them, no living shadows—it was damp, late and dark. And Deanna was ashen and still shivering.

"Mark…" Deanna murmured. She laughed. "I think he went off to fight the monster from my dream."

So much for Deanna being angry with him for attacking Jonas, Lauren thought.

"Well, as long as everyone is all right…" Janice said, and yawned.

"Fine. And I'm really sorry. Hope you all get back to sleep okay," Deanna said.

"Not a problem," Helen assured them.

"So can we go back to bed, too?" Heidi asked. "We'll block the door, Deanna, so you won't be able to get back out."

They went inside, and Lauren made a point of locking the door, then dragging a chair over and wedging it under the knob.

Heidi and Deanna watched from the hallway.

"Look good?" Lauren asked, determinedly cheerful.

"Looks good to me," Heidi said.

"Thanks," Deanna told her.

Then they turned and went into the bedroom.

Lauren curled up on the sofa bed, found the remote, turned on the television and flicked around until she found an old repeat of *Three's Company.*

She hugged her knees to her chest protectively as she watched.

They had to leave.

That was it. They had to go home.

Heidi would be upset at cutting her bachelorette trip short, but Lauren would make it up to her somehow. It was just insane to stay in a place where their neighbor was convinced he was a vampire hunter, Deanna kept sleepwalking and she herself thought she'd seen the darkness come alive.

And where a headless body had been discovered floating in the river...

Lauren stayed awake for at least an hour, staring at the screen, trying to concentrate on the TV, but she didn't see a thing.

She couldn't turn off her mind.

She kept remembering how Mark had gone chasing after that shadow and thrown some kind of liquid at it.

And back at the bar Big Jim had thrown beer at the fighters in the alleyway.

Vampires. Mark had insisted there were vampires.

Oh, please.

Mark Davidson was crazy. Gorgeous, but crazy.

She wondered if craziness was contagious, because even Janice had been convinced that she was being watched.

She tried, but she just couldn't make sense of any of it.

Somehow, somewhere along the line, she fell asleep. And she didn't wake up until, for the second time in a matter of hours, the sound of a bloodcurdling scream filled the air.

Second Day—Second Corpse.

Sean groaned as he stared at the headline. He had known it would be there, and he was afraid it would give rise to a general panic throughout the city.

Bobby entered the office. "You okay, Lieutenant?"

"Oh, yeah. Right as rain."

Bobby was silent for a minute. "We've got every cop on the force—and all up and down the Mississippi—on alert."

Sean stared at Bobby. "Yeah. Like that's going to stop this guy."

Bobby flushed. "Well, what *should* we do? Should I track

down the guy that woman was talking about last night? Mark Davidson?"

Sean sat back. "We need to find him. But I don't want him arrested and brought here. I'll deal with him, all right? If I need help, I'll let you know."

"Yes, sir." Bobby hesitated. "I've warned people, but I don't know how much good that will do." He walked to the door and looked back over his shoulder as he spoke.

"Good." Sean rose. "I'm going to hit the streets, ask some questions. I want you to call the hospitals. You know what we're looking for. Also, get someone to check out the missing persons bulletins. And I need to know about any reports of people acting crazy."

Bobby stared at him.

"What?" Sean said sharply.

Bobby shrugged. "Hey, this is New Orleans. People here pride themselves on acting crazy."

"Bobby, check the reports."

"I can't wake her up!" Heidi said, wide-eyed with alarm as she stared at Lauren over Deanna's prone body. "Look at her! She's not just pale, she's *gray*. She's really sick, Lauren. And she won't open her eyes."

Lauren strode straight to the phone and dialed 911. Then she sat down next to Deanna and tried to find a pulse.

Nothing at her wrists!

Then, at her throat, at last…

"She's alive," she breathed in relief.

Almost as she spoke, she heard the sound of a siren.

The next few minutes were a blur, as EMTs came rushing in, and she and Heidi tried to answer all their questions. The techs worked over Deanna, one of them in constant contact with an ER doctor through the entire process.

Lauren and Heidi scrambled into the bathroom quickly, one after the other, to get dressed, and Lauren found Deanna's purse, then made sure her ID and insurance information were there. The EMTs said one of them could ride with Deanna; the other would have to find her own way to the hospital.

With Deanna strapped to the gurney, they were just heading out when Helen and Janice came into the courtyard, already dressed for the day, to see what was going on. They had a car and were quick to offer a ride, along with their concern.

Lauren sent Heidi with Deanna and let the other women drive her over, thanking them profusely. At the hospital, as she exited the car, she paused.

"Please, you two be careful, okay?"

"Of course. Trust me, we're plenty streetwise," Helen assured her.

But Janice frowned. Something wasn't quite right, and Lauren could tell that she felt it.

Just like she did herself.

"Keep us posted," Helen told her, and Lauren promised that she would.

Lauren walked into the emergency room to find Heidi sitting in the waiting room.

"They're working on Deanna right now," Heidi said.

"Any word?" Lauren asked.

"They're transfusing her. She's dangerously anemic, that's what I've been told so far. This is so scary, Lauren. Maybe this is why she's been sleepwalking." Heidi shivered. "She would have died if we hadn't gotten her here when we did."

Lauren saw the sheer exhaustion and terror on Heidi's face and gave her a fierce hug. "She didn't die. She's here."

"It's my fault. I just know it is," Heidi said, and Lauren could tell that she meant what she said, but she was also perplexed as to just how it was her fault.

Lauren couldn't let her carry the guilt.

"If she's sick, there's no way it's your fault. And think about it. If you hadn't been with her and noticed that she'd passed out, she really might have died. We were there to get her straight to the hospital," Lauren said.

Heidi nodded, but she still didn't look entirely convinced.

"It's all right," Lauren promised.

And it was. Or at least it would be, because as soon as Deanna was strong enough to travel, Lauren was going to get her the hell out of here.

She just hoped they weren't followed.

She chided herself for the thought and told herself not to be ridiculous. It was all Mark Davidson's fault for trying to convince her that they were being stalked by something evil.

By vampires.

Bull!

"Hey…there's that guy," Heidi said.

"What guy?"

"The one who came in to watch the band last night. Didn't you say he's a cop?"

Lauren swung around. It *was* the cop. Sean Canady. He was at the triage station, asking questions.

As she stared at him, he turned, his eyes focusing straight on her.

He came toward her. "Miss Crow?"

"Yes, hello, Lieutenant. This is my friend, Heidi Weiss."

He nodded gravely to Lauren. "I hear your other friend is very ill."

"Yes."

He smiled gently at Heidi. "I'm sure they'll let you sit with her for a bit, if you ask." His voice didn't sound quite so gentle when he spoke to Lauren again. "I'd like to ask you a few questions, Miss Crow."

Was he suspicious of *her?*

Heidi frowned, but said, "Okay. I'll go in with Deanna."

The lieutenant took Heidi's seat once she had left.

"You followed us home last night. I can't imagine what else you might have to ask me," Lauren said.

He smiled and shrugged. "Sorry. I thought you'd appreciate the escort."

Lauren looked away to collect her thoughts. A man sitting across from them had a bloody bandage around his jaw. He stared at Lauren, unnerving her. Nurses were hovering over a little girl who had gotten her finger slammed in a car door. People here were sick, hurt, but the ER itself was busy and bright.

It made her memories of last night and the living shadows seem unreal.

"I want you to tell me more about the man who was involved in that bar fight," Canady said to her.

She turned and looked at him again.

"He's crazy," she said.

"Oh? Why?"

"He believes in vampires."

She waited for him to react, to shake his head in derision, to make a derogatory comment.

"Did you hear me? The man is nuts. I don't think he's dangerous, and he can be quite charming, but…he's crazy."

Canady still didn't say a word.

"Lieutenant?"

"I see you're still wearing your cross," he said.

Her hand flew to her throat. She'd forgotten all about it.

"It's not my cross," she said.

"Well, you should keep it on, anyway," he said solemnly. "It's very nice. And you won't lose it that way, will you? So do you know anything about the other guy? Jonas?"

She shook her head. "No. Only that Deanna talked to him a few times." She stared at him, once again feeling that something wasn't quite right.

"What on earth is going on here?" she demanded.

"I intend to find out," he told her. "Listen, I'm not sure you're safe where you're staying, and I don't have the manpower to look after you there."

"Why are you so worried about us?" she asked.

He was silent, looking across the room for a minute. Then he replied slowly. "I've been a cop a long time. It's just a hunch, but I think you three have been targeted by…well, by some lunatic, for lack of a better word. I know a place that's well protected." He shrugged and grinned. "One of my officers is there all the time. He's dating the manager. The owner is out of the country. I think you and your friend Heidi would be better off if you moved over there. It's called Montresse House. It's right on Bourbon."

He rose. "I'll have a man here watching your friend's room to make sure she's safe."

"I don't even know if they're admitting her yet," Lauren said.

"They'll be admitting her," Canady said softly.

A lump of fear rose to Lauren's throat.

"She can't be that bad. I need to take her home," she said.

"She has to get better first," he said. "Meanwhile, you two move over to Montresse House. And rest assured. I intend to get to the bottom of what's happening."

He handed her a business card, and Lauren took it from him

without looking. He gave her a smile of reassurance and headed for the door.

She stared after him for a moment, then looked across the room. The man with the bloody jaw was gone.

By his empty chair, she saw the day's paper.

And the headline.

Second Day—Second Corpse.

She froze, flesh, blood and bones.

She closed her eyes, opened them, then stared at the business card in her hand.

It was the same as the card Big Jim had given Deanna the night before.

7

Mark opened his eyes and groaned.

He'd been close. So damn close.

But he hadn't expected the trap, and that had been a serious—nearly fatal—mistake on his part. But when Deanna had screamed, he had *known* why. Pursuit had seemed the only possible option, even though he was working alone and had known Stephan had come with an army.

What Stephan's army didn't know was that their great leader didn't give a damn about any one of them; they were there to be sacrificed, and that was that. The more fools Stephan gathered around himself, the more fools he had to sacrifice along the way, security against his own capture or death.

It was actually a miracle, Mark thought, that he had managed to make it back.

He rolled, got out of bed and walked to the bathroom, where he stared at his face in the mirror.

He should have looked a hell of a lot worse. But he'd never given up his weapons. No matter how many hits he had taken after being led straight into an ambush, he'd kept hold of his weapons, weapons his opponents hadn't been prepared for.

Stephan had known, of course.

But his minions had no idea that Stephan knew his enemy, and so they had died for him.

Mark looked at his face in the mirror again, damning himself. There was no room for mistakes.

He had to get it together.

A shower would help.

It did. Half an hour later, he was showered, shaved and dressed, and he didn't look nearly as bad as he had. He was pulling a comb through his hair when there was a knock at his door.

He opened it to find Helen, from cottage three, standing there.

"Mark, you are here," she said breathlessly.

"Yes, what's wrong?" he asked her.

"I just thought you should know, one of the girls from next door was taken to the hospital this morning."

"Deanna?" he said, feeling his heart slam inside his chest.

She frowned. "Yes, how did you know?"

"I knew she'd been feeling a little off, that's all," he lied.

"Oh," Helen said. "Heidi rode in the ambulance with her, and Janice and I dropped Lauren off at the emergency room. It's been a while…. I knocked earlier, but you didn't hear me."

"I sleep pretty soundly," he told her. "But thanks for everything. I appreciate the information."

"You're welcome." She smiled. "Oh, and your newspaper." She handed him the daily paper, which was delivered to each door every morning.

He saw the headline.

Second Day—Second Corpse.

He thanked her again, then, after closing the door, threw the newspaper across the room. A few minutes later, he stepped outside, desperate to reach the hospital as quickly as possible.

Mistake number two.

He never saw it coming; he was too concerned about Deanna and the report of the second corpse.

And his attacker was prepared.

Whatever hit him, it was like a ton of bricks against his head.

As he crashed to the ground, he thought it must have been the broad side of an ax. A big one. Like a medieval battle-ax. Then he passed out and didn't think about anything at all.

"We're moving over to this place," Lauren told Heidi.

"What?" Heidi asked, distracted.

Deanna had been given a room, but she had yet to regain consciousness. She *was* regaining color, though, and the doctors kept assuring them that she was going to be fine, but the next twenty-four hours were critical. Her blood levels had been so low that she was close to death, but the transfusions seemed to be turning the tide, and they believed a full and perhaps even speedy recovery was not only possible but likely.

She was in a private room, with a police guard in the hall.

It should have felt safe, Lauren thought, but it didn't.

"That cop, Lieutenant Canady, said we'd be safer moving to this place," Lauren explained to Heidi.

"What is it to him, where we stay?" Heidi demanded.

Lauren took a deep breath. "He's afraid we've been targeted," she explained. "By a lunatic."

Heidi frowned.

"Maybe a lunatic who thinks he's a vampire," Lauren went on.

Heidi stared at her for a long moment in total disbelief, then started laughing. "Lauren, think about what you just said. A *vampire?* You've been reading too many freaky books."

"Heidi—"

"Deanna seems to have lost a lot of blood," Heidi explained

gently. "She's sick. She must have been sick when we got here, and that caused her sleepwalking. She wasn't attacked."

"Heidi, Lieutenant Canady said we should move, and I want to," Lauren said firmly. "Look, one of the lieutenant's officers is apparently always at this place, and he considers it really safe. If we *are* being targeted, we should move. We don't want to put anyone else—like Janice or Helen—in danger, right?"

Heidi arched a brow, considering Lauren's words.

"All right. Whatever you think. When do we move? I don't think we should both leave Deanna. Not now."

Lauren felt the same, but she didn't want to stay at the hospital all day, either. She decided to go back to Jackson Square later.

She was going to find Susan, the fortune-teller, and shake her until she said something that made sense.

She should tell the cops about Susan, she thought grimly. But tell them what? She didn't want the cops to think that she herself was crazy. There was nothing concrete to tell them. Best to talk to Susan first.

Lauren leaned forward. "All right, for now, you get going. Pack up our things. If you need to take a walk, shake off the hospital for a bit, do it, then come back. Okay?"

"I guess," Heidi said. She looked at the bed where Deanna lay, motionless and still ashen compared to anyone who was up and walking. She rose and touched her friend's forehead. "She's cool," she murmured. "Warm enough, though," she added quickly. "This morning, she was like ice." She looked across the bed at Lauren. "I'm so worried about her," she said.

"So am I."

"Was this all my fault somehow?" Heidi asked.

"No. Definitely not," Lauren assured her. "And she's going to be fine. That's what all the doctors have said."

Heidi stared across the room. "That's what they said about my dad, too. Right before he died of a second heart attack." She looked worriedly at Lauren. "I don't want to leave her right now. You go, okay?"

A rock tune suddenly started playing: Heidi's phone. She fumbled in her skirt pocket to retrieve it.

"Barry!" she announced, stricken. "What should I tell him?"

"He's *your* fiancé," Lauren reminded her.

"I know, but he'll get all worried. I just won't answer it. I'll call him back later, when I've figured out what to say."

"Just say Deanna got sick and she's in the hospital, but we're with her, and the doctors say she'll be fine."

Heidi nodded. "Right. That's what I'll tell him. *Later.* Go on, do what you need to. I'll stay here with Deanna. It will be fine."

"Okay. I'll be as quick as possible," Lauren assured her.

Heidi offered her a weak smile. "Hey, both of us sitting around here doesn't make much sense. I'll get out later. And this way you have to do all the work of packing us up." She smiled weakly.

"No problem. See you soon." Lauren smiled back, then left.

Mark came to slowly but didn't open his eyes. He tried to *feel* his surroundings first.

He was sitting up. Tied to a chair, wrists bound tightly behind his back.

He was *not* at a police station.

The temperature was pleasant, thanks to air-conditioning.

There was no noise, but someone was in the room with him; he could feel it. It wasn't Stephan, though. It wasn't a vampire at all.

His head was pounding.

He inhaled and exhaled, trying to ease the pain.

"You hit him too hard," someone whispered. The voice was feminine, soft. Concerned.

"I needed him unconscious."

He almost jerked up, giving away the fact that he was conscious. He knew the voice. Lieutenant Sean Canady.

He went on listening, trying to ascertain just where he was.

"Sean, you could have killed him."

"Maggie, quit worrying. This guy is pretty tough."

"You don't even know that he's guilty of anything."

"I do know that he knows what's going on around here."

He listened, trying to determine if there was anyone else in the room. But after several seconds of concentrating on his senses, he was certain no one else was with them.

He checked the ropes at his wrists, flexing imperceptibly, testing their strength.

He definitely wasn't under arrest. Things might be different in Louisiana, but so far it wasn't legal for the cops to crack your skull and tether you to a chair at a remote location.

He straightened, opening his eyes.

Canady was in a chair, facing him. A very attractive woman with dark eyes and dark auburn hair was standing by his side, her hand resting on his shoulder. Canady was wearing a tailored shirt and light jacket; the woman looked as if she had just returned from the gym.

He stared at Canady for a moment, then looked around.

Attic. They were in an attic. A big attic—they were in a big house. He recognized the architecture; his own home had been built in a similar style. They were out on Plantation Row somewhere, he decided, and this house was at least two hundred years old.

He arched a brow slowly at Canady and the woman. "I take it I'm not exactly under arrest," he said.

"Not officially. Not yet."

He waited, doing his best to hide his movements as he worked at the rope binding his wrists. Of course, Canady had a gun. Canady, he was certain, just about always carried a gun. Glock? Smith & Wesson? Whatever the cop was packing, his jacket covered it.

Mark, however, was certain that the gun was there.

"Your home?" he inquired.

Canady nodded. He didn't look particularly angry. He was more wary. And speculative.

"Hello," the woman said. "I'm Maggie."

"Maggie…Canady."

"Yes."

"I'd thank you for having me in, but…"

"What are you up to here in town?" Canady asked.

Mark lowered his head for a moment, stunned to find a half smile on his lips. He felt almost as if he had walked into an old western, and the sheriff was about to tell him to be on his horse, skedaddling, by sunset.

"I went to see you, if you recall," Mark said.

"To tell me there are vampires in New Orleans," Canady replied.

"I know who your murderer is. Trust me, if he's not doing the killing himself, he's responsible for it," Mark told him.

His hands were almost free.

"This man, Stephan," Canady said.

"Yes," Mark agreed.

"So you're saying there are real vampires in New Orleans," Canady said.

"Sean," Maggie murmured.

"Maggie, let him spell it out."

Mark shook his head and stared at the two of them. He let

out a sigh. "Yes, I'm saying there are real vampires in New Orleans. There's real danger out there. And I'm not it."

Mark frowned. Maggie Canady was staring at him as if she believed every word he was saying, even if her husband remained skeptical.

"You've got to let me go," Mark said. "I was trying to warn you."

"Where were you last night?" Canady asked skeptically.

Mark let out a sigh. "Battling a vampire." He decided to lay all his cards on the table. "Stephan is here. He's after Lauren Crow. I'm not sure if it's because he wants to torment me, or if he has some deep-seated psychological need to find Katie again."

"Katie?" Canady repeated.

"She was a woman he and I once knew," Mark said quietly. "I didn't know anything about vampires then—I would have laughed at the very suggestion—until I went to Kiev. I met her there. She was from Kiev, and she wanted to be married in one of the castles there. She had known Stephan…before. I believe he followed her here, and then back to Kiev. He tried to lure her away from me, but she came back."

"Where is this Katie now?" Sean asked.

"Dead."

Maggie and her husband exchanged looks.

"I've been trailing Stephan since I got here, but I know he's been close ever since. I ran into Lauren Crow in a bar. I thought I'd seen a ghost, she's so much like Katie," he told them.

"Deanna's the one who was attacked," Canady said.

Mark frowned, and a new sense of urgency raced through his veins. He was free of the ropes, but he didn't want to fight if he didn't have to.

"I'm telling you…" He hesitated, taking in a deep breath,

then letting it go. "Vampires exist, and Stephan is one of the most evil of them. Not only that, I believe he has a small army with him. I've tangled with a few of them. If you don't listen to me, if you don't help me, we're in for a serious slaughter."

"Let him go, Sean," Maggie said softly.

"You believe me?" he asked.

"Of course we believe you. Don't we, Sean?"

He stared at the woman. It was a miracle.

"You…you're willing to believe in vampires?"

She tossed back a length of deep auburn hair. "Of course I believe in them. I once was one. And we have several friends who are vampires right now. There are ways to survive without killing and turning innocents…" She sighed. "Sean has convinced your friends to move to Montresse House, by the way. It's owned by a vampire named Jessica, but she and some of the others have gone overseas to deal with a situation in Africa. Sean, please let him go." She gently touched her husband's arm. "We know he's telling the truth."

Lauren felt sorry and a little bit guilty checking out of their bed-and-breakfast, and she didn't say that they were moving on; she let their hostess think they had simply decided to go home early.

And it *was* time to go home. Past time. But they couldn't leave until Deanna could travel.

Packing up their things to move was a pain—both Deanna and Heidi were the type to throw everything everywhere. She actually tried to work on being annoyed; it kept her mind off the strange events happening around her.

When she had everything together, she lugged it all out to the curb and called for a taxi.

The driver, who mostly spoke an unidentifiable foreign

language, was definitely not happy that he had to pack his car with so much stuff just so one person could travel a few blocks.

She impatiently promised him a big tip.

The address on the card she had been given went with a house on Bourbon Street, one she had never seen before. There was a lawn, along with a pool in back; there were trees, flowers and a winding path. The gate was wrought iron.

The house itself stood back from the street and resembled a Southern plantation with its handsome porch.

The taxi driver deposited Lauren and her bags on the sidewalk.

When she tried to explain that she needed help getting to the door, he pretended not to understand English at all, just took his money and drove off.

But no sooner had he disappeared than she saw the front door to the house open. A slim woman of about five foot three appeared on the porch and hurried down the walkway.

She was followed by a cop. Lauren had seen him before; he was the officer who had been with Lieutenant Canady in the alleyway behind the bar.

He in turn was followed by Big Jim the sax player.

"Hey!" the woman called cheerfully. "I'm Stacey Lacroix. Lauren, right? Sean called about you. Come in. Come in. We'll grab all this stuff." She might have been tiny, but she seemed like a small whirlwind of energy. "Oh, and this is Bobby Munro," she said, introducing the cop.

"We've kind of met," Bobby said with a lopsided smile.

"In the alley," Lauren said. "Hello, again. I'm Lauren Crow."

"And this is Big Jim Dixon, best jazz sax player in all fifty states," Stacey interjected.

"That's an exaggeration," Jim Dixon said, taking her hand. "And we've kind of met, too."

"At the bar," she said. "And I think I saw you playing in a funeral procession the other day," she said.

"That was me," he agreed, and easily lifted one of the heaviest bags.

Despite the welcoming tone in Stacey's voice and the ease of her introductions, she looked around uneasily as she grabbed the canvas tote bag that was Deanna's carry-on.

So much for it being difficult getting everything up to the house; with the four of them, it would only take one trip.

But before heading up the walk, Lauren found herself pausing, looking around as Stacey had done.

The sky seemed to have taken on an ashen color, and clouds suddenly billowed darkly and menacingly overhead.

Birds suddenly took flight over the house.

"Let's go in," Stacey urged.

Lauren sensed a sudden urgency in the air, though it was unspoken. Big Jim was already halfway to the house. She followed quickly.

The place was wonderful. She fell in love with it the minute she stepped inside. She thought that it must be very old, which wasn't unusual for the area, but it had been meticulously maintained and restored. The banister was polished and gleaming. Woven rugs lay over the hardwood floors. A grandfather clock chimed as they entered, and a crystal chandelier cast a warm glow over the entry.

"My desk is back there in the hall," Stacey explained. "I'll have you sign in after you've seen your rooms. The owner is out of the country right now, but I think you'll be happy with your accommodations. We hadn't actually planned to have guests right now, but when Sean called…well, I could hardly say no. At least you'll have lots of room."

Bobby Munro and Big Jim were already heading up the

elegant stairway. Stacey locked the front door and followed. Lauren trailed behind her.

The stairs led to a long hallway that stretched in either direction. "Guest rooms to your left," Stacey advised, looking back. "There's a balcony that extends across the back, with a wonderful view of the pool. There's only one rule here. You don't ask anyone in—anyone at all—*ever*, unless you check with me first. It's Jessica's rule—she's the owner—and we all abide by it."

Stacey was looking back at her with a smile, but there was something strange about the way she spoke. As if the rule, if broken, could cause dire consequences. Like a carriage turning back into a pumpkin. Or worse.

"It's a beautiful house," she said politely.

"Yes, it is, isn't it?"

Big Jim and Bobby were just emerging from one of the guest rooms. "Don't know where you want what, exactly," Big Jim said. "We just put it all in the one room."

"I understand that there are three of you," Stacey said, "but one friend is in the hospital and the other—Heidi, is it?—will also need a place tonight. Anyway, this is you, Heidi is right there, and if and when you need a room for your other friend, she'll be right across the hall."

"I'm not sure we need quite so much room," Lauren murmured. The door to the bedroom she'd been assigned was still open, and the room was huge. There was a massive bed, a desk, French doors that led to the balcony, a wardrobe twice her size, and lots of space in between.

Stacey shrugged. "It's a big house. We make use of it when we can."

"Downstairs," Bobby offered, "you'll find the kitchen toward the back." He smiled, watching her closely. "I'm here most of the time when I'm not working." He took Stacey's hand. "We're engaged."

"Congratulations," Lauren said.

"I live in the caretaker's cottage out back. I don't really take care of anything, though, I just live there," Big Jim said.

"And Bobby is a cop, you know," Stacey said.

"Yes, I do."

Were the cops here sane? Lauren wondered.

The ones she had met so far had all seemed to study her as if she weren't quite right in the head. Then again, at least they took her reasonably seriously, seriously enough to station an officer outside Deanna's door at the hospital.

"I really think you'll love the room," Stacey said, gesturing for Lauren to step inside. Her pride in the house was evident.

Lauren did love it. It was exquisite, from the polished wood of the nineteenth-century dresser and bedposts, to the cherrywood desk and antique floral pattern on the bedspread. She hesitated, wondering if, no matter how highly Lieutenant Canady thought of the safety of the place, she could afford it. But before she could mention her reservations, Stacey mentioned a price per room per night that was absurdly low.

"How on earth can you afford to do business that way?" Lauren couldn't help asking.

"Oh, Jessica doesn't actually make her living running Montresse House," Stacey explained. "She's a psychologist, plus she has family money. She closes this place whenever she chooses."

"Are we the only guests right now?"

"We have another gentleman arriving later," Stacey said. "If you're ready, I'll sign you in downstairs."

"I have to go to work, but I'm usually here at night," Bobby said. "Nice to meet you for real."

"And I should get to the club," Big Jim said.

"Nice to see you both again," Lauren told them as they waved and started down the stairs.

She felt a moment of unease as she watched them go. Did they know too much about her, and were they a little *too* friendly? And what about that rule? *Don't let* anyone *in.*

Was it weird?

Oh, hell. What could be weirder than everything that was already going on? A gorgeous man had all but abducted her so he could tell her there were vampires in New Orleans. Deanna was in a hospital, receiving transfusions after sleepwalking and maybe being attacked. Tall-dark-and-handsome had disappeared, chasing after a shadow in the darkness, and a police lieutenant had ordered that Deanna's room be protected.

"I can sign in right now, if you like," she said to Stacey, shrugging off her worrisome thoughts. "In fact, I need to get moving."

"Of course," Stacey said.

It had all started with the fortune-teller, Lauren thought. And as soon as she finished signing in, she was going to find the woman and get a few answers.

Heidi had already been through three magazines. She had studied *Modern Bride,* reading up on the last-minute traumas that could lead to a problematic wedding, and moved on to *People.* Then she had looked through *Time.*

Deanna hadn't moved. She lay in her bed like Sleeping Beauty, stunning and sound asleep, awaiting her true love's kiss.

Why didn't she wake up?

Heidi took a moment to feel sorry for herself. She was with her best friends in a place they all loved, where they should have been having the time of their lives. Barry was at home with his crazy brothers and his friends. Nothing like a group of attorneys when they decided to cut loose. She thought about calling him, then decided that he'd be working now, and she never wanted to be one of those women who had to call a man just for reassurance.

No, they were fine. Deanna was getting the best care possible for…

Whatever this was.

Lauren would be back soon. One day, they would all look back on this experience as something that had brought them closer. And she had certainly never wanted her wedding or her bachelorette getaway to be boring.

She set down her magazine, stood, stretched, then smoothed Deanna's hair off her forehead. The nurse had been in just a few minutes ago, readjusting the IV, taking Deanna's vital signs. Everything was as good as it was going to get until her friend actually woke up.

Heidi walked to the door and peeked into the hallway.

A uniformed officer was sitting in a chair, reading the newspaper.

She went back to the chair and sat down. The chair could be converted into a bed. Either she or Lauren would probably stay in it through the night. For now, though, it was just a comfy chair.

"Mind if I turn on the television?" she said aloud. The sound of her own voice spooked her, and it wasn't as if Deanna cared whether she turned on the television or not.

She found the remote attached to the bed, but she could arrange the cord so she could control the set from her chair. She found a talk show on. She wasn't particularly fond of talk shows, but she couldn't find anything she actively wanted to see.

She closed her eyes and leaned back in the chair. As the voices droned on, she realized that she was actually kind of tired.

Fine. It wasn't as if she had company. She let herself drift off.

A few minutes later, she had the sensation that she was dreaming of being in a strange place. It was as if a man came on the television and began talking directly to her. A very good-looking man. She wasn't usually swayed by looks or charm, though she recognized them, of course. She was madly in love, but it was still possible for her to recognize when another male was handsome and charming.

But she found that this man had her full attention. She was certain that she was dreaming, but in her dream, she smiled. He was teasing her, flirting with her, and she found herself responding. He had very dark hair, and a very…*manly* face. And a very hypnotic voice. She wasn't sure what he was saying, exactly, but she felt flushed. Strange. He had a voice that seemed to…*touch* her. Excite her.

Arouse her.

How very silly…

It seemed that she was growing warmer. As if she could almost feel the brush of fingers against her inner thighs.

It was just a dream, she thought. She was closing in on her wedding day, and somewhere deep inside she was just having a few minutes of completely understandable panic.

After all, she was giving up other men forever, hence this erotic dream about a man on the television.

But now he was telling her to get up. To go to the window and let him in.

Of course, she wasn't really doing it. Seriously, what man came to a hospital window? And how could she really be up and opening it, letting him in…?

Letting him do things to her.

Sexual things…

While Deanna lay comatose on the bed.

8

Lauren signed the registration cards for the inn and left feeling filled with energy, determined to find the fortune-teller at Jackson Square.

But she realized, after walking around the square several times, that apparently many of the people who worked the area didn't show up until later, probably not until dusk, at least.

More upsettingly, she had the feeling she was being followed, even though it was broad daylight. The sun was strong, the air warm, and there was a slight breeze off the river. The world seemed calm, normal.

But it wasn't.

She returned to the hospital, thinking that Heidi was probably ready to wring her neck.

But Heidi wasn't irate in the least.

She was sleeping in the chair by the bed when Lauren arrived. She didn't wake up until Lauren touched her, and then she flushed and stretched, and seemed disoriented.

"Hey, how's she doing? Has anyone said anything?"

Heidi seemed a little flustered when she replied. "Um…yes, actually. The last nurse who came in here said that her vital signs are strong and that she's doing well. She hasn't come to yet, but she seems to be resting comfortably, and I guess the doctors are pleased with her progress."

"I'm sorry. I didn't mean to be gone so long."

"Were you gone long?" Heidi asked.

"Yes. But the new place is gorgeous."

"So was the old place," Heidi pointed out.

"You'll love Montresse House. I promise," Lauren assured her.

Heidi shrugged. "It's what you wanted."

"Thanks for humoring me."

"Some slave you are."

"Sorry."

Heidi frowned for a moment. "There's still a cop in the hall, right?"

"Yes, of course."

"Think we could go to lunch together? We missed breakfast, and I'm starving."

Lauren hesitated. It was broad daylight, she reminded herself. Deanna was in a hospital with a cop right outside her door. "Want to grab something in the hospital cafeteria?"

"Not really, but okay."

In the hallway, Lauren saw that the officer on duty was about fifty and appeared to be of French or Hispanic descent. He had a trustworthy face, a little haggard, but gentle and reassuring. When she told him they were going to grab a bite to eat together, he said, "Good idea. I'll sit inside with your friend. You take your time."

Lauren thanked him, noticing a heavy gold chain around his neck. "Crucifix?" she asked.

"Uh—yeah, actually." He drew it out from beneath his collar. "A gift from my missus. I always wear it. I like yours, too."

"So you are wearing Mark's cross," Heidi teased.

Lauren offered her a vague smile and thanked the officer.

In the cafeteria, they discovered that the hospital offered a pretty decent salad bar. They filled their plates, then sat down at a table.

"I really am sorry that your party has gone south. Mostly, I'm worried about Deanna, though," Lauren said.

"Oh, don't worry. I think that not being able to party hardy has been a good thing. I've had time to think about what I'm doing," Heidi said lightly.

"What do you mean?" Lauren asked.

Heidi shrugged. "I've been rethinking the entire marriage thing," she said.

Lauren, with a small wedge of lettuce halfway to her lips, froze. "What?" she said in astonishment.

"Marriage. I don't know if I'm ready."

"Heidi, your wedding is two weeks away."

"I know." Heidi, unconcerned, adjusted her napkin on her lap.

"Heidi, you love Barry."

"Well, of course I love him."

"Then…?"

"I've just been thinking. I'm not sure I'm ready."

"But you were so certain."

"There you go. Things change."

"Have you talked to him? Did you two get into an argument or something?" Lauren asked, perplexed.

"No, I wouldn't dream of fighting with him over the phone, and, anyway, we don't have fights. Disagreements now and then, but no big fights."

"Have you talked to him at all?"

"Not since yesterday."

"Then what…?"

"I'm just not sure I'm really ready for marriage." She flushed, staring at Lauren. "If you must know, it's occurred to me that I'm not entirely positive I'm ready for a sexually monogamous life."

Lauren just stared at her blankly. "Uh...well..."

"We don't need to discuss it," Heidi snapped.

"Okay."

Heidi set her fork down. "I'm not really hungry after all. Since you're here now, I think I'll head out. I'll go and make sure that we didn't leave anything at the old place and check out the new one. Okay?"

Heidi wasn't really asking; she was leaving. That was that.

"Okay."

Lauren wasn't sure that Heidi even heard her. She was already walking out.

Lauren discovered that she wasn't hungry herself and felt a sudden urge to get back to Deanna as quickly as possible.

She rushed back upstairs.

The friendly officer was still in the room. He blushed when she caught him reading Heidi's bridal magazine.

"Some really pretty pictures in there," he said. "My wife and I eloped to Vegas. Sometimes I think I cheated her out of a real wedding."

"How long have you been married?"

"Twenty-six years."

"I guess she was happy with what she got, then," Lauren assured him.

He smiled. A happy man. Feeling that maybe the world *would* be all right, Lauren took a seat at the foot of Deanna's bed.

The officer remained with her, and she never even noticed herself dozing off, but the next she knew, he was nudging her and telling her that the shift was changing.

She woke, blinked and realized it was twilight.

* * *

Lauren wasn't sure if she would really have left Heidi alone at the hospital all night in her determination to find the fortune-teller, but luckily she didn't have to worry about it, because Heidi reappeared in time.

Lauren's head was still reeling.

Deanna was holding her own, but Heidi's behavior was beyond peculiar. She had returned to the hospital in a very pleasant if somewhat…fey mood. Not a word Lauren usually used, but it was one that seemed to describe the way Heidi was acting. She had mentioned avoiding several calls from Barry, and said blithely that Deanna was going to be just fine and she would be happy as a little lark to stay with her and watch television or read for the evening. When Lauren promised that she would return as soon as she could, Heidi told her not to worry.

Lauren couldn't help but feel a little uneasy about leaving Heidi in charge, so to speak, then told herself that she was being ridiculous. There was a cop on constant duty at the door, and he was certainly capable of protecting both women if there should be any need.

After leaving the hospital, Lauren found the nicest taxi driver in the world and asked him to take her to Montresse House, because she'd decided to pick up a light jacket before hitting Jackson Square. The driver was a native of the area and sympathized with her for having a friend in the hospital. He also believed in the occult and told her that she should buy herself some serious mojo to protect herself against evil.

She thanked him while privately thinking there was no need to get carried away.

Unfortunately, as nice as he was, he wasn't able to get her

all the way to Montresse House or even to Bourbon Street. There had been an accident, and the streets were blocked off. He apologized profusely but suggested she get out a few blocks away and walk.

Lauren did, though she wasn't sure exactly where she was. There were people around, and there were lights, and she wasn't particularly worried. As she walked, she kept going over everything they'd done since arriving in the city.

A chill seemed to wrap itself around her suddenly, and she stopped walking. Frowning, she paused, looking around. The street was lined with old residences, with only a few storefronts here and there, and most of them were cafés that only served by day. Magnificent houses sat behind high walls, with bushes lining the sidewalk for added privacy, and it seemed they had all begun to rustle.

She quickened her pace.

Then she stopped.

Someone had stepped out from behind a high brick wall. Someone who was tall and formed a dark silhouette against the night.

She could hear the distant sound of traffic.

Laughter.

Even music.

She stood dead still. A breeze wafted by, strangely cool. She became aware that she was alone on the street. Doors and gates were closed. She wasn't far from Bourbon Street, but she might as well have been at the end of the world.

The silhouette wasn't moving, exactly, or at least not in any way she could identify, yet it seemed to be coming closer to her, almost floating just inches above the sidewalk.

Then, suddenly, the dark figure became a man, just a man. Tall, midthirties, athletic build, dark. He wore black jeans, a black polo shirt and a casual jacket. His hair seemed to be darker than the night.

And his eyes…

They might have been black, too.

Except there seemed to be some kind of a glowing golden light in them.

She told herself to move, to quicken her pace, to hurry past the man, then realized for the first time that she was standing dead still.

And he was smiling as he approached her.

She could hear the blare of a horn from somewhere, but it might as well have come from another world. It was followed by the plaintive sound of a jazz chord.

But it was so far away.

"Hello."

Her heart seemed to shudder as he spoke. She didn't understand why she wasn't moving. It was as if her limbs had become paralyzed. She was furious with herself. What the hell was the matter with her?

His voice was deep and smooth. She wondered if that was part of what held her so firmly where she was. But she had been standing still, just waiting, before he had spoken.

She didn't reply.

She just stared at him, and he stared back.

"I've been looking for you," he said.

He'd been looking for her? Ridiculous. She'd never seen him before. Or had she? At that moment, she knew that she *had* seen him before; she just couldn't place where or when.

To her amazement, she managed to speak. "I don't know you," she said. If she tried really hard, she thought, she could probably move.

"But *I* know *you*. And you will remember me in time."

It was the worst pickup line she'd ever heard, she thought.

"Excuse me, I have to get going," she murmured, and moved an arm.

She could move!

But when she managed a step, he was suddenly directly in front of her, even though she hadn't seen him move. *It was as if he had floated there.*

She stared into his eyes. They were gold. No, they were dark. No, there was some kind of fire that seemed to glow from within them.

That was it. She really had lost her mind.

"This time," he said softly, "I have the advantage. I will not lose you again."

She opened her mouth to speak. She wanted to protest that he couldn't lose what he didn't have.

But the fire in his eyes was so bright…

The cross, she thought. The silver cross. If she could just produce it…

No, that would mean that she believed in vampires, and that was ridiculous.

Besides, she couldn't move her arms again. She was held by the fire in his eyes. She willed her hand to move, pleaded with her body to function….

She found the cross with her fingers and drew it out from under her shirt.

A flash of fury seemed to tear through his eyes.

He opened his mouth.

His teeth weren't yellowed; they weren't horrid, rank or dripping with gore.

They weren't teeth at all.

They were fangs.

She willed herself to back away. Because now he was

coming right at her, furious at the sight of the cross. He started to reach out for her, as if he were in pain but planning to endure that pain. He was going to seize her cross and rip it from her neck.

And that was when Mark appeared.

She didn't know where he had come from; he was just suddenly there.

She felt his arms on her shoulders, felt him shove her out of the way. He was carrying, of all things, a squirt gun.

A child's squirt gun.

Then he lifted it and shot her attacker.

There was steam, a hiss, accompanied by a roar of fury.

The man with the burning eyes seemed to disappear in darkness and shadow, even as the sound of his voice remained.

And suddenly, there on the street, so near to Bourbon and yet so far, there were suddenly scores of shadows, like moving pools of darkness.

They took on form.

And life.

Mark tossed her something.

Another squirt gun.

She stared at him, still in shock, but somehow, she reflexively caught the toy.

"Don't let anyone get the cross. Start shooting," Mark ordered.

Shooting?

With a squirt gun?

They were crowding around her now. So many of them. They were people. They had been shadows, but now they were people.

A girl in a short skirt with a Bettie Page haircut and cute freckles. A twentysomething guy in a Grateful Dead T-shirt.

A man who looked like a James Bond wannabe. A woman who was a dead ringer for Ethel on *I Love Lucy*.

Someone almost pounced on Mark. He struck out with a kick that would have done Jackie Chan proud. His attacker went flying back and struck a wall—hard—then just picked himself up and started coming again.

Mark had whirled, and for a moment she thought he was shooting at *her* with the squirt gun, but he wasn't. She heard a cry of fury, followed by that awful hissing right behind her. She turned. A black form was turning to a pool of burning dust behind her.

A girl hopped on Mark's back. He caught her with both hands, throwing her over his shoulder to the sidewalk.

She looked like Pollyanna.

He took dead aim between her eyes with his water pistol. Shot.

She screamed.

The hissing came first.

Then there was a small burst of fire.

And she was ash.

Mark began to spin, a steady spray of water coming from his gun.

Somewhere, there was jazz music.

Somewhere, someone laughed.

A car horn blared.

The hissing continued, punctuated by screams of fury.

"Shoot!" Mark thundered. "Turn and shoot."

She spun around. A man who looked like a long-lost cavalier was almost on top of her. He looked so much like pictures of Charles II that shock almost caused her to hesitate.

Her finger twitched.

She pulled the trigger.

Hiss...

The man was just inches from her. He snarled and let out a cry of fury as he dissolved right in front of her, the picture of his open mouth, fangs gleaming, imprinted on her mind.

She thought that she saw fire, gleaming through a skull, as he burst into flame....

She felt something at her back. A man was there, reaching for her throat.

He touched the silver cross and screamed as his fingers burned. He stared at her, his face knitting into a hideous mask of fury.

Then she saw fire for an instant, and the mask of fury become a distorted skull. He exploded, and through the soot, she could see Mark, see that he had shot the man.

And then she heard what sounded like the flapping of wings, saw a rising of shadows.

In seconds the street was quiet again. The sounds from Bourbon Street seemed to grow louder. Become real. And near.

She was still standing on the sidewalk.

She was still staring at a man.

But now the man was Mark.

She was shaking, still holding her own water pistol. He bought the good kind, she thought dryly. They held a lot of water. Kids would have a great time playing with them at a pool.

But she wasn't a kid, and she wasn't at a pool.

And already she was finding it almost impossible to believe what had just taken place.

"Are you all right?" Mark asked.

Was she all right? What was he, out of his mind?

"Am I all right?" she repeated. "Hell, no!"

He took a breath and offered a rueful smile. "I'm sorry. I meant, are you hurt? Did anything... Did he touch you before I got here?"

She swallowed. She was suddenly shaking uncontrollably. "No."

He took a careful step toward her.

"I didn't see what I just saw," she whispered.

"You did," he told her.

It was impossible. It had all been so fast. *It couldn't have been real.*

She looked at the ground. It looked as if a careless gardener had lost dirt from a wheelbarrow as he had made his way down the street.

He reached out, taking the water pistol from her hand as carefully as if it had been a real gun.

"We should get to Montresse House," he said gently.

"The house," she echoed, frowning.

"At least you're not passing out," he murmured.

Those words suddenly gave her strength. And the little voice at the back of her mind that had whispered that there must be some veracity in the stories he had been telling her suddenly spoke up loudly.

They existed. *Vampires existed.*

"Of course I'm not going to pass out!" she snapped. Right. She was shaking so hard that she could barely stand.

"Let's go," he said.

"To Montresse House?" she asked.

"Yes."

"Of course," she said, the light dawning. "You have a room there, too, don't you?"

"Yes."

"Deanna's been bitten by a vampire, hasn't she." It was a statement, not a question. She was still having trouble digesting the fact that vampires were real.

"Yes."

"Will she live?"

"I hope so."

She started walking, her movements jerky. She felt as if she had become a puppet, a marionette, and wasn't really moving of her own volition.

As he walked at her side, it occurred to her that he had come in the nick of time.

That he had saved her life.

They were almost on Bourbon Street by then, and there were people everywhere, talking, laughing.

A drunk passed her, and he was wonderful. He was real. *Normal.*

"You've been following me," she said accusingly, stopping and turning on him.

"Whenever I've been able to," he said, stopping, too.

She was tempted to hit him. "You were late!"

"I thought you were at the hospital. I came as soon as I got word that you'd left," he told her.

She wanted him to hold her. She wanted to crawl into his arms. No, she wanted him to be normal, too. She desperately needed to take a step back.

She opened her mouth to speak. There was so much to say, to demand to know. But nothing came out. She didn't know where to start.

She took a step toward him, then another. She leaned against him. He seemed solid. Strong. His arms came around her, holding her, and she stood there, shaking.

Oh, God, it was so much better here....

She laid a hand on his shirt, feeling the strength of his body through the fabric. She had wanted to be near him, but she had been afraid.

Even now, she didn't dare trust him, even if...

Even if he had saved her life.

But she needed the clean, male scent of him, the vital strength of his form....

The sound of his voice.

Oh, God, it would be so easy to...

She pulled away from him and started walking again.

They reached the house on Bourbon Street, and all of a sudden the air seemed to be full of birds. Masses of birds. Or bats.

Or winged shadows.

Mark saw them, too, and his face tensed. But he didn't appear to be afraid. Instead, he looked angry.

"Open the gate," he said softly.

She did, and the birds or bats, *or shadows,* continued to hover overhead. But they didn't come closer.

She and Mark walked up the pathway to the house. The front door opened before they were even halfway there. "Come in, come in, and hurry, please," Stacey said.

It was evident that she'd already met Mark.

"What happened?" she demanded.

"Stephan made his first real play for Lauren," Mark explained.

"Oh, my God, where? When?" She looked at Lauren suspiciously. "He didn't...?"

"No," Mark told her. "But he's getting bolder. She was right off Bourbon."

Stacey let out a sigh. "Was he alone?"

"No. He has an army with him, just as I predicted," Mark said.

Lauren stared from one of them to the other. They were talking as if the city were under siege, and by an enemy they had fought before.

"A regular infestation," Stacey muttered. Then she saw the

way that Lauren was staring at her and smiled, shrugging her shoulders. "I assume now you understand the rule about not inviting anyone in, anyone at all."

"Yeah, I understand," Lauren said. Because she did. They were insane. And she was insane, too, because she was seeing what they saw.

"I'm sorry," she murmured. "I'm trying so hard to…"

"To believe what's unbelievable," Stacey said.

"So you *do* believe that vampires exist?" Lauren said.

"Of course," Stacey told her.

"But…"

Stacey shook her head, staring at Lauren. "But why doesn't the world know? You've just seen them—and you still don't completely believe. And," she said, and hesitated, looking at Mark, "I think that Mr. Davidson could tell you that there are plenty of vampires out there who are living their lives in as normal a manner as possible, hurting no one. But there are also those who…" Again, she paused. "There are people, regular people, who are psychotic. Cold-blooded killers. It's no different in the world of the undead."

"The undead," Lauren murmured slowly. "In other words, I may already know some vampires, good vampires, and I just don't realize it."

"Maybe," Stacey said. "Many exist without their closest friends knowing the truth."

"Sure they do," Lauren said skeptically.

"I know that this is a lot to take in," Mark said.

"But the important thing is, you're safe here," Stacey said. "Big Jim sleeps out in the caretaker's cottage, Bobby is here a lot of the time and I've been through this myself before. Our only weaknesses can come from within."

Lauren stared at them. "Lieutenant Canady told us to

come here. Are you telling me that a police lieutenant believes in vampires?"

"Yes," Mark told her.

"His wife used to be one," Stacey explained matter-of-factly.

"Used to be?" Lauren said.

"No one really understands what happened there, but Maggie was a vampire. For years and years. Then Sean came into her life, they had a major battle with a really vicious enemy, and then…she was human again. It was really great for Maggie, because she desperately wanted to have a family. It's different with Jessica Fraser, who owns this place. She's a vampire, too. A good one, of course."

"Of course."

"That's why Sean sent you here," Stacey explained. "We know how to fight evil. We've all fought vampires before."

"The bad ones, of course," Lauren murmured.

"Of course," Stacey said, gravely serious.

Could this nightmare be real? Lauren wondered.

When she'd woken up just a few days ago, the world had been spinning on its axis, and, though they'd had their problems, they had all been…

Sane.

But now…

Mark Davidson set a hand on her shoulder, and she looked up into his eyes. Serious eyes, striking eyes, eyes that had practically hypnotized her from the start.

"It will be all right. I don't intend to stop until I've taken Stephan down, and it won't matter how many servants he has running around, doing his bidding."

"Right." She knew she sounded exhausted and disbelieving, and she didn't care.

"I need a shower," he said. For the first time she noticed that there was black, sooty stuff all over his shirt.

She realized that she was covered with it, as well.

It was death.

Ashes to ashes.

Dust to dust.

She was literally wearing the evil of untold years.

Realization hit her, and suddenly she thought she *was* going to pass out.

She remembered where she had seen the man who had accosted her on the street before.

She had seen him in the crystal ball.

9

The shower felt good. Mark made the water as hot as he could, and the steam rose around him, and though he wondered if he would ever again feel that he was clean, really clean, given that he'd been doing this for so long, he certainly felt a hell of a lot better physically.

Maybe, if he ever succeeded in destroying Stephan, he would receive vindication, and in that, surely, there would be a little peace.

Thinking back, he had to admit that it had actually been an amazing day.

It wasn't often that you found out that a police lieutenant not only believed in what you were saying but actually had experience battling vampires. And then there had been the moments on the sidewalk.

He'd known that Stephan would eventually come after Lauren himself, but he hadn't known when, where or exactly how. And when he'd stumbled onto Stephan in the act of transforming, he'd thought he had a chance to rid the world of the man—the creature—forever.

But Stephan had no intention of dying. True, Mark had managed to take him by surprise with the holy water, but Stephan was going to be harder to kill than that. And like any

cult leader, Stephan had minions ready to die in service to him.
Mark knew he was lucky that, so far, those who had been
summoned to do battle with him while Stephan disappeared
were, for the most part, inexperienced. Old enough to know
how to do some hunting, foolish enough to be rash. None of
them had been around long—not even the cavalier this afternoon. That guy must have come from some costume party.

But then, that was always the way it was in any war. Send
out the expendable forces first.

He gritted his teeth in anger, curious that Stephan had
begun to bother keeping his population in check at all. He
thought about the poor murdered girls whose decapitated
corpses had been tossed into the river. It was possible but
unlikely that some of his newer minions were perpetrating the
crimes. He had a feeling that Stephan was doing this himself.

Stephan liked to create an aura of fear.

He liked it when the authorities thought they were going
after a heinous—but human—madman.

Of course, he hadn't planned on a man like Sean Canady.

In all honesty, Mark hadn't imagined encountering such a
situation himself. It wasn't just the cop who knew that
vampires existed. There was an alliance of people in New
Orleans who knew and made it their business to do something
about the dangerous ones. Unfortunately, most of them were
out of the country at the moment.

According to Sean's wife, Maggie, most of the real horrors
were occurring in Third World countries where people had
nothing, no money and no hope, and government coups were
constant, where AIDS was prevalent, and there was so much
hardship and sadness that the vampires could rule their
fiefdoms with little distraction.

But Sean was still here, as were a few others, though Sean

hadn't named them as yet. Mark knew he still had to tread carefully with the other man if he wanted to earn his trust. Maggie was more open. She had listened gravely to everything he had to say, then told him a few stories about some of their friends.

It had been an absurd conversation—or would have been, if he weren't who he was and the situation weren't so dire.

And now Stephan had shown himself.

Most of all, Lauren finally believed him about the existence of vampires. More, he prayed, he thought she was actually beginning to believe *in* him.

As he got out of the shower, he decided it was important to get over to the hospital.

As he towel-dried his hair, another towel around his hips, he heard a quiet tapping at his door. He hesitated, not quite ready for visitors.

"Yeah?" he said.

"It's me. Lauren."

He paused again.

Then he walked to the door and opened it.

Her eyes seemed to be even more brilliantly green than he had remembered. Her hair shimmered with an ever greater touch of fire. She was pale, but she appeared strong and wary.

And she was standing in his doorway.

"May I come in?" she asked.

"Um…sure." He moved outside, sweeping out a hand.

She walked in and perched at the foot of his bed. If she noticed his state of undress, she gave no sign.

She smelled erotically of shampoo, soap and perfume. She had chosen a plain black knit dress, and it hugged her curves in a way he couldn't help but notice.

"Did that really—I mean, *really*, happen?" she inquired.

"Yes," he said simply.

"It's impossible," she murmured, staring at him. He could tell that she wanted him to somehow deny the reality of it.

He strode over to the bed, taking a seat at her side, meeting her eyes but not touching her. "What's impossible?" he whispered. "There's all kind of evil in the world. Mostly it comes in human form. Today it came in vampire form, that's all. Stephan is real, and his little army of would-be assassins is real. I tried to tell you what was going on. And I blame myself for what happened to Deanna. At first I thought you would be the only one in real danger. But he's getting to you by going through Deanna."

"Will she get better?"

"There's definitely hope," he told her.

She stood and walked restlessly to the balcony doors. She pulled back the drape and looked out at the night.

"It's so beautiful," she said. There was a strange and poignant longing in her voice.

"It is," he agreed.

To his amazement, she let go of the drape and walked straight over to him.

"I should cut to the chase," she said softly. "There are things I have to do tonight."

"You mean, you want to go back to the hospital."

"Yes, that, and…"

She let her voice trail off, her eyes still on his. She was so close that he was practically breathing her in, and it was painful. Because she wasn't Katie.

She wasn't Katie at all.

It had been the familiarity that had first drawn him to her, but her deep russet hair was all her own, as were the ever-changing emerald and gold of her eyes. And her seductive smile…that, too, was hers and hers alone.

"Yes?" he asked softly. "And…?"

She slipped her arms around his neck and drew close. Her lips found his, while her body pressed tightly against his flesh. The kind of tight that caused the curves and hollows of their bodies to meet in perfect alignment. He was painfully aware of the fullness of her breasts, could feel the pressure of his instant erection and knew she could feel it, too.

She wasn't Katie, he reminded himself.

She was Lauren, and she was in shock. As strong as she might be normally, she was vulnerable right now. If he had any decency at all, he would step away and…

Who the hell could be that damned decent?

There was no hesitation in her lips. They molded to his, and her mouth was sweet, with a hint of mint, the sweep of her tongue an inducement and a tease, a hint of sheer enticement.

A voice spoke in his head.

Step away.

But he couldn't do it. Her fingers played across his chest, and her touch was electrifying. He was locked in a kiss that seemed to grow deeper and more passionate by the moment. Amazed that she had come to him, he cupped her face, needing more of her lips. His fingers threaded through her hair. Silk and velvet, a form of seduction all its own, it fell over his hands.

She stepped away from him then and, meeting his eyes, lifted the hem of her skirt and pulled her dress over her head. Then she stood before him wearing nothing except for strappy high-heeled sandals.

"You go out that way often?" he couldn't help but ask, his voice husky.

She smiled. "Only here," she assured him. And she moved back into his arms.

He didn't have to shed his towel. It managed to disappear on its own.

After that there was nothing between them, nothing at all, and he was touching her completely, savoring the feel of her flesh, trying not to give in to sheer insanity.

He had hungered for her, watched her, been awakened by her, and through it all, he had somehow kept his sanity, kept a clear head....

Until now.

His mouth lifted from hers, nuzzled against her earlobe, caressed the smooth flesh of her throat. She arched against him, fingertips running down his back. Along his spine. Over his buttocks. He felt his muscles flex and tighten.

Dear God.

Her lips pressed against his throat.

Her tongue teased his flesh, traced a searing line along his jugular.

He picked her up and made his way to the bed. They fell on it together, limbs already entwined before they even touched the mattress. His eyes met hers, and she smiled slightly; then she sought his lips again, and their mouths met in a kiss that was wet and searing and overpowering. At last his mouth left her lips and traveled down to her collarbone, where it taunted and explored. He drew his hand up from her thigh to her hip, moved to her midriff, then caressed her breast before he laved and teased with his tongue.

As he tasted her, he felt her fingertips, erotic, light, sensual, moving down his spine.

Around to his ribs.

Between them.

To his erection.

He groaned against her flesh, kissed his way along her skin, urgency racing through him. He wanted her right then; he wanted her forever. He wanted this to go on, and he felt he would lose his sanity if it did.

He moved lower.

Lower.

Teasing, tasting, the silken, fiery feel of her flesh creating a searing thunder in his mind, in his blood. She arched against him, whispered in longing and in protest, and moved with a subtle and sinuous grace that aroused his every muscle, every cell. His excitement was raw, carnal, soaring. Somehow he held on to his tenuous control as he teased and caressed her from the rise of her breasts to her abdomen, inner thighs, between. He heard her cries, felt the tremors of release shudder through her body, and felt her fingers dance across his flesh as she strove to drive him to an equal madness.

But he had been maddened from her first whisper.

From the first sight of her.

She moved against him, rising, finding his lips again, her body sliding against his. Their fingers entwined, and then she was on top of him, still moving, and her hair was a spill of red twilight and magic, enveloping them both in silk. He moved inside her in a reflex of motion and fury, and then his arms were around her and she was beneath him, and the world was filled with heat and the meshing of their bodies. When he felt her surge and shudder, he felt the explosion of his own climax rip through him like thunder, and he drew her to him again, savoring every shock and tremor that followed. The ragged pulse of his heart and lungs made a strange and staccato music in the night, and the pulse of her heart raged against his own, then eased slowly.

Lying at her side, he breathed in the scent of her, and when he turned, at last, meeting her eyes, her gaze was on him.

She smiled slowly. "I might have been a bit aggressive," she said, blushing.

"Please…feel free to be aggressive anytime," he offered.

She reached out, moving a damp lock of hair from his forehead. "You *are* sane," she murmured.

"Thank you. Not the compliment I might have expected or hoped for at the moment, but thank you."

Her smiled deepened, but then she sobered, staring into his eyes.

"There *are* vampires."

"Yes."

"Do you have any idea how incomprehensible that is to me?"

"Yes." He nodded, and stroked her cheek. "You're incredible."

She trembled slightly, her lashes veiling her eyes. "So are you. Is that the compliment you were looking for?" she asked, meeting his eyes again, a slight teasing note in her voice.

He smiled. "Evening is here," he said.

She nodded, rising up on one elbow. "I…I have to get to the hospital," she told him, fingering the cross around her neck. "Will this protect me?"

"To an extent. Stephan has ways of seeing that they're removed, but…don't go anywhere without a water pistol."

She started to laugh, and there were tears in her eyes. He sat up, sweeping his arms around her, holding her very tightly, cradling her.

"Hey," he murmured awkwardly.

"I'm sorry…it's just…a water pistol. It's holy water, right?"

"Yes."

She pulled away, staring at him. "If…the holy water kills so easily, how is it that Stephan is still…not dead?"

He let out a sigh. "So far, the second he's been injured, he's managed to disappear before my weapons can do their work. Because he has so many of his lackeys with him, they've kept me busy while he makes his escape." There was so much he still had to explain. And considering everything she'd had to accept so far, she was doing very well. He had to be careful, though, just how much information to impart and how fast.

She needed enough to keep herself safe, but not too much. Information overload could be a very dangerous thing.

"Young vampires are rash, impetuous and not very powerful. They think they're invincible, and they're not. But they *are* killers, and they kill easily, because most people are unaware of their existence. Because people tend to be trusting. Because vampires can…seduce."

She frowned. "Deanna kept telling me there were two men. She insisted that Jonas was good and that there was someone else. Someone who was evil."

"She might have been right."

"But you said Jonas was a vampire."

He hesitated. "Yes," he finally said.

"So he's evil."

"I don't know."

"I don't understand."

He lowered his head, wincing. How much could he expect her to believe?

"You know, of course, that terrible things have happened throughout history. The Spanish Inquisition was one of the worst instances of man's inhumanity to man, but it didn't make all churchmen evil. Stalin carried out a bloodbath, but all Russians weren't evil. Hitler was a maniac, but that didn't make all Germans bad. Terrorists kill in the name of Allah, but most Muslims are kind and compassionate and humane, as Mohammed taught."

She was once again staring at him as if he had lost his mind.

"What the hell are you saying?" she asked.

He lifted his hands. "That there are good vampires."

"Good vampires?"

He answered very slowly and carefully. "Vampires who want to coexist with humans in peace, who have retained the essence of humanity themselves. The woman who owns this house is actually a very wise…" He paused. "And good vampire."

She leaped out of bed, staring at him. He'd gone too far. Her eyes accused him of the absolute depths of madness.

"You—you know all this?" she said, her tone skeptical, her eyes enormous. And yet…he almost smiled at his own unconscious response to her. She was naked, staring at him, hair wild and beautiful, and his heart was pounding again. Of course, given what he'd just told her, she was undoubtedly thinking that she would never let him anywhere near her again.

"Lauren, there's so much…"

"I have to get to the hospital," she said curtly.

"I'll take you. I have a car," he told her.

Her features were tense. But she nodded, grabbing her dress, throwing it over her head. "Ten minutes. I need to shower and change. For the night."

He wasn't sure what that meant, but she was gone. He winced, then rose and headed back for the shower himself. He quickly rinsed off and dressed.

At least she was here, at Montresse House. At least she had agreed to let him drive her to the hospital. At least…

He had touched her. Made love to her.

At least now she had an idea of the mortal danger she was facing.

He wanted to think they could have a future.

He didn't dare.

There were a number of tourists wandering the Square. That was good, Susan thought. It was almost like old times. There was a caricaturist just a few feet away, sketching a young couple who were obviously in love. A young woman in a gypsy skirt and turban had set up on the other side of the artist.

She sat quietly at her own table for a moment, closing her eyes, her hands lying on the tarot card before her. She didn't turn over the cards; she just closed her eyes and listened.

She could hear the rumble of the mule-drawn carriages.

A sax playing to her left.

There was chatter.

Someone who was already a few sheets to the wind stumbled on the sidewalk and was helped by a more sober companion.

She concentrated harder.

Her full name was Susan Beauvais, and her family had been in the area for centuries. One ancestor had fled the bloody revolution that erupted in Haiti in 1791. Over the hundreds of years since, she'd accumulated all sorts of different ancestors. Someone had been white. At least one had been Native American. But it had been her mother, a Creole, who had told her about the magic that went untapped by most people throughout their lives. Reading tarot cards, palms and the crystal ball made for a decent living, but there was so much more a person could learn.

She didn't always feel comfortable with her power. Sometimes people were better off when they didn't know what lay ahead.

But there were other times when it was necessary for people to know what they were about to face. And this was such a time.

She'd sensed troubles like these before, but never so strong, so frightening.

She concentrated more fully, and at last it came to her.

A soft sound, a rustling on the wind.

Yes…she could hear it. The flapping of wings.

She looked up at the sky. Bats. There were often bats here. They rested high up in the eaves of the taller buildings.

She removed her hands from her cards, asked the artist to watch her table, then stood and hurried over to the church, looking around nervously as she went.

The great doors remained open, though they would be closed very soon.

Inside, she knelt down in the aisle and pulled the huge cross she always wore from beneath the cotton fabric of her shirt, then she held it tightly as she murmured her prayer.

Though she didn't look up, she sensed it when someone slid into the pew beside her. She shook her head. "You should not be here."

"It's my home," he said.

"There is a very fine line between good and evil," she said, turning to look up at the handsome young man in the pew. "You may get caught in the crossfire."

"There are very bad times coming," he said.

Susan bowed her head again. "Yes, I know."

"I have to be here."

"I will pray for you," Susan said.

"You must help," he said.

"And how can I do that?"

"You see things."

She turned and stared at him. "It's not as if there's a movie playing in my head. I see what comes to me. If I could choose, if I could see how to fight evil at every turn, there wouldn't be any evil. But you—you should go elsewhere."

"I can't."

"Many here don't trust you."

"I intend to prove myself."

She stared at him again. "You don't know what you're up against—on either side."

"Then I'll learn," he said grimly.

Susan watched him carefully as he rose to leave the church. When he had been gone for several minutes, she rose herself and found the holy water vessel. She dampened her fingers and drew the sign of the cross not just on her forehead, but on her arms, across her chest, above her heart, and in several places around her throat.

Belatedly, she noticed that there was a young priest at the back of the church, and he was staring at her in perplexed silence.

"Evening, Father," she said.

He nodded to her. Tongue-tied, maybe.

As she left, she smiled.

She returned to her table and again put her fingertips on her cards and closed her eyes. She could still hear the sound of wings beneath the laughter, beneath the carriage wheels and the clip-clop of the mules' hooves.

Should she keep her peace? Or try to contact the young woman? There was much she needed to know.

"I'd love a reading," someone said.

She looked up.

And her blood turned cold.

It was him.

* * *

Heidi seemed annoyed to see Lauren and Mark when they got to the hospital. Lauren was distressed to see that her friend was no longer wearing her engagement ring. But with Mark in the room, she didn't want to have a showdown with Heidi. She couldn't begin to imagine what had possessed her to forget how much she loved Barry. They'd been together since they had left college and moved to California. They'd been living together for two years. They wanted the same things: two children, another Norwegian elkhound, one cat and vacations spent hiking through the Redwoods.

"I'm fine here by myself, you know," Heidi said.

Mark, not really paying attention, had walked over to Deanna's side. He touched her brow and seemed relieved, then reached into the pocket of his jeans and produced another cross on a chain.

"What are you doing?" Heidi said sharply.

"Just saying a prayer," Mark replied, carefully slipping the chain around Deanna's neck and fumbling just a bit with the tiny clasp.

Deanna shifted restlessly in her deep sleep, then settled again.

"She doesn't want that!" Heidi snapped.

"It's okay, Heidi," Lauren told her. "I—I bought it for her," she lied.

"Well, that was stupid," Heidi said crossly.

"It won't hurt anything," Lauren said, disturbed by the strange way Heidi was acting.

"You should take that thing off her," Heidi said.

"Why on earth?" Lauren demanded.

Heidi didn't have an answer at first. "I think her mom is part Jewish," she said at last.

"Then we'll get her a Star of David, too," Mark said.

Heidi opened her mouth, apparently puzzled, then closed it again when she couldn't come up with anything to say.

"I think you need to get out of here for a while," Lauren said firmly.

"I…I'm needed here," Heidi said.

"Lauren is here now," Mark told her.

"Right. I can stay here, and you two can go have a nice meal in the Quarter," Lauren said.

Mark had never suggested such a thing, but surely he wouldn't want Heidi roaming around on her own. Not if everything he'd said was true.

Not if winged creatures could suddenly turn into vampires and attack just a few feet away from Bourbon Street.

"Um…sure," Mark said, offering Heidi his most engaging smile. "I'll take you out for a bit."

"I just feel that I should stay here," Heidi said stubbornly.

Actually, Lauren wished she could go out with Heidi herself, maybe get an idea of what was going on with her.

But would it be safe? Even forewarned and forearmed, with her cross and the somewhat smaller water pistol she'd stashed in her purse, could she really defeat what she could barely believed existed?

"Maybe I should take Heidi out for a bit and you should stay here," Lauren suggested.

Mark stared at her, just short of scowling.

Okay, bad idea.

He looked at Heidi. His voice was firm, his eyes meeting hers. "Heidi, let me take you to dinner."

"Okay."

To Lauren's amazement, Heidi rose as if she'd never disagreed. As if she thought it was the most natural thing in the world.

Mark set his hands on Lauren's shoulders. "You stay here. And be careful."

"This is a hospital. There's a cop in the hall," she reminded him.

"Be careful," he repeated.

"Of course."

What the hell could possibly happen to her in a hospital room?

"We won't be long. Come on, Heidi," Mark said.

Lauren nodded, picking up a magazine and dragging her chair nearer to Deanna's bed. As soon as the other two left, she touched her friend's forehead. Her skin seemed to be a normal temperature. She looked good, her breathing sounded even, and when Lauren rested two fingers on her pulse, it was beating regularly.

And still she slept like a princess awaiting her true love's kiss, Lauren thought whimsically.

She rose for a minute and adjusted the television set. She flicked around between channels, irritated as she came to one program after another that she didn't want to see, even shows she usually found entertaining.

Finally, she decided on the Cartoon Network.

SpongeBob SquarePants fit the bill for the moment.

She was half listening to the TV and flipping through the pages of one of Heidi's magazines when a nurse came in to check on Deanna. Lauren tensed, suspicious. Great. Was she going to start suspecting everybody now?

The nurse added a new bag to Deanna's IV and assured Lauren that her friend was doing very well and with luck would come to soon. All the signs were right, and her red-cell count was rising nicely.

Lauren thanked her and tried to settle back and get comfortable once the nurse was gone. She flipped a page, bored, worried.

What had she done?

Aggressive was actually an understatement when it came to describing her behavior earlier that night. But she couldn't be sorry. She had forgotten time and place and all the horrors that had so suddenly entered her life. He had made her feel erotic, sensual, beautiful. As if she had known him forever, as if the world was perfectly right and normal. As if...

As if they hadn't just battled the undead in an alley, as if one of her best friends wasn't lying there in a coma. He seemed to be everything right in the world, the perfect man, a man with whom she could easily fall in love....

"Lauren."

She nearly jumped from her chair, then looked over at the bed.

At first it didn't appear as if Deanna had moved. But then she stretched, as if in discomfort. Her hands fluttered, moved to her throat.

Her eyes remained closed, but her lips moved. She was murmuring something. Lauren went over to her, leaning in close.

"Deanna, I'm here. What is it."

"The fortune-teller."

Lauren's breath caught. "Deanna, I'm here. It's all right," she managed at last. "What about the fortune-teller?"

"The fortune-teller," Deanna repeated.

Lauren took a seat on the bed, holding her friend's hands, squeezing them with what she hoped felt like reassurance.

"It's all right. She isn't anywhere near us," Lauren said.

"Danger," Deanna mouthed.

Great.

Lauren looked around. The door to the hall was ajar. She

could hear footsteps in the hall, along with voices. She heard the cop directing someone to another room.

There was no danger anywhere near.

"It's all right," she soothed. "Deanna, I'm here. It's all right. We're safe."

Suddenly Deanna's eyes opened wide, and she stared at Lauren. She even attempted a weak smile.

"Deanna?" Lauren said, feeling greatly relieved but still slightly chilled. And wary.

She squeezed her friend's hands again.

Deanna looked like…Deanna. Lauren was stunned to feel tears stinging her eyes, she was so relieved.

"How are you? How do you feel?" she whispered.

Deanna tried to smile again, but the attempt failed. "Afraid," she said softly.

"Because of the fortune-teller?" Lauren asked.

Deanna frowned, as if she had no idea what Lauren was talking about.

"You don't need to be afraid. I'm here," Lauren told her.

Deanna looked away for a moment. "No. You don't understand. He comes to me. He comes *for* me," she said.

"No one is coming for you. You're in the hospital. I'm here. The police have even put a guard in the hallway. You're safe."

Deanna shook her head. "No," she murmured. "He comes in the darkness, in my dreams."

"I'm here, and I won't let anyone near you. I promise." Lauren paused, weighing her words carefully. "Honestly, I understand. He's evil and tries to slip into your mind, and you're afraid that…that he'll get through to you somehow."

Deanna stared at her. "You can't protect me," she whispered.

"I can," Lauren promised. "Deanna, there are…others who

know about his kind of evil. It's going to be okay, honestly. I *can* protect you." Her heart skipped a beat. Could she?

Yes. She could be strong, very strong. She knew she could. Even if she was afraid. Even if she knew a truth that couldn't be…

"Deanna, you said something about the fortune-teller." She hesitated, then asked, "Is she evil?"

Deanna only looked fretful and didn't seem to hear her.

Lauren felt a flash of anger at that damn fortune-teller. Everything seemed to have started with her. She had to find the woman.

"Deanna, listen to me. Everything is going to be all right."

Deanna suddenly started and cried out. "No!"

There was sheer terror in her voice.

Lauren looked down at her friend, who was looking fixedly toward the window.

Lauren followed her gaze.

A dark shadow, ebony against gray, seemed to hover outside in the night.

And from it, twin orbs of fire seemed to glow.

Like a pair of eyes…

Straight from hell.

10

Mark tried to reassure himself that Lauren would be all right alone in the hospital with Deanna.

It was amazing. She not only seemed to believe him, she seemed to *trust* him.

Of course, she didn't know the full truth. And that weighed heavily on him. But for now, the point was that he had to find Stephan's lair—and destroy Stephan. Taking Heidi—who was acting like a total airhead right now—out to dinner was not his idea of getting anywhere. But he hadn't wanted the two women out alone. Not at night.

He decided to take Heidi to the club where Big Jim Dixon played. Sean Canady had assured him that Big Jim was not only savvy but knew exactly how to defend himself and others.

Canady had also assured him that every man watching over Deanna in the hospital was aware of the existence of creatures beyond most people's awareness. Mark knew he had to have some faith in others, though his fury and determination were so great that he was still convinced he was the one who would find and destroy Stephan Delansky.

But he needed to help to defend the innocents who might otherwise be slain while he sought his prey. Stephan was powerful. He had survived many attempts to destroy him. He could hypnotize and mesmerize. And he healed quickly. Whatever wounds were inflicted upon him, it seemed he needed only minutes or at most hours to regain his full strength.

Mark nodded to Big Jim when he and Heidi entered the jazz joint. Big Jim nodded in return. It was a good feeling.

"I'm not really hungry," Heidi said, setting down her menu a few minutes later.

"You need to eat something."

"I need to be with Deanna," she countered.

She didn't seem at all like the same person who had been so sweetly flirtatious earlier, while still extolling the virtues of her fiancé.

"Look, Lauren is with Deanna. We'll get back soon enough. Lauren will be worried about you if you don't get some food into you and take a few deep breaths," Mark told her.

"Fine. I'll have a hamburger," she said. And when the waitress appeared a few seconds later, she followed through and ordered one. "I like my meat rare," she said. "Almost raw. Do you understand? Bleeding. Mooing."

Mark frowned. She was being demanding and rude, once again totally unlike the woman he had met earlier.

He ordered a hamburger for himself, also rare, and politely thanked their waitress after she took his order. Then he leaned back in his chair, staring at Heidi.

"Quit looking at me," she said irritably.

"He got to you, didn't he?" Mark inquired in a low tone.

She flushed, shaking her head. She seemed confused. "I—I don't know what you're talking about."

He leaned toward her. "Yes, you do. Think about it. Think hard. Somehow, he got in. Was it Stephan himself, or someone else?"

Color suffused her cheeks. "I don't know what you're talking about."

"Was he tall and dark—darker than me? And did he just appear to you? Did you leave the hospital? Or do those windows open? Did you invite him into the hospital room?"

"No!" Heidi protested, and shook her head, but tears were glistening in her eyes. "There was no one there. You're crazy."

He reached across the table, moving like lightning, cradling her head with his hand and twisting her chin up so he could get a look at her neck before she could stop him.

It was just as he had feared.

The puncture marks were there. Tiny, almost indiscernible. She hadn't been drained; she had merely been tainted.

It was a tease. A taunt. Stephan was sending a message loud and clear to tell Mark that he could get to anyone he wanted to.

And that, in the end, he would have Lauren.

Heidi jerked away from him. "Don't you touch me," she whispered to him. "Don't..." She stared at him, then bit her lip.

"It's not your fault," he said softly. "Give me your cell phone."

"It was just a dream!" she told him.

"No, it was real. Give me your cell phone. I have to call Lauren, and I don't have her cell number."

Heidi's eyes seemed to be glued to his. She fumbled in her purse for her phone, never looking away from him.

The waitress came with their hamburgers just as he found Lauren's number on Heidi's phone and called.

"That's not really rare enough," Heidi said, her attention finally drawn from him.

"They're just fine," Mark said firmly. "We'll take the check, too, please."

Lauren's phone rang and rang until her voice mail came on. She must have turned off her phone in the hospital, he thought.

"Forget dinner. We have to go," Mark said curtly.

"But—"

"Now!"

It was gone. The entire vision was gone in a split second, as if it had never been.

Lauren blinked, staring at the window. There was nothing there. Nothing at all.

Why the hell hadn't she thought to draw the drapes the moment she had come in? Shadows could play tricks. She must have seen lights coming from somewhere, the shadow of a cloud across the moon. It could have been anything.

"Deanna," she said, looking back to her friend.

Deanna's eyes were closed. She was sleeping as if she had never awakened.

"Deanna?" Lauren repeated.

She even shook her friend gently. But Deanna's eyes didn't open again.

"Hey, what's going on?"

Lauren swung around. Stacey Lacroix and Bobby Munro were there. Bobby was out of uniform, and Stacey was carrying a vase of flowers. She frowned as she stared at Lauren.

Lauren rose. "She was awake for a minute. She spoke."

They both stared at her, their eyes betraying the fact that they believed she had only thought Deanna had opened her eyes because she so badly wanted it to happen.

"Well, good, maybe that means she'll wake up again soon," Bobby said with forced cheer.

Stacey gave him a quick glance, then smiled at Lauren, too. Even standing still, she seemed like a whirlwind of energy and competence. "Where's Mark?" she asked.

"He took Heidi out for some dinner."

"Well, then, it's good that we stopped by," Bobby said.

"Yes." *Where the hell were you a few minutes ago?* Lauren wondered. You could have told me if there were really eyes in the night, or if I'm creating horrors in my mind because there just aren't enough real ones out there.

"Too bad we weren't a little earlier. You could have gone, too," Stacey told her. "But we're here now, and we've got some time. If you want, you can take a little walk down the hall, stretch, get yourself a soda or some coffee or something," she offered.

Lauren hesitated. She trusted these people. Sean Canady, a police lieutenant, had sent her to Montresse House. So if she couldn't trust Bobby Munro, another policeman, and Stacey Lacroix, the manager of Montresse House—assistant to a good vampire, she reminded herself dryly—who *could* she trust?

"You're sure you don't mind?" she asked. They were talking about a few minutes, she knew. Not the amount of time she intended to take.

But it seemed extraordinarily important that she find the fortune-teller. And she was only going to find her by night.

There are vampires out there, she reminded herself.

But she was aware. And armed. And she would be exceedingly careful.

"I really could use a walk, something to drink. In fact, I think I'll run down to the cafeteria and grab a snack, if that's all right," she said.

"Of course," Bobby told her, and smiled. He was thin but wiry, all muscle. He had a lopsided smile and seemed like a good guy, and just right for Stacey.

"You go right ahead," Stacey said. "Bobby and I know the officer on duty in the hall—he's a great guy. And we'd never leave your friend. You can trust us, you know."

I have to trust you, she thought.

"Thanks. I'll be back soon."

"Take your time," Bobby said.

She nodded, offered him a weak smile, and tried not to go tearing out of the room.

Lauren had been gone less than a minute when Bobby said, "What's that? I hear music."

Stacey, who had taken the chair by Deanna's bedside, paused and listened. "It sounds like 'Edelweiss,'" she said.

"I think you're right," Bobby said, "but where the hell is it coming from?"

"The bed," Stacey said, then started searching through the covers.

"Aha!" she said, producing a cell phone. "Lauren's phone."

Bobby frowned. "We should call back. It could be important. He reached for the phone, then hit the redial button. A woman who sounded strangely sulky and afraid, all in one, said, "Hello?"

"Heidi?" he said uncertainly.

"You called me," she returned irritably.

Bobby heard a note of impatience as someone else grabbed the phone. "Lauren?" a man's voice said anxiously. "It's Mark."

"This is Bobby Munro. Stacey and I are here with Deanna. Lauren went to get some coffee, but she forgot her phone."

"Find her. Get her back with the two of you. Stephan is getting into Deanna's room somehow. Heidi has been tainted."

"All right," Bobby said. He flipped the phone closed and looked at Stacey. "I'm going after Lauren," he explained. "You be careful. *He's* getting in here somehow."

"Heidi must have *let* him in. Don't worry. I won't."

Bobby nodded grimly and hurried out of the room. No

frigging good deed goes unpunished, he thought. Great idea, to help out, give the girls a break.

And now…

A killer had access to the room.

And Lauren was gone.

Luckily, a taxi was available right outside the hospital, and Lauren immediately flagged him over.

The driver had a Southern accent and spoke English perfectly. He assured her that traffic was quiet, and he gave her a card so she could give him a ring if she needed a ride back later.

He made his way through the traffic easily enough and was able to let her off on Decatur Street, right at Jackson Square.

She walked around.

And around.

Back where they had originally met Susan the fortune-teller, Lauren saw that there was an empty table with tarot cards laid out.

No one was there.

There was no tent set up, either. Maybe Susan hadn't had a chance to replace her crystal ball.

A young artist was seated near the empty table, sketching idly. She had an easel displaying a number of very good caricatures, but when Lauren approached her, she saw that the woman was working on a realistic sketch of a man.

He was a man like any other, except that…he wasn't. He wore stylish jeans and a casual tailored shirt, but even in the sketch, his eyes were…strange, arresting.

And frightening.

She couldn't pinpoint why, but the impression was there. Even in a sketch.

"Excuse me," Lauren said to the artist, who jumped, gasping.

"Sorry, didn't mean to startle you," Lauren said.

The girl flipped her sketchbook closed.

"You saw that man tonight?" Lauren asked.

The girl nodded. It seemed she was trying to collect herself. "Would you like a caricature? I'm really good. Just twenty dollars."

"I'm sorry, I don't have time, but…" Lauren dug in her purse for a twenty. Once she had been just like this girl, just trying to make enough to get through school. "Here…. When did you see that man?"

The girl looked confused. "I…" She laughed suddenly and admitted, "I don't know."

"Think. Please?"

The young woman tried, then shook her head. "I don't know. I honestly don't know."

"Has anything…strange happened here tonight?" Lauren asked.

The girl smiled with real amusement then. "Come on, this is New Orleans."

"Please. I could really use some help," Lauren told her.

"I don't…I don't know. I've kind of been in a fog all night."

"What about the woman next to you?" Lauren asked.

The artist frowned. "What woman next to me?"

"Over there. That table. It belongs to a fortune-teller named Susan."

"Oh, of course."

"Please, have you seen her? Do you know where she is?"

"I saw her go into the church earlier. But it's closed now, of course."

"Thank you."

Lauren walked quickly toward the church, which indeed looked closed. But at the entrance to the alley that ran beside the church, she saw a sign. She walked over to it, frowning, scanning the announcements.

Choir practice! And it was going on right now.

She hurried to the front door. It was locked. She raced down the alley and found a side door, and managed to slip in. She wasn't sure where she was, but quickly wandering along the hall brought her to the side of the main altar. In a small chapel off to the far side, someone was indeed leading choir practice. The sound of the hymn they were singing was beautiful.

She looked toward the rear of the church, searching the pews.

And there was her fortune-teller, just sitting there, staring at the altar.

Lauren made her way down the aisle, then hurried in to take a seat in the pew beside Susan.

"What have you done to us?" she demanded in a heated whisper.

Susan turned to her. "This is a house of God. You will not bring venom in here."

"What have you done?" Lauren repeated.

"Me? You have brought danger and a curse on me, young woman. You shouldn't have come here. And you should have left when I told you to go."

Lauren inhaled, wondering just how absurd she was going to sound. "I know there are vampires here. But it isn't my fault. You knew it, and you didn't warn us."

"I told you to leave," Susan said softly. "But you and your friends refused to believe. You think you are safe in your ignorance, but I will suffer for your stubbornness and arrogance. You bring danger to me just by being here."

"Susan, my friend is in a coma. But she came out of it for two minutes and mentioned you. What do you know? Why did she talk about you?"

Susan turned on her, her eyes narrowed. "Perhaps because she realized that you had all put me in danger. I am afraid to work. How will I live? I have become a target. Because of you."

"What are you talking about?"

Susan stared at her. Her face seemed impassive, but her voice was harsh. "Stephan. Stephan Delansky."

Lauren was so taken by surprise that she just stared.

Maybe this was all an elaborate ruse. Susan was in on it with Mark. And apparently the cops were in on it, too.

If she hadn't seen the wings in the sky, the shadows that took form and came after her, fangs bared...

Susan looked toward the altar again. "There will always be evil. There will always be those who combat it. There will always be those, like me, who see it, sense it, are touched by it...but do not have the power to best it." She stared at Lauren again, though she seemed to be talking to herself. "Evil has come before, and it will come again. Such is the way of the world." Her eyes cleared and met Lauren's. "But you have ruined me."

"You're the one who had the crystal ball!"

"And through it, he saw you."

"But he was here already," Lauren argued angrily, afraid.

"Yes. But now he will stay. Until he has you."

"This is ridiculous," Lauren said harshly.

"Is it? Is it ridiculous when a mother wakes in the night and knows that her child has died? Is it ridiculous when a husband suddenly knows his wife is in danger, when a twin knows her other half needs help? Right now *you* need help."

"I have help," Lauren whispered.

Susan ignored her and went on. "Forget what you think of as real, what you see as sanity. Forget it all—if you want to live. I am alive now only because I know that what we don't

see is real, that what we don't admit can be true. If you want
to survive, realize that for your friends, and for yourself."

"I'm not your enemy," Lauren protested. "You brought
this down on me. You and your crystal ball."

"He would have found you," Susan said. "The crystal only
let you know he had done so. You should have run while you
had the chance." She shrugged. "He might have followed
you, but the danger would have been gone from my life."

Lauren felt oddly as if she had been slapped, the woman
spoke so coldly, with such a dismissive determination. But then
Susan turned back to her. "You have help, you say? Take that
help and cherish it. You cannot win on your own. Even an army
could not help you win if that army did not see and believe. As
for your friends? Keep them safe if you can." She stood up,
clearly anxious to get away. She pulled a folded paper from one
pocket of her long skirt and thrust it toward Lauren. "I do not
know everything, but I research what clues come my way. Read
that. It's a copy of a newspaper article, and it may help you. But
don't read it now. Get away from here. Go back to those who
will help you. If you care anything for others, keep away from
me. And when you leave here, *bathe* yourself in holy water."

Susan hurried up the aisle.

Lauren rose, more confused than ever. "Susan, wait!"

But Susan was gone.

Lauren hurried from the pew herself. In the aisle, she genu-
flected and crossed herself. And she didn't forget to dab
herself liberally with holy water before she made her way
back to the side aisle and out into the alley.

It was quiet.

Dark.

Shadowed.

Surely there were people nearby, she told herself. It was

early, especially by New Orleans standards. Carriages would be clip-clopping late into the night and musicians playing on street corners.

But the narrow alley seemed ancient, shrouded in a strange sense of decaying elegance. There was a breeze, and it whispered in a strangely cool tongue.

She heard something in the air.

Like a flock of birds overhead.

Or bats.

She looked up into the darkness of the sky.

Once upon a time she would have thought only that the night was merely alive with creatures who rested in the eaves by day and hunted by night.

But now she knew better. Now she knew…

That she was their prey.

Bobby Munro was in the lobby when Mark and Heidi returned to the hospital. He looked distraught. Downright ill.

"What's wrong?" Mark asked anxiously.

"Lauren's missing. She's not in the hospital. I've looked everywhere," Bobby told him.

Tension tightened Mark's muscles, and he clenched his jaw tightly, fighting against fury and fear. "I'll look for her. You need to get back to Deanna. Heidi, go with Bobby."

Heidi looked at him, a slow smile curving her lips as she rolled a strand of blond hair around her finger. A look of purely wicked lasciviousness crossed her face.

"He's coming, you know. He's coming back. He's going to kill you."

"Do something with her, will you?" Mark said to Bobby in frustration. Something was clearly wrong with Heidi, but he had no time to worry about her right now.

"I'll do my best," Bobby told him, but Mark was already gone.

Mark left his car in the lot. It was imperative that he find Lauren immediately, and in the crowded Quarter, he would do better on foot.

Leticia Lockwood finally signed off on her last patient. She bade good-night to her fellow nurses and headed out to the parking lot. She was probably the last person on her shift to leave, but she didn't mind. She felt herself blessed to have gotten through nursing school. She loved her work and was happy to do what she could to help others—and get paid for it.

She smiled as she headed for her car. Aunt Judy didn't know it yet, but they were going to church tonight. She thought her aunt would be pleased. Thanks to her, Leticia had managed to keep her goal in mind and ignore many a temptation. Like Tyrone Martin, back when they were in high school. Tyrone had been about the best-looking guy ever to run down a football field. But he had gotten into drugs. Then shoplifting. And now he was doing six years in the state pen. While others had fallen for him, she had not. She had refused his cocaine, his pot—and his determination to get her into bed, and she was glad of it. He had several illegitimate kids, and their mothers were all on welfare. Aunt Judy's forceful resolve had made her stick to her books. Her aunt had never threatened her with violence, but Leticia had wanted to please her aunt, so she'd tried hard to do the right things.

But tonight…

She'd promised the new deacon at their Baptist church that she would be there. She was going for the singing. And for Pete Rosman, the man she'd been looking for all her life. And he liked her; she knew it. They were both people who liked to *do* things. They were proactive and believed that if everybody just put some elbow grease into life, things would be better for everyone.

As she headed for her car, she saw a man. He was bent over by a tree, and he didn't look well. She frowned, instantly concerned.

"Are you all right?" she called.

He put a hand out and waved weakly at her. She hurried over to him. He was handsome, she decided. Too pale, obviously sick.

She took his hand. "Come on… Emergency is right over here. I'll help you."

"No, no…." He flashed her an engaging smile. "I'm so sorry. I'm all right. I just need to sit down for a minute. I was out with friends, and I guess I had too much to drink."

"It's a familiar story around here," she murmured.

"You disapprove. I'm sorry. I'm okay. You can… I'll be all right. I'm going back to my hotel to crash for a while. You're a nice lady, though. Pretty, too," he assured her.

She blushed.

"I'll be all right," he said. But he was leaning on her heavily. And those eyes of his!

She chastised herself. She was going to help him. And not because he had nice eyes and had paid her a compliment, she assured herself. She was going to help him because he needed help. It would only take her a few minutes out of her way to drop him at his hotel.

"Come on. I'll give you a ride home."

"You're too kind."

"Come on."

He held on to her, accepting her aid. She got him over to her car and into the passenger seat. When she sat next to him, ready to put her key in the ignition, he suddenly looked out at the sky and cursed.

She frowned. He was staring toward the cathedral, so she looked in that direction, too. It looked like there was a swarm of birds overhead.

In fact, even at this distance, it seemed that she could hear their fluttering wings.

"It's just birds, maybe bats," she said, intending to reassure him. But in fact he didn't look nervous. He suddenly looked like a great cat that had realized its prey was trapped nearby.

He looked at her. There was something very odd about him. "Sorry, I'm out of time," he told her.

"What are you talking about?" she asked, disturbed.

She saw his eyes again and opened her mouth to scream.

Too late.

The bats were coming. Circling overhead, then dipping low, their wings brushing Lauren with just a touch…a terrifying touch.

Yet…

They didn't settle, didn't land on her, though she knew it would be a struggle to make it the short distance back to the Square.

Where there would be people. Lots of people. Police cars, maybe even mounted officers.

Help.

She judged her distance.

It would be closer to walk back to the church. *Sanctuary.*

She clung to the wall, sliding back to the door as quickly as she could.

She tried it.

Locked. Now it was locked. She banged at it. But no one came.

She was armed, she reminded herself.

Yeah, right. With a water pistol.

She drew it out of her bag and she took aim at the next winged creature that came her way. She held the child's toy with both hands.

And she fired.

The thing fell to the ground with a horrible hissing sound, and there was a small explosion, a puff of smoke in the air, and then...

A pile of dust. As she stared at it, she noticed that there was a figure at the back of the alley. Standing there. Watching her.

The other bats hovered above her, so she ignored the mysterious figure in favor of the immediate danger and began to shoot. She shot and shot, ignoring the shrill hissing and rain of dust, until she suddenly realized that she was going to run out of "ammo."

She stopped.

The figure in the alley was still watching her.

And then she heard the low sound of chilling laughter.

Mark combed Bourbon Street first, going from bar to bar. He moved as fast as he could, his sense of fear growing greater with every second.

He'd put a call through to Canady, and he knew the cop would be out looking for her, and that he had patrolmen on the hunt, as well. He'd done everything he could conceivably do, but even so, he felt as if he were being torn apart, as if he had failed again.

He didn't know where the hell she was.

He would find her. By God, he would find her. She was strong. Even in danger, she would be strong. She believed. She knew the truth.

Exiting a bar, he plowed straight into another man.

Jonas.

"You," he breathed, and reached into his pocket; he couldn't miss this time.

"Sweet God in heaven, man, will you just listen to me?" Jonas pleaded.

"I have an entire vial of holy water," Mark informed him quietly. "And if you make one wrong move, I *will* destroy you."

He spoke quietly, because there were people all around them. From inside, he could hear the band playing and a waitress shouting something to the bartender.

As he and Jonas stood there glaring at each other, a woman flashed a smile and asked them to move aside just a smidge— she wanted to get into the club.

Mark caught the younger man's arm and pulled him out to the street.

"I am not the one you're looking for!" Jonas said earnestly.

"Where the hell is Lauren?"

"Lauren?" Jonas demanded with a frown. "Deanna's the one in the hospital. Would you just listen to me for a minute? I'm not evil."

Evil? Maybe not, Mark thought, but he was certainly a vampire.

Mark drew out the vial of holy water. The other man stared straight at him without flinching. "Hit me if you have to, but I'm telling you the truth. I want to help you. I...I care about Deanna. I've never met anyone like her. She's...she's..." A flicker of fury lit his eyes. "She's too fine to become the plaything of a vicious bastard like...*him*."

"No one here knows you," Mark told him curtly. "The cops here know that vampires exist—some of them, anyway. But no one knows *you*."

Jonas lifted his hand and pulled a chain out from beneath his T-shirt.

He was wearing a cross.

"Could I wear this if I were associated with that monster, Stephan?" he demanded.

Mark arched a brow.

"Look, I *am* new to the area," Jonas went on. "I've been in New York City for a long time. No one there notices anyone else, there are blood banks up the kazoo… I came here to work the music scene. That's all. Not to hurt anyone." He offered a rueful smile. "Hell, there are enough rats around, you know?"

"Make sure you stay out of my way," Mark warned him.

"I can help you. I want to help you. Look, I haven't been…what I am now for very long, and I'm not very powerful, but I'd give my…existence to help Deanna. I'll do anything. *Anything.*"

"Just stay out of my way," Mark repeated.

He started walking away, his anxiety for Lauren rising to the surface again. He wasn't going to kill Jonas—though letting him live might be a serious mistake. But he didn't have the time right now to figure out the best way to handle the situation. He had to find Lauren.

"How the hell can I prove myself to you?" Jonas called after him.

Mark kept going without answering.

He moved with long strides, eager to quit Bourbon Street. It felt as if he were screaming on the inside.

He had to find her.

Now.

The figure at the end of the alley continued to stand there, staring.

She stood dead still and stared back.

She was almost out of holy water, and she was trying des-

perately to remember everything that Mark had said. This was
Stephan, she was certain. Mark had said he was very strong.
She could hit him with what remained of the holy water, and
undoubtedly she would hurt him, but would it be enough? It
might only serve to enrage him and make him all the more
certain that the time to sink his teeth into her throat was now….

"I am not Katya!" she shouted.

"You are the one I will have," he said softly in return.

It seemed as if the entire world had gone still. As if time
itself had stopped. She was alone in the alley with him,
wrapped in darkness and shadows.

"No," she said softly. "You don't know what it is to really
have anyone. You will never have me. And in your brutality
and your cruelty, you will find your own destruction."

He started walking toward her.

How far would her water pistol shoot?

"Put down that weapon. And take off your cross. Because
I *will* have you. I will have you in the way I want to have you,
and that's all that will matter. When I tire of you, well…maybe
you'll be lucky and that won't happen."

She took a step backward.

He seemed closer than he had been.

As if he had floated.

But now he was walking casually toward her, as if they
were old acquaintances, just chatting after a chance meeting
on the street.

She sensed, more than felt, a sudden fluttering.

A shadow in the air. Darkness…

Like wings.

Lauren realized that Stephan was frowning.

Then, suddenly, another man materialized in front of her,
standing between her and Stephan.

It was Jonas, the young, dark-haired stranger who had so captivated Deanna.

"Leave her alone," Jonas said.

Stephan paused, then almost immediately started laughing. "And just what are you going to do about it?"

Jonas turned slightly toward Lauren. "Run!" he yelled to her.

She realized that Stephan probably had the power to tear the young man apart. Young *man?* He was nothing but a creature himself; she had just seen him create substance from shadow.

"Don't fight him," she said vehemently.

"Go!" he urged.

Stephan was coming swiftly closer, floating….

He reached Jonas, lifted a hand. It was a casual movement, but his touch sent Jonas flying across the alley, slamming hard against the wall of the church.

Then Stephan was walking toward her again.

And she found she was having difficulty moving. She could see his eyes. They were dark, and they were light. They were blackness, a Stygian pit, and they gleamed with something like fire. She wanted to move, but…

She forced herself to blink, then she aimed the water pistol.

"You won't shoot," he said.

But she did.

His hiss grew into a bellow of fury as the spray hit him, but he didn't stop. Jonas recovered, straightening from where he had slumped to the ground. He raced back, leaping on the older vampire's back.

"Go, Lauren! Don't let him into your mind!"

She nodded, backing away. Stephan was already reaching around and plucking Jonas from his back as if he were no more than a pesky mosquito.

"Let him go!" she commanded, firing her water pistol again. When the spray hit Stephan, he once again roared in fury. She squeezed the plastic trigger again. Nothing happened. The gun was empty.

"Go!" Jonas told her.

Stephan said something she couldn't understand, but it felt as if she was hit by a cold and paralyzing blast of air. Her feet seemed leaden. She opened her mouth to scream as Stephan pounded Jonas to the pavement. Then he kicked him aside like trash and started toward Lauren again with determined strides.

But just before he reached her, before his fetid breath could wash over her, there was a whirlwind of energy in the street. Suddenly Stephan was hit by an enormous streak of energy and power.

Lauren couldn't begin to imagine the source, and then she saw that it was a man.

Mark.

He threw himself at Stephan in an attack so violent that he seemed to be the very wrath of God himself. His onslaught caught the vampire off balance. For a second Stephan teetered, and then the two of them became a melee of flying limbs and went down, rolling across the stone pavement of the alleyway together, a black mass of fury and rage.

At that moment the sky came to life again, wings appearing from the darkness, then fading back into it again.

Something swept down toward Lauren, and she heard a shout. Mark's voice. He was talking to Jonas.

"Get her out of here! Get her the hell out of here!"

Jonas moved like a flash of lightning. She felt his arms around her. "Run! Help me, Lauren, damn it. Run!"

They ran.

Shadows took form in their wake, as if wings and darkness combined to become tremendous hands, reaching out….

They ran….

And ran.

And burst out onto the Square and joined the sea of humanity once again. People were strolling around, talking, laughing. A guitarist played a country song, a respectable imitation of Johnny Cash.

In the light, in the throng, in the music and chatter and *life* of the square, Lauren stopped running at last. Jonas was still holding her as she turned back and looked down the alley.

All she saw was…

Nothing.

No wings, no shadows. No sign of Stephan.

And no sign, either, of Mark.

11

"We shouldn't have left him," Lauren argued.

They were standing on the edge of the Square. A nearby sign advertised the Pontalbo Museum. A Civil War cannon stood behind a fence, just to her right. If she looked across the green, she could see the statue of Andrew Jackson on horseback.

If she looked around, she could see a world that was normal in every way.

Jonas turned to her, shaking his head sadly. "We had to leave him. Don't you see? He would have been more vulnerable if you had stayed. He would have had to defend you."

She looked at him. He looked like a regular guy. And yet she knew he was anything but.

She had just seen him materialize from shadow.

He was a vampire.

She inadvertently took a step back.

He groaned. "I was ready to give my life for you back there," he said softly. "Why are you afraid of me? You can trust me, you know."

She frowned, shook her head, and then spoke ruefully. "You do realize I still think I'm insane for believing that vampires exist, don't you? Trusting a vampire may take a bit of effort."

"If people only knew how many totally decent vampires actually walk among them," he began.

"Vampires aren't exactly known for their good works," she pointed out, then looked toward the alley again, her concern growing. "Where did they go? How did they disappear so quickly?"

He shook his head. "I don't know. All I *do* know is that I have to watch out for you until Mark reappears," he said firmly.

She couldn't help but look anxiously toward the alley again.

"What should we do?" she asked.

"We should go to the hospital," he said.

She frowned. "You want me to let *you* into Deanna's room?"

"I swear to you, I'm not the one who hurt her and I never would. I give you my word."

"Forgive me, but I'm not sure about trusting the word of a vampire."

"I was ready to die for you," he reminded her again, sounding genuinely hurt.

"Maybe that was just a ploy," she said. "Maybe you're on Stephan's side, and you're just stringing us all along."

"Look. What he wants is you. That's pretty evident. And he might have had you, right then and there. I'm pretty sure the only reason he didn't just swoop right in and take you is that he thrives on the chase."

"Why not chase us right into the Square? What could these people have done against a host of vampires?"

He shook his head. "If everyone believed—no, knew—that vampires are real, that they exist right here alongside you in what you think of as your safe little world, they'd try to exterminate them. Us. The good *and* the bad. The good would die first, because they try not to hurt other people. Then you'd be left with the bad. And the bad could turn the tide enough to kill everything. You have to realize that there is an entire underworld out there. Some people sense it. Some even know that it exists. Some people, like Sean Canady, know it and know they need our help in the fight for human safety. If Stephan had carried his battle into the Square, if enough people had seen him and been attacked, the truth would have been revealed and a real war would be on. A bloodbath. Creatures like Stephan exist because they prey on what human beings consider to be *real* fears. If he tires of his victims and decides not to accept them as members of his flock, he decapitates them and discards their bodies. When he came here, he began throwing them in the Mississippi." He hesitated for a moment. "Once there was an entire hierarchy system, a code of vampire law. A vampire could only create three more of his own kind each century. There was—is—even a…a *king* if you will. Of course, there were always monsters who broke the law, and their behavior threatened exposure for everyone. They were dealt with by their own, or occasionally by a vampire hunter or a guardian. This king actually resides here in New Orleans."

"Then where the hell is he?" Lauren demanded.

"Out of the country, apparently." He shook his head. "Look, I came here because of Lucian, the king. He leads an alliance of those who work against evil and believe that they can find redemption and be part of a better world. I swear to you, what I'm saying is the truth."

It couldn't be.

It could. Either that, or she was suffering from the most real and ridiculous delusion that had ever plagued a person.

"Please. Let's go to the hospital and wait there for Mark. I'm sure he'll come find you. I ran into him earlier, when he was looking for you here in the Quarter."

"Was he with Heidi? My…our other friend."

"No. She must be back at the hospital."

Lauren was afraid. Afraid to trust him and equally afraid not to. It was night. If she got into a taxi with him…

"Shall we get a cab?" he suggested.

She hesitated.

"I swear to God—and I do believe in Him—that I am not going to bite the taxi driver and kidnap you," he said.

Deanna had told her that there were two. One who was evil. Stephan. And Jonas?

She looked around the Square. Bourbon Street would still be buzzing, but the artists here were closing up. The guitar player was already gone.

"All right," she said. "But I need to warn you. I'm wearing a cross."

He smiled. "So am I."

As they walked to the through street, she asked him, "How is it you can wear a cross?"

He offered her a shy smile. "Because I'm not evil. Because I have no desire to harm anyone."

"So…the fact that they're evil makes crosses and holy water poison to the others?"

"Of course," he said. "It makes sense if you think about it."

They found a taxi, but even as they climbed in, Lauren still felt nervous. She was worried, as well. Worried about Mark.

Worried about Deanna.

She kept her distance in the cab, and Jonas didn't pressure her, and they reached the hospital without incident. She started to pay, but Jonas insisted on covering it.

When they reached Deanna's room, Bobby was at the door. "Sweet Jesus, there you are!" he exclaimed, holding her for a minute. Then he drew back. "Where's Mark?" He looked over her shoulder at Jonas, arching a brow.

"Mark is...otherwise engaged," she murmured, then introduced the two men before looking past Bobby into the room. Stacey was in a chair near the bed, and Heidi was there, too, sitting as straight as a ramrod, wearing a frown of irritation.

"What's wrong with Heidi?" she asked quickly.

Bobby looked unhappy. "I guess you never spoke with Mark."

"No. Not really." There were too many people in the hallway and beyond who might hear their conversation for her to explain what had happened.

Jonas, ignoring everyone else, walked to Deanna's bedside. He took her hand and stared at her, and he was either as concerned as he claimed or a fabulous actor, Lauren thought.

"What's wrong with Heidi?" she repeated, returning her attention to Bobby.

He dropped his voice to a whisper. "She's been tainted."

"Tainted?" she asked, but her heart sank. She was pretty sure she knew what that meant without a lengthy explanation. "How?" she asked.

Bobby shrugged unhappily. "Um...well, I guess she let him in."

"Oh, God. Then...?"

"She isn't really all that...ill. I think we can deal with it," Stacey said, rising and walking over to join them. "I just have to get her to Montresse House. She needs to be guarded. Kept safe from...from bringing more harm to herself."

Stacey fell silent as a nurse walked into the room. She had a sour face and was clearly not pleased to see all of them. "This is a hospital room, not a bar on Bourbon," she said irritably. "Please keep it to two visitors."

"We can take care of Heidi if you want to stay here with Deanna," Bobby said.

Lauren hesitated. That meant she would be left alone with Deanna—and Jonas.

He seemed desperately sincere. Did she dare trust in him? Did she have a choice?

And, anyway, weren't Bobby and Stacey practically strangers, as well?

Bobby's cell phone rang as she hesitated. The nurse gave him a disapproving look and started to lecture him on the hospital's prohibition against cell phones, but he just flashed his badge at her and took the call. When he flicked his phone closed, he looked at her authoritatively.

"We'll be leaving shortly. Lieutenant Canady is on his way in, and we won't leave until he gets here."

The nurse looked at him disapprovingly, sniffed and departed.

Bobby looked at Lauren. "Mark is at Sean's place," he told her.

He and Stacey sat down to wait, and Heidi continued to sit in silence, as well, staring at the window as if she could see out of it, despite the fact that the curtains were drawn.

There was no way out of the fact that he'd behaved rashly, Mark thought.

Far too rashly.

But what the hell else could he have done, under the circumstances?

At the very least, Lauren was safe. He had to believe that. Had to believe that Jonas could be trusted. The other man had taken quite a blow.

But could it all have been an act?

It was a small point compared to the fact that, once again,

Stephan had escaped. The violence of their fight had taken them down several streets, and when Stephan had managed to pull his disappearing act, Mark had found himself staggering onto Bourbon Street, where the cops had found him. He had assumed—correctly—that they would think he was a drunk who had been involved in a barroom brawl.

When they had argued over whether to arrest him or take him to a hospital, he had convinced them to call Sean Canady instead.

Canady had collected him and taken him back to his own home, where Maggie had patched up his wounds, even though he had assured her that he was going to be all right. He had been worried sick about Lauren, but Canady had quickly gotten hold of Bobby Munro and found out that she and Jonas were safely at the hospital.

When he had started to rise, Canady had stopped him.

"You need to recover. Give yourself time."

"I can't."

"You have to. Or you'll be worthless."

That was true.

"Look, I'll go to the hospital myself," Sean said. "You stay here and get your strength back."

"We have a great guestroom upstairs," Maggie told him. "You can lie down and rest now that you're patched up and you've had something to eat."

They were right. He felt suddenly grateful to have met them.

So he agreed, though he still felt frustrated and useless as he watched Sean leave.

Maggie sat with him while he lay down. "I realized after we met the other day that I'd seen you before," she told him after a minute.

He looked at her. Studied her and thought about where he was. "Yeah, I guess you have."

She smiled. "You're originally from here."

"Near here," he agreed. He shook his head. "I don't get it, though. You *were* a vampire. And you're certain that you're not anymore?"

"Oh, Lord, yes. Sometimes I'm glad, but sometimes…sometimes I wish I could do a few of the things I used to do. But I have Sean, and we have our family. I've never heard of this kind of reversal happening with anyone else, but…my case was different." She rose and walked around the room restlessly. "It was all so long ago, but my father and some of his friends killed the vampire who created me while he was still in the process of turning me. That kept me from actually dying, and I think that somehow made the difference. But Sean and I have good friends who are in mixed marriages. And as Sean told you, Jessica Fraser, who owns Montresse House, is a vampire, and though they aren't married, her partner is a guardian, as ancient as she is, who's sort of like an angel of death against evil vampires. It's a crazy world, huh?"

"What do you think about Jonas?" he asked her.

"You said he fought Stephan," she reminded him.

"Yes, but…I just worry about leaving Deanna and the others alone with him."

"Don't worry. Sean will be at the hospital soon. You've got to rest. I'll leave you alone now so you can get some sleep."

She was right. He needed his strength.

He closed his eyes.

When Sean Canady arrived, so clearly the voice of authority, Lauren couldn't help but be glad he was there.

She felt far more secure. His faith in Bobby and Stacey became hers. She watched while they escorted Heidi from the room, promising to keep an eagle eye on her.

Jonas didn't move from Deanna's side, sticking so close that there was no way for Lauren to actually get near her. But there was also no way she was leaving her. Not even if Sean Canady was the one sitting guard.

However, the rest of the night passed without incident.

She discovered that she had fallen asleep when the nurse came in at the crack of dawn to change the IV and check on Deanna's vital signs.

Lauren felt a hand on her shoulder. It was Sean Canady. "Come on. I'm taking you home."

"I can't leave her," she whispered, indicating Jonas.

"Yes, you can. Bobby is on duty. He'll sit right here in the room, and he won't be alone."

She looked over Sean's shoulder, to the very attractive, auburn-haired woman standing behind him. She introduced herself as Maggie Canady, Sean's wife.

"I swear, your friend will be safe," she vowed.

Lauren was exhausted and knew she really did need to sleep. She might be insane to be so trusting, but if she didn't accept these people, she might as well lie down and die then and there. They were all she had.

The sun was out as Sean drove her back to Montresse House. Birds were singing. Pretty ones, in beautiful colors.

He let her off at the end of the walk.

"Aren't you coming in?" she asked him.

He shook his head. "Stacey knows you're here. Look, she's got the door open already."

"You have to work?"

He looked away. "I have an autopsy to attend," he said wearily.

"The second girl who was found in the Mississippi?" she asked.

He paused for a moment, then handed her a newspaper from the backseat. She saw the headline as he spoke.

"Third victim," he said briefly.

"It's like…one a night," she murmured.

Sean shrugged. "Actually, it could be worse. Stephan Delansky is apparently keeping his minions in check and killing just enough to make sure that law officials up and down the Mississippi wind up chasing their tails."

"He has to be stopped," Lauren said.

"Yes, he does. But not by you, especially not now. Go get some sleep," he told her.

She started to exit the car, then paused. "Mark?"

"Mark will be all right. Go on in."

She obeyed at last. Stacey was waiting for her at the door, and when Lauren entered, Stacey stepped outside, waved to Sean, then looked around—upward. Seemingly satisfied that no one was there, she followed Lauren inside and closed the door.

"Coffee's on," she told Lauren. "Except maybe you don't want coffee. It would just keep you up. But I made waffles, and they're delicious. Eat, grab a shower, curl up and get some sleep."

"What about Heidi?" Lauren asked her.

"Heidi's doing well. I gave her a sedative, enough to keep her out for a while. She won't be doing any communicating until she's had some time to get rid of the…infection."

Lauren looked around warily. "How do you know that, er…*evil* can't get in?"

Stacey laughed. "Take a good look around. See the planters? We water them very carefully—with holy water. And if you take a good look at the way the windows are constructed, you'll see that the beams are crosses. There's also garlic powder worked into some of the molding. Trust me, we have any number of protective devices here. Of course, you still have to be careful."

Stacey led the way to the kitchen, reached into the microwave and produced a plate for Lauren. "Sit down. Eat."

Lauren discovered that she was famished, and the waffles were as delicious as Stacey had promised. "Are we safe by day?"

"Saf*er*," Stacey said. "Vampires—good and evil—are at their greatest strength at night. And I sincerely doubt Stephan will attack by day. He's not some idiotic young vampire, out to feed his way through the city. Not that many would be that stupid—this being the home of the Alliance."

"What?" Lauren said.

"The Alliance."

Lauren frowned, shaking her head. "So Jonas was telling the truth."

"That there is an alliance of…shall we say…otherworldly beings who make their home here? Yes. Unfortunately, Stephan knew right when to hit this area. Almost everyone's away. I just hope they'll return in time."

"You hope?"

"Don't be afraid. Mark clearly knows his enemy. And Sean and Maggie—well, no one knows more than they do. It's really too bad that Brian MacAllistair, Jessica's partner, isn't here. Guardians are…are ancient and because of that, they're powerful. Very few…people have survived since the Middle Ages. Look, it's all right. Sean's officers are more than capable of handling vampires. I mean, he doesn't give classes on Fighting Vampires 101 or anything like that. There are just some guys on his squad who naturally…know. It's not so difficult, really. If you believe in a higher power, you believe in good. If you believe in good, you have to believe in evil. I'm sorry. I'm getting very complicated here, and you probably just want to get some sleep. Would you like more waffles?"

"What?" Lauren realized she'd been drowsing and had barely heard whatever Stacey was saying.

"Waffles. Would you like more waffles? You've cleaned your plate."

"Oh, no, thank you. They were delicious. I guess...I guess I'll just peek in on Heidi and then get some sleep myself, if that's okay?"

"Sure."

They went upstairs, where Stacey opened one of the bedroom doors. Heidi was soundly sleeping, cradling a stuffed teddy bear.

"Bobby won it at the fair," Stacey explained.

"Nice. Thank you," Lauren told her.

"No prob. Call me if you need me," Stacey said, heading back downstairs.

First things first. In her own room, Lauren took a long, hot shower after realizing just how...grimy she was. The thought that the specks of soot on her flesh and in her hair were the remnants of evil beings was not a pleasant one. She scrubbed herself vigorously, then repeated the process.

At last, though, sated from the waffles, clean and warm, she practically crashed down on her bed, images spinning through her mind. Vampires. Shadows. Darkness. Bats. Amorphous shapes that solidified in the night. Terrible things. Evil creatures...

And Mark.

Mark last night.

She curled into the mattress. Mark was all right. Sean Canady had assured her that he was fine. Safe.

At last she slept.

And later…he came to her.

She thought she was dreaming at first. That she heard his voice because she longed to hear it. That he was touching her, his fingers running through her hair, because she wanted to be touched.

"Lauren."

She realized that he was really there, at her side. Blue eyes deep as midnight, yet brilliant as the day. The contours of his face as rugged and strong as ever, but the look in his eyes so tender.

Then he was kissing her.

Lips moving on hers, coaxing, powerful. His hands sliding over her, cupping her breasts, traveling down to her hips.

She wasn't dreaming. He was with her.

Making love to her.

And, oh, God, it was good.

She curled into his arms, returned his kisses with searing wet ardor, broke away, kissed and teased and laved his flesh. Somehow the nightgown she had donned after her shower was gone. Somehow his naked flesh was erotically close to her own. She felt the hardness of his arousal against her, the vitality of him, the pressure of his muscles and movement. The drapes were drawn, only a touch of the sun entering, and it seemed he was bathed in gold. It was as if real fire emanated from her when he touched her, that the elements themselves combined to arouse and seduce her.

She had never known such a lover. He had clearly decided to go slow. She had met his first caress so easily, only to discover she was firmly pressed back again and again, that he wanted to stroke each niche and curve of her, the brush of his fingers followed by the pressure and caress of his lips and tongue. He traced a slow pattern on her flesh, making her ache and writhe as he moved from her throat to her collarbone, breasts, midriff, belly, thighs…until he delved intimately between them, driving her to a point of madness, a point of searing climax…and then took her there again.

His lips were forceful, his entire body thrusting in a way that seemed to penetrate her every pore, even her very mind. She thought she might well die as she arched against him, seeking more and more and more of him, or at the very least that she would go mad. But then the sweet delirium of climax burst upon her again, and his flesh against her flesh, their hearts thundering, pulses racing, breathing coming in gasps of wind…

Then dying down.

She didn't lie quietly at his side, waiting for the wonder to subside. Instead she sat up, staring at him, frowning, worried. "You're all right?" she asked anxiously.

"I thought I was much more than that, actually," he teased.

She almost hit him.

"I'm serious. You escaped him, but you were hurt. How in God's name…?"

"I'm all right," he said quietly. "Really."

She hopped up, comfortable with him, heedless of her nudity, anxious to see him clearly and assure herself that he really was completely well.

She turned on the light and went back to his side, then searched him head to toe, anxiously, with her eyes, with her touch.

"You…you're not even bruised."

"I'm tough," he told her. "Worn, rugged and tough," he added with a soft laugh.

"I was so worried when you didn't come back."

He reached up, his eyes on hers as he touched her cheek. "You were worried? So was I. Trusting Jonas wasn't easy."

"He took me straight to the Square."

He nodded, looking down for a moment. "Sean had told me he was pretty sure the guy was decent."

"Deanna...liked him," she murmured.

"Yeah, well, I guess he was there at the right time last night," he said. "Still...I don't like it. The thing is, though, I have to find Stephan's hideout. His lair."

Lauren frowned. "You're certain that he has...a lair?" she asked slowly.

"Of course."

"Well, excuse me if I'm asking silly questions, but...accepting that vampires exist is still new to me. So...does he have a coffin somewhere? Native earth and all that?"

He was looking at the ceiling, his expression serious, and he gave no hint that she was asking something bizarre. "It's not as complicated as you think. He has native earth somewhere. A place where he can go to rest...to heal, if he's wounded. But he has to have a place large enough for his followers to go." He turned and looked at her, suddenly almost angry. "Where the hell did you go last night? Why did you leave the hospital? You know it's not safe for you to be out alone."

She was startled by the question. And though she didn't know why, she didn't want to tell him the whole truth.

"I...I thought it might be important to find the fortune-teller."

He frowned. "The woman in your sketch?"

She nodded.

"Did you find her?"

"No." Why had she lied? She wasn't sure. Then she knew. Susan had given her that paper, the copy of whatever she had found at the library, and Lauren realized that she wanted to read it herself. To see if it was something that made some kind of sense. Her meeting with the woman had been unnerving.

She felt very guilty about the lie, however, so, without prompting, she began to explain. "I don't think I ever told you. I…I saw Stephan in her crystal ball. The night we arrived, Heidi and Deanna wanted to have our fortunes told. Susan had a little tent and a crystal ball. And when I looked into it, Stephan appeared."

His expression grave, he asked, "Why didn't you tell me this before?" He was still angry, she realized, but trying to keep his temper leashed.

"I'm sorry—but you didn't exactly seem sane at first."

"But since then…" He closed his eyes, shook his head. She could almost hear the grating of his teeth.

He sat up, then rose, reaching for his pants. "So that's when and how he found you," he said quietly. "I'll see if I can find the woman. See what else she may be able to tell us. And *you*—you have to be extremely careful. No—I mean *no*—wandering off on your own. Please, Lauren, I'm begging you."

She nodded, watching him. "He's killed again, you know. They found a third body in the river."

He swore, pulling up his jeans. "He has to be found. And stopped," he said grimly.

"What do I do…what *can* I do, about Deanna? And Heidi?" she added.

"Stacey will know how to manage Heidi. I imagine she's already acting a great deal more like herself already."

"So being seduced, bitten…doesn't automatically make you become…a vampire?" she asked.

He shook his head. "You become a vampire when the kill is complete," he said. "Unless you're staked. Or beheaded."

"How can there be so many vampires and only three murders? I mean…don't they need to feed?"

He slipped into his shirt. "They can feed on many things. Rats, small animals…and a good glut can last a very long time. I'm sure, if we checked the surrounding area, we'd find that a few blood banks have been ransacked." He hesitated. "Stephan is a monster. Cruel, power-hungry, and he thrives on the pain and torment he causes others. But in the end…he wants to live. He wants me to die, because I'm an enemy who has been on his trail for a long, long time. But he wants you first—and he wants me alive to see it. Maybe he believes he can seduce you, that you'll live a long and happy—and blood-thirsty—unlife together. Maybe he only wants you because he knows he can cut me to the quick again. Maybe it's both. I can tell you this, though. He's using Deanna and Heidi to torment you, to get to you. And I have to stop him."

He went still when he finished speaking.

She frowned. "What is it?"

He groaned. Suddenly, instead of buttoning his shirt he was pulling it off again. The jeans fell to the floor.

And then he was back beside her, eyes meeting hers, fingers caressing her hair.

"I need to go," he murmured.

She nodded.

"But not yet. Not just yet."

Nor could she let him go. They were both fevered, hasty, making love with a fierce and desperate passion.

She was falling in love, she thought. With his face.

With his hands.

His touch.

His kiss.

Not just in love with being in love, with making love. No, with a man.

She barely knew him.

She had to believe that she knew enough.

She ceased to think. She soared; she reveled in sensation. Together, they were cataclysmic, explosive. She could not get close enough to him.

Her heart pounded; her breathing rasped; her flesh was slick and wet; and the moment of culmination was shattering and sweet.

In the end, he held her close for a moment and sighed deeply. Then he was up and gone.

And she was left alone with her thoughts, to wonder if what she felt could be real or was only a dream.

A dream…when all else was a nightmare.

12

Mark headed to Jackson Square. He had noticed Susan, the woman Lauren had sketched, when he had first come back to the city and had wandered through the Square, seeing what had changed, what had remained the same.

It always amazed him. Take away a few signs, add a few cosmetic details, and the Square was just as it always had been. There were a few musicians out, a few artists and one tarot card reader. There was no sign of Susan.

He walked on to the police station, where, with little difficulty, he was ushered in to see Sean Canady, who was at his desk, bent over some paperwork.

He studied Mark as he came in. "You look refreshed," he said.

"You got a minute?"

Canady indicated a chair.

"Was there anything unusual about the autopsy?" Mark asked, cutting right to the chase.

"Would you call it unusual to find three headless bodies in the Mississippi in three days? Because I would," Sean said. "It's obviously the same killer. You can only see one puncture mark on the latest victim—the other went with the head when it was severed. I don't know if Stephan is leaving the marks on purpose—to let those who know in on what he's up to—

or if he's just being careless. Thankfully, the M.E. says they were all dead prior to the decapitations. The state police have set up a task force extending up and down the river."

"They having any luck?"

"There's nothing to go on. No prints, nothing left behind, and the water is doing a number on any evidence that might have been left on the bodies. They brought in a profiler, who believes we're looking for a man in his mid- to late twenties, maybe early thirties, someone with feelings of inadequacy, and a menial day job. May or may not have a wife at home. Everyone is baffled by his ability to decapitate his victims and hide the heads, although it's likely they're in the Mississippi, as well—it can be merciless. Everyone agrees it will be a major breakthrough if we can discover *where* the crimes are taking place. They're looking for something like an abandoned slaughterhouse, since the victims have been practically bloodless."

"Did you make any suggestions?" Mark asked him.

"Of course. I suggested we were looking for a vampire."

Mark arched a brow. "And you're still employed."

Sean smiled ruefully. "I've spent many years now knowing that what we're up against doesn't always fit the normal expectations. Sorting out the crazed human from the crazed *in*human. Since we've had cultist activity here before, sometimes people listen to me. I've told them that I'm personally convinced we're up against a cult, and that they should think as if they were up against real vampires, because that's what this group thinks they are."

"Good call," Mark said. "What about your own men?"

Sean shrugged, his smile deepening. "The nonbelievers have thought for years that I'm a little bit crazy—worse, they believe I can think like a deranged killer. But they've seen things come to a satisfactory conclusion before by thinking my way, so… The men I put in the hospital to watch over Deanna…they've been on similar duty before. They believe."

"What's your take on Jonas?" Mark asked him.

"Seems like he's on the right side. But I don't personally know him."

"Neither do I."

"Truthfully, I don't know *you,* either," Sean said.

Mark almost said, *Your wife knew me,* but he refrained. She had really only known *of* him, and that had been a long time ago.

"Stephan is holed up somewhere. The problem is, I don't think it's in your jurisdiction. He's got to be out of the Quarter somewhere, maybe even out of the city and the parish. I was thinking of taking a closer look down Plantation Row, out past your place. I already took a quick ride out that way, and I didn't see anything that looked empty—that looked like some cultist group was sneaking in and out of it."

"Maybe it won't look empty," Sean suggested. "Maybe Stephan made a few contacts before he came here. Maybe, by day, it looks like any other house."

"Have your guys keep their eyes and ears open, huh?"

Sean just stared at him.

"They're already doing that, huh?" Mark said.

"Yes."

"I'll be in touch," Mark assured him, rising.

"By the way, we've got IDs on all the girls. They all have records for prostitution. One from Baton Rouge, one of them from Lafayette and one from Poughkeepsie."

"Poughkeepsie?"

"New York State. Maybe she was relocating. She didn't have a known address down here, anyway."

Mark shrugged. "Working girls will always go off alone with a man," he said. "It makes sense."

"Yes," Sean said simply, then drew a deep breath. "I've got men watching the bars and strip clubs. But I don't think you'll find Stephan that way. He's more subtle. If he's committing the murders himself, I think he's having the women brought to him."

Mark nodded. "Makes sense. I found one of his minions in a bar when I first arrived. I followed him when he took a woman to a cemetery and killed him."

"I guess he found someone who thought that doing it in a graveyard would be exciting."

"Even young vampires can be seductive," Mark said.

Sean nodded. "We're on the alert for anything unusual. I'll call you right away if I hear anything at all."

Mark thanked him and left the police station.

Stephan and his followers were targeting easy prey, he thought. Women who were ready to be seduced—for a price. They just didn't know that they were the ones who would be paying.

Well, he'd hit the bars, and he had found one of Stephan's lackeys, though the young woman he'd gone after had been just a tourist.

But Stephan had an untold number of followers. They could be anywhere. Not one of them, so far, seemed to have acquired the kind of strength and power Stephan had learned over the years, though. By day most of them were probably resting. But maybe not all of them.

During the day, the city was quieter than it was by night. Most people spent their time checking out the historic district, the museums, the restaurants and the shops. Parents took children for carriage rides. The aquarium and the zoo drew crowds.

But the bars were open.

And so were the strip clubs.

He wandered in and out of a few of the bars, catching

snatches of live music along the way. At one place, the group was so good that he wanted to forget his quest and stay to listen, but he resisted the urge. Everywhere he went, he sensed nothing, saw nothing. Everything was quiet.

He decided to try a few of the strip clubs. At the Bottomless Pit he found worn carpets, cheap patrons and tired strippers. No one appeared the least bit menacing. In fact, performers and audience alike seemed to be asleep.

He moved on and found a neon sign that promised *Bare, Bare, Bare!*

A hawker with bad teeth was out front, trying to lure people in. Mark decided to pay the cover charge and take a look.

It was quiet.

There were a few scattered patrons, including a heavyset man in the front row, with a prime location right next to the pole. As Mark entered, a weary announcer was trying to make his voice excited as he raved about Nefertiti, goddess among women.

She appeared on the walkway, and in contrast to the rather cheesy atmosphere of the place, the ennui of the announcer and the shabby appearance of most of the patrons, she was good-looking to the point of beautiful. Tall, golden-skinned, with long, sleek dark hair. She made her way to the pole and eyed the heavyset man who had taken up the catbird seat.

She twisted and writhed. She started out wearing spangly harem pants and a jeweled bra, with finely meshed material connecting the skimpy bits. The mesh went quickly, then the top, and before long, just as promised, she was *bare, bare, bare,* and everything was gone.

She elicited a fair amount of applause for her act, considering the room wasn't particularly well populated.

Then Nefertiti stepped down, and the announcer called

out the next girl, Annie Oakley, with a faux hearty "Ride 'em, cowboy."

Annie Oakley had clearly been around a while. Her breasts were definitely silicone, and gravity was establishing dominance.

Few people were watching her.

Nefertiti had gotten dressed, though she wasn't exactly ready for church, and gone over to the man in front, offering him a lap dance. Mark kept one eye on the stage and the other on Nefertiti. It was the usual stuff, but the heavyset man was evidently enamored.

Mark's phone rang. Still watching Nefertiti negotiate, he answered with a soft "Yes?"

"I've got something." Sean's voice.

But Mark barely heard him; he swore and snapped the phone shut, staring at Nefertiti. Her hair was a good foil, but not good enough to hide the fact that she was just about to take a bite out of the beefy flesh and pulsing jugular of her heavyset client.

Heidi did seem more like Heidi, Lauren thought. She seemed confused by her own actions, though, almost as if she didn't really remember a thing about the day before.

"Hey," Lauren said, giving her a hug when she found her downstairs at the breakfast table.

"Hey," Heidi echoed, then asked anxiously, "Do you think Deanna is going to be all right? I can't...I can't seem to make much sense of yesterday. I guess I was coming down with something. And you're not going to believe this. It's awful."

"What?" Lauren asked, her heart thumping.

"I can't find my engagement ring. How in God's name did I lose my engagement ring?"

"It might show up," Lauren said.

"Barry will kill me," Heidi said.

"No, he won't. And…you're still going to marry him?"

Heidi frowned. "Of course I'm going to marry him."

"I'm glad."

"When did I say I wasn't going to marry him?" Heidi pressed.

Stacey, coming to the table with fresh coffee, answered flatly, "Yesterday."

"Never!" Heidi protested.

Lauren looked at Stacey and then at Heidi. "Uh, yes," she murmured.

"Tell her. You have to tell her the truth," Stacey insisted.

Lauren stared at Stacey again. Just what "truth" was Heidi going to believe?

"You were bitten by a vampire," Stacey said. "You have to know all this, and you have to get with the program."

Heidi's jaw fell. She looked at Lauren accusingly, as if Lauren had forced them to move to a crazy house.

"A *vampire?*" Heidi demanded. Stacey was quiet. Heidi picked up her coffee cup, and her fingers were shaking. "A vampire," she repeated tonelessly.

"Yes, actually," Lauren told her.

"Who's the vampire?"

"We think you were bitten by a vampire named Stephan," Lauren told her.

Stacey took a seat at the table and leaned toward Heidi. "Think about it. When you were at the hospital, *you* let him in. Thankfully, he went after you and didn't suck the remaining life out of Deanna."

Again Heidi's jaw dropped. "You are all stark raving mad," she said, and started to rise.

Stacey set a hand on Heidi's arm. "Think hard. Make

yourself remember yesterday. Remember Bobby and me coming in. Remember Lauren! Think about going to dinner with Mark and then coming back to the hospital. None of it was a dream. None of it was in your imagination. It was all real."

Heidi looked pale and uneasy. "All right, yesterday was strange. I'm sure I had a fever. Maybe a bit of whatever made Deanna so sick."

Lauren started to reply, but she didn't get a chance to. Stacey had decided there was going to be nothing gentle about getting Heidi to see the real picture and kept going.

"You bet it's the same thing. Deanna would have died if she hadn't gotten to the hospital when she did. And she could have died again when *you* let that monster into her room. Fortunately he decided he would try poisoning *you,* as well. But luckily Mark recognized your symptoms right away, and we were able to get you back here before anything worse happened. But he's still out there, and you're weak—"

"I am not weak!" Heidi flared.

"Wait!" Lauren spoke at last. "Stacey, this...man is extremely powerful, and Heidi had no idea what she was up against. Stephan has hypnotic powers. I was almost frozen myself when I came across him, and I was armed and knew what I was up against."

"You were *armed?*" Heidi demanded.

"Water pistol," Lauren told Heidi. "Holy water."

"Forget that for now," Stacey interjected. "It's incredibly important that you think back and remember everything," Stacey said to Heidi.

"Vampires really do exist, and Deanna and you have both been tainted. He has a gateway to you now, unless you really understand the danger and fight against him," Stacey said firmly.

Again Heidi just stared.

"I do remember going to dinner with Mark. He wouldn't let me eat my hamburger," she said thoughtfully.

"He knew, once he was with you, that you'd been tainted," Lauren told her gently.

Heidi shook her head. "You guys have all had a few too many. I know something is very wrong, but *vampires?*"

Before either of them could answer, Heidi's cell phone began ringing. It was Barry, Lauren knew. She recognized the ring tone.

"Hey, sweetheart," Heidi began.

Both Lauren and Stacey could hear the anger in Barry's voice, though they couldn't make out what he was saying.

"No!" Heidi said. "I didn't! It must have been someone's idea of a practical joke. I would never—"

The phone went dead in Heidi's hand. Tears were apparent in her eyes as she stared at the other two women.

"He…he says I called him yesterday and said that it was off, that I was sorry, but I wanted to sleep with other men. And then I hung up on him!"

"I'll call him," Lauren said quickly. "I'll think of something to say. I mean, we all know how much you love him. And how much he loves you."

"He hates me!" Heidi said, distressed. "I didn't call him. I would never have said those awful things."

"You did call him. And that's the problem. He's your fiancé—he knows your voice."

Heidi burst into tears.

"It's going to be all right," Lauren said, the words hollow in her own ears, but they were the only ones that seemed appropriate at the moment.

Stacey was harder and firmer. "You need to start out by being glad you're alive, and then you need to start believing what we're saying. You are going to do every single thing I tell you to do, and then, when we've all survived this, we'll work on getting your fiancé back."

"I'll call Barry today," Lauren told Heidi, handing her a napkin to dry her eyes. "Don't cry, Heidi. It won't help any."

"Don't cry?" Heidi exploded suddenly. "You're telling me I was bitten by a vampire—because I'm weak—and that I called my fiancé and trashed the prospect of my marriage. And you don't want me to cry?"

"No, don't cry, get mad," Stacey said. "You need to be angry. Take a good, hard look at what the creature trying to seduce you made you do. Wake up!"

"I am awake. Believe me, I'm awake," Heidi retorted angrily. She wiped her face and stared at the other women. "If this is some kind of practical joke…"

"I wish it were," Lauren said softly, reaching across the table to gently touch her friend's hand. "I'll call Barry. We'll convince him your phone was stolen by someone who over-heard you talking about him and decided to be cruel."

"Will he believe it?" Heidi asked.

"Will he believe it if you tell him you were under the in-fluence of a vampire?" Stacey asked curtly.

"You will call him? You'll convince him?" Heidi said to Lauren.

"Of course. You love him, and he loves you. He's just angry right now—but he loves you."

Heidi was quiet for a minute. "So…what now?"

"I have to get back over to the hospital," Lauren said.

"Yes, of course, we need to go back," Heidi said.

"Not you," Stacey told her firmly.

"What?" Heidi protested.

"You're with me. You need another day to replenish what you lost—and you need to learn the ropes," Stacey told her.

"What ropes?" Heidi asked.

"Vampire-killing ropes," Stacey said in a tone that left no room for argument.

Mark leaped up, knocking a table over in his haste to reach "Nefertiti" before she could sink her fangs into the man.

"Stop!" he shouted, and threw himself at the woman.

She went flying down to the stage beneath him. Her eyes— a deep brown with a hint of the light that gave her away seething fire—met his.

Then the heavyset man had him by the arm and was dragging him up.

"He's a psycho!" Nefertiti shrieked.

"Bastard! Pay for your own entertainment," her big client bellowed.

"Call the cops," Nefertiti said.

"I'll handle this asshole better than the cops," the man said, drawing back his massive fist.

Mark easily dodged the blow. "She's diseased!" he shouted as he ducked. The other man had put so much weight into his attempted attack that it carried him down to the floor with an oomph.

"Diseased?" he said. "Oh, God!"

Nefertiti took that moment to race backstage. Mark leaped over the big man on the ground and followed her.

A half-dozen not-so-hot-looking showgirls in various stages of undress shrieked as he went flying through the dressing room in pursuit.

Nefertiti grabbed a silk robe and kept running, heading for the back door.

She pushed through it; Mark was right behind her.

The door led to a long hallway.

She reached the door to the street just a split second before he did. She burst outside, and he followed, catching her by the arm.

She spun around, fangs bared, ready to shape-shift. By then he'd drawn a small little squirt gun from his pocket. He fired and hit her squarely between the breasts.

She screamed.

People stared.

"Cops! Somebody call the cops!" came a cry.

"He's got a gun!" someone else roared.

"It's a frigging water pistol!" a third person chimed in.

One way or the other, Mark couldn't afford to stick around. They made a pretty ridiculous picture, the stripper in her heavy makeup and robe, him with a water pistol shoved against her side, a wave of smoke rising from her chest.

He had to move, and quickly. He didn't want to lose his hostage, but he also didn't want to destroy her.

He wanted answers from her.

"Come with me—now. And quietly. You know what I have here. You can die for real, or you can help me. The choice is yours," he said.

"I'm hurt," she said pathetically.

"You'll be more than hurt in two seconds if you don't shut up and do what I tell you," he assured her.

She slipped an arm around his shoulders, pretending to be with him. Onlookers would probably just assume they'd had a lovers' quarrel, he thought.

"I'm nearly…gone."

"Nearly, but not quite."

"You need to show some mercy," she whined.

"Like you were about to?" he suggested.

"I wasn't going to kill him."

"We'll never know, will we? Just shut up and come with me, or the cops will be here. And then I'll have to kill you, because I can't let you go," he promised her swiftly. "Let's go."

She complied without further complaint.

The older woman sitting across the desk from Sean Canady was very upset. The desk sergeant had tried to explain that she couldn't fill out a missing persons report, because the missing person hadn't been missing long enough.

But the woman had been persistent.

Her name was Judy Lockwood, she said. She had raised her niece, Leticia, since she had been a small child and Judy's brother, Leticia's father, had passed away. Leticia had grown up to be a fine young lady. She worked at the hospital as a nurse, and she hadn't been sick a day since she started. She went to church; she always came home at night.

But she hadn't come home last night. And she hadn't reported in to her job at the hospital.

Because Sean had insisted on being told about absolutely anything even slightly out of the ordinary, Judy had been shown into his office.

He had put through a call to Mark Davidson the minute he had heard the two keywords *disappeared* and *hospital*.

The woman in front of him was straight and slender, wearing a flowered dress that was clean, smelled of fresh air and was perfectly pressed. She wore dignity about her like a cloak; she sang in the church choir, and she lived by a code of right and wrong.

Sean's heart seemed to squeeze as she spoke to him. He prayed her niece was fine. He doubted that she was, though. From all he was hearing, she was a far cry from the previous victims whose pitiful remains had been pulled from the mighty river.

"When was your niece last seen, Miss Lockwood?" he asked.

"Just yesterday evening—and I know, I know, she hasn't been missing long enough, but I'm telling you, something's wrong. She said goodbye to Bess Newman, who was taking over her patients. Bess said she left late, because Leticia always stays longer, just to make sure all her paperwork is filled out and all her patients are in good shape. She's a really good nurse, Lieutenant Canady," Judy assured him.

"But no one saw her after she left the hospital?" Sean asked.

"No," Judy said.

"Did she drive to work?" Sean asked.

"Yes, sir, I was getting to that. Her car's not in the parking lot."

"And you don't think she drove somewhere, and that…something came up?"

She stared at him as if only a complete idiot could have made such a comment. "Lieutenant, you haven't been listening to me. Leticia is a very good girl. She goes to church. She has never missed a day of work. What can you imagine that would suddenly make a woman like that just decide she wouldn't go to work?"

"Miss Lockwood, I *am* worried about your niece, and that's why I'm taking this report myself."

Huge tears suddenly filled her eyes. "She's a good girl. Not that I wish any ill on anyone, but from what I read in the papers…those other girls took chances. My Leticia didn't. She went to church. She went to work. She'll go out on a date now and then, but with a good boy, a boy from the church. She's never had any truck with boys in gangs. So she couldn't have been taken by…by whatever horrible monster…killed those other girls…could she?" she asked weakly, hopefully.

Sean covered her hand with his. "I'm going to follow up

on this, Miss Lockwood. I promise you, I'll do my very best to find her."

As Judy Lockwood started to rise, there was another tap on his door. The desk sergeant stuck his head in. "A friend of Miss Lockwood's is here, Lieutenant," he said.

Another woman walked in. She was almost Sean's size and, like Judy, beautifully dressed, down to her straw hat. "Excuse me, Lieutenant Canady, and thank you for your time. Judy, I just got a call from Leticia. She ran late into work, and that was all. She's sorry you were worried, Judy, and she'll talk to you tonight. But she's fine, and that's what matters, right?" She turned to Sean. "I have a cell phone, you see. The grandkids bought it for me last Christmas. Judy doesn't like them, so she never got one."

"Thank the Lord!" Judy said, rising, clapping her hands together. She turned sheepishly to Sean. "Lieutenant Canady, I thank you for your time. And I am so sorry I wasted it."

"I don't think it was a waste of time, Judy. We need answers around here right now, and I'm hoping anyone will come in when they're afraid, just as you did."

"You're a fine young man, Lieutenant."

He smiled. He was pushing fifty. He wasn't sure that made him a *young* man at all.

They left his office, and he had just started to pick up his phone when there was yet another tap at his door. The desk sergeant was back.

"I'm sorry, sir."

"No. You did the right thing," Sean said.

As soon as the sergeant left and closed the door behind him, Sean picked up his cell and called Bobby Munro. "Stay there. Stay in that room and don't leave until I get there."

"Right, Lieutenant," Bobby said.

"Jonas still there?"

"Sir," Bobby said very softly, "he hasn't left even to take a leak."

Let's hope to hell he's as decent as he seems, Sean thought, then asked, "So what's going on there? Everything fine?"

"Yup. The doctor was in this morning. He hopes she'll come to soon, and that she'll be fine. It's looking good. Well, as good as it can look, at any rate."

"Can you see the chalkboard that lists the nurses assigned to the room?" Sean asked.

"Yeah, I can see it from here."

"Is someone named Leticia coming on?"

"Yeah, how did you know?"

"Don't let her in the room," Sean said.

"Um, actually, that would be a problem, Lieutenant."

"Why is that?"

"She just walked in. She's here right now," Bobby told him.

The pulse in the throat, he had told her. "Find the pulse in the throat. You're a nurse, so you won't have any problem. You're starving, and you will be in this pain until you fill yourself with what you need, but you must be careful. There is only one who can stop your pain. You must go to her room. There will be someone there, so you must be careful, but you are a nurse, and you can go right in and ease your pain."

The words pounded in Leticia's head. She had very little memory of exactly what had happened; she only knew that she was supposed to do as she had always done. Go to work. Sign in. Once she had done what he had commanded, all would be well. He would find her again. She would be rewarded as she had never been rewarded before.

She found the patient, Deanna Marin, who was lying there in silence. There were also two men in the room, one sitting by the bed and watching Deanna intently. The other was a cop, but he was on the phone. She had seen him in the room before. Bobby. The cop's name was Bobby. For some reason, even though so much was a blur, she knew his name.

She walked over to the bedside and replaced the IV drip, just as she normally would. Then she leaned lower. She could hear the pounding of the woman's heart, could see the pulse in her throat.

She felt a streak of agony worse than anything that had plagued her so far. A hunger unlike anything she could have imagined before. It tore at her insides like a razor blade. It demanded satiation.

She opened her mouth, and she felt another stark and terrible pain as her teeth actually…stretched. Somewhere, in the very back of her mind, she knew that biting another woman and seeking to drain her of the very last drop of her life's blood was wrong.

But the hunger…

The hunger was unbearable….

She paused suddenly, terrified.

The pain continued to brutally tear at her stomach, but something worse, something as powerful as an atomic bomb, had exploded within her mind.

She was nearly blinded.

Yet she saw.

There was a chain around the woman's neck.

A chain and a cross.

Leticia remembered Aunt Judy and Pete, how she'd wanted to be a nurse to save lives, how she had loved to sing with the choir and…

No! The pain raked her and made her bleed inside. She was insane with hunger, ravenous. She had to feed.

She leaned lower, her fangs closer....

And then heavy hands fell on her shoulders, and she screamed at the agony tearing her apart.

It took Lauren so long to smooth things over between Barry and Heidi that she was ready to scream at them both when Barry at last agreed to speak with Heidi again.

They were on the phone, cooing away to each other, when she finally felt able to leave, Big Jim Dixon accompanying her.

She was glad of his company. Big Jim seemed to take everything in stride, and he didn't talk much; she was happy just to be with him.

He drove her right up to the front door of the hospital. "Are you coming in?" she asked him.

"I want to get back to the house. I don't like to leave Stacey alone," he told her. "Heidi seems just fine," he said, noticing the way she quickly looked at him. "Honestly," he added firmly.

"Of course," Lauren said. "Thank you for driving me here."

"We watch out for one another here. You go on up and see your friend. She won't be alone. Bobby will be with her."

Lauren walked through the halls and down to the elevator. People said hello all along the way, and she greeted them politely in return. New Orleans really was a great place—if you just discounted the vampires.

She reached Deanna's floor, where there was the usual activity at the nurses' station. It was a busy place. Doctors, orderlies, nurses, all going about their business.

She walked down the hall.

There was no officer outside the door.

She felt a little leap of fear, then remembered that Bobby was on duty, and he would be in the room with Deanna.

But when she reached the room and walked in, there was no one there.

Just Deanna, sleeping as usual. So beautiful, so peaceful, like the fairytale princess awaiting her lover.

The windows were open, the drapes blowing inward.

There was no sign of Bobby, or even Jonas.

As she stood in the doorway, puzzled, a scream echoed from down the hall.

13

Mark didn't dare take "Nefertiti" to Montresse House—there was no way he would invite her into the home where Lauren and her friends had found safety. Nor could he take her out to Sean's house, for the same reason. He would never risk the lieutenant and his family's safety by bringing such a creature in.

At least she seemed to have decided that he was dangerous to her, and she was quiet and well behaved, accepting his lead as he moved down the street, trying to find a café with a courtyard and plenty of room—and sunlight.

She protested when he chose a place and picked out a table. His chair was in shadow. Hers was not.

"Sit," he commanded.

"I'm sitting."

"Talk."

"What do you want me to say?"

"I want to know where you go to sleep."

"I sleep…different places."

"Who did this to you?" he asked her.

She waved a hand in the air dismissively. "Who knows? Someone with money."

He leaned back, shaking his head. "You're a liar. You never

worked in that club until you became a vampire. And you go
somewhere in particular at night."

She stared at him sulkily just as a waitress came to their
table and looked inquiringly at Mark. "Order," he said with a
shrug. Nefertiti smiled at the waitress. "He's so rude. But
he's so good in bed that I don't care," she said sweetly.

The waitress, an older woman with graying hair, stared
at the two of them as if she'd just been faced with the dregs
of society.

"An iced tea, please," he said.

"I'm hungry," Nefertiti whined.

"Then eat."

"He really is so commanding," she told the waitress. "I'll
have a hamburger."

"Medium? Medium-well?" the waitress asked.

Nefertiti offered her a sugary smile. "Raw, please."

"You mean...rare? The health code suggests—"

"Not rare. Raw. No bun, thanks."

"I can't give you a raw hamburger. The health code—"

Mark slapped a large bill on the table. "Please just bring
her a raw hamburger."

With a disapproving look, the waitress left them.

"Where are you from?" Mark demanded, leaning closer to
her.

"Bourbon Street."

"Where are you from?" he repeated.

She smiled. "Houma, originally. But now I'm from Bourbon Street."

"So you were created on Bourbon Street?"

"Ooh. Smart fella."

"So where do you go at night?"

"Wherever I choose."

He had the water pistol aimed at her beneath the table and let go with a short spray. She nearly jumped out of the chair. "Bastard!" she hissed at him.

The waitress returned with a plate holding a raw hamburger. It was barely on the table before Nefertiti was digging into it with her fingers. The waitress made a soft sound, clearly not intended for them to hear, that was filled with disgust.

"Maybe you can be helped," Mark suggested when the waitress had gone.

Nefertiti stopped eating for a moment and stared at him, then shook her head. "No. I died, and I rose. There is no help."

He realized suddenly that she was looking past him, over his shoulder. He turned around but saw nothing. In that split second, she was up and running.

"Stop!" he shouted.

She only kept running. He followed, practically leaping over a table to keep up with her. She turned down a side street, then into an alley. "Stop!" he yelled again.

At that moment a toddler came running out of a door onto the sidewalk in front of her.

Nefertiti stared, then grabbed the child and turned to look Mark straight in the eye.

The little boy started to cry. From inside the house, they could hear a woman's voice calling, "Ryan? Ryan! Where are you?"

Nefertiti shook her head at Mark with a curious, almost wistful smile.

"Don't!" he cried.

She opened her mouth and began to lower it, fangs extended, to the crying toddler's throat.

He shot her with a long, continuous spray. She let out a screech of agony and dropped the boy. Smoke and steam rose from her skin, and she fell, hardly recognizable anymore as a human being but instead a writhing, shifting form, wretchedly decayed.

He heard the sound of police sirens.

Disgusted, Mark turned and quickly escaped the alley. He heard the mother shouting, calling the boy's name, then screaming in bone-chilling horror, no doubt as she stumbled onto Nefertiti's remains.

As he turned onto Rue Delphine, Mark saw a police cruiser, lights flashing, pass him.

And he heard the flutter of wings overhead.

As he walked quickly away, he thought over what had happened and realized that the woman who called herself Nefertiti had preferred extinction at his hands to facing her master and being branded a traitor.

As he walked, he remembered hanging up on Sean back at the club. Cursing, he drew out his phone and punched in the lieutenant's cell number.

Lauren was torn. The scream demanded—*self-preservation demanded*—that she run. At the same time, she needed to know why someone was screaming. But most of all, she knew that if Deanna were to have a chance, she couldn't leave her alone again.

That last option won out. She rushed over to Deanna's bed, wondering if whatever was happening was only a ruse to trick everyone into leaving her friend alone and vulnerable.

Deanna's IV was still connected to her arm. She still lay on her white pillow and sheets as she had for what seemed like forever. The princess. Unmoving.

Swallowing, her fear nearly paralyzing her, Lauren picked up Deanna's hand and fumbled for the pulse in her wrist.

It was there, regular and strong. She breathed a sigh of relief. *But what the hell was going on?*

Lauren had been concentrating so hard on Deanna that it was several seconds before she realized that someone had come into the room behind her.

As she turned around, wary and tense, she heard the door to the room slam shut.

He was there.

Stephan. Stephan Delansky. Standing now at the foot of the bed. Ink-dark hair fell over his forehead, contrasting with the doctor's white coat he was wearing. "How is my patient?" he asked very softly.

Lauren looked toward the open window. Shouts and cries were coming from the hallway; the hospital seemed to have turned into Bedlam. But Stephan Delansky seemed oblivious to all that. She didn't know where he had come from, if he had stepped into the room from the hall, or if he had come through the window.

But it didn't really matter. All that mattered was that he was there.

She stared at him and flipped the cross she was wearing out from under her shirt.

He smiled. "That will not stop me, you know."

"Maybe so, but you're there, and I'm here."

"Because you must come to me."

"I will never come to you."

"Eventually, you will." He laughed softly. "I have my ways of doing things. Methods. Even madness, you might say. You see, this is a war. Whatever skirmish I may lose to my enemy, in the end, it is a war, and I will win. And you *will* come to me, because I know you."

"You cause suffering and death," she told him. "You hurt

people. You nearly killed my friend. You're evil, and you will not win."

He smiled and shook his head, as if explaining things to a small child. "What in life has ever led you to believe that what you call 'evil' cannot win? Take that silly cross around your neck. I have seen it before, and it failed to stop me then, just as it will now. *He* is not the salvation you think he is. And I am not death, but rather, eternal life."

"Tell that to the women you've beheaded," she said softly.

He made a dismissive sound. "They did not deserve to live."

"You're wrong. They didn't deserve to be murdered."

They could both hear footsteps then; someone was running down the corridor toward Deanna's room.

"You *will* come to me," he told her again, his smile cold and certain.

There was the sound of something slamming heavily against the door. Instinctively, Lauren looked in that direction just as the door burst open.

Mark was there, standing in the doorway, his gaze quickly darting around the room. He rushed over to her, drawing her close to him, his arms around her.

"He was here," he said huskily, his tone certain.

"Yes." She couldn't help it. She was trembling, even though Stephan had vanished as suddenly as he'd appeared.

"Deanna?"

"She seems to be all right."

"And…you?"

"I'm fine, too."

He let out a sigh of relief. For a moment he seemed so weary that she longed to hold him forever, but now, more than ever, she was afraid to leave Deanna's side.

"What's happening here?" she demanded.

As if in answer, another scream echoed from down the hall.

* * *

Even between them, Sean realized, he and Bobby couldn't manage to hold the woman.

Leticia Lockwood was slim and delicately built, but at this moment her strength was unimaginable.

"I can't hold her!" Bobby cried.

Sean had gotten off the elevator just in time to see Bobby trying to wrench Leticia away from a gurney, where she was rabidly attacking a bag marked Type O Positive that was attached to a line transfusing into an apparently post-op gentleman of advanced years. Bobby was already sporting a swollen jaw, and hospital employees were scurrying just to get out of the way.

"Hey," Sean said firmly, grabbing hold of Leticia's shoulder as she writhed like an animal beneath Bobby.

She screamed, a bloodcurdling sound that was horrible to hear. Then, with astounding ease, she threw Bobby clear across the hall.

"Damn it, stop! I don't want to shoot you!" Sean roared.

He might as well not have bothered. Leticia was up and flying at a hapless intern who was standing by, aghast.

"Shit!" Sean swore and went tearing after her.

He tackled her, and they hit the floor together.

She shoved him, and he fared no better than Bobby.

She was off again, this time making a leap for the frozen and panic-stricken head nurse, who was standing behind the desk.

Wincing, Sean drew his weapon and fired a warning shot.

Everyone screamed—except Leticia, who didn't even pause.

Before Sean had a chance to shoot again, Mark Davidson came running out of Deanna's room. He saw Leticia, saw her intended victim, and took a flying leap over the desk. He caught Leticia by the shoulders and shoved her forward, crashing into a rolling cart filled with medications. Bottles and vials went flying everywhere.

Sean waited, expecting Davidson to go flying just as he and Bobby had, but there was only silence.

Nothing.

He strode to the desk and looked over. Mark was straddling the girl, staring down at her and talking soothingly. "Someone get her something quickly—a major-league tranquilizer," Sean said.

The head nurse, who had appeared almost catatonic with fear, suddenly sprang to life. She fumbled on the floor, searching through the wrapped needles and the different vials. In a second she was at Mark's side. Leticia began to thrash again, forcing her back, but Mark seized the hypodermic from her and quickly inserted the needle. In a second, Leticia's wild and frantic eyes closed, and she went limp.

Mark stayed as he was for several long seconds. Then he eased back.

Sean strode over to him. "You all right?"

"Yeah."

Suddenly hospital personnel were everywhere.

"I can't believe it," the head nurse said, stricken. "It's Leticia. She's one of our finest nurses."

"She went insane," one of the interns said.

"Like a rabid dog!" another claimed.

"Let's get her into a bed," an intern said.

"You're going to find that she needs a transfusion, and she needs it fast," Mark said.

"Are you a doctor, young man?" the head nurse demanded.

Mark looked up at her. "I know what she needs," he said quietly. The nurse frowned as Mark rose and lifted Leticia into his arms. "A room?" he said.

The head nurse just nodded. The young intern who had first suggested that she needed a bed followed Mark into an empty room and spoke quickly to the nurse. "Pull up her chart. Her blood type must be on record."

The nurse stared at him.

"Do it. Now."

She jumped, shooting a disapproving glance at Mark, and hurried back out to the hall.

Sean stood in the doorway, watching, then felt a tap on his shoulder. He turned to see Bobby standing behind him.

"Lauren is here, in Deanna's room. I'll be with her."

"Thanks, Bobby."

Sean looked at Mark, who was standing next to the bed where Leticia now lay, completely out. "Will the transfusion do it?" he asked quietly.

Mark shook his head, his uncertainty clear.

The intern, who was checking Leticia's pulse, said, "I think she'll be all right. She must have been under the influence of some heavy-duty drug. We'll do a tox screen and find out what the hell is going on. She's one of our best nurses. I can't imagine Leticia... She never even smoked pot, sings in her church choir..."

A commotion in the hallway began to grow into a din. Sean stepped out to see what was going on and found patients milling around curiously and the staff trying to get them calmed down and back into their rooms.

"Folks, it's all over. Everything's all right," Sean said.

A middle-aged woman in a hospital gown that left her more than a little exposed suddenly pointed and started screaming.

Sean turned toward the gurney with the post-op patient. The man was still unconscious, but Leticia had apparently gotten her teeth into the blood bag, because blood was sprayed all over the man and the wall.

"It's all right. It's all right, Mrs. Ruben," a nurse assured her.

An orderly quickly went over to the gurney. "I need help here," he called.

"People, please," Sean said. "Get back into your rooms. Let the hospital staff get things cleaned up."

"Someone stabbed him!" Mrs. Ruben screamed.

"He wasn't stabbed," Sean said patiently. "It's just a spill."

"A spill like murder! Blood-red murder!" the woman shouted.

"Murder!" someone else repeated.

Sean groaned. "Stop it!" he snapped, using all his authority. "There's been no murder," he said, all the while knowing the words might well be a lie. "Get back to your rooms."

To his relief, the patients began to obey.

With Mark in with Leticia Lockwood and the staff suddenly finding both courage and their senses, Sean strode across to Deanna's room.

Lauren was perched by her friend's side.

Bobby was standing, hands on his hips, looking like a crouched tiger ready to spring in any direction.

Sean walked over to the bed. "She all right?" he asked Lauren.

"No change," she told him.

As he nodded, Mark Davidson returned to the room. "We have to get Deanna out of here," he said flatly. "Sean, there's a Judy Lockwood across the hall with Leticia. She wants to talk to you."

Sean walked to the door, pausing on the way to ask Mark, "And what the hell do I tell her?"

Mark took a deep breath. "I have absolutely no idea," he admitted, then smiled. "Hey, you're the cop." Then he turned serious again. "But we have to get Deanna out of this place."

He frowned. "Where the hell is Jonas? He was like a bad penny, but suddenly there's no sign of him."

"I don't know," Sean said.

"All right, let's just move," Mark said.

Sean, wincing, strode across the hall.

What the hell was he going to say to the woman? *Your niece, your decent, sweet, God-fearing niece, was possessed by a vampire?*

He just hoped he wouldn't end up having to stake her.

Lauren wasn't quite sure how Mark managed to convince Deanna's doctors that she would be better cared for at home. At first the doctor in charge—called back in from a day's fishing excursion, wearing a cap with a bouncing bass—was adamant that she wasn't ready to be released, not while she was still in a coma.

Lauren swore she could care for her, but the doctor kept shaking his head.

Then Mark began to talk. He didn't say anything she hadn't said herself, but somehow he was more convincing. Maybe it was a guy thing. She usually hated that. But at the moment she couldn't be too upset, because she was getting what she wanted.

The release papers were signed, and arrangements made for a registered nurse to come by three times a day. An ambulance was hired to transport her from the hospital to the house on Bourbon Street.

Lauren rode in the ambulance with Deanna. Sean, Bobby and Mark followed by car. The paramedics helped settle Deanna in, then left.

Heidi was still upset and on edge, but she was behaving normally again, and she was ready to be a little mother hen, clucking over Deanna. She assured Stacey and Bobby that she would be taking over Deanna's care and would make sure they didn't impose on anyone, and that she would protect her friend against any evil.

Lauren noticed that Mark seemed to find that final claim especially, doubtful. He had a hushed conversation with Stacey in the hallway, and Lauren suspected Stacey was assuring him that she had gotten Heidi to understand the danger facing them.

"I really think Heidi is going to be okay," she whispered to Mark, as he came back into the room. She kept her voice down because Heidi was close by, concentrating on making sure that Deanna's pillow was properly plumped.

He stared at her as she spoke, seeming distant and tense.

"Really," she said, catching his arm and leading him toward the door. "She's herself again."

Mark sighed, shaking his head. "And Sean told me about Judy Lockwood saying Leticia wouldn't stay out all night or miss work. Don't you see? He gets to the people he uses. He literally gets into their blood."

Sean Canady came up the stairs, staring at Mark. "We've got another corpse," he said.

"Headless?" Lauren asked, swallowing.

"No," he said to her. "And found in a courtyard, not the Mississippi." He turned back to Mark. "They're having a hard time discerning how she originally met her demise. She's pretty well decayed. Apparently she's been dead for months."

"A fraternity prank?" Lauren asked, hoping against hope. But then she saw the way Sean and Mark were looking at each other.

"Vampires only explode and turn to dust if they've been dead long enough that their body would have decayed already. Apparently we have a few fairly fresh kills on our hands."

"I think Lauren's idea of a fraternity prank makes sense. At least, that's the story I'd go with for the press," Mark told Sean.

"Hell," Sean groaned.

"We should go, don't you think?" Mark said to him.

"To the morgue?" Sean asked.

"To the hospital. We've got to see if we can talk to Leticia." He turned to Lauren. "Stay here. And please, don't leave this house."

"I won't. Deanna and Heidi are both here," she said.

"And Bobby and Stacey," Sean told her. "And I'm going to tell Big Jim that the band will have to do without him for a few nights. Call me if anything, anything at all, happens."

"Absolutely," she swore.

She nodded, turned and took a seat on the bed next to Deanna, as if to show both men that she wasn't going anywhere.

Sun streamed in from the balcony. The air conditioner hummed.

The only odd thing at all was the fact that Stacey had strung cloves of garlic all the way around the windows and the French doors that led to the balcony.

The room smelled like a pizzeria. But there were far worse scents, Lauren had discovered.

Like blood.

Sean was quite a helpful guy, Mark noted dryly to himself. The cop was his passage into the places he needed to go.

Like Leticia's room, where Sean had stationed an officer by the door while Deanna's release was being handled.

When they entered, Mark saw that Leticia was shackled to the bed, and Judy Lockwood was still there, seated by her niece's side in the big hospital chair that turned into a bed. She was humming as she knitted a sweater.

Mark noticed that Judy had brought her own kind of defense. The windowsill was littered with a bit of dirt, which he knew was some kind of mojo Judy thought might work to keep her niece safe. There was also a huge cross on the bedside stand.

"How's she doing?" Sean asked.

"Sleeping like a baby," Judy told him. She didn't miss a stitch as she answered, then smiled at Sean. "Thank you for listening to me."

Sean nodded. "This is a friend of mine, Miss Lockwood, Mark Davidson. I think you met him earlier."

Judy studied him. "All right," she said after a moment. "Are you going to help us, then, Mr. Mark?"

"I'm going to do my best. I'll need to speak with Leticia when she wakes up. I'm hoping she can tell me something about where she's been."

Judy nodded. "You may take a seat, young man."

"I'll leave you, Mark, and get down to the mor—station," Sean said. "Judy, feel free to call me anytime."

"I will, Lieutenant," she said firmly, her eyes on Mark. "And I thank you again," she added softly.

Sean left with a nod to Mark, who turned to Judy. "Miss Lockwood, are her clothes in the closet?"

She nodded.

"May I look at them?"

She stared at him for a long time. "They say you calmed her down. The cops couldn't hold her. No one could. You calmed her down."

"Um…yes."

He was startled when she reached out and grabbed him. "Is she going to be all right?" she demanded tensely.

This woman was somehow in the know, Mark thought.

Maybe she didn't even know what she understood; maybe she just had special instincts. But somehow she knew that more was going on here than it seemed.

"I sincerely hope so," he said.

"I love this girl," Judy said with quiet vehemence. "Understand this—I love this girl more than my own life. I love her enough to kill her if need be. Do you understand what I'm saying, young man?"

"She needs a lot of blood," he said softly. "A lot."

Judy leaned back, eyeing him warily. "She's been getting that."

"She needs to be…watched."

"I won't leave her side."

He hesitated. "You have to be very careful. You have to…watch whomever comes in here."

"I can do that," Judy assured him.

He nodded.

"Her things are all in the closet," Judy told him.

He thanked her.

Judy's uniform gave him little to go on; it was splotched with blood, but he had expected that. Then he checked her shoes. The soles were thickly caked with dark muck and swamp grass.

He set the shoes back where they'd been. He was surprised that Stephan hadn't made a clean kill of the nurse. A small miracle, he thought, then winced, thinking about the day.

About the decaying corpse that was now at the morgue.

Nefertiti.

"I'll be praying for my girl," Judy said, her fingers busy at her knitting once again. "I'll be praying for her. You'll be praying, too, won't you, Mark?"

She stared straight at him.

"Yes," he said simply.

"You go on now," she told him. "I'll be here. Day and night. Come what may. You can count on me," she said.

He smiled, then walked over to the table, found paper and pen, and scribbled down his number. "If she wakes up…"

"I'll call you."

"Thank you."

Mark left the hospital. As he did, he saw night was coming. His cell phone rang. It was Sean.

"Meet me at the morgue."

"Now?"

"It's as good a time as any."

"Lauren."

Lauren jumped. She had dozed off in a chair.

She looked across the room, thinking Heidi, who was relaxing in another chair, had spoken.

Heidi stared at her.

Then they both stared at Deanna.

Lauren blinked.

This time it seemed Deanna really was conscious. Lauren and Heidi both leaped up, almost crashing into each other in their rush to reach Deanna's side.

"Hey!" Heidi said.

"Deanna," Lauren breathed.

"I'm thirsty," Deanna murmured.

"I've got it," Heidi immediately said.

Lauren smiled and lifted Deanna's head so Heidi could hold the glass in place. Deanna took an eager sip.

"Go slow," Lauren warned.

Deanna nodded, drank and sagged back against her pillow. Her eyes closed for a minute, then flew open again. "Jonas," she said.

"Jonas," Lauren repeated blankly. Then she frowned. Where *was* Jonas? He had stayed by Deanna's side for so long, but today…

Deanna had been alone, all alone, while Bobby had battled with Leticia, while pure madness had broken out….

Where had Jonas been?

"He's been with me, hasn't he?" Deanna asked softly.

"Yes, honey, he hung around," Heidi assured her, smoothing back her hair.

Deanna stared at Lauren. "Jonas is *good,*" she said firmly.

Then why the hell had he disappeared right when Deanna needed him most? Lauren wondered.

Bernie Gibbs was on night duty at the morgue. His job was to sit at the desk and deal with whatever the doctors might need help with, and sign the paperwork for whatever dear souls might depart this world in the darkness. Since the doctors never needed help at night, mainly he read books and signed for bodies when they were brought in.

He was often on night duty. Actually, he liked it, liked the silence. He'd gotten through three years at Tulane by working here. He heard about some weird stuff now and then, but it didn't bother him any. He'd always been the kind of kid who could sit through the most gruesome horror movie. Now that he was premed, he'd already seen a hell of a lot worse than anything Hollyweird could come up with.

Tonight he was in pretty good shape. He had borrowed a popular new spy thriller from the library, and it was just as engrossing as the reviews had promised. He was actually glad to be at work, where the stiffs never interrupted him just when he was at the best part of a book.

He'd gotten one call from Lieutenant Canady, who'd said

he would be coming by. He hadn't explained why, just told Bernie to keep an eye out for him. But that was cool. Canady was a good guy. He was hell on wheels if you were a crook, but if you were just an average Joe, schlepping along, he didn't mind what you did with your free time. But Canady hadn't shown yet.

There was a sudden noise—right when his spy was meeting up with his Asian nemesis. It startled him from his concentration on the book, and he cocked his head to listen.

Nothing.

He wondered what the hell the noise had been. Something must have fallen out back. He turned his attention back to his book, but he couldn't help wondering what could have fallen?

He set his book down, swearing softly. Had a door been left open? Or did they have rats or something?

Shit.

He decided he'd better check it out.

He stood, and looked around. He didn't have a weapon. Attendants at the morgue didn't usually have problems with their…charges. But what if some jerk had broken in? He looked around and saw his book. "Great," he muttered aloud. He could just see the headline. Courageous Night Attendant at Morgue Foils Thief with Spy Novel.

No, the book wasn't good enough.

There were all kinds of scalpels and saws in the autopsy rooms, but he didn't want to take a chance of coming across an intruder before he could get to a weapon. He opened the drawer to his desk. Aha! A letter opener.

Clutching it in his hand, he stood. He looked toward the door to the street and noted that it was securely locked. He started down the hallway.

A glance into the first room showed him that everything was sterile and pristine.

And smelling...sanitized.

Like a morgue.

A place of death.

Hardly a surprise, he thought with a shrug, and he moved on.

He found nothing. At last he came to the large insulated stainless steel doors that led to the morgue's current occupants.

He opened the door to what was essentially a giant refrigerator and looked around. Nothing. No, wait.

Something.

Shit!

There was movement on one of the gurneys. Damn it, they did have rats! Big rats, if the movement he was seeing gave any clue.

Rats—or a frat brother, trying to freak him out, he thought. He shook his head and walked to the gurney.

"Asshole," he said, pulling back the sheet.

But no frat brother was waiting to leap up and yell "Boo!"

He'd seen the corpse earlier. It was the one that had been discovered by a woman chasing after her kid, and it was months dead and decaying. The eyes were...gone. Eaten by insects or who knew what. Most of the flesh had been rotted away, and what was left clinging to the bones looked as if it had been burned. In fact, the smell of burning flesh had hovered around the body. She—because it was a she—had scarcely been recognizable as a human being.

But now...

A sound like...like insects gnawing on flesh and bone was coming from the corpse, but that wasn't the cause

It *was* flesh and bone, all right. Flesh and bone that

appeared to be repairing themselves. As he stared, watching blood vessels appear, muscles take form...

Her eyes—eyes that hadn't been there at all earlier—suddenly opened, and she stared at him.

Stared at him.

And then she smiled.

Smiled, only it wasn't a smile, it was like a snarl, and she was baring her teeth, but they weren't teeth at all, they were fangs. She looked like a huge asp, her horrid maw of a mouth opening, and he knew that she meant to sink those fangs into his jugular.

He screamed.

And he struck, batting at her face with his hand and trying to stab her with the letter opener. But those teeth were still coming....

Then, suddenly, he felt something heavy smash down on his head. Stars burst before his eyes, and he crashed to the floor.

He thought vaguely that he heard someone groan "Son of a bitch," but he wasn't sure. And then the world went quiet, as if a black curtain had fallen from the sky, and all seemed to be eternal darkness.

14

Mark was certain the morgue was empty when he arrived, but as he stood at the door of the seemingly deserted facility, it opened, and Sean Canady was standing there in the dark.

"Took you long enough," he said, then turned and walked away, calling over his shoulder, "Come in. Quickly."

Mark followed, his eyes adjusting quickly to the darkness. There were security lights, but they offered dim illumination at best.

"No night attendant?" Mark asked.

"He's…here."

"Oh?"

"I knocked him out," Sean said impatiently. "I had to."

"Really?"

"Come see."

"I thought you wanted me down here because of that body the cops brought in today?" Mark asked with a frown.

"Yes."

"I destroyed her today."

"She *should* have been destroyed," Sean said.

"What? If she's coming back, we need to talk to her. We need to know where she's been sleeping, who—"

"I'm sorry, but it's too late now."

"What the hell are you talking about?"

"Come on back. You'll see."

He did see. The morgue attendant was out cold on the floor, and the corpse....

She was half-covered in flesh again, looking like a Hollywood movie prop. Her eyes were open but unseeing. Her mouth was distorted in a snarl.

Her fangs were glistening.

And she had a literal death grip on a stake that was protruding from her chest.

"You certainly did take care of her," Mark said, looking at Canady.

"I had to. I know you were hoping she could be brought back to help us, but it's not going to happen. And after what I saw here tonight, we've got to be very careful." He indicated the morgue attendant on the floor. "She nearly had him. There seem to be some fairly new recruits in Stephan's flock. We can't count on dust to dust to get rid of them. If you make a kill, be damn sure you cut the head off. I'll take care of any explanations."

"Like Stephan, when he throws his refuse into the Mississippi," Mark said bitterly.

"You've got to make sure they're down for good," Sean said firmly. "I have a community of the living to protect. I know you need information, but you can't get it at any risk to others."

Mark looked down at the fallen morgue attendant. Poor guy looked well and truly out. "How hard did you hit him?" he asked Canady.

"He'll come to soon enough."

"How much did he see?"

Canady shrugged. "Too much. But with the bump on his head, he won't say anything. Who the hell would believe him?"

"She should begin to rot again quickly," Mark said.

"I want her more than rotted," Canady said curtly.

"If she *were* to come back…"

"Mark, we can't take chances like that. She almost put paid to Bernie. I barely got here in time."

Mark winced. "All right. What next?" he asked Canady.

Sean handed him a bone saw. Mark nodded and got to work. Decapitation was not an easy process, he thought halfway through.

When they were done, he asked Canady, "How the hell are you going to explain this?"

"I'm not. I'm going to pray she rots again by morning."

"What about the morgue attendant?"

"I'm going to prop him back at his desk. With any luck, he's going to think he's worked a few hours too many alone with the dead at night."

"I guess you know what you're doing."

Canady shrugged. "It's the best I can think of, anyway. When I leave here, I'm heading back to the hospital to check on things there. Where will you be? Back at Montresse House?"

Mark shook his head. "No. I can't just sit around and wait. I have to find Stephan's lair. He's using guerilla tactics, going after different people, trying to keep us so busy and scattered that he'll eventually succeed in getting to Lauren. I have to find him first."

"What do you think he'll do next?" Canady asked.

"I don't know, but I hope to God I can find him before he does it," Mark replied.

Deanna remained very weak, and she was also fretful, worried about Jonas.

Lauren was worried about him, too, though not, she suspected, for quite the same reason.

Stacey managed to cook up a delicious soup that Deanna was able to keep down, so at least her strength was improving, even if the danger was still out there.

But that night, with Stacey, Bobby and Big Jim around, it seemed to Lauren that the situation was on the upswing, at the very least.

Deanna actually made it to the shower by herself, with one of them waiting, ready to hand her a towel and support her back to the bed.

Big Jim suggested they gather in Deanna's room for a game of Trivial Pursuit, and though she felt listless about the idea at first, Lauren was pleased to see how eagerly her friends agreed. Still, though she tried, she couldn't get into the game herself; she felt strangely restless and unnerved. Finally she excused herself and went downstairs to brew a pot of tea.

As the tea steeped, she suddenly remembered the paper Susan had given her, which she'd forgotten in the welter of events. She raced upstairs to her own room and found it in the pocket of the jeans she had worn the day before. Eagerly, she sat down on the bed to read.

It was a newspaper article, written ten years earlier about strange events in Louisiana history.

Lauren was perplexed. The event in question dated back to 1870. A plantation owner who had survived the ravages of the "War of Northern Aggression" had been returned to his home for burial after traveling abroad to attend the wedding of his son in Kiev, where he had apparently gone berserk and used a bow and arrow to kill the bride and several of the guests.

On the day of his funeral, the house—a beautiful, graceful home on the river—had gone up in flames. The shell had remained for years. As of the article date, the ruins were still abandoned, and the property had reverted to the state.

Lauren read the article over and over again, unable to puzzle out why Susan had given it to her.

Perplexed, she refolded the sheet of paper and tossed it on the nightstand.

Mark spent more than two hours just driving around.

He had been certain at first that Stephan would have chosen a place along Plantation Row for his refuge, but he had apparently been wrong, because he didn't see anything suspicious the entire time.

He headed back to the hospital, anxious to see how Leticia was doing, but all seemed quiet when he reached her room.

For whatever good it might do, Sean had stationed an officer on duty outside the door. And Judith Lockwood was right where he had left her, the knitting project in her hands beginning to look more like a sweater.

He noticed there were more crosses in the room. Several of them—all wooden—lined the window frame.

"Hello, Miss Lockwood," he said quietly.

She looked up calmly and nodded at him. "He's been here already, been here and gone."

"He?" he murmured.

She returned her gaze to her knitting. "Folks can poke fun at some of the old beliefs, but you know, way back in the old days, in the jungles and deserts, folks knew. They knew about good, and they knew about evil. My girl here, she just happened into the way of evil. But she's a good girl. And I don't intend to lose her to any spawn of Satan. I was ready." She smiled. "Well, I have to admit, I'm a little bit afraid to be leaving this place myself now, but I was ready. He showed up at that window. And I gave it to him good. You see that silver cross there? I blazed my light on it just as soon as I saw the golden orbs of his eyes at the glass." She chuckled softly. "He was gone, lickety-split. Yessir, I think we're going to be fine."

Mark walked over to Judy and took her hands. "Good for you. You're saving her life, you know. But you're right—you mustn't leave here. Not at all. Not until it's…safe."

"Not until you've killed the bastard, huh?" she asked.

He nodded. "He needed Leticia because she's a nurse, but she's also a very beautiful young woman. You've kept her from him. She's not the one he's after, but he'll hurt you, hurt you badly, if he can, because he doesn't like people denying him anything. You understand, don't you?"

She stared at him. "Oh, yes, young man. I understand. I understand much more than you imagine I do. And I won't be leaving. Do you see stupid in this old body? I think not!"

Mark had to smile. "I do not see stupid," he agreed.

"Get out there, then. Get out there and stop the monster that did this to my girl."

"Yes, ma'am," he told her, and left.

Outside, he swore. If only he knew where the hell the bastard was going to strike next.

Deanna still didn't have much strength, though she was doing much better than Lauren would have expected. By midnight, however, she was sleeping again, apparently peacefully.

In her chair, Heidi yawned.

"You all go on to bed now," Big Jim said, looking around the room. "I'll take first watch. Bobby can spell me in a few hours. And Stacey is always up by six."

"I can watch Deanna," Lauren said. "You're already doing enough, giving up your job to stay here with us."

"You listen to me, Lauren. I know what I'm up against. You go get some sleep. You won't be any good if you're overtired."

Heidi stood. "I'm sorry, but I really am exhausted." She grinned. "It's very tiring, convincing your fiancé that you don't want to sleep with the entire roster of the New Orleans Saints. Big Jim, bless you. I'm going to bed."

"Okay, I guess I'll get some sleep, too," Lauren said.

"We'll do it as Big Jim calls it," Bobby said, rising as well, and holding out a hand to Stacey. "Come on, kid."

They all filed out of Deanna's room.

"Maybe I should bunk in with you," Lauren told Heidi.

"No, thank you."

"But—"

"Lauren, the room is protected. And I have a feeling someone will come home to you eventually. And though I think it's great you're getting some at last, I don't want to be around for it," she said, laughing.

"All right," Lauren agreed. "I'm right next door. If you get nervous, if anything so much as goes bump in the night…"

"I'll scream my head off so you can come save me," Heidi swore, then gave Lauren a warm and reassuring hug. "I swear, I almost lost Barry, and there's no way I'll let that happen, especially now that I know what I'm up against. I'll be ready for anything that comes my way, I promise."

Lauren watched Heidi disappear into her room, then headed for her own.

She took a long shower, with plenty of hot water, before dressing in a soft knit nightgown and curling up in bed.

The silence of the house seemed to weigh on her, and she realized that she was listening. Waiting.

Listening for the sound of wings, fluttering in the night. Waiting in fear.

It was exactly what he wanted, she thought. He had been at the hospital. He had wanted to prove that he could go

anywhere, that he could injure them when they didn't eve
know they were vulnerable. And that he did want her.

Why?

Because she looked like Katie?

It was all so ridiculous.

She got up and decided to read the article Susan had give
her one more time. But she still didn't understand what th
seer had been trying to tell her. It was a sad story, and it ha
all happened in 1870, shortly after the Civil War had torn th
nation apart.

She noticed that several sources were cited at the botton
of the article. She wondered if she could find any of them o
the computer, or if she would have to go to the library.

It was almost 2:00 a.m., and though she couldn't sleep
she was exhausted. She decided to see what she could fin
in the morning.

She lay down again to try to get some sleep.

Although it seemed futile, Mark decided to try barhop
ping again.

Big Jim wasn't playing, he quickly discovered. But h
stayed for a beer, and listened to the remainder of the group

He was still bothered by everything that had happene
with "Nefertiti." She had wanted him to destroy her. He wa
certain she hadn't seized the child because she reall
intended to take his life; rather, she had wanted death an
had forced his hand. But he was still frustrated, thinkin
that she might have known something that could hav
helped him.

He straightened suddenly and looked around. Nothing i
the bar looked different, but something had changed.

He sipped his beer and carefully observed those aroun

im. Three college boys were sitting at one of the high tables
near the bar. There were eight people on the dance floor. They
weren't dancing as couples, just moving to the music.

At the table next to him a young woman was seated with
an older man. He homed in on their conversation; it was a
father and daughter. She was going to Tulane, and he was
down visiting.

The bar was sparsely populated. Several people appeared
to be alone. There were two attractive women in their early
fifties enjoying conversation, margaritas and the music.

A couple was at the far end. The man had sandy hair, and
was broad-shouldered, tall and dressed in a black tailored
shirt and jeans.

He looked like he might be the quarterback on his college team.

The girl was pretty. She looked sweet, radiant and innocent.
Also very young. She had dark eyes and long brown hair, and
wore a tube top and a short plaid miniskirt. They had their
heads bowed toward each other.

Suddenly the girl laughed a little too loudly, probably the
result of too much to drink.

He saw the man set money on the bar and whisper to her.
She smiled and flushed.

They started out the door together, hand in hand.

Mark followed.

There was a loud boom, like a burst of thunder.

Lauren started up, alarmed, awakened from a deep sleep.

The French doors had crashed inward. The drapes, white
and billowing, were floating like ethereal clouds.

A flash of lightning brightened the darkness.

And he was there. Stephan. He was tall and impossibly for-

bidding. He wore a black cape that billowed behind him, dar
against the white of the drapes.

"Ask me in. Ask me to come for you," he said.

"No. I'll never ask you in."

"I know you read the article," he said softly.

"What does that matter?" she demanded sharply.

"I know the fortune-teller," he assured her.

"Susan…" she murmured, fear leaping into her hear
Susan had been terrified. She had known about Stephan.

"I haven't hurt her—yet. But I know she gave you the article

"It says nothing about you," she told him.

"You didn't read it properly," he said, and smiled, th
gleaming gold of his eyes offering something that was almo
tender. "You want to come with me. You know you do. Yo
know what I can offer. With me, you'll have everything. Yo
need to turn away from him. *He* is the evil one."

"No."

"He's a liar, you know."

"No."

Then he began to laugh, that awful laughter she had fir
heard issuing from the crystal ball.

"I'm coming for you…. I'm *here* for you."

The couple seemed to be heading for one of the large hote
on Canal Street.

At first it was easy enough to keep his distance and sti
keep them in sight, but the closer they got to Canal, the mor
difficult it was for Mark to keep track of them in the crow
without being spotted. Eventually he saw them enter the lobb
of one of the hotels, and he had no choice but to follow closel
He walked to the desk and asked the clerk on duty for dire
tions to the Square. As he pretended to listen to what the ma

was telling him, he watched the elevator as they entered it, glad that no one else got in with them, and saw where it topped. The fourth floor.

Mark pretended to head nonchalantly away, then made for the stairs. Taking the steps two at a time, he reached the fourth-floor hallway and swore softly. It was a big hotel and there was no indication what room they were in.

There was nothing to do but tread lightly and listen.

A television blared from one room; rock music sounded from another. He kept moving. Then he heard it again.

That too-loud laughter. At least she was still alive and well. Even enjoying herself, apparently.

He found the room from which the sound had come and paused. He heard the low hum of teasing voices. More laughter.

And then a gasp.

Followed by a scream.

Mark burst into the room.

For a moment he paused, frowning.

The guy was on the floor, the girl straddling him, pressing his arms down. For a moment Mark was about to back out of the room in embarrassment. How the hell could he have been so wrong?

Then saw that he hadn't been wrong after all. She laughed again, and in the soft light of the room, her fangs glowed. Dripped saliva…

She stared at Mark as the man beneath her began to let out a terrified mewling sound.

Mark swore, tore across the room and tackled her, forcing her off the man on the floor. She was strong and tough. She fought hard, trying to grapple him to the ground as she had the other man, while he tried to reach into his pocket for his weapon.

She shoved, and he crashed into the wall but quickly recovered. She let out a screech of fury and threw herself at him

He was dimly aware of it when the guy rose, staggered to his feet and went stumbling from the room. Then Mark looked into the gleaming, maddened eyes of his miniskirted opponent as she started snapping at him, trying to sink her fangs into any part of his flesh that she could.

He threw her off and nearly reached the holy water in the pistol in his pocket, but she came at him again.

He ducked, but not quickly enough, and they both crashed down together. The water pistol went flying. He swore.

She was on top of him, but he gritted his teeth, flexed his muscles and threw her off. She landed on the water pistol With a howl and a hiss, she leaped up, staring at it, then him

She started to laugh again. "You are no match for Stephan," she told him. "You...with your silly weapons He will have you. He will torment you. He will take all that you love. You think you can hurt him? You think you *have* hurt him? Never. He knows how to move in the world, how to feed. He knows how to take what he wants. You are nothing! Nothing at all. In the end, you will be nothing but blood. Blood, blood and more blood. There will be a spill of blood, a rain of blood. It will be just like a blood wedding," she cackled.

"Your woman will die. And then she will live. Not like Katie. Katie is dead. Katie is blood. Just a memory of blood But he will have her, and we who have served him will reign."

Enough.

He made it to his feet and practically flew across the room

He hit her with such force that they slammed against the window together and shattered it. Then they were falling...

Falling into the night, into the abyss.

* * *

No, no, no! It wasn't happening. She had to fight it.

At last, with a jerk and gasp, Lauren managed to shake erself awake. In a raw panic, she stared around the room.

The windows were closed.

The drapes lay still.

There was no man standing inside her room.

She inhaled, exhaled, and realized she had tangled the overs in her nightmare. She was sweat slicked and clammy, nd her heart was thundering.

"It was a dream," she told herself aloud.

Just a dream.

But she remained afraid. She rose and turned on the light, en went into the bathroom and turned on the light there, efore splashing her face with cold water.

She breathed deeply again, staring at her face in the mirror. he looked like a wild woman. She smoothed down her hair, ashed her face a second time for good measure, and looked gain. The wide-eyed panic was at last fading from her eyes.

But a sense of somehow being violated stayed with her.

She left her room and went down the hall. Heidi's door was jar. She peeked in. Heidi was curled beneath the covers, ugging the extra pillow. She appeared to be sleeping peacefully.

Lauren continued down the hallway. The door to Deanna's om was open. Big Jim was no longer on duty, but Bobby as there, reading a gun manual.

He looked up. "Hey," he said softly.

"Hey. Is everything all right?"

"Fine. Deanna woke up hungry again. She seems to be oing just fine."

"Thank God."

"Are you sure *you're* all right?" Bobby asked her.

"Yes. I just can't sleep is all." She walked closer to Deanna. Her friend's color was much better. She was breathing deeply and seemed to be sleeping peacefully. No dreams were plaguing her.

"I told you. She's fine," Bobby said.

"I believe you," she said, smiling as she turned and stretched. She was still tired, but there was no way in hell she was going to go back to sleep. "Hey, why don't you go to bed? You have to go to work in the morning, I assume."

He grinned. "Actually, I'm assigned to the house right now."

"I can't sleep, Bobby. You might as well get some rest."

"Are you sure?"

"I promise you, I'm not going to be able to go back to sleep."

"All right, then. The house is protected. And if anything happens—and I do mean anything at all—just let out a good loud scream. One of us will be with you in two seconds. Okay? And don't worry about a false alarm. It's better to get us up for nothing than to second-guess your fear and end up dead—or worse."

She thought about telling him about her dream. No. She didn't want anyone to worry about *her* when there was so much going on. Besides, talking about it would make it seem more real in her own mind, and she wasn't about to make Stephan any more real than he already was.

When she saw Mark again, she would tell him. Then again, maybe she wouldn't. Maybe, by day, she could get to a library. She would ask someone to go with her, find some excuse.

Was she actually distrusting Mark? she asked herself. Because of something that Stephan had said to her in a dream?

No, she assured herself, though it was true that she didn't really know him.

Yes, she did, she argued with herself.

"Are you sure you're all right?" Bobby asked.

"Absolutely. Honestly. Go—get some rest."

He nodded and left her.

For a few moments she moved restlessly around the room. But then she decided to read for a while. Bobby's manual didn't seem very interesting, but there were all kinds of things to choose from in the bookcase. She chose one on pirates in New Orleans and took a seat in Bobby's chair. She glanced at Deanna again and was glad to see that her friend was still just fine.

With a sigh, she began to read, then gave herself a shake and realized she wasn't comprehending anything she was reading. She was falling asleep.

Great. She had to stay awake.

She turned on the television that sat on top of the dresser, glad that every room had a TV and cable. *Robin Hood: Men in Tights* was on. A comedy. Good.

She looked at Deanna again to make sure the television wasn't disturbing her. It wasn't.

She sat down again. Between the book and the television, she should manage to stay awake.

And she did. But when the movie ended and *Bram Stoker's Dracula* came on, she rose quickly and switched the channel to the news.

But the news was about the fact that police up and down the Mississippi River were still looking for the murderer responsible for the deaths of at least three women, and she quickly changed the channel again and found an old episode of *Lassie*. Big surprise, she thought. Timmy was in trouble again.

She tried to read, but once again her lids grew heavy.

I will stay awake, she vowed to herself. I will.

* * *

Down, down, down…

They crashed to the pavement, and he landed on top, but despite that, she was apparently unhurt and only laughed again.

Mark looked up and down the street. Far away, down near Harrah's, there seemed to be activity. In the other direction, the T-shirt shop next to the hotel apparently never closed. Light was streaming from the door.

But there was no one immediately near them.

She started clawing for his throat again, so he put his fingers around hers.

She fought. She struggled.

He used all his strength. All the tactics he had learned. She was unbelievably strong, but finally he felt the snap. He'd broken her neck. She was still looking up at him, but now her head was tilted at a gruesome angle.

"Blood, blood, blood!" she repeated.

There was some discarded construction material lying out by the curb. He kept a grip on her and rolled toward it.

She saw his intent and tried futilely to straighten her head.

Too late. He found a ragged two-by-four and thrust it into her chest as hard as he could.

From somewhere nearby, a woman screamed in horror. "Murder!"

The girl beneath Mark stared up at him, her eyes growing wide. Her deep gasp sounded like a balloon being deflated. Blood gurgled from her lips as she began to turn black….

And exploded into soot beneath him.

Covered with it, blackened, Mark rose. He heard the wail of a police cruiser in the distance, and he turned and ran into the shadows, seeking an alley.

He found one, aware of footsteps pounding behind him as he disappeared into the darkness.

He couldn't be accused of anything, because she had been old. Very old. There would be no murder charge because there would be no body....

He headed down the street. In the distance, he could still hear the woman screaming about murder.

She could hear a rapping.

No, it was a pounding.

It broke into the deep and dreamless sleep into which Lauren had fallen, curled into the comfortable chair.

She opened her eyes.

Yes, it was pounding. And it was coming from...

The front door.

Her eyes flew open, and she immediately looked over to the bed.

Empty!

Lauren sprang to her feet and raced into the hall, then down the stairs. Deanna was standing at the front door. And it was open.

Hair disheveled, looking barely awake, Stacey—with Bobby at her heels—nearly crashed into Lauren.

"Deanna!" Lauren cried.

As she spoke, a man stumbled in. He was wearing jeans and a Killers T-shirt.

He was covered in blood, and he crashed to the floor in the entryway.

Jonas.

15

Mark thanked God that the city hadn't changed much. He was able to make his way back into the Quarter easily enough. Once there, he realized what time it was.

Daylight would come soon. He needed to get back to Montresse House on Bourbon Street, steal a few hours of rest and get moving again. It occurred to him that he should be circling the lake looking for Stephan's lair.

It was a huge lake, so he needed to get started early. If he could just manage a little sleep and then get going, he could cover a lot of ground.

It wasn't yet morning when he arrived at the house, but he felt every muscle tense as he stared up at the beautiful old manor on Bourbon Street.

It was ablaze with light.

He started to run, opened the gate and sprinted for the front door. He was shocked to find it unlocked.

He pushed it open, then frowned as he closed it and looked around the foyer.

They were all there: Big Jim, Bobby, Stacey, Lauren, Heidi—and Deanna. Along with someone else.

Jonas.

The vampire, bare-chested as Stacey washed his wounds,

sat in a chair, evidently describing whatever had brought him to his current state. Deanna was seated at his feet, holding his hand, looking up at him with wide and adoring eyes.

Big Jim and Bobby noticed Mark first, followed by the others. Lauren let out a little cry, staring at him.

"I'm all right. It's…grime, that's all," he said. Then he looked at Jonas and knew his voice was thick with suspicion when he asked, "What the hell happened to you?"

"I killed him!" Jonas said triumphantly.

"Stephan?" Mark said.

Jonas's smile faded. "No," he admitted. "But one of his right-hand men. And he's dead now. Deader than a doornail. He went up in a puff of…" He paused, getting a good look at Mark. "Soot," he said weakly.

"He's hurt," Deanna said reproachfully. "Leave him alone."

Mark stared at her sharply. She looked much better than someone who'd just woken up from a coma had a right to.

He stared at Big Jim. "Who let him in?" he demanded. Too harshly, he thought with a wince.

"I did," Deanna said, carefully getting to her feet.

"Oh?" He looked at the others.

Lauren stepped closer, staring at him. She was tall, wearing a plain nightgown, yet she looked as elegant as a queen. Her eyes were so brilliant, and her hair was like a cascade of the sun's rays down her back. *If she were differently dressed, if it were a different time, she really might have been Katie.*

But she wasn't Katie. She was Lauren. Just as beautiful. Articulate, talented, her own person. He knew that. And she had come to mean everything in the world to him.

Life, love…salvation.

"I fell asleep," she said. "Then Jonas knocked…and Deanna heard him first."

"I'm glad to see you're doing so well," Mark told Deanna.

"We've got everything under control," Big Jim told him. "In case you want to shower." He looked pointedly at Mark's grimy clothes.

The sun would come up soon, and they did seem to be fine, Mark thought. Apparently Jonas had been in the house for a while, and nothing dire had happened. And Big Jim was there—ready to rip him to pieces if he caused any trouble.

"All right. I'll shower." He turned to Jonas. "Then you and I are going to have a talk."

"He's hurt!" Deanna said again.

"He'll be just fine by the time I'm out of the shower."

"I've got some clean clothes you can wear," Bobby told Jonas. "You might want to wash away some of the stuff on you, too. The blood and the, uh…whatever."

Mark nodded curtly to the lot of them and started up the stairs to his own room, where he stripped off his clothing, knowing he wouldn't wash it or have it cleaned—it was going in the incinerator. He stepped into the shower.

As he turned the water on, he heard the door to his room open. And he knew who it was.

He waited, standing beneath the hot spray, grateful for the sheets of water raining down on him. And the heat. The heat seemed to cure all the little aches and pains.

"Mark?"

He didn't say anything, just watched her come closer.

"You're angry at everyone, but you shouldn't be. Jonas coming into the house…was my fault."

Finally he said, "He's in now. Fault doesn't matter."

"But I thought you believed Jonas was…good. Not evil."

He ignored her implied question and said, "If you're going to torment me, you might as well get in here."

She hesitated, but a second later she stepped in beside him. The water seemed to heat up a notch. Hotter, harder. No. It wasn't the water. It was his senses. It was *her.*

Suddenly he didn't care about anything but the moment and having her there and safe.

"I'm sorry," she told him, her arms encircling his back. "Honestly, you don't know how sorry I am," she whispered. She started to speak again, but he turned into her arms and found her lips with his own.

The soot that had covered him was gone. It had washed away down the drain like a bad dream. The heat was good, and Lauren's skin was sleek against him. The soap smelled clean, like the woods, like pine. It was a pleasant, subtle, earthy scent. Like the lithe, supple vitality and life of her in his arms, it was completely arousing. Like the feel of her flesh, so hot and slick, it was an aphrodisiac. The pressure of her body against his was almost unbearable. The taste of her was erotic. He buried himself against her, holding her, kissing her, caressing her curves, everything heightened by the time and place, the water, the heat and the steam. He felt her lips against his flesh, felt her move against him, touch him…. God, she knew just how to move against him. Knew when to keep her touch light. Knew when to make it rough.

When and where to caress and kiss and torment…

He lifted her against the tile. She held tight and settled onto him, like liquid steel as she arched and moved and rode to his urging, clinging to his shoulders, legs wrapped tightly around his waist. Her fingers stroked his shoulders and back. Her whispers and kisses fell against his throat and shoulders and earlobes, and when they had both climaxed to the music of the steam and their own heartbeats, she found his lips, desperately clinging while he eased her back to the ground.

And still the spray fell around them.

He held her soaked, glistening body, smoothing back her hair, looking into her eyes.

He almost said the words he had said once before, what seemed like eons ago....

I love you.

But he held back. Instead he cupped her chin and stared at the beauty of her face, the fine lines of her profile sculpted by the water.

"We have to be more careful than ever," he said softly.

She swallowed. "It's my fault. And I was thinking...we should leave."

He felt as if someone were squeezing his heart, but when he spoke, it wasn't because he was afraid. It was because he couldn't bear to let her go.

He spoke the truth.

"It won't help if you leave," he said wearily. "He'll follow you."

Fear lit her eyes, but she blinked it away quickly. "All right. But maybe Heidi and Deanna should go."

Maybe they should, he thought. Except that once they were gone, there would be no Sean Canady, no Bobby Munro, no Stacey and no Maggie, no Big Jim, to keep them safe.

And now Jonas was in the mix, too.

"I'm afraid this has to be solved here, now, or else you'll all be in danger for the rest of your lives," he told her.

And it was the truth.

She lowered her eyes and nodded, her hair teasing his chest.

"I'm not lying just to keep you here," he said softly.

"I know you're not," she told him. "So where do we go from here?"

"We find him. So you're never in danger again."

* * *

As he listened to the half-hysterical woman on the street, Sean Canady nodded politely and reminded himself that he had asked to be told when anything odd occurred.

"I'm telling you, the two of them fell from the fourth-floor window," she said indignantly. "It's broken. Even a blind man can see that."

The window *was* broken. That much was for sure. The hotel manager had told him that the room was registered to a Rene Smith. She had listed her address as New York City. Sean wasn't from New York and hadn't spent that much time in the Big Apple, but even he knew there was no such thing as Eighteenth Avenue in Manhattan.

"They fell from the window—and got back up?" one of the detectives with Sean inquired skeptically.

The woman, who was in her midsixties and wrapped in self-righteousness, looked at the officer and inhaled deeply. "I'm telling you what I saw," she said. "With these two eyes."

Sean lowered his head, wincing. The officer who'd spoken was Jerry Merchant. Night shift. Detective Jerry Merchant. This was really his case.

And he knew Jerry.

Knew what Jerry was about to say.

"I'm sorry, but do you usually wear glasses?" Jerry asked politely.

Not unexpectedly, the woman exploded. "I wear glasses to read a menu, young man, not to see at a distance. I was right across the street. Over there. And I'm telling you that two people came flying out of that window. They hit the ground. Then the man took one of those construction beams and slammed it into the woman's chest. *I saw it.*"

"You mean like that beam lying in the pile of soot on the sidewalk over there?" Jerry asked.

The woman pursed her lips. "Harry was right next to me. He saw it, too. Didn't you, Harry?" She gave her husband a light smack in the arm with her handbag.

"Uh…" Harry said, looking at his wife and wincing. "I was concentrating on Harrah's—that's where we were headed. It's our fortieth anniversary, right, Sonia?" He attempted a weak smile. If he'd wanted a happy anniversary, he wasn't getting it now.

"Harry! How could you have missed it?" she demanded angrily.

"Honey, if you say they fell from the window, I know they did," Harry said gallantly.

She sniffed. "They're going to be pulling that girl out of the Mississippi, too, you mark my words."

"Now, now, since she would have been dead if a two-by-four had gone through her chest, she'd have to be here, wouldn't she? They won't be pulling her out of the Mississippi. I'm sure of that," Jerry said.

Sean knew that Jerry was right, but he was also feeling a fair amount of sympathy for Sonia, who had undoubtedly seen it all exactly the way she was telling it.

Which was unnerving. It looked like Mark was right. Stephan *had* brought an army.

"You have to find that man and arrest him," Sonia said.

"You'll describe him for us, right?" Jerry said.

He was humoring her, thank God, Sean thought.

"Of course. Get me one of those police artists," she said.

"Just give us an overall description, if you will, please. We'll start from there," Jerry said.

At that point Sonia hesitated. Then she sighed. "I think he was tall and dark. That's all I can really say."

The desk clerk chimed in at that point and told them the woman who had taken the room had come back with a man, but he hadn't been dark. He'd been young, college age, and he'd looked like an all-American football hero.

Sean left Jerry and the night crew to their work. Then he started pounding the streets, even though he was afraid he was already too late. Still, it never paid to give up before starting.

Thirty minutes later, he found a tall man with broad shoulders and sandy hair sitting alone in a nearby—and nearly empty—bar. One proudly advertising that it never closed and had remained open throughout Hurricane Katrina.

Sean took the seat next to the man, whose fingers were threaded through his hair as he stared into his untouched beer.

"Bad night?" Sean asked.

The guy started and stared at Sean, fear in his eyes. "Uh, yeah. Bad night." He picked up the beer and consumed nearly the whole glass in a single swallow.

"I'm a cop," Sean told him. "What happened?"

"I didn't do anything, I swear. I'm an honor student."

"Quarterback?" Sean said.

"Fullback."

"You any good?" Sean asked.

"You bet," he said proudly, seeming a little more at ease.

"Want to tell me about tonight?"

"You wouldn't believe me."

"Tell me."

"Can a cop buy a guy a beer?"

Sean motioned to the bartender, who set another beer in front of the blond man. "This is it," he said, wincing. "I may never drink again. Worse than that, I may be afraid to get laid for the rest of my life."

"Tell me."

"She was gorgeous. We met in some bar. Started talking, drinking. She knew music…we danced. Drank some more. Then she told me she had a room. Next thing I know, she's trying to rip my throat out."

"And then?"

"Some guy bursts into the room and they go at it—and I got the hell out. She was scary crazy. She'd had her teeth sharpened or something. And she must have been on steroids, because she was stronger than any guy I ever met. Stronger than the entire football team."

"What about the guy who burst in on you? What happened to him?"

"I don't know. Like I said, I got the hell out. That's the truth, I swear it. Please…that's all I know. I've never run so fast in my life. Please, don't arrest me. I wasn't doing anything illegal."

"I'm not going to arrest you," Sean told him.

The kid lowered his head. "After this beer, I'll never drink again, and I'll never pick up a strange girl again, either. I don't care how good she looks."

Sean set a hand on the other man's shoulder. "I wouldn't go telling all your buds on the team about this, if I were you."

The young man looked at him with sheer horror. "Oh, God, no!"

"Good. Here's my card. You have any more trouble, give me a call."

"Thanks." The kid offered his hand. "I'm Nate Herman. And…thanks. I don't know who that guy was, but…he saved my life. I'm telling you, she had *fangs*. And she wanted to rip my throat out."

"Why don't you finish up that beer and I'll drop you off at your dorm?"

When they left, the sun was coming up.

Sean was relieved but still wary.

The sun was no guarantee the world was a safe place. He knew that all too well.

Lauren wouldn't have believed it was possible, but she actually fell back to sleep. Mark was glad; she had seemed keyed up but, beneath that, extremely tired.

As for Deanna…

With Jonas in the house, she seemed to have made a miraculous recovery. The nurse who'd come by a little while ago had told them that she didn't think Deanna needed continued medical visitations. That was a relief, Mark thought. He didn't like having outsiders in the house.

It was midmorning before he got the chance to talk to Jonas. And that was after he spent some time on the phone with Sean Canady, who asked him to try hard not to break any more windows. Or to fall four floors from a building and then put a stake through what appeared to be a young woman's heart in public.

"Glad you're all right," Sean said as the conversation drew to a close. "And, by the way, I've asked Maggie to stop by Montresse House later today. She can take some of the stress off the others, let them have a little break."

Mark let out a breath, thinking how grateful he was to the cop. With Maggie in the house, he wouldn't be so worried about leaving. He felt tremendous faith in this woman who had actually *been* a vampire, though he still didn't understand how it was possible that she had reverted to humanity.

I never actually died, she had told him.

Therein must lie the difference. He'd seen a lot through the years, but nothing like Maggie Canady. However, once they had talked, he hadn't been able to doubt her.

"All right, where were you?" he asked Jonas, when he was alone with him at the kitchen table at last.

"I'd been at the hospital, and something didn't seem right."

"As in…?"

Jonas looked at him, cocking his head at an angle. "I just…sensed something wasn't right. So I went into the hallway and I saw a doctor. But he wasn't a doctor, you know? Anyway, I started following him. He headed out to the parking garage. It was a trap. A whole gang of them lit on me. I managed to get away, but I was messed up pretty bad, and I didn't think I'd make it. Anyway, I must have passed out. I wound up in the emergency room. As soon as I could, I escaped, but by then…the whole hospital had gone nuts. I was on my way here, 'cuz I overheard someone saying Deanna had been taken here, when I ran into Stephan's…general, I guess you'd call him. And I took him out."

Jonas sounded proud, and if what he said was true, Mark supposed he had a right to. But was it true?

Or was it all a clever act?

Mark leaned back, staring at him. He looked fine right now, wearing one of Bobby's freshly pressed shirts and chinos.

What he looked like didn't mean a damned thing.

"So how are you doing now?" Mark asked.

"Good. I'm in good shape," Jonas said.

Mark drummed his fingers on the table, studying the man. He wasn't leaving him here. Not when he was going out, even if Maggie Canady was coming by.

"So you think Stephan got into the hospital by dressing up in a doctor's uniform?"

"I'm willing to bet. Who wouldn't open the door for a doctor?"

Mark pulled out his cell phone and made a call to the hospital. He asked for Leticia Lockwood's room.

Judy Lockwood answered. She sounded pleased to hear his voice. "Leticia seems to be doing much better. She isn't actually coherent yet, but she *has* opened her eyes a few times. She seems bewildered, poor dear. But we're just fine. Mighty kind of you to ask."

He hesitated, then said, "Miss Lockwood, you have to be careful about letting anyone into the room—including the doctors. Never actually ask anyone in, okay?"

He heard her soft chuckle on the other end. "Silly man, I know that," she assured him. "And I have that nice officer's card if I get worried, and your number, too. Don't you go being worried about me. I know what I'm up against."

"I'm glad to hear it, Miss Lockwood. Thank you."

He closed his phone, studying Jonas again.

"We're going to take a ride."

"Shouldn't I stay here?"

"Hell, no."

"You still don't trust me."

"I don't know you."

Jonas shrugged. "Fair enough. Where are we going?"

"I told you. For a ride. No questions. You still look a little rough around the edges, so you can rest while I drive."

"Mind if I tell Deanna I'm going out?"

"Sure. I'll walk you up there."

He watched from the hallway while Jonas went in to talk to Deanna. Heidi was sitting with her, which didn't seem to be the safest combination in the world, but Big Jim was there, too, so he decided things would probably be fine.

He left Jonas to his goodbyes and went into his own room.

Lauren was still sound asleep in his bed. She was so beautiful, her hair like sunshine splashed across the pillows. He leaned down and kissed her brow. She smiled, as if even in her sleep she was aware he was there.

He met Jonas in the hallway. "Let's go," he said.

"I'm right behind you."

"I like it better when you're right in front of me," Mark countered.

Once they were out of the city, Jonas looked at him. "What are you looking for?" he asked.

Mark hesitated. "Anything that looks like it's been abandoned but is suddenly in use. Like a car in front of a condemned building, anything like that."

"Like beer bottles on an overgrown lawn?" Jonas asked.

"Yeah, exactly," Mark said.

"Turn around then. We just passed one."

Lauren was surprised when she woke and walked into Deanna's room to find Deanna asleep and a strange woman sitting with her. She had auburn hair, darker than her own, and fantastic eyes that seemed both green and gold. She had been reading, but she set her book down and stood.

"Hi. You have to be Lauren. I'm Maggie Canady."

"The lieutenant's wife?"

"Yes." Maggie offered her a hand, and Lauren took it. "Actually, I think I've seen you before."

"Oh?" Lauren murmured warily. Had this woman known Katie, too?

"You've been in my shop. I own a clothing store."

"Oh, my God, yes!" Lauren said. She should have recognized the woman's face, she thought. There was a painting of her in the store, wearing a costume. Civil War era, Lauren thought. It was a beautiful painting. She had admired it often.

"Great shop. I go there practically every time I come here. I feel like I've been going there since I was a child."

"It's been in the family," Maggie said.

Deanna moved on the bed but didn't awaken.

"She looks great," Maggie said. "Especially for being nearly drained by a vampire."

Lauren blinked. "You…know?"

"Yes, and I'm here to help," Maggie told her. "Trust me, I know what I'm doing."

There was something about the way she spoke; Lauren did believe her.

"I'm glad you're here. Is…Mark still here?"

"He left with Jonas."

"Oh. Heidi?"

"Asleep in her own room." Maggie smiled. "It's a very tired household this morning. Bobby is puttering around in the kitchen. At least he's awake." She smiled. "He's assigned to watch the house. I'm not sure how Sean manages stuff like that with his superiors on the force, but…he's a good cop, and they give him a lot of leeway."

Lauren nodded, feeling more secure knowing there were cops who knew what to watch out for. Mark had been right. They didn't dare leave until Stephan was stopped. She was more afraid than ever, after last night, certain that sooner or later he would find her.

"Well, I'm awake, but I have to admit, going back to sleep this morning was wonderful. Right now, though, I need to go to the library."

Maggie frowned instantly. "You can't go anywhere alone."

"Since Big Jim and Bobby are here, do you want to come

with me?" She smiled. "I'm willing to bet there are tanks of holy water in this house. I have a water pistol—and I know how to use it," she said lightly. "I'm sure you do, too."

Maggie looked thoughtful as she studied Lauren and said, "I have a feeling you're going to the library with or without company. Why?"

"There's something I have to look up. It's important. This all began with a fortune-teller. She made a few comments about things I need to know."

Maggie's brow furrowed. "It's so important that you'd leave the house now?"

"Yes," Lauren said firmly.

"All right. I'll get Big Jim up here. We'll go together. Go get your purse, or whatever you'll need. I'll meet you downstairs in a minute."

"Thanks."

Apparently there really was a vat of holy water in the house somewhere, because when Lauren got downstairs, Maggie was supplied with a number of water pistols, four in all, two for each of them. She handed Lauren a small container of something else.

"What's this?" Lauren asked.

"Toothpicks," Maggie explained.

"Toothpicks?" Lauren repeated, confused.

"They don't kill, but they hurt a vampire like hell. Especially if you catch one in the eyes. I always keep a few in my pockets. So…you wearing your cross?"

"I am."

"Are you two off?" Bobby Munro asked, coming in from the kitchen. "I'm not sure this is such a great idea. Don't be gone for more than a few hours," he said firmly.

Maggie laughed. "Don't worry, Bobby. I have to be back before church camp ends. My kids," she explained to Lauren.

"I have three. And I wouldn't leave them at all right now if it weren't for church camp."

"Call," Bobby said. "If you need me."

"You bet," Maggie assured him.

With a wave, she started out the door. Lauren gave Bobby a cheerful wave, as well, and followed.

Mark made a U-turn. A minute later he saw the place Bobby had been talking about. It was dark, two storied, and looked as if it had been built in the Victorian era. There had once been a wraparound porch, but most of it was gone now. There was still evidence of gingerbread trim. One step leading up to the front door was gone.

But the lawn showed signs of activity.

A rum bottle. Two beer cans and a half-dozen beer bottles.

As they walked across the lawn, Mark noticed that someone had recently created a makeshift barbecue; an old oven grill had been placed between sticks over a bed of coals.

"Are they cooking their meat?" Jonas murmured.

"I don't know what they're cooking," Mark muttered in reply, and stared at Jonas. "Are you ready?"

Jonas lifted the flashlight, heavy hammer and the shoulder bag of stakes he was carrying, taken from the trunk of Mark's car. Mark was similarly armed.

"I take it you always travel with these?" Jonas asked.

"Always."

"What happens if you get pulled over for a traffic stop?"

"So far, it hasn't happened," Mark told him. "Let's go."

He looked up at the sky, glad that it was one of those days when the sun was brilliantly shining. The house was close to the water; the ground underfoot was soft. When they reached the porch, he lifted his foot and checked his shoe.

The sole was covered with marshy mud and strands of grass.

Just as Leticia's white nurse's shoes had been.

"Go on," Mark said.

Jonas stared at him, shaking his head ruefully. "Sure, I'll go first. Though if I *were* a traitor, that would just make it easier for me to warn the others."

"Maybe. But you also wouldn't be behind me, ready to trap me," Mark replied. "Go."

Jonas preceded him up the stairs, ably—and silently—leaping over the missing step. He landed on the porch. When he tried the door, it was locked.

He looked back at Mark, who came up beside him and nodded.

"Count of three?" Jonas asked.

"Why not?" Mark said quietly.

Jonas mouthed the count, and then they rammed the door together. It opened, and they were in the house.

An eerie darkness rose to meet them, along with the fetid stench of death.

16

Heidi was asleep, and yet...

She felt as if she were awake.

Awake and...

Being seduced. By someone—something—deliciously wicked. Something unknown, that couldn't—shouldn't—be. Something tainted with an irresistible touch of sin. It was as if the covers had been drawn back and a stranger had joined her. A known...stranger. She felt the air, warm and arousing, against her flesh as the covers were stripped away. She felt fire against her flesh as his hands teased along her thighs, fingers dancing delicately across her flesh. He spread her legs, and she couldn't believe the things he did to her then, the intimacies that were being taken. But, oh, God, the excitement that was growing in her, the heat rising in her center, hot, wet...

All while she was sleeping.

"Let me" came a voice.

And she knew she couldn't bear it if she didn't.

It was a dream, she told herself, only an erotic dream.

More and more intimate as that husky whisper repeated the words. "Let me... Let me...in. Let me into you."

She burned. Ached. Writhed.
"Let me" came the whisper against her flesh.
"Yes," she whispered. "Yes."

Although Maggie accompanied her, Lauren could tell that the other woman wasn't pleased about going to the library. She didn't seem easy with Lauren's research, either. But she sat there at a neighboring computer and uncomplainingly looked up various dates or pieces of information at Lauren's request.

Lauren found the process frustratingly slow. It seemed that every reference led her to another reference, and another, then finally to a dead end.

"Hey…I think I found one of Mark's ancestors," she said at last, skimming a newspaper article that had been written before the Civil War. "'Randolph Davidson and son supply regular cavalry.'" She looked at Maggie with excitement, then went on. "Davidson was the owner of Innisfarm, and he financed a militia group. He was apparently quite wealthy…look! His son's name was Mark!"

"You know families, they're always reusing names," Maggie said.

Lauren kept scrolling through the now-defunct local paper. So much of what she read was so sad. Lists of the dead and pleas for information on missing sons. Then the man called "Beast" Butler came to New Orleans in 1862, and the city remained under Northern control from that point on.

She was about to give up on finding any more information on Mark's ancestors when she was startled to come upon a social page dating from 1870. The city was still struggling; the war had ended, but not the loss and the bitterness. Even so, engagements and weddings were still being listed. She read aloud. "'Mark Davidson arrives in town with future bride.' His bride-to-be was named Katya Bresniskaya, from the Ukraine. The wedding was supposed to take place in the bride's homeland."

She turned and stared at Maggie. "How ridiculous! This is more or less the story Mark told me about his past," she said, infuriated.

Maggie stared back at her, then sighed. "There's more."

She reached over and scrolled down the screen.

"'Tragedy strikes again. Noble house falls to madness,'" Lauren read aloud. She looked over at Maggie, who wasn't even looking at the screen as she began to tell the story.

"Father and son, and all the family who were still alive after the war, traveled to Kiev. On the day of the wedding, Randolph Davidson shot his daughter-in-law in the back with a silver-tipped wooden arrow. Katya's family's revenge was instantaneous. The wedding turned into a bloodbath. Davidson was killed first. It was assumed his son was killed, as well, although his body wasn't returned for burial, as the father's was. It was a terrible day when Davidson was buried. He was put to rest on family land, and while the service was going on, the house burned to the ground. The land still lies vacant."

Lauren shook her head, staring wide-eyed at Maggie. "I don't understand. Is Mark suffering from some kind of delusion? Does he think he's this Mark Davidson? And if the father killed Katya, why does he claim Stephan did it?"

"I think you should talk to Mark," Maggie said. "But he doesn't just think he's that Mark Davidson, he *is* that Mark Davidson."

"I'm not so sure I should be talking to anyone here," Lauren said, dismissing Maggie's comment as the craziest thing she'd ever heard, and glanced quickly away, then back at Maggie. "I'm sorry."

"I can tell you one more thing, because I've known creatures like Stephan before. If you don't end this now, you will live in fear all your life. Either that, or you can just accept the life he wants for you." Maggie shook her head. "I wish the others were here. Lucian would be especially helpful."

"Lucian," Lauren said, frowning. "Jonas talked about Lucian. About coming to see Lucian so he could work here…find a home here."

Maggie went on as if she hadn't heard Lauren, as if her thoughts were elsewhere. "It would be great to have Brent here, too." She turned to Lauren then and said, sounding quite sane, "Brent is a werewolf."

Lauren blinked. They were all crazy, including this woman.

"Mechanically enhanced," Maggie added. "The war, you know."

"The Civil War?"

"No, no. World War II."

Lauren stared at Maggie. "If I'm following what you're telling me… No, it's just insane. That would mean that Mark was a Confederate soldier in the Civil War. And that he survived the battles and Reconstruction, and in 1870 he married a girl named Katya whom he'd met in New Orleans, a girl from the Ukraine. But…his father, not Stephan, went mad and killed her, and somehow Mark is more than a century old."

Maggie looked uncomfortable. "You really need to talk to him."

"Were you alive during the Civil War?" Lauren demanded.

Maggie lowered her head, wincing.

"You're telling me that you were."

"Please, Lauren, talk to Mark."

Lauren suddenly felt as if she had to escape. Sitting in the library, surrounded by students and retirees busy at the computers, patrons searching for books and mothers with their children, she felt as if she alone had entered a world of insanity. Vampires were bad enough, but all this…

The dream that had haunted her now seemed far too real. Had Stephan somehow entered her mind? She wouldn't have come here, to the library, if it hadn't been for the dream.

Could it be possible? Had Mark been chasing Stephan for more than a hundred years?

Since just after the Civil War?

No, it was impossible.

But what if it *were* real? Then she could understand the build-up of hatred, of his desperate longing to find justice. But that still didn't explain why he blamed Stephan, not his father, for Katya's death.

She shook her head as if to clear her mind. She really couldn't take any more of any of this right now.

Maggie was blithely talking about a friend who was a werewolf and had apparently been "enhanced" in some way during World War II, but she couldn't bring herself to listen. She was too busy obsessing over the possibility that Mark had been around for more than a hundred years.

She stood up, feeling ill. Had Mark been lying to her all along? Evading the truth all along? Had he mistrusted Jonas when he was really no better than the other man?

At least Jonas admitted what he was….

She stood up, angry, confused, and thinking there was really only one person she could trust.

Herself.

"Let's go," she said, hoping her agitation wasn't evident in her voice.

"Lauren, please, I wish I knew how to convince you that Stephan has to be stopped."

"I do believe he has to be stopped." *I just don't know what else I believe,* she thought.

Maggie turned her phone on as they left the library, and seconds later it rang. She answered, and Lauren watched her face grow pale.

"What is it?"

"We have to get back to the house."

"What's happened?"

"Heidi is gone."

From the moment he and Jonas entered the house, Mark knew that something wasn't right.

There were vampires here, that was for certain. As the door closed behind them, Mark felt the flutter of wings. He turned his flashlight toward the sound. The creature veered slightly, shrieking with pure fury. He swung the heavy hammer he carried, stunning the creature. It fell to the floor. His stakes were honed to razor-sharpness, and his aim was excellent; he speared it instantly. A smell rose as it let out a dying gasp and disappeared in a puff of dust and grime, a flash of fire. It didn't totally disintegrate; its skull rolled and crashed into an arm bone. As he watched, there came another fluttering; this time one of the hideous beings was heading for Jonas.

Jonas cried out and ducked, but he swung as well, replicating Mark's earlier move. They had to catch the things in the air, knock them down, then impale them instantly. That seemed to be the method.

Mark aimed his light across the room. The flooring was gone in places, and he could see down into the basement below them.

"Most of them will be down there," he told Jonas. "Hopefully asleep."

Jonas swallowed hard. "Let's go."

They found the stairs. Jonas almost crashed through a rotten step on the way down, but Mark caught him. The basement turned out to be filled with coffins, some relatively modern, some ancient and decaying. "Go for the old ones first," Mark told Jonas.

"Shouldn't we do them together?" Jonas asked thickly.

"Do you see how many there are?" Mark asked him.

"Um…yeah."

"No time to partner up." Mark went for what looked to be the oldest coffin and opened it quickly. The woman sleeping inside was young and beautiful, dressed in an elegant gown that spoke of a long-ago time in a distant place. She had become as she was in the late 1700s, he guessed.

"My God," Jonas breathed from just behind Mark. "That…angel can't be a creature of evil."

Mark stared at him.

The woman's eyes suddenly popped open, and she stared at them in shock and fury. Her lips curled back as she hissed out a terrible sound of hatred.

"Shit!" Jonas said.

"You should know," Mark told him harshly.

He lifted his stake over her heart just as she started to move. Not fast enough. He hammered the point into her. Her mouth opened again, but this time no sound came. Instead, blood spilled out. She had feasted quite recently. She began to change, her beautiful face turning skeletal, and then she was soot.

Mark heard a rustling in the next coffin and turned on Jonas. "Damn you, *move!*"

Jonas swallowed and came to life.

"The old ones. Go for the older ones first," Mark reminded him, then headed for the coffin where he'd heard the rustling. When he swung it open, the dignified and elderly Edwardian vampire was ready.

But so was he.

The creature never growled, never let out so much as a shriek. He simply exploded in silence, with nothing but a puff of black.

Mark began to move more quickly. After a moment he heard Jonas let out a moan. He turned instantly, worried. But Jonas was all right. He was standing over an open coffin, his features twisted into a grimace of disgust.

"Ugh," he murmured. "I hit a juicy one."

Mark grated his teeth with impatience. "Move, and quickly. They're waking up."

While he was speaking, he was hastily flipping open lids, mindless of the noise he was making. By the time they reached the last two coffins, the vampires were out and ready for battle. Jonas let out a cry of surprise when one caught hold of his shoulders and prepared to cannibalize him.

Mark drew out his pistol of holy water.

The creature, struck, let out a cry like the Wicked Witch of the West. Mark shot again, but by then Jonas had gathered both his wits and his strength. He turned, his stake dripping blood from previous kills, and slammed it into the writhing creature.

Mark dealt with the last vampire the same way; a stream of water, followed by a fierce impaling.

"All right," he told Jonas. "Go back now. Wherever the head is still attached, well, you know what to do."

As they continued to work, Jonas asked, "How the hell is anyone ever going to explain this?"

"That's Sean Canady's department," Mark said. "Apparently, he's handled situations like this before."

"Oh, God," Jonas moaned again. "This is just gross."

Mark stepped back, playing his light around the room. They had taken care of every coffin in the place and destroyed at least forty of the deadly creatures, but something was still wrong.

"I don't know how he does it," he said.

"What?" Jonas asked absently, working on the last corpse, "a juicy one," as he called the younger vampires.

"This place…it's a decoy," Mark said. "These were Stephan's sacrifices." He stared at Jonas. "He wanted us to find this place—wanted *me* to find it."

"Why?" Jonas asked.

Innocently? Mark wondered.

"So he could be busy elsewhere," Mark said angrily, and turned toward the stairs. He had to get back to Montresse House as quickly as possible.

No sooner had Maggie hung up than Lauren's cell rang. She didn't recognize the voice at first.

"Don't speak to anyone. I don't know where you are or who you're with, but you have to come to me now. Do you understand?"

It was Susan, the fortune-teller, she realized.

"No," she said harshly.

She could hear a note of misery in the woman's voice. Like a sob. But was it real?

"I'm the messenger, just the messenger," the woman said. "He has Heidi. And he says he'll kill her, and that her death will be on your head."

Maggie was staring at her questioningly.

"It's nothing," Lauren lied.

"Come to the Square," Susan said, then made a strange sound. A sound of pain, Lauren thought.

Don't do anything stupid, don't act insanely, she warned herself.

It was as if Stephan knew what she was thinking and was using Susan to make sure she knew it. "You can get help, maybe even eventually bring him down. But Stephan wants to know if that will really matter, because, if you don't come now, Heidi will definitely be dead."

How the hell had he gotten to Heidi?

She remembered her own dream. He had that power. He could enter the mind.

"What is it?" Maggie persisted.

"Nothing, just a call from back home," Lauren lied.

She heard Susan's voice again, a whisper this time. "Don't come. He wants you, but you can't give him what he wants. You—"

Susan's voice suddenly broke off in a chilling, gasping sound. Lauren realized that Maggie was still staring at her and knew she couldn't let her face betray her fear.

"You sure nothing's wrong?" Maggie asked.

Lauren covered the phone. "A client's not happy with a project, that's all," she said, then returned her attention to the call.

But the phone had gone dead.

They were nearing Maggie's Volvo, and Lauren realized she had to act fast, so she said, "Damn. I can't find my wallet. It must have fallen out of my bag. I'll be right back."

She turned and raced back into the library.

Then out the back door.

The call came the minute Mark and Jonas stepped out onto the broken-down porch. It was Stacey, and she was frantic. "I don't understand. The house was completely protected. There was no way he could have forced his way in."

"But Heidi is gone?" Mark asked.

"Yes," Stacey told him miserably.

His heart thundered. "Lauren?"

"She should be back any minute," Stacey told him.

"Back? From where?" he demanded.

"She went to the library with Maggie, but they're on their way back here."

"We're on our way, too," he told Stacey.

"Wait!" Jonas cried. "Deanna?"

"Deanna?" Mark said into the cell.

"She's fine."

He nodded to Jonas, who was actually shaking. And, still, Mark couldn't help but wonder whether this supposedly good vampire was for real. After all, he was the one who had spotted the house where the creatures were resting. A house that had been a decoy.

He hung up. "Let's go," he told Jonas and sprinted for the car.

Lauren found a taxi that took her down to the Square.

It was still light, but twilight was coming soon. It had been a beautiful, brilliant, sunny day, but now glorious streaks of pink and crimson were making their way in waves across a sky still lit by the glittering orb of the sinking sun.

But what did daylight matter in the end? Stephan could move freely by day when he chose.

Darkness simply gave him even greater power.

There were people everywhere and no shadows yet, but even so, Lauren felt a rising sense of fear as she looked around the Square, then headed to the spot where she had first met Susan.

Where she had first seen Stephan in the crystal ball.

She stood in the Square, facing the cathedral, and felt a breeze that blew across her skin like a chilling caress.

She turned and looked around—and wondered how she had missed it.

A small tent had been pitched near what she thought of as Susan's spot.

The same tent she had entered that first night, which now seemed ridiculously long ago.

A lifetime ago.

Her hand shaking, she drew back the flap.

And found Susan.

Deanna didn't know what was wrong with her. She certainly didn't feel sick. She did feel...vindicated. She also felt as if she were truly falling in love for the first time.

With Jonas...

Talk about a mixed marriage.

Even so, as she stood in the living room of Montresse House, knowing Jonas was on his way, she felt compelled to leave. Something was telling her that she had to get out. And that she couldn't tell anyone where she was going.

She heard Bobby and Big Jim talking on the other side of the room. "Maybe we shouldn't have trusted that bastard Jonas," Bobby said. "Maybe Mark would have been back by now if it weren't for him."

"I'll kill him," Big Jim said angrily.

Get out, get out now, a voice in Deanna's head commanded. *Get out. Come to me.*

She could see him in her mind's eye, a tall, dark man, and he was beckoning to her.

"Looks like we'd better get ready for a major fight,"

Bobby said. "I'll call Sean. It looks like this is going to be the showdown."

Big Jim asked, "How do you know?"

"I don't *know*," Bobby admitted. "I just feel it, I guess. I've learned to go on intuition sometimes."

Big Jim stared at him, then nodded knowingly. "Yeah," he said simply, then headed for the back of the house, followed by Bobby.

Deanna looked toward the front door.

Come to me. Help me. I need your help. Please...

She glanced around quickly. No one in sight.

She opened the door and walked out.

Susan was lying on the floor, bleeding from a gash on her head....

Bleeding profusely from her throat.

Lauren let out a soft cry and knelt down beside her, desperate to find a pulse. She fumbled with her phone while she sought the woman's wrist and hit 911 instinctively. "Susan, oh, Susan...I'm so sorry," she murmured. An operator came on, and Lauren quickly gave her location. There had to be officers on the street. There had to be help nearby.

"Oh, Susan..." she said miserably.

The woman's lips moved.

Lauren bent close to her, her heart in her throat. She was torn. The woman was badly hurt, maybe even near death. But she had to try to get her to speak. Had to find Stephan and save Heidi.

"He was here, wasn't he? Stephan was here. He hurt you. And now I have to find him. I have to help Heidi. Susan, where is she? Please, you have to help me."

She could hear a siren. Thank God. Help was coming.

"Please, Susan!"

Again the woman's lips moved.

Lauren bent lower and finally realized what Susan was saying, the words she was repeating over and over again.

An address.

Judy Lockwood, aware that idle hands and idle minds were never good, kept up with her knitting, hour after hour. But as she looked down at her stitches, she suddenly had an uncanny feeling and looked up.

Leticia was awake.

She wasn't just awake. She was straining against her restraints and staring at Judy. "The hour has come."

Judy frowned, then hurried to her niece's side. "Leticia, thank the Lord, you're awake."

Leticia didn't seem to see her, though. She only repeated, "The hour has come."

"What hour, Leticia? What hour?" Judy asked, frowning.

Leticia stared straight at her then, as if noticing her for the first time. "I saw him. He was killing a woman in the Square."

Judy thought that maybe she should call for a doctor.

But she didn't.

She made a different call instead.

Mark practically flew into the house. Jonas was right behind him.

"Where's Lauren?" Mark demanded of Maggie, who only stared at him, stricken. The others were there, as well, Big Jim, Bobby and Stacey. But there was no sign of Lauren, or of Heidi and Deanna.

"She got away from me at the library," Maggie said.

"Deanna?" Jonas cried.

No one moved. They only looked guiltily away. Mark finally paid attention to his surroundings and realized that the grand entry hall of the mansion looked like a strange arsenal, with all kinds of bizarre weapons arranged in rows. There were a slew of water pistols. Bows and arrows. Stakes and hammers. Everyone was wearing a large cross. They were prepared.

But they were alone.

He turned, ready to accuse Jonas, but the man looked so stricken that Mark could only conclude that he really was good, or else he was such an accomplished actor that he should have been a stand-in for Benedict Arnold.

"Exactly what happened?" Mark demanded, looking from face to face.

"Heidi was sleeping. I checked on her every few minutes," Stacey said.

"Deanna was downstairs with us," Bobby said.

Heidi and Deanna had walked out on their own, Mark knew. Stephan hadn't gotten in—except into their minds.

He swung around to stare accusingly at Maggie.

Where had Lauren gone when she left the library? The nightmare that had plagued him forever was alive and vivid in his mind's eye.

A bride in white, walking down the aisle, her eyes aglow with love.

And then the blood, the rivers of blood…

"Has anyone gotten hold of Sean?" he asked.

"Yes," Maggie said.

Just then Mark's phone rang. He answered and heard Sean Canady's voice. "The Square," he said simply. "A fortune-teller was attacked in her tent."

Mark turned around, heading for the door. "The Square!" he shouted.

"Wait!" Bobby yelled.

But Mark wasn't waiting.

"Catch up with me!" he commanded.

Lauren was torn. The ambulance would be there any second. She couldn't leave Susan.

But she had to leave Susan. Because she had to save Heidi.

What if Susan died—as she probably would—because she had tried to warn her away when Stephan had been with her?

Stephan was a vicious bastard. He killed for his own pleasure and amusement. He only let his victims "live" sometimes so he could enjoy their even greater torment.

Or to create his army.

And Heidi would never have been one of Stephan's victims if not for her.

There was no help for it. She had to find her friend.

As she left through the back flap, she heard the paramedics approaching the tent and prayed they weren't too late.

Mark reached the Square to find a scene of utter chaos. An ambulance and two police cars were parked in the middle of the pedestrian area. Artists, singers, musicians and tourists were standing around in awkward groups, some being questioned by the police, others just curious to see what all the fuss was about.

Mark forced his way through the crowd to where an officer was holding everyone back and fielding questions.

"She was attacked," one bystander said. "I saw them bring her out. She was covered in blood."

"Was it him? Was it the man who threw those women into the river?" someone else asked.

He had to get into the ambulance, Mark decided. And it didn't matter how.

Just then Sean Canady pulled up in his car. He saw Mark and beckoned him over.

"I have to speak to Susan," Mark said. "I have to get to her. I *have* to."

They strode over to the rescue vehicle. The back door was still open; Susan was inside, lying on a stretcher.

"You'll have to question her later, Lieutenant," the med-tech said. "She's in bad shape, lost a lot of blood. The wound on her head… It's amazing her entire skull wasn't caved in. We're getting ready to take off."

"This man needs a minute with her," Canady said.

"All right. Come in. But she's probably dying. She's hanging on by a thread."

Mark leaped up and took Susan's hands in his own. He willed strength into her, prayed that she would open her eyes.

She didn't.

But her lips began to move.

He leaned close to her.

She could barely form words.

But he managed to understand.

17

It seemed to Lauren as if she'd been in the cab forever.

The beautiful pink light of twilight had gone to deepest red, and now it was fading altogether. No, that wasn't true. There was still light. Red light. Blood-red light, like a mist over the moon.

Suddenly, the cabdriver stopped and turned in his seat to stare back at Lauren. "We're here. Twenty-two fifty," he told her.

They were there?

Where?

Then she realized that she was in front of what should have been a lovely home and saw that it had been destroyed by the Katrina flooding. In fact, the whole neighborhood had been flooded out.

That was why there were no lights...except one street-light. The connection was weak, though, or maybe the bulb was about to go, because it kept flickering on and off.

"Twenty-two-fifty," the cabby repeated. "Look, lady, this is where you asked to be let off, and now I gotta go. Give me your money and get out of the car. I'm not staying here. If you're crazy enough to, be my guest. If not, it's another twenty-two-fifty back to civilization."

She dug in her purse for the money. At the same time, she

tucked two of the water pistols into the waistband of her jeans and pulled the tails of her tailored denim shirt down to cover them. Then she paid the cabbie, but apparently she hesitated too long for his taste.

"Lady, I'm getting out of here," he warned her.

"Sure. And thanks. Thanks a lot. Service with a smile," she countered.

She was barely out of the cab when he gunned the motor and shot away.

She stared up at the dark house. It had been beautiful once. As she moved closer, she could see a faded advertisement for the development the house was part of. It had been called Arcadia. Old luxury with modern convenience, the billboard explained. Every house a variant of the original mansion—the one she was standing in front of. It must have dated back nearly two hundred years, and it had been meticulously restored.

Then abandoned.

As she stood in the darkness, she saw that there *was* light inside. Pale, barely showing behind the drapes that covered every window.

Lauren fingered the cross that Mark had given her. She needed strength so badly. Her knees were giving out on her. She felt a rush of fear and knew she couldn't give in to it.

As she stood there, staring at the house, the night changed abruptly.

The sky darkened, and when she looked up, it seemed that the moon rode across a sea of red.

The darkness around her seemed to swoop and swerve. Giant shadows, changing, forming, coming close to her.

The breeze whispered.

Grew louder.

And then it wasn't the breeze whispering at all. It was the sound of laughter, soft and throaty and all around her.

A strand of her hair rose, and she shuddered; it felt as if one of the shadows had touched her face.

She gritted her teeth and fought the urge to run. The din seemed to grow, laughter rising.

Her hair was tugged.

Pulled.

The shadows began to take form, and then, suddenly, people were standing before her, at least twelve of them, all men. They were all dressed in black. Black jeans, chinos, even dress pants. Black T-shirts, polos, dress shirts. Some were young, others older. And they were all amused.

One man stepped forward. Stephan, standing tallest, and very dark. He was wearing a black poet's shirt and trousers that clung to his muscular legs. He wore black boots, as well, that covered his calves.

"Welcome," he told her.

"Don't welcome me. You know I don't want to be here. But you have my friend."

"I have both your friends, and if you're lucky and very well behaved, they just may live. Come. Come closer."

"No."

He shrugged. "Take her," he said casually.

The others closed in around her. She heard someone moving at her back, and he was close, far too close. She thought she could feel his fetid breath, teasing at her nape.

Her fear peaked and she realized that she had to move— or die.

So she moved.

She drew out her water pistols and began to shoot.

She turned to her rear, desperate to rid herself of the

creature breathing down her back. He was close, and she aimed straight into his eyes. She smelled burning flesh.

He screamed, and as he sizzled and burned, he tried to change back into shadow. He morphed...there, not there. She saw a patch of skull. She saw wings.

She fired again, and he collapsed at her feet.

She stomped on him, and he exploded into dust and soot. An old vampire, she thought. Very old.

Ashes to ashes. Dust to dust.

The others moved on her then, and she began to spin, her water pistols working. She tried, in the midst of her terror, to remember to aim. She couldn't waste her holy water; she had no idea how long her "ammunition" would last.

All around her, the night seemed to explode with cries of pain and shouts of fury. The cacophony rose to a crescendo; there was fire, mist...explosions of unnameable filth all around her.

And then there was a roar of fury.

"Enough!"

It was Stephan.

"We can't take her while she's shooting," one of his minions said. She couldn't tell where the sound had come from and tried to find the speaker, longing to see him die.

But Stephan roared out a command again.

"Enough!"

There was stillness all around her.

Shadows formed shapes again. Only five remained standing, and they lined up at Stephan's side.

"She will drop her weapons," Stephan said.

"Why would I do that?" she demanded.

He smiled. "Because if you do not, your friends will die. I will kill them slowly, one at a time. The little blonde first, then

the dark beauty. You will watch them suffer, and I promise
you will hear them scream and curse you as they die."

She froze, swallowing.

"Drop your weapons, my dear," Stephan said pleasantly.
Then he snapped out a single word in a terrible fury.

"Now!"

Time.

Time was of the essence, Mark knew.

Stephan had been toying with them all along. He hadn't
cared how many he sacrificed on the way to his ultimate
showdown. Mark even knew that Stephan had planned for him
to discover his lair at last. Planned for him to feel desperate.

Planned for him to come alone.

But there was no help for it.

He slipped from the ambulance and disappeared into the
crowd.

He could see Canady standing in the center of the storm,
fielding questions, commanding men, and he dialed the lieutenant's cell number.

"Canady speaking."

"It's Mark."

"Where the hell are you?"

Mark didn't answer. Instead he gave Sean an address and
said he was on his way.

"No! That's what he wants you to do."

"I know. But it's also what I have to do," Mark said, then
hung up before Sean could voice a further protest. Then he
punched in a number for Montresse House, passed on the information he had received from Susan, then said, "Tell Jonas.
He can get there faster."

Then he hung up—and moved.

* * *

As Lauren stared at Stephan, the front door of the house opened and she was stunned to see Heidi and Deanna walk calmly down the steps to flank him.

"Let's go inside, shall we?" Stephan suggested.

"What are you two doing here?" Lauren asked her friends, ignoring Stephan's words.

Neither one appeared to even hear her.

Stephan smiled knowingly at Lauren. "Actually, they're both rather happy to be with me. They're both so lovely...." He ran his fingers down the sculpted angle of Deanna's cheek. "She really is a beauty. And, I'm sure, very talented. And this little one...I love a pale blonde."

"If I drop my weapons," Lauren said, "we'll all be in your power."

"A cab brought you out here, and a cab can take them back," Stephan said, as pleasantly and easily as if they were eager to leave a party early.

She held on to her weapons and saw a flash of anger cross Stephan's face.

"I want guarantees."

"You don't have the right to ask for anything," he told her coldly.

"You have to let them go. Both of them."

They were at an impasse, staring at each other. She thought she could use every last drop of water she had on Stephan. But would it be enough?

Five of his followers were still "alive." And Stephan himself was so strong, capable of healing himself of wounds that would kill a lesser...creature.

Even as the thought passed through Lauren's mind, Deanna silently took up a position in front of Stephan, and Lauren

realized that the friend she was trying to save was willing t
protect him with her own life.

"Shall we go inside?" Stephan asked.

"No, not until I see the two of them safely away from you

Stephan shrugged. "You have a phone. Call a cab. Go ahead

She hesitated, then carefully kept the one pistol in her han
as she stuffed the other into her waistband and fumbled fo
her phone. Stephan simply stared at her, politely smiling, a
she ordered the cab and hung up.

His smile deepened. "You've been so hard to find, Laure
Somehow I knew, though, that you were out there somewhere
I must have sensed you would be here when I came to Nev
Orleans. And then I saw you, through that crystal ball, and
have been patiently waiting for you, aching for you, ever since.

"Patiently waiting?" she said. "Interesting. As far as I ca
tell, you've been running all over town seducing women."

"Only to get your attention," he told her.

"You have my attention. What you don't have is my trust.

"You called for a cab yourself," he reminded her. "Wh
knows? Maybe the fellow who dropped you off will just tur
around and come back."

"Maybe he'll report this place to the police."

"I rather hope not. It's tricky when you kill an entire polic
force," he said conversationally.

"You know that the police here know exactly who an
what you are," she told him.

"You're stalling for time," he said softly. "You're waitin;
for Mark to come to your rescue, like a hero of old, riding u
on a white charger. But surely you know the truth by now.
have been maligned. He is the liar, the evil one."

"Somehow, I just don't believe that."

He shrugged. "You will."

To Lauren's surprise, she was startled by the sudden glow of headlights. She turned around, shielding her eyes.

The taxi had arrived.

Stephan lifted his arms. Like zombies, Deanna and Heidi walked toward the car. Lauren stared at Stephan with mistrust.

"Speak to the driver yourself, my dear. But you will hand me that water gun, and then you and I will walk inside together. If not, the cab—and your friends—will not be allowed to leave."

Her fingers itched, but she didn't dare pull the trigger. Five of his goons were still grouped around him. She knew that none of them would think a thing of killing the driver and the girls.

She walked with Stephan over to the cab. "The ladies need to get back to Bourbon Street," Stephan said pleasantly, producing a large bill. "Get them there safely, please."

He made sure that the back door was properly closed, then patted the top of the cab. It drove off.

Lauren felt the gun twisted from her hand.

"Let's go in."

She still had the cross around her neck, she reminded herself.

And the toothpicks.

She was in the monster's lair, and all she had were toothpicks.

Mark arrived just in time to see the two girls get into the cab, then watch Stephan put his arm around Lauren and lead her toward the house.

He held still, desperate to control himself; if he wanted to save her, he couldn't behave rashly. That was what Stephan was counting on. If he played his hand too quickly, he would lose.

He had to be careful not to betray himself; he didn't

want Stephan's goons knowing he was there. He had to get into the house.

As he waited, he got a look at the taxi driver and cursed silently.

The driver wasn't really a man at all. Not in the customary sense of the word. Lauren had just sacrificed herself so that Heidi and Deanna could become a gourmet meal….

He cursed fate, but just as Stephan knew *him,* he knew Stephan. Mark waited.

Then he went after the cab.

She still had the cross, Lauren thought, but she didn't dare touch it; she didn't want Stephan to remember that she was wearing it around her neck. She prayed that when the ambulance had reached Susan, the woman had managed to speak and tell someone where Lauren had gone.

"Come in, come in," Stephan said welcomingly, as if she had finally agreed to a date, and he meant to do his charming best to seduce her.

She entered the house. The glow inside came from candles set in holders on the floor. There was nothing else, not a stick of furniture, in sight.

But there were more shadows. The sound of whispering. The flutter of wings.

Suddenly the ceiling came alive. With a sinking heart, Lauren realized that at least twenty or thirty more vampires were hiding in the dark confines of the house.

"The basement is my real domain," he told her. "I think you'll find it quite inviting."

"Really? I find a beach in bright sunlight inviting, actually," she told him.

He smiled at that. "You'll see."

He waved his hand, and the empty room seemed to come to life as shadows dropped to the floor and fluttering wings became feet against hard wood.

"Go," Stephan said.

And they all began to move, taking up defensive positions outside.

"Downstairs," Stephan invited her, opening a door. There was light coming from the basement—more candles, she thought.

She walked down the stairs. She would be alone with him down there, she thought. Maybe the chance to kill him would somehow arise.

And maybe he would cease teasing and playing; maybe his fangs would sink into her throat at any second.

She banished the thought and tried to focus on escape.

The instinct to survive was quite incredible, she realized.

His basement had been turned into an elegant salon. There were comfortable sofas, and a pool table stood to one side, separated from the sitting area by support pillars. Music played softly from somewhere, and she saw a large-screen television in one corner of the room. She wondered if he had a generator to provide power.

He led her to the sofa. She didn't want to sit, but she could tell that he wasn't going to give her a choice.

"Watch the screen."

"No."

"You are afraid."

She refused to answer and looked deliberately away from the screen, so he simply caught her chin between his thumb and forefinger and forced her to watch as a portrait came into focus.

It was as if she were staring at herself. "You must understand. She was mine, always mine. I watched Katya when she was a child. I watched her grow. I was the one in love with her. Then…she came here."

The French Quarter appeared on the screen in a series of old photographs. There were no cars, no taxis. No neon lights. The roads were dirt. Carriages were traversing them. Men and women in nineteenth-century costume were walking past shops, gentlemen tipping their hats to the ladies….

And there she was.

Except that it wasn't her. It was another woman. Katya. And there was Mark. His hair was longer; he had sideburns. He was laughing, showing the woman something in a store window. They were walking, her hand, delicately encased in white gloves, on his arm.

The scene changed. They were in a castle, a fire burning in the hearth. There was a daybed, covered in fur.

And the woman…

Katya.

Katya was on the daybed with a man who looked like Stephan. They were together, naked, making love….

Lauren gazed at the image in horror.

She was stunned when the screen suddenly went blank and a rough, angry voice said forcefully, "Actually, that's not how it happened at all."

She turned to the stairs, her heart leaping. Mark was there, and he wasn't alone. Heidi and Deanna were behind him.

"See!" Stephan cried as he stood, and smiled triumphantly. "*He* is the evil one. I sent your friends to safety, but he has made them his creatures."

Mark continued down the stairway, followed by the women. They still seemed to be acting like zombies, Lauren thought.

"Tell her the truth, Mark, or don't you dare?" Stephan asked mockingly.

"The truth? Why don't *you* tell the truth for once? You never intended to free her friends. You sent them off with one of your lackeys as a reward for serving you."

Lauren hadn't realized that Mark was holding something behind his back until he tossed it down before Stephan, and then, even after everything she'd seen, she cried out.

It was the taxi driver's severed head.

Stephan ignored the gory trophy and looked at Mark. "She's mine now. Just as Katya was mine."

"Katya was yours because you used the evil power that fuels your existence to seduce her. She was never with you willingly. And you could never bear the fact that she came back to me."

Stephan turned to Lauren. "I didn't kill Katya."

She was torn, unsure what to believe. She knew for a fact that Mark hadn't told her the truth, or at least not all of it. Then the moment passed as she realized what must have happened all those years ago, at the same time wondering why Mark didn't seem to understand that they were in grave peril, that neither Heidi nor Deanna would be any help in a fight. That in fact they would probably try to kill him.

She spoke softly when she finally responded to Stephan. "I know that Mark's father killed Katya. Because he knew she was a vampire. He might have even known that she had, in turn, made Mark a vampire. But you caused her death. You killed her. Because you made her a vampire. It was the only way you could win her. Maybe at first you did try simply to get her to care about you…for you. But you failed. So you tainted her, and then you murdered her, made her just like you. Except *she* wasn't like you, because when she came back to life, she still despised you. And she went back to Mark. And he loved her, was willing to love her…no matter what."

Stephan let out something like a snarl, staring at her, and she had to fight not to tremble. He was close, so close.

She could be dead in seconds.

"The real truth is this—I have the power, the greatest power."

"You don't know what real power is, Stephan," Mark charged him.

"The only question now is who to kill first," Stephan said softy.

Then he lunged. Faster than light. Lauren shrieked, certain his fangs would rip into her at any second.

But just when she thought there was no hope, that no one could save her, the room seemed to explode. Darkness burst between them like the beating of a massive wing. But it wasn't darkness, it was Mark. He struck out at Stephan, and the force of his blow sent the other man flying across the room. For a second Lauren felt a sense of sheer triumph, but it was quickly gone, because Stephan was up in a flash.

Worse, howling like a pair of banshees, Heidi and Deanna came flying across the room, and while Stephan and Mark were locked in a vicious struggle, Lauren was left to face her two best friends, both of whom seemed intent on killing her. Heidi was so tiny that Lauren was able to shove her away with a swift push. Deanna, however, was tall. And strong. And she had her fingers around Lauren's throat and was squeezing tightly.

Lauren fumbled desperately in her pocket and found the toothpicks. She managed to get her fingers around one and jab Deanna forcefully in the rib cage.

To her amazement, the hands around her throat relaxed.

When Heidi moved, Lauren jabbed her. A toothpick in each hand, she managed to rise and face the two of them, her eyes searching the room to see where Stephan had dropped her water pistol.

She saw it and managed to grab it—then shot both her friends. Crying out, they ran to a corner of the room, and huddled together, arm in arm, staring at her as if she were a creature from hell.

She spun around. Mark and Stephan were still fighting bitterly, the battle so frenzied that they were literally flying around the room. Stephan clung to the rafters, trying to kick Mark when he sprang for him. There was a burst of power so great that the whole house shook when Mark dodged Stephan's maneuver and slammed into the other man.

Darkness shadowed the room in tandem with a blast of hot air as Stephan fought back.

Lauren decided she must be going mad, because she thought she saw wings, thought she saw wolves, golden eyes gleaming, canines dripping, fur flying….

She sensed someone behind her and spun around.

Deanna had found her courage and was getting ready to reach for her, to attempt to throttle her once again.

She didn't have to defend herself, because before Deanna touched her, someone else came hurtling into the room.

Jonas.

"Deanna!" he shouted, and Deanna froze.

Suddenly Lauren felt hands clutch her from behind and whirl her around.

Stephan.

He opened his mouth, and she saw his fangs. They seemed to gleam, and they were almost on her. Then he was ripped away from her, as something huge and black exploded in the room.

For a split second there was a blinding flash of light, and in its brilliance she saw Mark grasp Stephan and force the other man to his knees, his hands tight on Stephan's head.

Mark twisted…and there was another explosion.

The explosion was Stephan.

Lauren choked and coughed and staggered back.

As the dust began to clear, she saw Mark, flesh bloodied, body torn, standing there.

Then he crumpled to the ground.

She raced over to him and dropped to her knees. Blood was oozing from wounds on his arms, on his forehead. She used the tail of her shirt and dabbed at the blood. She was barely aware of Deanna speaking nearby.

"Where the hell are we?" Deanna asked, confused. And then, "Jonas!"

But Jonas was already hurrying to Lauren's side. He knelt down by her.

"He's going to die!" she cried.

Jonas squeezed her hand reassuringly. "No, he's not. He's going to be all right. See? He's healing already."

Lauren stood and drew away from Jonas.

"How did you get in here? How did he get in here? There were dozens of…them outside. But you…you're both just like them, aren't you?"

Jonas stood up and looked down at her. "Yes, I'm a vampire," he admitted. "But I'm not like them. What do I have to do to prove myself?"

There was a groan from the floor. Mark.

Lauren fell back to her knees and helped him to sit up, then stared in amazement. The wound on his forehead already seemed smaller, and he was no longer oozing blood.

She stared at him.

He winced, lowering his head. "I should have told you the truth right from the beginning. I just…I just… There was so much you had to accept and understand first…."

She drew back. "We're still in danger. There were at least a dozen vampires out there."

"It's safe," Jonas said.

"I don't believe you," Lauren said. She was scared. No, not just scared—terrified. Shaking. And that made her angry.

She was so grateful that he was alive.

But she had just watched him twist off a man's head like a bottle cap. No, not a man's head.

A vampire's head.

An evil vampire's head.

Jonas let out a groan of impatience, reached for her water pistol and thrust it toward her. "Go ahead. Shoot me."

When she just stared at him, horrified, he turned the pistol toward his chest and pulled the trigger himself.

Deanna screamed.

Nothing happened, except that Jonas got wet.

He turned the gun on Mark and shot him. In the face. Mark started, then stared at him with a fierce scowl. "Come outside," he told Lauren firmly. When she refused to budge, apparently stunned that the holy water had no effect on him, he said curtly, "We're good. It can't hurt us. Now come on."

He got to his feet without asking for help and he strode toward the stairs.

Deanna gave Lauren a distrustful glance. Even Heidi shuddered as she walked by.

With little choice, Lauren followed Mark

The room above was empty. It was dark, the candles out, but it didn't matter. She could feel that it was empty.

She followed him out into the night.

The moon was no longer shadowed and red. It was a huge, glowing orb in the heavens, casting a gentle glow.

Then she looked around and was amazed by the sight that met her eyes.

There was Big Jim, a huge wooden lance in one hand, the tip dripping blood, and a machete in his other hand.

And there was Stacey, armed with a mega-water pistol, like the Uzi of squirt toys.

Sean was there, and Maggie, and Bobby and the cop who had been watching over Deanna when she had first gone into the hospital.

To her amazement, there was also an older black woman there, carrying a huge cross and a machete, and flanked by a handsome black man and a stunning young black woman. Lauren realized that she had seen the younger woman before, at the hospital. She was Deanna's nurse, the one who had gone mad, although she seemed to be just fine now.

The older woman stepped forward. "It's over, then?" she asked Mark.

He reached out, drawing her to him. "It's over, Miss Lockwood. Thank you."

"I told you I knew what I was up against," the woman told him, drawing away and shaking a finger at him. "You've just got to have a little more faith in folks, you hear?"

"Yes, ma'am." Mark looked at Sean. "How are you going to explain this one?" he asked.

Lauren took a good look around the yard and gasped.

There were dust piles and soot streaks everywhere.

There were also bones, and a fresh headless body. She winced.

"I think it'll be poetic justice if we pin it on the taxi driver," Sean said. "Though I'll have to think about how to explain him ending up without a head."

"Really, Sean," Maggie protested. "Sometimes you can be so…"

Sean sighed. "Maggie, his ID is false. The guy's real name was Wayne Girard. He was found guilty of twenty-seven murders, then escaped—I'm sure with our pal Stephan's help. I'll have some fast-talking to do, but he can take the blame."

Lauren walked over to Maggie and Sean, and everyone from Montresse House. They all hugged her—hard.

"Cop by day, vampire hunter by night," Bobby said lightly, winking.

"You all need to get the hell out of here," Sean said. "Except for you, Bobby, Mr. Fearless Vampire Hunter. You get to stay and help me clean this mess up. More cars are on the way," he said quietly.

His wife gave him a quick kiss on the cheek and headed for her car. By then the others had come up from the basement, and Mark beckoned Heidi and Deanna closer.

"You three," he said, including Lauren, "go with Maggie. Jonas and I will get back on our own."

"Jonas…" Deanna murmured.

"Jonas will be fine," Maggie called. "Get in the car. Come on. It will be much easier for Sean and Bobby if we get out of here."

Deanna exchanged one last long kiss with Jonas before Maggie sighed and grabbed her arm, almost throwing her in the car.

As they drove away, Lauren looked back. Mark and Jonas were still there with Sean and Bobby. Maybe they meant to help with the cleanup. But how would they explain their presence when the rest of the cops got there?

"What will the other cops say when they see Mark and Jonas?" Deanna asked worriedly.

"They won't," Maggie said.

"They'll fly back," Heidi said cheerfully
Lauren waited for Maggie to correct her.
She didn't.

It was over, Mark thought.

By the time he returned to Montresse House, it was very late and the house was quiet.

He spent a long time showering, and as he tried to wash away more than just the soot—seeking to dispel the hatred and bitterness that had ruled him for so long—he kept telling himself that it was over. Really over. Stephan was dead.

But he felt hollow. Drained.

When he stepped out of the shower, he saw that he was just about healed already. The outside didn't matter, though.

He felt as if his insides were all torn apart.

He should have told her.

But he hadn't been honest and she'd found out on her own, and now he'd lost her.

No, he'd never really had her.

He lay down in bed, glad that he could open the doors to the balcony and feel the soft breeze wash over him. Maybe when he closed his eyes he would no longer dream.

No longer see her walking toward him, all in white. See her smile.

Katya had loved him, trusted him enough to tell him the truth about what had happened. And though he hadn't believed her at first, he had believed *in* her. He had fought with Stephan over what he had done to her, and it had been he who had turned him. It was something Stephan had relished...until he had realized that it didn't matter to the two of them. They would have their wedding, and they would have it in a church. When she had been vulnerable and unaware, Stephan had

een able to hypnotize Katya. But not after she had realized
vhat he was and what he was doing. She'd had a will of steel.

But his father…

God, his father! So strong, so loving, so proud. He'd told
Mark what had happened, but Mark had never imagined his
ather would so willingly give up his own life to slay Mark's
ntended bride. He hadn't known that his son had been turned,
s well, or that there were ways to fight the evil nature of their
ew way of being.

So what now? Mark asked himself. Now that it was over.

Lauren would leave. She would be going home with Heidi,
hough Deanna…

There was no question. She was staying.

With Jonas, who had turned out to be the real deal.

He closed his eyes; he needed to sleep. Needed to stop tor-
nenting himself.

He froze suddenly, aware that his door had opened. He
arefully opened one eye.

Lauren was walking toward the bed. Softly, silently. She
melled of soap and shampoo and simple sweetness. She
as wearing a white silky nightgown, her hair like a sunset
gainst it.

She paused, then lay down at his side and rose up on one
lbow, staring at him.

"There will be no more keeping the truth from me—the
osolute, complete and total truth—ever again," she told him.

He opened his eyes. She had sounded so fierce, but there
as a slight smile curving her lips.

"Lauren…"

"Shut up and listen. I thought I'd never been more afraid
 my life than when I first got out there tonight. But then…I
ought I had lost you, and it was a fear that was ten times

more terrible. So here's the thing. Don't protect my feeling
Even if I'm going to be angry."

"I was, er, actually a little worried about you being mo
than angry if I told you the truth about myself," he said softl

"I admit it. At one point I might have been afraid of you
But now…I think we've gotten to know each other really wel
even if it's been in a short but very intense amount of time."

He smiled, then turned on her fiercely. "What part abo
me telling you to stay in this house didn't you understand?
he demanded.

"I had to go," she protested.

"Not without telling me."

"But you might have stopped me," she said.

"Damn right."

She smiled, and her lashes fell; then her eyes rose to me
his again. "Seriously, Deanna and Heidi…I couldn't risk the
lives. We still don't know if Susan is going to make it or not

"I believe she will," he said firmly.

"The point is—" she began.

"The point is that you don't listen," he teased her.

"The point is that from now on I always get the truth from
you," she told him.

"Because intelligent people believe in vampires?" h
asked wryly.

"When they can't help but see what's happening," she tol
him softly.

"From now on, will you swear to tell me before you ru
off trying to save anyone? And will you have faith in me?
he demanded.

"Yes," she said. And then she touched his face, leane
closer to him and spoke against his lips. "Now…hold m
please. Because I don't care who—or should I say *what?*–

u are. I have never known love like this before. So...please,
ow me that you feel the same way."

He did.

And the hollowness was gone.

He was whole, as he had never thought he could be again.

Epilogue

It was the most gorgeous wedding. The church was filled w
flowers in dozens of colors. A royal-blue runner ran down t
aisle and out through the church doors.

There were old friends in attendance.

And new ones.

The groom was handsome, tall and dark.

The bride was far more than beautiful. Her happiness l
erally glowed.

She entered to the strains of a beautiful love ballad.

"That's gorgeous," Deanna whispered to Heidi where th
stood waiting at the altar.

"He wrote it," Heidi whispered back.

Lauren kept walking down the aisle on the arm of Big Ji
who was giving her away. He wore a smile broader than Tex
as he handed her over to the groom.

The vows were as beautiful as the song that had accomp
nied the bride's progress. Mark and Lauren had written th
vows themselves. Not everyone in attendance fully und
stood them, but many there did. The promise to love throu
eternity, come what may. The vow that love was undying. T
usual words in some ways…dramatically different in othe

They left the church in a rain of rice and cheers.

The reception was held on the grounds of Montresse
ouse, where the smells of barbecue and gumbo fought for
minance. As afternoon turned to evening, Big Jim's band
nmed, and the groom even joined them for a while, until he
w his bride watching him with something private in her eyes.

Then he was done playing. He left the stage and walked
er to her.

"The truth, the whole truth," he told her, "is that I love you."

She laughed and said, "I would never doubt you."

The moon glowed down, and it seemed as if they were
ncing on brilliant white clouds and that they would do
forever.

Perhaps some things *were* eternal.

Turn the page for a sneak peek at
THE SÉANCE,
the next paranormal thriller from
New York Times *bestselling author*
Heather Graham.

Available in October 2007
only from MIRA Books.

1

An autopsy room always smelled like death.

And it was never dark, the way it was in so many movies. If anything, it was too bright. Everything about it rendered death matter-of-fact.

Facts, yes. It was facts they were after. The victim's voice was forever silenced, and only the elegant, hushed cry of the body was left to help those who sought to catch a killer.

Jed Braden could never figure out how the medical examiner and the cops got so blasé about the place that they managed not only to eat but to wolf down food in the autopsy room.

Not that he wasn't familiar enough with autopsy rooms himself. He was, in fact, far more acquainted with his current surroundings than he had ever wanted to be. But eating there? Not him.

This morning it was doughnuts for the rest of them but he'd even refused coffee. He'd never passed out at an autopsy, even when he'd been a rookie in homicide, and he didn't feel like starting now.

Whenever a cause of death was suspicious, there had to be an autopsy, and it always felt like the last, the ultimate, invasion. Everything that had once been part and parcel of a living soul was spread out not just naked, but sliced and probed.

At least no autopsy had been required for Margaritte. She had been filled with morphine, and at the end, her eyes had opened once, looked into his, then closed. A flutter had lifted her chest, and she had died in his arms, looking as if she were only sleeping but truly at rest at last.

Doc Martin, the M.E., finished intoning the time and date into his recorder and shut off the device for a moment, staring at him.

He didn't speak to Jed, though. He spoke to Jerry Dwyer, at his side.

"Lieutenant. What's *he* doing here?"

Inwardly, Jed groaned.

"Doc…" Jerry murmured unhappily. "Well…I think it's his…conscience."

The M.E. hiked a bushy gray eyebrow. "But he's not a cop anymore. He's a *writer.*"

He managed to say the word *writer* as if it were a synonym for scumbag.

Why not? Jed thought. He was feeling a little bit like a scumbag that morning.

Doc Martin sniffed. "He *used* to be a cop. A good one, too," he admitted gruffly.

"Yeah, so give him a break," Jerry Dwyer told him. "And he's got his private investigator's license, too. He's still legit."

This time Martin made a skeptical sound at the back of his throat. "Yeah, he got that license so he could keep sticking his nose into other people's business—so that he could write about it. He's working for the dead girl? He knows her folks? I don't think so."

"Maybe I want to see justice done," Jed said. "Maybe the entire force was wrong twelve years ago."

"Maybe we've got a copycat," Martin said.

"And maybe we got the wrong guy," Jed said quietly.

"Technically, we didn't get *any* guy, exactly," Jerry reminded them both uncomfortably.

Martin grunted and turned the tape recorder back on. Jerry gave Jed a glance, shrugging. He'd warned Jed that they might have trouble. He'd told him right out that if Martin said he had to leave, he had to leave.

An autopsy was a long, hard business, and Jed knew it. In his five years in homicide he'd learned too well just how much had to be done meticulously and tediously. And messily.

He'd never expected to attend one when his presence wasn't necessary in solving a case, and the truth was that he didn't have to be here today.

Except in his own mind.

The woman on the table was already out of her body bag. There had been no need to inspect her clothing. She hadn't been found with any.

The discovery of her body on I-4 had been not just a tragedy but a shock. Her name was Sherry Mason; she had come to what the locals called Theme Park Central in the middle of the Florida peninsula because she'd wanted to be a star. The police knew her identity because her purse—holding not just her ID but fifty-five dollars and change, and several credit cards—had been found discarded near her naked body.

She had been found not just lying there but carefully displayed, arranged, stretched out on her back as if she were sleeping, her arms crossed over her chest, mummy-style. They were assuming, results to be verified during the autopsy, that she had been sexually assaulted.

Just like the other victims—those who'd been slain twelve years ago.

An ancient vampire,
a blood-sucking near-
deity and a battle for
the existence of the
human race continue
with the third book in
the Blood Ties series
from *USA TODAY*
bestselling author

JENNIFER ARMINTROUT

Pick up a copy July 24.

SAVE $1.00

off the purchase price of
**BLOOD TIES BOOK THREE:
ASHES TO ASHES**
by Jennifer Armintrout.

Offer valid from July 24, 2007, to October 31, 2007.
Redeemable at participating retail outlets. Limit one coupon per purchase.

52607934

5 65373 00076 2 (8100)0 11427

MJABT3CPN

nocturne™

**DON'T MISS THE RIVETING CONCLUSION
TO THE RAINTREE TRILOGY**

RAINTREE: SANCTUARY

by *New York Times* bestselling author

BEVERLY BARTON

Mercy, guardian of the Raintree
homeplace, takes a stand against
the Ansara wizards to battle for
the Clan's future.

*On sale July,
wherever books are sold.*

SNRT2

HEATHER GRAHAM

32424	THE ISLAND	___ $7.99 U.S.	___ $9.50 CAN.
32343	KISS OF DARKNESS	___ $7.99 U.S.	___ $9.50 CAN.
32277	KILLING KELLY	___ $7.99 U.S.	___ $9.50 CAN.
32218	GHOST WALK	___ $7.50 U.S.	___ $8.99 CAN.
32137	DEAD ON THE DANCE FLOOR	___ $7.50 U.S.	___ $8.99 CAN.
32134	NIGHT OF THE BLACKBIRD	___ $6.50 U.S.	___ $7.99 CAN.
32133	NEVER SLEEP WITH STRANGERS	___ $6.50 U.S.	___ $7.99 CAN.
32132	IF LOOKS COULD KILL	___ $6.50 U.S.	___ $7.99 CAN.
32074	THE PRESENCE	___ $6.99 U.S.	___ $8.50 CAN.
32010	PICTURE ME DEAD	___ $6.99 U.S.	___ $8.50 CAN.
66864	SLOW BURN	___ $5.99 U.S.	___ $6.99 CAN.
66750	HAUNTED	___ $6.99 U.S.	___ $8.50 CAN.
66665	HURRICANE BAY	___ $6.99 U.S.	___ $8.50 CAN.
32131	EYES OF FIRE	___ $6.50 U.S.	___ $7.99 CAN.
32321	THE VISION	___ $7.99 U.S.	___ $9.50 CAN.

(limited quantities available)

TOTAL AMOUNT	$ _____
POSTAGE & HANDLING	$ _____
($1.00 FOR 1 BOOK, 50¢ for each additional)	
APPLICABLE TAXES*	$ _____
TOTAL PAYABLE	$ _____

(check or money order—please do not send cash)

To order, complete this form and send it, along with a check or money order for the total above, payable to MIRA Books, to: **In the U.S.:** 3010 Walden Avenue, P.O. Box 9077, Buffalo, NY 14269-9077; **In Canada:** P.O. Box 636, Fort Erie, Ontario, L2A 5X3.

Name: _____
Address: _____ City: _____
State/Prov.: _____ Zip/Postal Code: _____
Account Number (if applicable): _____

075 CSAS

*New York residents remit applicable sales taxes.
*Canadian residents remit applicable GST and provincial taxes.

MIRA®

www.MIRABooks.com

MHG0707BL